The Tears of the Rose

THE TWELVE KINGDOMS

Books by Jeffe Kennedy

The Twelve Kingdoms:
The Mark of the Tala

The Twelve Kingdoms:
The Tears of the Rose

The Twelve Kingdoms:
The Talon of the Hawk
(coming June 2015)

The Master of the Opera
available as an eBook serial
Act 1: Passionate Overture
Act 2: Ghost Aria
Act 3: Phantom Serenade
Act 4: Dark Interlude
Act 5: A Haunting Duet
Act 6: Crescendo

Published by Kensington Publishing Corp.

The Tears of the Rose

THE TWELVE KINGDOMS

JEFFE KENNEDY

KENSINGTON BOOKS
www.kensingtonbooks.com

KENSINGTON BOOKS are published by

Kensington Publishing Corp.
119 West 40th Street
New York, NY 10018

All Kensington titles, imprints, and distributed lines are available at special quantity discounts for bulk purchases for sales promotion, premiums, fund-raising, and educational or institutional use.

Special book excerpts or customized printings can also be created to fit specific needs. For details, write or phone the office of the Kensington Special Sales Manager: Kensington Publishing Corp., 119 West 40th Street, New York, NY 10018. Attn. Special Sales Department. Phone: 1-800-221-2647.

Kensington and the K logo Reg. U.S. Pat. & TM Off.

ISBN-13: 978-0-7582-9445-6
ISBN-10: 0-7582-9445-X
First Kensington Trade Paperback Printing: December 2014

eISBN-13: 978-0-7582-9446-3
eISBN-10: 0-7582-9446-8
First Kensington Electronic Edition: December 2014

10 9 8 7 6 5 4 3 2 1

Printed in the United States of America

To Teddy,
who shouldn't be in the ground

Acknowledgments

Many thanks to everyone at Kensington who has been so amazing to me about celebrating this book and the trilogy, especially Peter Senftleben, curmudgeonly editor extraordinaire; Vida Engstrand, delightful diva of communications; Jane Nutter, a paragon of a publicist; and Rebecca Cremonese, for being such a dedicated, enthusiastic caretaker of the pages and the story. If anyone gets to dinner & movie Ash, it will be you.
Everlasting gratitude to my critique partners: Marcella Burnard and Carolyn Crane, for the insightful, under-pressure reads and tireless support.
Thanks to my longtime friend, Marin Untiedt, who taught me to value knitting, gave me what I needed to know, and would probably be very much like this.
Thank you from the bottom of my heart to all the incredible reviewers and readers who loved *The Mark of the Tala* and immediately demanded this book. I hope you all like Amelia's story, too.
Finally, thanks to my family for being the love and balance in my life.
And always, to David, for all the little things, every day.

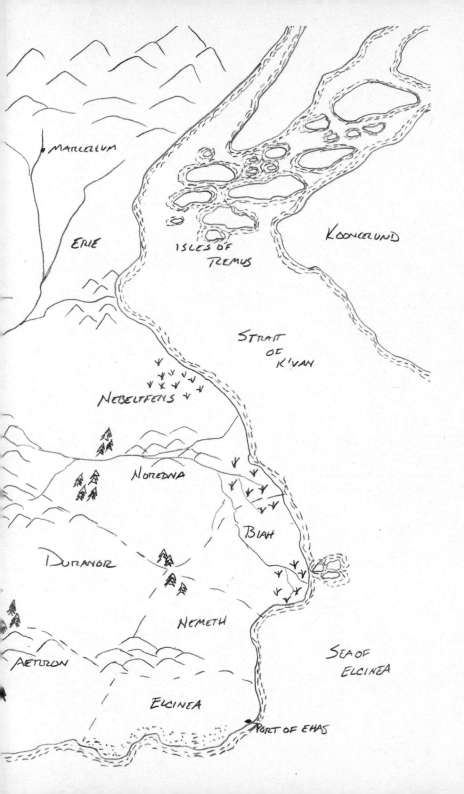

1

When they brought Hugh's empty body home to me, I didn't weep.

A princess never lets her people see her cry.

Father expected that much, even of me.

It wasn't even that difficult. My grief, my rage, they bloomed large in my heart, too huge to escape through such a small channel as a tear duct. All that he had been, so glorious, so handsome, full of life and love . . . gone.

The procession climbed the winding road to Windroven, lined by Hugh's people, all dressed in the ashy gray of mourning. The folk of Avonlidgh don't call out with their mourning. No, they observe it with silence, as stolid as their remote and rocky coastline. Fittingly, however, the wind wailed instead. It tore at my griseous cloak with pinching fingers and snapped my hair painfully against my skin.

When we first received the news, I'd tried to cut it off, the long tresses Hugh had loved so much. But my ladies stopped me, saying I'd regret it later.

They didn't understand that I only had room for one regret. It edged out everything else. I couldn't understand how anyone could imagine that any other thing mattered or would ever matter again.

Hugh was gone.

Even though the words circled my mind in an endless cruel march, I couldn't quite believe it.

The members of the procession struggled against the ferocious wind, full of bits of biting ice off the churning ocean, my sister and her elite squad, Ursula's Hawks. Now her Hawks served as pallbearers, carrying the pallet at shoulder height despite the added effort, a gesture of highest regard. Not enough regard to have prevented his death, however. As they passed, the people and soldiers of Avonlidgh fell in behind, a drab parade in their wake.

Not so long ago, before winter set in, Hugh and I had ridden up that hill, bringing my other sister, Andi, with us. We'd given her protection, the shelter of our home. Sacrificed the armies of Avonlidgh to save her—and failed.

Hugh had gone to rescue her and died for it.

A sour ball of frozen guilt and hate choked me, the gorge rising every morning. That channel wasn't big enough, either, so it grew inside me, monstrous and vile.

They reached the top and Ursula's steely gaze found mine. The eldest and heir to the High Throne of the Twelve Kingdoms, she looked more gaunt than ever. In the past, some might have called her passably attractive, in her hard-edged way, but not at this moment. Her normally clear gray eyes clouded dark with defeat and her thin lips pursed tight with exhaustion.

She dismounted, saying nothing, gesturing for her Hawks to lay Hugh's shrouded body at my feet. They hadn't had the appropriate cloth to work with—I'd fix that—so they'd wrapped him in his cloak. I'd thought my heart had already died, but it clenched at the sight of the sigil I'd embroidered for him. Still, it could all be a lie.

Couldn't it?

"Show me." My voice croaked out, and Ursula, the brave one,

she who never flinches, blanched ever so slightly. Then she dropped to one knee and did the honors herself, touching the fabric tenderly with bare fingers the color of ice. The frozen wool resisted, then tore with a sigh that could have been a man's dying breath. One of my ladies broke into hysterical sobs that quickly faded as someone led her away.

I wanted to say it wasn't him. Surely this lifeless *thing* couldn't be my golden prince. When he first strode into the audience chamber at Castle Ordnung, he'd won everyone's hearts in an instant. We all fell in love with him, with the way the sun walked with him, radiant and perfect.

The light had abandoned him now.

There was nothing left to say good-bye to. Just a frozen husk.

Ursula stared at him, too, hands folded over her armored knee. The sourness of guilt and metallic shame filled the air. Of course she felt it, too. Ursula never failed. Especially not in such a spectacular way. I saved some of my hate for her. If she'd arrived in time to stop the siege, if she'd taken Odfell's Pass as was meant, Hugh would still be alive.

"Tell me what happened." I spoke to her only, where she still knelt by Hugh's pallid corpse, even his sunny blond locks sapped of color.

King Erich, who'd stood in silence behind me this whole time, stoically observing the delivery of his dead son, stirred. A gnarled oak tree coming to life and moving its creaking limbs. "Perhaps we should go inside and—"

"No," I interrupted him. Someone gasped in shock, but I was beyond caring. "I want her to say it out loud right here. So everyone can hear. And bear witness."

Ursula measured me with her eyes. Maybe seeing someone besides her flirty, flighty baby sister for the first time.

"We attempted to take Odfell's Pass. King Rayfe and his Tala armies stopped us. Hugh fell in the battle." Her voice choked on the words, the burnt smell of lies floating up from them.

"Was Andi there?" I demanded.

Ursula hesitated—so, so unlike her—and inclined her head.

"Why didn't you bring her back with you, then?"

"We could not," Ursula answered in a voice devoid of emotion.

"So the mission failed." Old Erich sounded weary. He'd traveled to Windroven in the dead of winter to keep vigil for his fallen heir. Now all Avonlidgh had was me. Having the most beautiful woman in the Twelve Kingdoms for your son's wife sounds great, until you realize she's the one who will be making the decisions when you're dead. Who wanted a girl who cared only about pretty dresses and picnics running a kingdom, after all?

Yes, I knew what they were thinking. The stink of their doubt filled the castle. Worthless, useless me.

And soon I wouldn't even be beautiful, my one claim to importance. With every day, that famed beauty flaked away, dying on the surface of my skin and sloughing off like moss deprived of water. I felt it and didn't care. *Let it wither and die with everything else.*

"Princess Andromeda elected to honor her marriage to Rayfe and her commitment to the Tala," Ursula was telling Erich. "The pass cannot be taken by force. There is a magical barrier that cannot be breached. We tried and failed. It's over."

"I've heard such ridiculous rumors for decades." Erich's exhausted tone held a world of regret, possibly larger than mine. "You should not believe everything you're told, Princess. Especially by such tricksters as the Tala."

"I witnessed it myself," she replied.

"I highly doubt High King Uorsin will be so convinced."

"I will convince him, King Erich," Ursula answered. "I shall go to his seat at Castle Ordnung next and confess—"

"How did he die?" My voice cut through their conversation like a rusty knife.

Ursula rose. Met my eyes. So stoic. So steady.

"He fell in the battle at Odfell's Pass."

Her words smoldered, stinking of the lie. How I was so certain, I didn't know, but I was.

"Whose hand wielded the blade?"

Erich laid a hand on my shoulder. "Princess Amelia, in the heat of battle it is rarely easy to—"

"*She* knows." I hissed it at her. "Don't you? Tell me what you're not saying."

Ursula's shoulders dropped, her hand finding the hilt of her sword, fingers wrapping around it for comfort.

"Hugh went for Rayfe and Andi stepped between them. She asked me to give you her confession: that he died at her hands."

A murmur ran through the erstwhile silent crowd, growing larger the farther it rippled away. I closed my eyes, listening to it spread. This. This was what I'd known. The burning ball in my gut turned, wanting to rise again. Andi. How could she?

"She offers you her grief and great sorrow. One day, when you're ready to hear it, she will offer you her apology. She knows well that it is nothing you will accept at this time."

"This is true, then?" Erich's voice was ashen, weakened by the shock.

"It was never intended," came Ursula's reply, "but yes. In his zeal, Hugh thought to slay the King of the Tala. He died a brave and noble death."

I felt the sneer twisting my lips and opened my eyes to gaze down at the rotting shell of my true love. "There is no such thing as a brave and noble death."

"No." Ursula spoke the quiet agreement. "I erred in saying so."

"Yes." I swallowed, my mouth filling with the saliva that presaged vomit. I couldn't be ill in front of my people.

"She asked me to give you three other messages—in private."

"I don't want to hear them!" The world darkened at the edges.

Ursula frowned at me. "Ami—are you all right?"

The childhood endearment nearly broke me open. I couldn't do this.

"I have to lie down." I fumbled to stay on my feet, and my

hand found Dafne, solid and steady by my side. I leaned on her before I remembered that she had been Andi's friend first. Before Andi had betrayed me so foully.

"Shh," she soothed me, though I hadn't said anything to her. She wound an arm around my waist. "Let's get you inside. I'm sure it's not as bad as it sounds. Your sister loves you. They both do. Princess Ursula—would you care to accompany us?"

"I don't want her to—"

"Now, now. Save your energy, Princess." Dafne sounded all concerned, but I knew they were worried about offending Ursula. As if anything touched her hardened heart.

I was beyond protesting, though, and my ladies swept me along, a sea of soft hands and gray silk skirts. As if my stomach knew we'd entered my chambers, it heaved in earnest just as I reached for the washbowl. Lady Dulcinor held my hair away from my face and I emptied myself into the basin. My eyes watered from the vicious spasms, but still I did not weep.

"How long has she been ill like this?" Ursula was talking to Dafne in lowered tones, and I couldn't make out the librarian's reply.

I lost the rest of their conversation in the rustle of silk and comforting murmurs of the other ladies as they swept me away from my sick and eased me onto the glorious bed I'd shared with Hugh for such a brief marriage. As I stared up at the fanciful draperies of lace and ribbon, his teasing words came back to me. *A beautiful princess bed for the most beautiful princess of all.*

Our story was not supposed to end this way.

Ursula sat on the bed beside me and I let her sinking weight draw my eyelids closed. I didn't resist when she took my hand, though hers was still as cold as melting ice. I felt nothing.

"Ami—"

"Don't call me that." My voice was dull, but she heard me.

"Let me help you, Amelia. I want to be here for you."

"I don't need anyone killed today, thank you. I've had enough of that."

Her fingers tightened on mine. A low blow, but a direct hit. Funny that she was trying to mother me now. She'd never wanted to before. Always our father's daughter, obsessed with sword fighting, strategy, and law, she'd never even seemed to miss our mother. Ursula had always been studying or practicing in the yard, telling me to stay out of her way when I toddled after her. Andi had been the one to care for me, my substitute mother. Andi had always been the moderator between me and Ursula, too.

Andi, who had betrayed me and now was as gone from the world as Hugh.

"I can't imagine the kind of grief you're feeling, Amelia, but you must think of the babe. Take care of yourself for your child's sake."

What in Glorianna's name was she talking about? I squinched my eyes open to glare at the lacy canopy and pulled my hand out of hers.

"I'm sick over Andi's betrayal and Hugh's murder, Ursula. I'm not pregnant. I realize it's not in your realm of expertise, but a woman needs a living man's member inside her to make a baby. It might have escaped your notice, but *my* husband is dead."

"I'm going to ignore that and write it off to you being out of your head. But you need to get a grip."

There was Ursula's usual impatience—and a shadow of hurt in those steel-gray eyes. I was on a roll today. Normally nothing pierced her heart.

"Hugh left only a month ago. You could easily be two or three months along. I realize it's not *your* realm, but I think you can do the math."

My ladies had discreetly retreated into the antechamber, giving us privacy to squabble, so I scooted my own self up to sit against the pink-satin-padded headboard. Ursula made no move to help me.

"You think I'm with child?"

She nodded. She'd cut her hair short for the campaign—all the better to fit under her helm. The ragged cut set off her sharp cheekbones. "More, Andi said you were. No, don't shake your head. This is one of the things Andi asked me to tell you."

"I don't want to hear it. I hate her. I'll hate her forever!"

"I don't care. Enough with the drama. Be your father's daughter and pull yourself together."

"I am, Ursula! I've held up for days and days and *days*. You have no idea how it is! But I stood there and let you lay my husband's body at my feet and I didn't break. Now you want me to listen to the words of the woman who killed him in cold blood?" The poison wanted to rise again, but I choked it down. I didn't want Ursula to see me sick again.

"It wasn't cold blood." Ursula's voice was the flat of a blade. "It was chaotic and frenzied and horrible. Impossibly fast and excruciatingly slow. If I could take back that moment, if any sacrifice I could make would change that dreadful sequence, I would in a heartbeat. We could have hidden the truth from you, but Andi wanted you to know she takes responsibility for it. Even if it means you hate her forever."

She let the silence hang between us, full of the weight of expectation. She'd learned the trick from our father and wielded the weapon with the same mastery. I'd never been able to bear it. I plucked at my gray skirts.

"Fine. Then tell me and have done."

Ursula held up her blue-veined hand and showed me three points, as if I were still the five-year-old to her fifteen and she was explaining the three goddesses. "First, she said that you were with child and that she will bear the mark of the Tala also."

"How could she possibly know that?" The question ripped out of me. "I'm still not sure it's true! Besides—why in Glorianna's name would she wish such an evil thing upon her niece? That thrice-cursed mark brought her only misery and destroyed her life."

Ursula shook her head, seeming to notice her cold hands for the first time, because she rubbed them vigorously together, then stood and paced to the fireplace, holding them out to the fire.

"She's not wishing—she simply said what she believed to be true. Andi has changed. Whatever she's gone through, she's . . . more than what she was."

"How?" My throat felt raw. It bothered me how much I ached to know. I'd hated that she'd been forced to marry that demon spawn, hated that she'd done it to rescue me. I didn't want her to change. All I wanted was to go back and make it so none of this had ever happened.

Ursula gave me a wry look over her shoulder. "She's uncannily like our mother now."

"I wouldn't remember." Hard to recall much about a woman who died giving birth to you.

"I do." Ursula spoke softly to the flames. "And Andi has that about her now. Something witchy. I saw her do things . . ." She shook it off. "Hugh thought he was lying when he told her you were with child. She didn't want to come with us and he believed that she would do that for you."

I scoffed at that, but she ignored me.

"Then, after he . . . Afterwards, I told her it had been a lie and she got that look in her eye—you remember how she sometimes did? Like when we argued with Father that Hugh was for you and not for me. And she said, 'Pairing either of them with anyone else would be an exercise in futility. This is how it will be.' "

I remembered it word for word, just as Ursula did. Andi had always hung in the background, preferring to be invisible, but she'd stood before our father—who'd been so, so angry that my cursed face had distracted the match he'd planned for his heir— and told him what he wanted was futile. *Nobody* told High King Uorsin what he wanted was futile.

He'd been so angry with her.

He'd recognized her disloyalty to the kingdom and the family long before anyone else. Maybe he'd recognized her murderous heart when I had not.

"She was that way, only more so," Ursula continued, as if I'd replied. "More confident. She said your daughter would bear the mark and—"

"Whatever *that* means."

"Whatever that means," Ursula agreed, "and that you should send the girl to her. That your daughter will need what she can teach her."

"Is she out of her mind?" Ursula didn't answer me, so I scrabbled off the high bed in a tangle of skirts and grabbed her by the arm. Her metal-embedded leather sleeve was still icy wet from the gale outside. "Why in Glorianna's name would I trust Hugh's child with his murderer?"

"I'm only passing along the message, Amelia." Her remote calm made me want to grind my teeth, as it always did. Princess Ursula the Heartless, they called her. No man would ever have her because she loved her sword the most.

"Then tell me the third thing and go."

"She said to find the doll our mother left you."

"Doll? What doll?" I shook her arm. The whole thing enraged me. Why would she taunt me in my grief with all this nonsense?

Ursula looked down at me and gently peeled my clenched fingers off her arm. "I don't know, Ami. She gave me the same message. Remember that horrible little hair doll Andi always kept, on the high shelf in her room?"

"No." I spat it out, as I wished I could spit out all this rage. But I did remember. She'd let me play with anything of hers but that. It was ugly anyway.

"She took it with her, I guess."

That surprised me. Andi had fled Ordnung disguised as one of my maids right after the Tala attacked. She'd been crazy acting, screaming about dogs howling. I didn't think she'd taken much. She'd been so heartbroken, so afraid our father would kill her mare. She loved that horse. More than she loved me. If she'd ever loved me. I hardened my heart against the sympathy. I should be more like Ursula. Funny, since now I'd be a widow—my bed as cold as my spinster sister's. So ironic.

"So?"

Ursula sighed, the hard smell of her impatience hitting me. She'd delivered her messages, done the requisite comforting, and was ready to be on her way.

"So, just that. Andi thinks our mother made each of us a doll and that we need them. She said to find yours."

"Hard for a dead woman to make a doll."

"I said the same thing, but I had a lot of time to think on the journey here." Ursula turned her head and pinned me with a pointed look. "I remember now—her making it while she was pregnant with you. She spent months on it. Singing and talking to you. I'm sure it's a sorrow to you that you never knew her, and maybe I should have told you this before, but she loved you and talked to you all the time. Maybe some part of you knows that, deep inside."

"I don't know that." It hit me then, unexpectedly hard, and I sank to my knees, not feeling the warmth of the fire. I was all alone now, with no one to love me. Not my mother, not Hugh, not even Andi. The pain of them all mixed together and a high keening sound rose from my throat. The people of Avonlidgh might not cry out at the ravages of death, but I was a child of Mohraya, a daughter of Glorianna, and we do wail out our grief.

"Amelia . . ." Ursula put her hand on my shoulder.

"Just go. Leave me alone for a while." I sounded like I was begging her. In fact, I was. I couldn't bear for anyone to see me this way. So lost and broken. "Dulcinor can show you your rooms."

Another person might have argued. Andi likely would have, as much as she hated my hysterics, but Ursula always respected someone's desire to be alone. Without another word, she left, softly pulling the door to behind her.

I sat on the floor in front of the fire, my dry eyes baking while soothing tears remained in some distant, cutoff place. Alone.

2

W e buried Hugh the next day.
   In keeping with their silence in the face of loss, the people of Avonlidgh hold neither wakes nor elaborate services for the dead. How brilliant Hugh, so full of life and laughter, had come from these grave people, I didn't know. He had been the sunlight streaming through a break in the storm clouds. Now there was only gray.

The rock carvers had been working since we'd heard the news, and they had Hugh's final resting place ready. He would be entombed with the rest of his line, the royal stone sarcophagi each in their niches, then sealed in. Though Erich's seat was at Castle Avonlidgh, a much more central location, on the Danu River, Windroven was the ancestral home of their family. This rocky, desolate shore was where they were born, if it could be arranged, and where their bodies were laid to rest, Glorianna willing.

Ursula and Old Erich flanked me, slightly behind, as if I might turn and run, a child bolting from punishment. I fixed my eyes on Kir, High Priest of Glorianna, who'd traveled from Ordnung when the news spread, for the express purpose of laying the hope of Avonlidgh to eternal darkness. The only one not in gray, he wore Glorianna's vivid pink, a color undimmed by grief or death.

I found myself clutching my golden pendant, Glorianna's rose, for . . . something. I couldn't call it comfort, for there was none to be had.

All too soon, Kir finished with his benedictions and they covered Hugh's body in the open sarcophagus with a blanket of pink roses woven by the chapel priests from their carefully tended hothouse. Glorianna is eternal, thus Her roses bloom year-round. It's Her gift to us, that nothing truly dies, but lives on.

The pendant bit into my palm as I prayed fiercely for it to be true. But Glorianna did not answer.

"Princess Amelia?"

Oh. They all waited on me. I took a step and faltered. Ursula put a hand under my elbow, but I yanked it away. I didn't need her support. I needed only one person and he was forever torn from me. Feeling the cold damp of the caves in my bones, I moved like a corpse myself, to gaze down on Hugh's waxy, bloodless face.

Though his skin was dull, devoid of life, his golden hair flopped over his brow, as it always had, gold spun into silk. Someone had washed it. But they hadn't fixed it right. Of its own accord, my hand reached out to tidy it, the way I'd done so many times. Always he would turn his head and kiss the palm of my hand and say, *You might as well not bother. My wife is the most beautiful woman in the Twelve Kingdoms. No one will notice how I look ever again.*

Part of me waited for it, for him to complete our little ritual. But he was gone.

Someone muffled a cough—one of those winter lung diseases, wracking and wet—though the rest of the assembly held their silence. With a sigh, I reached up and unclasped the necklace my father had given me for my fifteenth birthday, Glorianna's rose worked in precious gold dangling from the chain with sparkling light, even in the gloom. I tucked it in Hugh's clasped hands. His fingers felt like stone already.

"Glorianna's love go with you, as mine always will," I whispered.

High Priest Kir led me out of the niche, patting my hand on his arm. The assistant priest, in mourning gray over a white monk's robe, a deep cowl covering his head, closed the sarcophagus and returned to his master's side. His eyes flashed from the shadows of his hood and I got the searing impression of their unnatural green color, like apples in the early spring. Scar tissue distorted the shape of his face and I understood why he wore the cowl.

My fingers spasmed, crumpling the fine velvet of Kir's sleeve. He didn't protest, but he smoothed my hand, then whispered that we need not watch the stonemasons close the tomb.

I shook my head, pressing my lips together. I would stay. Stay until they had sealed Hugh forever away from the light.

High Priest Kir and his assistant withdrew with deep bows and murmured prayers, drawing Glorianna's eternal circles in the air. Behind me, people left as quietly as they could, the whispers of their clothing marking their passage. There was some bit of fuss in helping Old Erich into the chair they'd carried him in. His aged joints couldn't navigate the narrow and uneven cliffside path.

Silence settled, broken only by the splat and scrape of the stonemasons building their wall. Someone still breathed behind me and I looked to see Ursula, standing military straight and somber, at my right hand.

"You can go," I told her.

"I'm staying with you." She said it in that tone, the one that meant I'd never argue her out of it.

And though I thought I hadn't needed her, a rush of gratitude filled me to have her there as witness. Then, one day, if I needed to ask her if we'd really buried him, she could tell me and I'd be able to tell what was true.

I tried not to think about how Andi should be there, on my

other side. Never did I imagine we three wouldn't always be together.

Much less that Andi would murder my one true love.

I worried at that, a tongue returning again and again to a sore tooth, unable to help myself, despite the sick, spiking pain each time I touched it. I pictured her face, those stormy eyes burning out of the wild mess of her rusty black hair. In my mind, she plunged her dagger into Hugh's breast. There, the pain. I played the scene again, Andi's sweetly mysterious smile twisting into an evil grimace of delight. Oh, the pain. I clung to it, reveling in it, needing it.

The stonemasons had finished. They gathered up their tools and bowed their way out, leaving us alone in the tomb, with only the gusting wind whistling through the alcoves, worming its way through the cracks.

Ursula never stirred. If I stayed here all night, she would stay with me. With her fit warrior's body, she would long outlast me.

With a last prayer, I made myself move. Ursula followed me, giving me space and the courtesy of her quiet, something I'd never before appreciated. The wind hit me like a closed fist when I stepped out of the tombs, taking me by surprise, and my gray-kid-slippered foot slid on the ice that formed on the rocks. My stomach flew and the precipice loomed beneath me, white, foaming waves churning below.

Ursula, fast as a striking snake, grabbed me and steadied me. "Watch that step, Ami."

I stared down at the waves. "You should have let me go. It would be fitting."

She pushed me against the rock wall, the stones biting into my back, and gripped my shoulders, steely eyes sharp as a blade. "Never. I will never let you go. Neither will Andi."

Andi's face, gleaming with unholy joy as she plunged in the knife.

"Andi wouldn't care."

"She does." Ursula's fingers dug into my shoulders like talons.

"I don't care if you believe it or not. But she made me promise to see that you survive this blow. If not for us, if not for yourself, then live for the child you carry."

"I'm still not sure that—"

"I don't care if you're convinced. I am certain enough for both of us. Now, can I trust you to walk up this Danu-cursed trail on your own, or do I have to truss and carry you?"

"You shouldn't swear by Danu."

"You're not in a position to be giving me advice. Choose."

I sagged, deeply chilled and ever so tired. Only her strength held me up. "I'll go. Suicide is against *Glorianna's* plan."

"At least we have that." Ursula's tone held a hint of her usual dry wit, but she sounded tired, too. I hadn't asked her how the last months had been for her, chasing Rayfe's demonic armies through the Twelve Kingdoms, taking our father's and Avonlidgh's troops after the Tala, only to fail in the end.

Drained, feeling as empty as Hugh's corpse, I still didn't ask.

That night I lay alone in our huge bed, the fire casting lurid shadows against the looping lace above me. It seemed the satin rosettes, cunningly formed to echo Glorianna's roses, mocked me with their loveliness. Outside the wind howled in the turrets. A full gale had hit just after Hugh's burial, sealing us inside Windroven as surely as the castle's dead were entombed below.

I curled on my side under the extra blankets my ladies had piled on. Surely I'd never be warm again. They'd covered the glazed windows with tapestries to keep out the chill, but the wind is clever. It snuck through, as it had snaked through the tombs. It seized me that Hugh would be cold down there, all alone.

Here I lay in our bed, while he had only the freezing comfort of stone and rotting roses. It gnawed at me. My fingers curled with the gut-wrenching need to tear the stones apart, to unbury him from the crushing weight of the tomb. He should be here with me, cuddling against my back.

The tapestry rippled, the wind clawing at it.

In a flurry, I hurtled out of the covers, pulling on my heavy velvet robe. It wasn't mourning gray, but Hugh wouldn't care. I burst into the anteroom, looking about for my boots. Ursula sat in a chair by the fire, a wine goblet dangling from her hand. She'd been staring at the flames, deep in some memory, but her keen gaze found me.

"Where are you going, Ami?" She spoke gently, as she had when Andi had been so afraid, when the Tala first found her.

I wrapped my arms around myself. "Where are my ladies?"

"Asleep. As you should be."

"Why aren't you?"

She grimaced. "Can't. So I volunteered to sit with you."

"I'm not a baby who needs to be sat with."

"You're grieving, Amelia. People go out of their heads with it. There's no shame in needing people around you."

"What do you understand about it?" As if summoned by her words, the grief rose and caught me around the throat, choking my voice away.

"Enough that I'm not letting you go anywhere near those cliffs."

"That's not where I was going . . ."

She only gazed at me, eyes dark with sympathy, the salt scent of it soft on the air. I couldn't say that I meant only to visit him, to keep him company. The wind howled, mocking me.

"I'm going back to bed."

"Or you can sit with me by the fire. Have some wine and talk."

She and Andi used to do that—sit up late after feasts and have long, wide-ranging conversations. First I was too young to stay up with them; then . . . Then what? I'd had better things to do, I'd thought. I starred in my own sonnet by the time I was twelve. After that it seemed there had always been some entertainment,

some far more exciting thing to do. The court social life at Ordnung had circled around me and I'd loved it. So odd that I was
the one left out now.

What would we talk about? I nearly asked her.

Instead I mutely shook my head and returned to my cold bed.

The sick hit me before I fully awoke. I managed to roll to my
side, to at least spew on the floor, but only dry heaves racked me.
When had I last eaten? I wasn't even sure if it had been last night
that I'd talked to Ursula by the fire. It might have been a dream.

Hearing me, my ladies rushed in, all dressed for the day, flowers looking toward spring. No extended mourning. The people of
Avonlidgh give death its nod and move on. There's always more
work to be done.

Lady Dulcinor clucked in sympathy, tucking the pillows behind
me and setting an empty washbasin on my lap. "Oh, Princess! So
terrible how wan you are. It's a tragedy for you to be widowed so
very young. And poor Hugh! Cut down in his prime. They're already writing the songs, I hear, of your tragic, young love."

She babbled on. I nearly hurled the washbasin at her. Would
have, but the surging queasiness hinted I might need it yet. Suddenly I understood why Andi had called her empty-headed.

One of the other ladies set coddled eggs, pickled fish, and some
of my favorite jasmine tea on a lap tray. The scent curled into my
gut, wrenching it in its sickly-sweet fragrance, and I gagged into
the basin, coughing up bitter bile.

"Take that away," Ursula ordered from the doorway. "Isn't
there a midwife around here?"

They gaped at her. No flower, she. Instead she wore her fighting leathers, a tall and lean woman, a hawk among doves. She
looked haggard and I wondered if she'd slept at all.

"But Princess Amelia isn't—" one of the younger ladies ventured.

"This is nonsense," she snapped at them, making scooting motions with her hands. "The lot of you are useless. Go find a midwife or at least a castle woman who's had the morning sicks. Someone who knows how to deal with this. Surely *someone* knows. Danu knows I don't."

"Get Dafne—the librarian." I rolled my head on the pillow, damp with cold sweat.

Ursula raised an eyebrow. "You think she'll know?"

"Really, Princess Ursula," Dulcinor fluttered at her, "Lady Mailloux has no real royal status. She's not fit for Princess Amelia's—"

"Go get her." Ursula jerked her head at the doorway. "And take that stinky tea with you."

They darted out, songbirds scattering before the talons could strike them also. Ursula went to the water pitcher and poured some into a goblet, handed it to me, and took the basin away. She rinsed it out into the chamber pot and set it on my lap again.

"Drink the water," she ordered.

"I'll just puke it up."

She shrugged. "Gives your stomach something to do. And some of it might soak in. Drink it—you look like hell."

I nearly choked on the water. "I don't think anybody has said that to me in my entire life."

She grinned, tucking her thumbs in the waistband of her leather pants. "That's what older sisters are for."

Sipping the flat, metallic-tasting stuff, I stared into the dull gleam of the washbasin. It helped not to have the smell. Surprising that Ursula would know that.

"You don't have to take care of me. If you hadn't run my ladies out, they'd be doing this."

"I don't mind. I take care of myself most of the time. It's not as if I can take handmaids to battle with me."

I'd never thought about that. Ursula had always been . . . Ursula.

"I want you to come to Ordnung with me." She tried to make

it sound casual, but the steel in her gaze told me this wasn't a suggestion.

"Why? Because you're afraid I'll do myself harm if you're not here to watch me?"

"There are other reasons, but in a word, yes."

At least she was honest.

"Is it me you're worried about or this babe I'm carrying?"

"Right now you're a package deal," she returned evenly, not responding to the petulance I heard in my own voice. "At least you're acknowledging that you're with child."

"I'm not, necessarily." There. Stubborn felt better.

"How long since you've had your monthlies?"

"You know I've never been regular. I can't ever keep track." But a while, I thought. Months maybe? I'd been so afraid for Andi; then there was the kidnapping and Hugh leaving. Then the news. I'd hardly been thinking about my monthlies.

"Knock-knock?" Dafne stood in the doorway, burdened with a tray. "Am I interrupting?"

"No." Ursula eyed her. "What did you bring?"

Dafne set the tray down and busied herself with a teapot. "I've sent for the village midwife. In the meantime, quick research says this gingerroot eases the morning sicks. I've also got some dry toast for you to nibble, Princess. Small bites, until your stomach settles."

Dubious, I tried a bite. It was bland, but at least my gut didn't rebel. The tea smelled a bit of the spiced cakes we always ate during Moranu's Feast at midwinter, a thought that made me cringe, but the cramping sick didn't rise to it. Feeling braver, I drank some, sighing as the comforting warmth relaxed my belly.

"Well done, librarian," Ursula said. "She actually looks as if she might live."

"I told you. Dafne knows *everything*."

"No wonder Andi likes you." Ursula gave her an approving nod.

"Because Andi never studied a day in her life? Yes." I smiled, remembering, and Ursula grinned at me. Then I realized I'd forgotten, for a moment, to hate Andi. We all should hate her. "Thank you, Dafne. That will be all."

Dafne curtsied and backed out with perfect manners, but she didn't look properly humble. Just for show, then.

"There was no call to order her out like that." Ursula folded her arms and frowned at me.

"She's little better than a servant. You ordered my ladies out with less kindness."

"They deserved it. Dafne helped you when she didn't have to. And she is decidedly not a servant."

"She's probably Andi's spy," I grumbled, knowing I was being unreasonable but unable to help myself. I felt sick and miserable and alone. If Hugh were here, he'd gather me into his lap and hold me, stroking my hair and telling me over and over how much he loved me. Now nobody loved me. The knowledge knotted low in my throat, where all those unshed tears had lodged.

Ursula sighed, clearly out of patience. "I'll send your ladies in to tend you. If the midwife says you can travel, I want to leave tomorrow. Day after, at the latest."

She turned to go and I wanted to call her back. To apologize, of all things. But what for? She said she wanted to help me in my grief, but all she did was kick at me. Same as always.

"I'm not going!" I yelled that at her back instead.

"Yes, you are. As I outrank you, I'm commanding it."

"That's not fair. This is *my* castle!"

She ran a hand through her uneven auburn shag. "Danu—you sound like you're five, not eighteen."

I gasped, outrage filling me, and threw the teacup at her head with an incoherent scream. She plucked it neatly out of the air and I found myself gaping at her. She'd always been fast, but I hadn't seen her hand move. Giving me that *look*, she poured more tea into the cup and set it on my tray.

"This is the second time I'm cutting you slack, Ami. This is a horrible thing for you to go through, and I know it's our fault for always spoiling and petting you. Still, you're going to have to find it in yourself to come through this. I can only do so much."

She turned and closed the door behind her with a soft and significant click.

Furious, I hurled the teacup at the door, enjoying the satisfying smash of the delicate ceramic. For good measure I followed it with the plate of stupid toast. Then I flung myself on my pillows, willing myself to cry.

But the tears refused me.

I was as dry as stone.

3

Three days later—at least I managed to delay an extra day—we left for Ordnung.

Ursula always gets her way. I might as well have tried to stop a stampeding bull. None of my protests swayed her. She insisted she had reasons for me to make the journey. But by the way her sharp eyes rested on me, I knew she mainly wanted to keep me off the cliffs.

And in the dark of night, when the wind howled, I could admit to myself that she might be right to worry. The irrational thoughts plagued me. Hugh couldn't be alone among those stones, with the weather so cruel. *It's only his body,* I told myself, staring up at the flickering shadows that turned the cheerful rosettes into death's heads. *He doesn't feel it. He's gone.*

Still, I saw the desolation in his summer-blue eyes, wondering why I didn't come for him.

I tried praying to Glorianna, but She was as silent as She'd always been.

Like crumbling mortar, my rational mind gave way, bit by bit, until by dawn, I felt wrung out and exhausted with the effort not to go to him. Then the sickness rose and I never wanted more to die. It made getting through the nights that much harder. That's why I delayed only one extra day, to prove I could.

Ursula was right to make me leave. Not that I'd ever tell her that.

The morning we left, I paid a farewell visit to Hugh's tomb. High Priest Kir accompanied me, to bestow a last blessing, as he and Old Erich planned to accompany us to Ordnung. His strange assistant followed behind. Thankfully he wore that deep cowl as before, keeping his head bowed to spare us the sight of that disfigured face.

Ironically, the sun had chosen that day to shine in the cold winter sky, and the wind, though never gone, blew with teasing pulls of my hair—almost gentle, hinting that spring might indeed arrive someday. We went early, the rising sun at our backs, then lost behind the bulk of Windroven.

The tombs felt none of the warmth. Already Hugh's matched the others—the stones in the arch of his crypt as worn, equally limned with frost. For a panicked moment I wasn't even sure which was his. The morning sick—as if it felt my fear—swirled up, and I fumbled for one of the mint candies that seemed to help. I might not have Ursula's dignity or responsibility, but I'd be mortified to barf on the High Priest's pink slippers.

Kir's assistant, however, went unerringly to one farther down than I'd thought. Clutching the wreath of Glorianna roses they'd given me, I trailed behind, ready to tell him that he was wrong. But then I saw the mortar marks, the bits and crumbs leading to the sealed door.

My legs wouldn't hold me, so I knelt, pretending to a reverence that eluded me while Kir chanted Glorianna's blessing for the dead. Instead, I counted the archways, so I could find Hugh's again when we returned. It's not Avonlidgh's way, to etch the names or sigils of the dead on their graves. The dead are gone, once more faceless and returned to Glorianna's arms.

Or to Moranu or Danu, if you belonged to Them. But High King Uorsin had declared Glorianna ascendant, a practice Avonlidgh had long embraced—if only to pacify their conqueror. Hugh hadn't much cared either way, except that he always said that I could be Glorianna incarnate, in all Her delicate radiance. When I scolded him for the blasphemy, he'd kiss and tickle me until I couldn't draw breath.

He wasn't the first to call me Glorianna's avatar, but I loved it from him best.

"You may lay the wreath, Princess." Kir's reminder, followed by a cough, yanked me back to the frozen present, making me realize this wasn't the first time he'd said it. The assistant shifted restlessly and I caught that eerie flash of green-apple eyes, glimmering with hatred.

Hastily I looked away, down at the lushly pink roses. Surely I had imagined that, too.

"I need some time alone." My voice sounded frail. Not the High King's daughter, future Queen of Avonlidgh. I laid my finger against a rose thorn, pressing so it pained me. Tried again. "Leave me."

"Princess, the caravan—"

I stood, fixing High Priest Kir with my best imitation of Ursula's stern expression. "The caravan can wait. I highly doubt Her Highness will leave without me." *I should be so lucky.*

They both bowed with perfect manners and backed their way out—far better than Dafne had done. The assistant seemed so quiet and respectful that I wondered if I'd imagined that look in his eye.

Then I was alone with Hugh, alone for the first time since he'd left our bed that last morning, kissing me sweetly and promising to rescue my sister. Had it been that night that I'd conceived? He'd been so passionate and tender. We'd made love three times—a first—because he'd wanted to make sure I wouldn't miss him too much.

Oh, how I missed him.

I set the wreath before the crypt, as I was meant to, then—tentatively—touched the stones walling him in. My fingertips found the mortar, as I'd imagined them doing so many nights, digging in so it bit into me, a sick ache where I'd pricked myself with the thorn.

"Hugh?" My whisper echoed like the voices of ghosts. "I'm saying good-bye for a little while. I must travel, but I'll be back. Your child—do you know about our babe? I'll make sure to have my lie-in here, at Windroven, as you would have wanted. I promise you that."

My voice hitched, choked with the tears that couldn't escape. For the first time, the babe seemed real to me. Would this child also be entombed here someday? It seemed so much easier to envision that eventuality, rather than a living child. I put a hand over my belly, more settled now, and kept the other on the stones, clinging to them. I imagined Hugh on the other side, perhaps also leaning his cheek against the wall, pressing his palm to mine. Death didn't separate us—only this barrier. That was all.

"I think of you every minute." The ice on the stones melted beneath my cheek, almost like the feel of the tears I longed for. "This shouldn't have happened. I don't understand how it did. I don't know what to do."

I closed my eyes, seeing his handsome face again. "You said you'd love me forever, and now"—my voice cracked—"I'm nothing. How could you leave me?"

"Princess Amelia?"

I knew that voice. Dafne, likely playing Ursula's messenger girl. How much had she eavesdropped? I refused to open my eyes.

"Go away."

"I can't, but I'll wait back here."

I pried open an eyelid to see she stood as far away as possible. The strange echoes of the tombs had made her sound so much closer. She held her hands folded in front of her, encased in traveling gloves, her expression somber. Nothing about her indicated that she found what I was doing strange. Not a messenger, but yet another babysitter.

"I'll leave when I'm ready." Already the stones dried under my cheek. I could no longer see Hugh, just on the other side of the wall.

"Of course, Your Highness. It's only that Princess Ursula grows . . . impatient."

"She can't grow impatient. She's always full-fledged impatient."

Dafne made a wry twist of her mouth. "True, Princess."

With a long breath, I let go of the wall and bent to pluck a rose from the wreath, to take with me. The blossoms seemed far too pretty to leave here. But death doesn't respect beauty any more than anything else. Plucked from Glorianna's gardens, they'd begun to die at that moment. Nothing could stop it.

"What do you think happens, after death?"

Dafne paused. I'd surprised her. "I am no priest of Glorianna. Surely you should ask High Priest Kir."

"I know what his answer would be. I want to hear yours."

"Why me?" She asked it bluntly, failing to call me Princess, as if to call me out for the extraordinary nature of my question. I'd called her little better than a servant and felt a flush of shame over it, though she couldn't know that.

"You're Andi's librarian. If she thought you knew . . . things, then I want to know what they are."

"That's a curious way to ask for my thoughts on death."

"Fine," I snapped. "Don't tell me. I know I'm not my sister. You owe me nothing. You probably hate me as much as she does."

I pushed past her and she laid a hand on my arm, then snatched it back at my outrage.

"Forgive me, Your Highness." She ducked her head. "But I can tell you, when Andi was here and we . . . discussed how things might go, were she to . . . have to marry King Rayfe—her greatest concern was you. She loves you and never wanted to cause you any pain. That hasn't changed."

I watched her lips move and smelled that burnt scent in the air that lately seemed to mean lies. Why was she lying to me? Not in the words necessarily, but running beneath, like an underground river.

"That's a lie. She murdered my husband in cold blood. That's hardly failing to cause me pain."

"I wasn't there, but she wouldn't have done such a thing in cold blood. She agonized over whether you'd be hurt."

"What aren't you telling me?" I asked, watching the flinch of response. To her credit, she held my gaze, steady, unapologetic.

"Secrets that aren't mine to tell."

Andi. My sister had secrets. It made me burn with rage to think it. Never had I kept a secret from her.

"Keep them, then. I want nothing of hers, ever again."

I stepped out onto the path, looking out over the endless ocean. I'd miss it, the constant roar of the surf, the way the light changed on it. The tips of the waves sparkled, catching the rising sun. I'd felt safe here, high up on the cliffs, protected and cherished.

"I suppose I don't believe that anything really dies." Dafne said, standing beside me, gazing at the vista. "I think life cycles into life again. It just . . . changes form."

Putting my hand on my still-flat belly, I mulled her words. Where did this new life come from? Not from nothing.

"Thank you," I finally replied. "I realize I'm an empty-headed twit and not always as kind as I should be. Your words help."

"You must understand you have my deepest sympathy, Princess. We all feel a bit of your loss. Prince Hugh was . . . larger than life."

I nodded, the salt sting in my eyes only from the breeze off the water.

"I can press that for you."

For a moment, I had no idea what she was talking about, then realized she'd indicated the rose from the wreath.

"It's a way of preserving it, so it dries with the petals intact. Something you can keep."

"But it will never be what it was."

"No." Her voice seemed full of sincere regret. "It can't be. But it will be a way to remember what it was."

"Thank you." I handed it to her and she cupped it in her gloved hands, as if it were something precious. "That's two kindnesses you've done me."

She curtsied. This time there was no lie behind it.

The ocean stretched on, endless and deep. So much more than the surface. I'd called myself empty-headed. Nothing without Hugh. Maybe it was true. Glorianna knew I'd seen it in the faces of everyone around me. Perhaps, like the ocean, I could be more than the surface, what they saw every day.

I could be Glorianna's avatar, not just in appearance, but in other ways.

Andi had changed, had she? *More than she was.* I could be more, too. I would show them all.

🌹 🌹 🌹

I rode in the chariot, letting Dulcinor's chatter wash over me. High Priest Kir rode with Erich, and Ursula stayed on horseback, though I couldn't understand how she didn't freeze. The early sun had disappeared behind a solid bank of clouds, gray as my gown. Bits of snow fell, only to skitter over the hard ground in small drifts of ice.

The midwife, Marin, rode with us. It seemed that I was to be monitored at all times. I told Ursula I felt sure the babe would grow on its own and didn't need to be watched, but Ursula pulled rank, yet again, and dismissed my complaints.

Dafne made up our fourth, though I couldn't imagine why she'd return to Castle Ordnung. It seemed to me the librarian had been all too ready to flee with Andi when she left home and had taken shameless advantage of Hugh's generosity in starting a new library at Windroven. Hugh had laughed, saying Mohraya's loss was Avonlidgh's gain, then stroked my cheek in that way he had, reminding me that the principle applied with me, also.

He'd been incorrigible that way.

I pressed my lips against the nausea—the rocking of the carriage did not help—and stared fixedly out the window, the carriage curtains open because the cold air helped me. Winter held the land in a firm grip, the fields barren, no livestock in sight. It seemed so wrong, even with the season. When we passed a burned-out farmstead, I frowned at it.

"What happened here?" I wondered out loud.

Dafne looked up from the book she was reading and peeked through her curtain to see what I looked at, then gave me a grave look. "The war."

Rayfe and his horrible armies. "The Tala did all this? Why would they attack innocent farmers?"

"That's how demons do," Dulcinor assured me. "They don't care a whit for innocence. They slaughter everything in their path. I hear their foul creatures even eat people alive." Marin said nothing, her needles clicking as they wove the yarn piece she worked on.

Dafne cleared her throat. "In truth, most of these outlying farms were cleared by the armies defending Windroven."

"Why?" The concept flabbergasted me. Had Hugh mentioned this to me? Surely not. But then, we never discussed unpleasant things. He hadn't liked to see me distressed.

"Because, in a siege situation, the defenders must make sure the attackers lack as many resources as possible." Dafne closed her book, using a finger to mark the page. "The people inside the castle can only last as long as the supplies do. It's good strategy to limit what the attackers can access."

It made sense, though I'd never thought about it before. "But the siege didn't last that long."

"Because Andi's marriage to Rayfe stopped it. That's the only reason. It could have gone on much longer." Dafne's round face looked pinched and I vaguely recalled she'd lost her family—and heritage—to a siege during the campaigns that made my father

High King. "She couldn't bear to have this kind of devastation occur to protect her."

"She married him to rescue me," I argued.

"You're so lucky those wicked Tala didn't harm you, Princess!" Lady Dulcinor fanned her flushed face, though she kept the fur robe mounded on her lap.

I nodded as if I agreed but wondered if it was luck. For all that they'd kidnapped me, King Rayfe and his men had been careful with me, even kind. They were terrifying, of course, all long, wild hair and fearsome beastlike eyes—and all those wild, strange animals around them!—but Rayfe had promised I wouldn't be hurt. And I hadn't been.

Instead Andi had traded herself for me. Wasn't that what had happened?

Dafne watched me, seeming serene, but that undercurrent of lies wafted through the back of her gaze, the burnt-toast scent in the air turning my stomach. She knew something about it. Secrets that weren't hers to tell.

Andi's secrets.

Feeling the chill, I closed the curtains. Better not to look.

Alarmed shouts and the bellowing cry of a horse in pain jerked me from a sleepy doze on the second afternoon. Dulcinor emitted a thin wail and began praying to Glorianna so loudly that she drowned out all outside noises except for Ursula's sharp commands, cutting through the tumult.

Dafne, who'd had her curtain open, shook her head at me. "I can't see anything."

On the other side of the carriage, the clang of weapons burst out, with crackling ricochets of orders and a tumult of incoherent yelling. Full of dread, yet burning to find out, I twitched my own curtain. Marin leaned over and put her sturdy hand on mine.

"Best not, Your Highness," she said quietly. "Sometimes the mouse best avoids the cat by staying in its hole."

A thunder of hoofbeats roared up and past our carriage, rumbling off into the distance. We waited, Dafne, Marin, and I staring at one another, while Dulcinor wept, face buried in her skirts—which would surely be ruined by her tears and makeup.

The curtain jerked open and we all jumped, Dafne pressing a hand to her heart.

Ursula's sharp face filled the opening, quickly surveying us for damage. "All is well. We can continue on in a few minutes."

"What happened?" I asked.

Her narrow lips pressed together in annoyance, though not at me this time. "Highway robbers. And on the King's Road, too. But we've run them off easily enough."

Angry voices drifted down the road and I recognized one as belonging to Old Erich. Everybody else was out there, deciding things. I should be, too. Not a mouse. "I want to see."

"You have legs. Come out and see, then." She dropped the curtain, and the hoofbeats of her warhorse faded.

I glanced at the other women, uncertain, but Dafne nodded at me. "I want to see, too."

Dulcinor didn't seem to hear us, just kept weeping into the fabric she'd be sorry she ruined, now that we'd survived. Dafne made the decision and popped open the carriage door. After a quick glance about, she stepped out and held a hand up to help me down. At first there didn't seem to be much to see, just a lot of dirt scuffed through the snow. But there—a man lay dead in a snowbank, long, dark hair snarled, several of the Hawks' arrows protruding from his chest. Other shadows marred the snow in unsightly heaps.

Down our caravan, King Erich was indeed shouting at the lieutenant of Ursula's Hawks, and it seemed Ursula had just joined them.

". . . an abomination against Avonlidgh that I cannot travel through my own kingdom without being attacked by riffraff!"

"We may have crossed into Mohraya, King Erich." Ursula stared him down, diverting him from her lieutenant. "In which case the failure belongs to me."

He turned more purple than his expensively dyed robes. "The fault for all of this lies with the High King! For what did we trade our wealth and independence if he's going to cower inside Ordnung and let the rest of the Twelve fall into chaos?"

Ursula's eyes glittered brighter gray than the overcast sky. "You're edging into treason, King Erich."

High Priest Kir, bright pink robes the only other color in the wintery landscape, smoothly stepped up, making the circle of Glorianna in the air, which everyone echoed dutifully. "Praise Glorianna that we are all safe, and our gratitude to the brave escort that protected us! King Erich, it grows colder and I believe it may snow. Shall we retire to our conveyance and discuss these atrocious events?"

His assistant, white robes tainted by a spray of bright blood, stood close behind, head bowed so the cowl hid his face. Odd that he'd been so close to the fighting.

"An excellent suggestion." Ursula nodded, giving her Hawks hand signals. "We shall leave the slain robbers as a caution and continue immediately."

With that, we were escorted to the carriage. I should have said something. Led a prayer. Next time I would.

"At least it wasn't the Tala," I said, as much for Dulcinor's peace of mind as anything. Marin gave me a long look as she picked up her discarded knitting. "What?" I asked her.

"They likely were Tala, Princess." Dafne's tone was gentle but firm. "Those men had the right coloring. And it makes sense."

"Why haven't they gone home, then? They should all go back to the Wild Lands and leave us be. They've done enough damage here."

"That's a good question." Dafne looked contemplative. "Seems that they would, if they could."

When we reached Louson, to stay at the small but decent manse of one of our father's oldest friends, the fertile river valley looked lovely and peaceful under a blanket of pristine snow. It had taken three days of travel to fully escape the signs of the Siege of Windroven. It would not make Old Erich any happier to see this part of Mohraya looking so well.

I understood better why Andi had restlessly paced the turrets and high walls of Windroven, no matter how I begged her to stay inside. Remembering how my ladies and I had treated the first battles as a spectacle, I groaned at my foolishness. No wonder Andi hadn't wanted to be around me.

All that time, I'd thought she'd been afraid only of being forced to marry our enemy. Instead she'd been thinking about the lands outside the walls, the dead bodies lying about the country-side. Hugh had told me not to fret about the siege and I hadn't.

And then Kir had been the one to soothe Erich, by calling on Glorianna, after Ursula saved us all. My uselessness ate at me.

After a welcome feast I barely touched—in fact, I excused my-self early because the smell of the poached fish nearly made me lose the little I had eaten—I went to Glorianna's chapel, to pray for guidance.

I'd been here before, when I'd paid the priests to perform a High Protection for Andi, to save her from Rayfe and the Tala. It looked much the same as it had that night—except that the rose window over the altar had since been repaired. The sight of it brought back all the emotions of that night, my desperate fear for Andi's safety and the stark terror when the black wolf crashed through. My utter shame that I ran, leaving her behind.

"Do you pray, Princess?"

I jumped nearly out of my skin, half expecting the wolf to attack again. But no—that was done and he wouldn't come for me. It wasn't me he'd wanted. The assistant priest lurked in the shadows, white robes an echo of the marble walls beyond the flickering candles, still wearing that deep cowl. I hadn't heard him speak before and now I imagined his twisted whisper came from a reptilian face, scarred into a monster's visage.

Standing, I put a hand over my belly. "Yes. I prefer to be alone."

Instead of leaving, he sidled closer. "They did a good job of replacing the window. It's even grander this time—a great tribute to the glory of our goddess."

"Yes." I held my ground, though he came nearer. My heart thumped, but I had no reason to be afraid. Or did I? That flash of utter hatred in his eyes had seemed so vivid in that moment. Surely those dark memories of the past, on top of the attack today, had made me jumpy. My personal guard was right outside. Besides, no harm could come to me here, under Glorianna's gaze.

"All hail Glorianna." He spoke to the rose window, and I started to echo the prayer, until I broke off, realizing he'd said it with irony, not reverence. He turned his head in an abrupt, liquid movement, and I startled, jumping back and losing my footing on the risers. His hand snaked out and seized my shoulder, steadying me. "Don't fall, Princess. You wouldn't want to risk the precious burden you carry."

"Unhand me."

He let me go and held up his hands, surprisingly brown and weathered for a priest. "No offense, Your Highness. I meant only to assist in your time of need."

"With my balance or with prayer?"

"Yes."

"Are you playing games with me?"

"With the future Queen of Avonlidgh and she known throughout the land as Glorianna's avatar? Why would I risk myself in such a way?"

"My sister does that—answers a question with a question."

"Indeed."

"So which is it, balance or prayer?"

"Prayer is a form of self-reflection that leads to balance, but you don't need my help. Glorianna is within you. She hears you without assistance from such as me."

"That's close to blasphemous."

"And yet Glorianna does not strike me down for my words."

"Who are you?" I tried to demand in my usual way, but my words came out sounding frightened.

"What more do you need to know, but that I am a priest of Glorianna and thus trustworthy?"

"Who once again refuses to answer my question. I could have you punished for your impertinence."

His gaze flashed from the shadow of the cowl, like a cat's eyes at night. "But you won't do that, will you, Amelia?"

"I won't, if you leave me in peace."

"Peace is an expensive commodity—I highly doubt you can afford it."

"What in Glorianna's name does that mean?"

"Only that peace—true inner peace—comes from seeing yourself clearly and accepting who you are."

I looked away, bothered that I couldn't see his face. Bothered that there might be nothing in me to see. "You presume far too much for a lowly assistant priest. You understand nothing about me."

"Looking in a mirror to fix your pretty face isn't the same as seeing yourself."

The impertinence—and the uncomfortable parallel to my own thoughts—made me gasp, and I swung on him, full of imperial rage.

"Your Highness!" High Priest Kir called from the rear of the chapel. "Had I known you intended to come here, I would have been here sooner. I will assist with your prayers."

The assistant priest faded back, but a breath of a laugh made me think he mocked Kir and me both.

"I shall retire, then, sir." He'd folded those coarse, tanned hands into his loose sleeves and bowed his face.

"Yes, yes." Kir waved him away, busying himself with preparations at the altar.

When I looked again, he was gone.

4

"Who is that?" I asked Kir, who frowned a little, losing his count in the infusion of Glorianna's wine.

"My assistant, Your Highness. I believed you'd seen him before, but perhaps in the, ah, aftermath of Prince Hugh's tragic passing and your extreme grief—"

"Not that." I gave rein to my irritation. Better than letting the sorrow take me over at Kir's careless words. Just when I thought the edge had dulled, it swamped me, a wave wanting to drag me off the rocks at Windroven, cold, bitter, and irresistibly powerful. "I mean what is his name? His background."

"Ah." Kir smiled, composing his features into that beatific expression he favored. "These things are not known to me. He is of the White Monks."

I'd vaguely heard of that order, over in far Nebeltfens, but I couldn't recall why they sounded familiar. A special cult of Glorianna?

"And that means?" I prompted Kir, who had to conceal his frustration at losing his count again. "You can leave off on that— I don't care for the full ceremony tonight."

"But, Your Highness, if you wish to pray in the Temple, then—"

"Tell me about the White Monks." I didn't care if I sounded like a spoiled drama queen right then. Especially if it got me the answers I sought.

"They consecrate themselves to Glorianna's service very young. They give up their names, their previous identities, all the better to make themselves vessels for Glorianna's pure and holy presence."

"Why are they called the White Monks—for the robes?"

"The robes are secondary, Your Highness. The White Monks spend the first three years of service under a strict vow of silence, and the name of their order reflects the stillness and purity they believe that brings. Many never speak again."

"But this one does."

"Did he speak to you? He rarely does."

"He did."

Kir looked at me expectantly and I nearly said how impertinent—even rude—the assistant had been. Then closed my lips over it. *But you won't do that, will you, Amelia?* He'd called me by my name and I hadn't noticed. How odd.

"I hope he didn't bother you, Your Highness. You're something of a legend among the younger priests—in truth, among the older ones, also. This one asked to accompany me in my journey here, but I trusted his taciturn nature to restrain him."

"I'm a legend? Restrain him from what?" A flutter of pleasure threaded through me, the first since I'd heard the tragic news from Odfell's Pass. I used to feel this, it seemed ages ago, when some troubadour sang a new song composed to me. Though I would never have told Hugh so, in my heart of hearts I'd missed it. Windroven is well off the traveled routes. And nobody writes poetry about wives.

"They see you as the incarnation of Glorianna, Your Highness." He bowed to me, a deeply respectful and ceremonial gesture. "Her avatar, sent to us in our time of need, to combat the demonic forces that threaten to tear us asunder."

My heart rose, painfully. "The Tala."

He nodded. "Already they tore Princess Andromeda from our

breast, leaving a gaping wound for their poison to flow in and rot us from the inside out. You fought to save her."

"I did." How did he see what no one else had? "I fought for her with all my might. And so did Prince Hugh."

"Which is why she killed him." He made the sign of Glorianna, a circle in the air. "Like a viper at your bosom, she struck at you, attempting to destroy you, also. But Glorianna protects Her avatar. She's blessed you with the child who will save us all."

"She will?"

"*He* will." Kir made the circle again. "We have seen visions. He will be the next High King, and the Twelve Kingdoms shall flourish under his rule. We will destroy the Tala, utterly and for all and forever. We shall take back Annfwn, the paradise that should have been Glorianna's, that *Her* sister stole from Her. And you shall lead us there, Glorianna's chosen one."

Kir's visage gleamed with a glowing, nearly fanatical light. Could this be true? It would mean that Andi—and Ursula—were wrong about the child being a daughter. But then, they had already tried to mislead me in other ways. And Dafne, making out that Andi had been so noble—was that more misdirection? After all, Andi's actions had spoken very loudly.

High Priest Kir came closer, then knelt before me, kissing the tips of my fingers. "Do you see the parallels in your story?"

"I'd never heard this, that Moranu stole Annfwn. I'd never heard of Annfwn before those Tala showed up."

He nodded gravely. "It's a wound to Glorianna's children and so we don't speak of it. Annfwn is said to be paradise, where we once all lived. Shouldn't paradise belong to Glorianna?"

"But Her sister Moranu stole it?"

"Through vile treachery. It was High King Uorsin's lifelong quest to recover Annfwn for Glorianna."

My mouth was sticky, the scent of roses too strong with the burning candles. "What happened to his quest?"

Kir glanced from side to side, as if checking for eavesdroppers, and lowered his voice. "Salena of the Tala."

"My mother?" And Andi carried our mother's mark. It all began to make sense, Andi's change, her betrayal. The half-breed blood showing through.

"You are wise, Your Highness. Uorsin sacrificed his dream of gaining Annfwn to make a lasting peace for Glorianna. And, some of us believe, so that you could be born. *You*. The third, most important daughter. Glorianna made flesh."

My heart thumped with the wild possibilities of it. I'd prayed for guidance and Glorianna had answered. Could this be my purpose? "Prince Hugh always said he thought my beauty came from Glorianna's touch."

"Yes, Your Highness. Her radiance is visible in every aspect of your grace and loveliness. Small wonder the poets told tales of you. They will again, as you lead Glorianna's church to greatness. As you lead her children into Annfwn."

That night, I sat in front of the mirror in the grand guest room set aside for my use. Ursula had been given the master's suite, which seemed unfair. Truly, our ranks were equal now. Though she might be heir to the High King, I would be Queen of Avonlidgh sooner than that, as Old Erich couldn't possibly last much longer.

And, if Kir had spoken truly—which I believed he did, for he spoke in Glorianna's chapel, surely at her behest—I carried Uorsin's true heir. Even Ursula—as much as she tried to be a son to our father—she knew as we all did that he'd longed for a boy to take his place. It had been a last trick of Salena's to saddle him with daughters.

Though no one said this aloud.

Kir, though, had put a new spin on our family history. Perhaps Glorianna had guided Salena to our father so that I might be born. Then, her role complete, she passed on. Perhaps she redeemed her devil nature before her death and now rested in Glorianna's arms.

For the first time since I heard that Hugh was forever gone from me, I brushed my hair before bed. I'd started when I was five, when my nurse taught me to do it for myself. My beauty, she'd said, was a tribute to Glorianna, so I owed it to the goddess to maintain that.

One hundred strokes every night, to keep the shine.

I should never have stopped. I counted them as I drew the brush through the red-gold locks, sinking into the peaceful, even feel of it. The woman looking back at me in the mirror wore the same face I'd always known. Still beautiful.

Not ugly as I'd imagined. All that had happened had failed to touch me. Nothing dimmed the fiery river of my hair, the translucence of my skin, the twilight blue of my eyes, enormous in my delicate face. I'd heard myself described in poems before I knew half the words to assign to the features the mirrors showed me.

The most beautiful woman in the Twelve Kingdoms. Then and still.

My gift from Glorianna and a sign of Her favor. She would no more strip me of that radiance than She could tear it from Her own being. Though Glorianna's enemies had torn Hugh from me, I would not give up Her fight. His death would not be in vain. Our child would be High King and cleanse the land of the Tala.

Glorianna willed it.

I would honor her will.

🌹 🌹 🌹

If Ursula looked at me strangely the next morning, I put it down to the fact that she hadn't seen me out of mourning since we'd reunited. Of course, she was angry that I'd delayed our departure by hours while Dulcinor recruited the Louson maids into sewing my new pink gown. Not that I cared a whit for Ursula's moods.

I belonged to Glorianna and I would honor Her.

"Done primping?" Ursula asked, looking me up and down.

"And puking, yes, thank you."

She had the grace to look chagrined, and I enjoyed the score. Even though the queasies were much better thanks to Marin's concoctions. I sent Dafne to ride with some of the other ladies, so Kir could talk with me more about Glorianna and his plans to recover Annfwn for us and for Glorianna's greater good.

For all I knew, Dafne was one of them. Who said the shape-shifting demons couldn't masquerade as humans, too? It seemed more and more likely that she was a spy and her supposed concern for me a clever ruse to gain my confidence. But I would be more clever than she.

As for the midwife, she simply spent her time knitting, humming to herself, and glancing up from time to time to check my color. She seemed to know when the carriage movement was getting to me, handing me well-timed mints or thin toasts to chew on before I realized I needed them.

Time passed quickly with High Priest Kir's excellent conversation. I hadn't recognized before what a well-educated and intelligent man he was. And so devout. His allegiance to Glorianna practically glowed from his countenance. Never before had I understood the true foundation of the war the Tala had waged—and catastrophically won—to wrest Andi's loyalty from us.

More and more I understood how they'd clouded her mind with half-truths and used her emotions against her. As I'd suspected, she didn't love Rayfe. Even if she believed she did, it would be impossible because he wasn't even human. It made so much sense—though the Tala appeared to be people, they were truly animals and thus without souls.

"Love is the expression of the soul, Your Highness," Kir explained. "It is the pure and true animus of us as Glorianna's children. In Her wisdom, Glorianna gave us love to connect our souls together, to give us solace until we return to Her encompassing light. Thus, love must be given to be received, and received to be given. It's an eternal cycle."

"So the Tala cannot love."

Kir shook his head, looking somber and sorrowful. "No. You are as insightful as you are beautiful, Princess. You are correct: the Tala cannot give or receive love because they aren't Glorianna's children."

"Whose children are they?"

"Some say Moranu's. Others say they belong to none of the trinity but are simply animals that have learned to mimic humans."

"Then Andi has been bewitched."

He considered that, then leaned forward. "Your compassionate nature does you credit, Your Highness. You are indeed Glorianna's avatar on this earth. You carry within you all of Her goodness and thus you can't bear to think ill of others. But you are also brave and strong. You may have to face that the woman you thought was your sister was never truly human at all."

The even click of Marin's needles hitched and she muttered about dropping a stitch.

"I've heard tell"—High Priest Kir lowered his voice, turning a shoulder to the midwife—"that those in Princess Andromeda's presence sometimes felt a strange creeping sensation, a visceral fear, perhaps, such as when one sees a poisonous spider."

The staunchly loyal part of me protested. Sometimes the people at Castle Ordnung had whispered cruel things about Andi. But I had always, *always* defended her. They just didn't understand her. Andi had been shy, preferring to ride her horses instead of participating in the feasts and dances. Even when I encouraged the men waiting for their turn to dance with me to at least talk to her, she hadn't tried to be pleasant to them.

She always had to be difficult, it seemed. Still, she was human. Wasn't she?

Kir read the confusion on my face, because he took my hand,

folding it between his in a fatherly gesture. "Such loyalty. You have no ill thoughts in you, so you cannot imagine them in others. But we all heard the truth of it from Her Highness Ursula's own lips. Glorianna's spirit in you drives you to absolve the creature who carelessly, viciously murdered your husband. Your son will grow up without a father. Is there any way this cannot be the manifestation of a cruel and malicious will?"

My throat clogged, all of those unshed tears still trapped in there, locked in forever, stuck with pieces of my destroyed heart. I didn't feel like Glorianna's avatar. I felt more the five-year-old that Ursula scornfully accused me of being.

"Your mother was one of them," Kir continued, his smooth voice relentless. "Many are the tales told of how she beguiled High King Uorsin and forced him into her devil's bargain. Ask yourself this—what did she get out of the marriage? They had no love for each other. What was her demonic plan?"

My stomach churned and Marin handed me a cup of tea from her flask. I might have imagined it, but it seemed she cast an angry, sideways glance at Kir. Taking the cup allowed me to withdraw my hand from the priest's grip, and I wrapped my own around the delicate mug, wishing my fingers weren't so cold.

"I don't know," I admitted. "I never knew her. She's always been a cipher to me. No one would ever talk about her." So much so, in fact, that I'd never heard of the Tala until Rayfe demanded our father make good on their old treaty to give him Andi for his bride, much less that our mother, Salena, had been one of them.

"There is a school of thought in Glorianna's temple that explains much about the late queen."

"What is it?"

"Perhaps Your Highness should have a bit of a rest," Marin interrupted. Kir flushed angrily at her lack of manners, and she cringed. "Your color isn't what I'd want it to be, is all, Princess."

In truth I felt ill. The tea wasn't helping. But I needed to hear this. Nobody had ever said to my face that I killed my mother by being born, but they didn't have to. I knew when they lied about it. How they told me it wasn't my fault, that I bore no guilt for it. All the time the stink of lies ran beneath.

"I want to hear this." I handed the mug to Marin. "This isn't helping."

"You see, Your Highness"—Kir templed his fingers and bowed to me over them—"Glorianna created you to fight these battles for Her. Once the demon spawn Andromeda was born, Glorianna saw what a great evil had been released into the world. So She created *you*, perfect in every way. Your beauty is a guiding star for those who would serve your cause.

"Your very goodness burned through the womb and released your mother from the chains of evil. She died, yes, but she passed over redeemed, infused with Glorianna's nature from contact with Her spirit via you."

I wanted to believe that, this idea I'd been mulling over. Maybe Glorianna had whispered it to me. That was how I'd known.

"You *saved* her, Princess Amelia. They named you for the love you brought to the world in her place. Now we are crying for that love. We need you to lead us. Everything that has happened has led to this moment. Do not let your mother's death be in vain. Don't forsake Prince Hugh, who sacrificed himself that your eyes might be opened."

My head swam. "I don't feel well at all." I missed Hugh, bitterly and profoundly. I needed to ask him what he thought of all this. He'd always known the right thing to say to comfort me. Now it seemed I was beyond comfort. How had the world changed so utterly?

Or not changed. From Kir's words, it had been this way all along and I had been simply too blind to see it. How Andi must have laughed at me, watching me indulge in fripperies and romance while she plotted all along to defeat me.

"What of Ursula?"

Kir shook his head, then slid a significant glance at Marin, whose needles flew furiously. "We should perhaps speak of such things at another time. We must do all we can to protect Glorianna's sacred cause. High King Uorsin's great quest."

Did he mean to imply that Ursula wasn't on our side? But it was true—she had defended Andi's actions. My head pounded and my stomach lurched. "Stop the carriage!" I cried out.

In a flash, Marin had me around the waist, supporting me out of the halted carriage. I fell ignominiously to my knees in the half-frozen mud, retching up toast and tea. She patted my back, soothing me, murmuring that babes take their toll and I must keep peaceful.

The cold filth soaked through my skirts and I knew the pink gown would be forever stained.

5

We arrived at Castle Ordnung a day later.

The High King's seat and my childhood home, Ordnung had been built fairly recently—completed not long after Ursula was born, in fact. It didn't look as if it had grown out of the old volcano as Windroven did, constructed of the same dark rock, towers and wings added over time. Instead, Ordnung gleamed brilliant white, with perfect, straight lines and solid defenses. Both a monument to our father's immense achievement in uniting the kingdoms and a fortress in case of attack, Castle Ordnung was, by definition, the finest castle in the land.

Out of long habit, my heart rose to see it, with its uniformed soldiers standing guard and all the bright pennants flying—one for each of the twelve kingdoms—and High King Uorsin's rampant bear above them all. I'd always thought of Ordnung as my true home.

Oddly, though, I missed Windroven, in all her dark rock and ungainly sprawl.

Uorsin received us in the grand audience chamber. As heir to the High Throne, Ursula preceded us and Erich escorted me on his arm. High Priest Kir and that creepy White Monk followed behind.

The last time I was here, I'd been on Hugh's arm and we'd been bursting with fun over our surprise visit—my first since our wedding. With a start, I realized that my wedding anniversary would be soon, when true spring came to Mohraya. We hadn't had even a full year together.

No doubt it would still be wintery on the cold coast of Avonlidgh, but that would be fitting. I would celebrate by myself, perhaps holding vigil at Hugh's tomb, so he wouldn't be alone. My stomach clenched and Old Erich patted my hand, where I dug my nails into his bony forearm.

Uorsin glowered at us. Or, more precisely, fixed his angry gaze on Ursula.

"So you come home with your tail between your legs, do you?"

If that insult struck home, Ursula didn't show any sign. She stood at attention, her spine rigid. Because it was court, she wore a gown, dark and severe in cut, but well made. Had she dragged it with her on the long campaign? Someone had trimmed her shaggy hair, too, and attempted to make it look put up like a proper court lady's instead of just short. She wore the simple gold band across her forehead that proclaimed her heir to the High King's throne. Despite myself, a thrill of pride ran through me. Ursula was nothing if not admirable.

"Yes, my King." Ursula curtsied deeply, keeping her head bowed. "I bring grave news indeed."

He flicked an irritated hand at her. "We have already heard your news. Every damn person in the Twelve Kingdoms and beyond the Wild Lands has heard the news. You can explain your many failures to me in private."

A susurrus of speculation ran through the assembled court. I'd never seen Uorsin so mightily, so fulminously and broodingly enraged. Not even when we first received the message from the Tala. It did not bode well for Ursula. Then he surprised me again by stepping down from the throne and calling my name. He opened his arms, as he had when I was a little girl.

I couldn't possibly embarrass him by not responding, no matter how odd his actions for formal court, so I did what he expected of me—and ran to him, leaving Erich to lean on his valet and brushing past Ursula, who'd stepped aside to clear my way. Uorsin embraced me in his bear hug, nearly crushing me. He rubbed his bristled chin on the top of my head and held me tight.

"My flower, my precious rose. Always you have been the best of us. The sweetest, most innocent, and most beautiful of my daughters. It is a tragedy beyond speaking that *you* should be the one to suffer for your sisters' many sins. First, one betrays me; then the other fails me. You alone have been all that a dutiful daughter should be."

He finally released me and I drew a long breath, feeling more than a little dizzy. Uorsin smelled as if he hadn't been bathing enough—and like the greasy meats he ate for breakfast. I concentrated on breathing through my mouth as Marin had taught me, to master the sickness. It would not do to hurl on the High King's shiny boots.

"You will stay in Ordnung with me," he declared. "I have need of a proper hostess, as my heir seems to be useful neither as a woman nor as a man."

I winced for Ursula, though she did not reveal a flicker of expression on her face. Meanwhile the Avonlidgh contingent behind us began muttering unhappily. Old Erich came forward and bowed to the High King, then put a hand on my shoulder to steady himself.

"King Erich." Uorsin acknowledged his obeisance and assumed a concerned expression. The smoldering scent of lies tinged the air. "My deepest sympathies on the loss of your son—my heart-son—and Avonlidgh's heir. It must be a grave blow in your old age."

If the insensitivity of the remark bothered Erich, he didn't show it. For all that he was terribly old and frail, he was a shrewd man. Hugh had often spoken of how much he admired his father's wisdom and strategy. I'd never given it much thought, but I marked it now, how he gathered a regal air around him—and showed with his arm around me that he, too, called me daughter.

"My gratitude, High King. Your grace and bearing in this time of Avonlidgh's trial simply demonstrates yet again the wisdom of your leadership over us all. Truly, the Twelve flourish under your evenhanded and just rule. I feel confident we can trust in you to right the many wrongs we've suffered and restore peace, bounty, and lawfulness to our lands."

Uorsin frowned, that beefy anger seething below the surface of his skin. He didn't appreciate being taken by surprise. Perhaps Erich had lost some of his wisdom to the dementia of grief. It hit people that way sometimes—they thought they were being rational, but they weren't.

"It is so unfortunate that the unrest in your household resulted in Avonlidgh's loss," Erich continued. "However, I and the people of Avonlidgh wish to assure you of our continued fealty and utter faith that Your Highness will make recompense."

Uorsin's bushy eyebrows knotted. Derodotur, his long-time adviser, moved up surreptitiously and caught the High King's eye. In the court were ambassadors from all the Twelve Kingdoms, save Mohraya, since Uorsin claimed kingship of that land also.

"Of course, Erich." Uorsin took on a boisterous mien. "I shall determine the appropriate recompense and give it to the people of Avonlidgh with love and respect."

Erich bowed. "You are indeed a great and good High King, but I do not wish to impose. To save you the trouble of casting your mind upon us and our troubles, when you have so many greater tasks to attend to, we have determined the small boons we ask of you."

Ursula pretended to be casually scanning the room but caught my eye with a bit of a raised brow. No, I hadn't known about this plan. She was the type to be included in strategy discussions, not me. Something I'd have to change, if I wanted to be taken seriously.

"Princess Amelia came among us as a stranger and has become family. She is Avonlidgh's daughter, in truth. Our heart-daughter. A princess and wife beyond reproach, she inspires the people of Avonlidgh equally with her grace and loveliness. The child she carries in her womb shall be my heir. Thus does joyful news mitigate the terrible and grave."

Uorsin barely hid his astonishment, and I felt more than heard Ursula's impatient sigh. She'd planned for us to tell our father the news in private. But crafty Old Erich had outmaneuvered us. He'd also added a nod in Ursula's direction, as if offering her his respect despite Uorsin's rejection.

The whispers of surprise rippled around the room, growing in volume until they became shouts and cheers. The third generation of Uorsin's reign was in sight. At Derodotur's signal, musicians struck up a triumphant and joyful avalanche of sound while everyone shouted Uorsin's name.

All accomplishments belong to the High King.

When the tumult settled, Uorsin had recovered enough to beam at me with paternal joy. So clever of Derodotur to arrange the distraction. My father pulled me into his arms again, and I held my breath, hoping the embrace would not last so long this time. Fortunately he let me go quickly, but kept me under the drape of his arm. Reasserting his role as my father.

"If the child is a boy, he shall inherit the throne of the High King!" he declared.

Behind me, Kir shouted praise to Glorianna. I didn't dare look at Ursula. Somehow this moment wasn't as sweet as I'd expected. Erich nodded, seeming to agree, applauding with the others. "Avonlidgh shall be gratified to become the seat of the High King," Erich shouted, and the Avonlidgh contingent cheered.

"Mohraya is the seat of the High King. That is how it's always been." Uorsin's powerful voice cut through the cheering. Beside him, Derodotur sidled forward, into the High King's peripheral vision.

Erich appeared befuddled. "Always? But you are the first High King. Mohraya has been and continues to be your seat of power. As the patron country of your successor, Avonlidgh will be honored to serve. The High Throne will move to Castle Avon-lidgh."

Uorsin shrugged Derodotur away. "The only seat of power is here. The child will be born in Castle Ordnung and rule from here—under my hand, until he learns his way."

Erich staggered a step, leaning on his valet heavily, appearing devastated. "Avonlidgh must lose yet another heir?" He projected sorrow and horror. "Already our ravaged land must yield up more. Our people slaughtered, slowly starving, and continually preyed upon by bandits the High King's armies seem to be unable to contain. Has Glorianna turned Her back upon us all?"

The ambassadors around the room looked angry, and several ladies dabbed at their eyes. Mutterings turned from joyful to unsettled.

"I fear the worst is true." The Duranor envoy stepped up beside Erich. "We, too, have suffered from the effects of your war, High King. Even still, escaped Tala prisoners raid our farms, raping our daughters and stealing the bread from the mouths of innocent children. All for a treaty you signed in good faith and declined to honor."

Uorsin glowered, clenching his fists. The unclean, meaty smell of his twisted rage thickened.

"You understand nothing of the situation, Lord Stefan," Uorsin ground out.

"Do we not?" Stefan spread his hands to include all the ambassadors. "You promised us peace and prosperity. Instead you've brought the Tala down on our heads. Again. And this after years of decline. Every season, the fields yield less, the livestock grow more gaunt. Instead of gaining bounty for us, you've carelessly lost one of your daughters. What shall we sacrifice next, High King?"

Shocked silence fell heavy over the room, followed by the wintery smell of fear and despair.

Mastering himself, Uorsin took me by the hand and guided me up the steps to the dais with the High King's throne, my mother's empty throne, and the three for my sisters and me. He settled me into Ursula's seat at his right hand with a great show of solicitude. I couldn't look at her.

Tension creased the rims of Derodotur's eyes, before he smoothed his face into his diplomat's blandness. Even I understood that Uorsin had transgressed several political lines here in seizing Avonlidgh's heir from them. It seemed . . . unlike him. That deep anger rumbled through him, and I had to steel myself not to lean away from the greasy smell.

Instead I focused out over the hall and the assembled people, dividing into various factions, already aligning themselves. Here, too, Glorianna's window had been replaced. Twice the Tala had shattered Her rose windows—both times seeking Andi. I'd been frightened at the time but had never suspected that it would be that moment when the foundation of the world would shift—and keep shifting.

I prayed to the goddess for guidance. Surely being Her avatar should come with more certainty about what I should do and say.

Kir must be right. The Tala had brought the seed of evil to us, and the poison continued to spread. Even my father, who had always been so strong, so certain of his rule and his ability to bring peace to all the lands, seemed uncertain. Unstable. I needed to give him the gift of Glorianna's confidence and the brilliant future before us.

Derodotur placed himself in front of us. "It will be months before we know if the child is a boy or a girl. We need not settle this right this moment."

"When is the babe due?" That from a voice in the crowd.

"Yes! Are we even sure it will live?" someone else called out. I kept my eyes on Glorianna's window. *May She protect my child.* As Her avatar, surely I deserved that much from Her. Though it hadn't prompted Her to save my one true love. The grief sucked at what little confidence I had. Was I favored by Glorianna or not?

Some people shifted in the rear of the hall, a stirring and muttering, and I glimpsed Dafne pushing Marin forward. The woman looked overwhelmed by the grand hall, far more elaborate than anything at Windroven, to be sure.

"Who are you?" Uorsin demanded. "Why is a commoner approaching my throne?"

"She is my midwife, High King," I answered in a quiet tone, not sure where I found the courage. Except that Marin had been kind to me and the way she'd knitted her fingers together bothered me. "I believe she seeks to answer the questions put forth."

"Hmph." He rapped his knuckles impatiently on the arm of his throne. "This is hardly public business."

I would have laughed, if such a sound could make it past the knot of tears that clogged my throat. It felt as if all those tender moments between Hugh and me, those shadowed, firelight kisses and touches, had been trotted out for display before all these people. They watched me with avid, hungry faces. No longer a person to them, but a means to an end.

They'd warned Andi about that—that the Tala wanted her only for her womb. Now it was me. By my own people.

"High King Uorsin," Erich said, "these matters concern us all. Avonlidgh awaits these same answers."

I hadn't thought Old Erich could be so stubborn. Despite his stooped profile and white hair, he seemed like a hunting dog on the scent. He would not give up.

"Speak!" Uorsin demanded, and the midwife braced her shoulders and caught my eye. An apology. How odd that she understood. "Princess Amelia, despite the great emotional blows she has suffered, is healthy and strong. There's every reason to expect a vital babe, born about a month after Danu's midsummer feast—as long as Her Highness is careful to remain rested and at peace."

"And is the child a boy or girl?" One of Erich's retainers this time.

"Only Glorianna knows," Marin answered. "It's not for us to guess such things, especially so early on."

"The princess was ill on the journey—that's a sign of a boy," someone said.

"The witch Salena cursed Uorsin's get to throw only girls!" another shouted, from the dubious anonymity of the crowd.

"Glorianna may know, but so do I." Lady Zevondeth tottered forward from where she'd been sitting in a chair to the side. She leaned heavily on her cane and took Marin's measure. From the corner of my eye, I caught Ursula stepping forward, then checking herself.

Lady Zevondeth hitched her way toward me, the gold-wrapped oak cane thumping on the marble tiles, and my skin crawled. Suddenly I didn't want her to touch me, which made no sense. She'd always been kindly to me. But the acute way her nearly blind, milky eyes shone, the greedy reach of her hand—and the way Ursula deftly inserted herself between us—upset my mind much as my gut had been.

"Lady Zevondeth," Ursula greeted her, formally, as if our father hadn't disgraced her.

"Your Highness." Lady Zevondeth dropped a deep curtsy, showing more respect than the situation currently warranted. "How fares Queen Andromeda? I hope she discovered some answers to her questions."

That hit me like a spark from the fireplace. Andi was a queen now. That is, if we acknowledged the sovereignty of the Tala and Rayfe's claim as king. How odd that Andi and I might both be queens and Ursula forever a princess.

"What questions?" Uorsin growled, and Zevondeth beamed at him, unafraid.

"I cannot answer that, Your Highness."

"You can if I command it." His tone held menace, but it seemed to roll off her.

"Not if you've previously commanded us all never to speak of it in this court." She grinned, showing a few missing teeth. Horrible. Especially when she turned it on me. "I need only to touch your hand, Princess Amelia. Remember—I was there when you came into this world. I meant you no harm then or now."

"Do it," Uorsin ordered, likely to both of us.

Ursula gave way but rested her hand on her sword hilt. Bizarrely, it comforted me, the way she stuck by my side even still. As if she would cut down Lady Zevondeth in the midst of court. Really she shouldn't be wearing her sword with that dress—the lines were all wrong—but no one short of Uorsin could make Ursula take off her sword.

Thus all the jokes about her sword being Ursula's only lover.

Not looking in Zevondeth's black gaps, I held out my hand and gazed up at Glorianna's window, praying to Her for strength. I wished that if Glorianna was whispering Her will to me, She'd speak more loudly. Though I'd claimed to have visions of Glorianna—mostly when I was younger—I'd never gotten a real message from Her. Part of me felt fragile, like that brittle glass about to be smashed. She offered me none of Her strength now.

Zevondeth's hand grasped mine, tight enough that the palsy that shook her spread up my arm. Hopefully it was from age, not disease. I imagined my skin shriveling like hers, my eyes turning into white marbles. The rose window seemed to mock me with Glorianna's silence, and I scanned the sea of faces avidly watching the spectacle.

My gaze snagged on an apple-green stare. The White Monk, with his face hidden by his monk's cowl, but somehow that color penetrated the shadows, laying me open with his hatred and scorn.

"It is a boy," Zevondeth declared. And, oddly, she winked at me.

Rather than looking devastated by the news, Ursula furrowed her brow in confusion. Why she'd believed Andi could predict the future, I didn't know.

I was getting tired of this.

"Then my grandson shall be born here, at the seat of my power," Uorsin declared. "Princess Amelia shall stay by my side, where she belongs." He took my hand and held it, strangely making me feel more captured than cherished.

"And what of Avonlidgh and justice, High King?" Erich demanded. Several angry voices joined in, forming a chorus of unrest. "Are we to remain a defeated people, continually plagued by our enemy?"

"We are at peace with the Tala," Derodotur spoke firmly. "The alliance of the royal houses is intact and all treaties hold. There is no defeat."

"Then my son gave his life for a treaty that did not change?" Erich made it sound absurd. "I find it hard to believe, High King Uorsin—and remember that I was there when you sacked Aerron and gave no quarter to your enemy—that you would accept this so calmly."

The regal ambassador from Aerron, of an age to have been there also, inclined her head, a bitter line to her mouth.

"You were also there when I took Castle Avonlidgh, weren't you, Erich?" Uorsin's tone held deadly threat. "You fought me and failed then. Do you care to pit yourself against me a second time, now that I have all the might of the eleven other kingdoms behind me?"

Erich made a show of looking around the court room, which had fallen mostly silent, save a few whispers here and there, to better hear every word of this exchange. Then Old Erich's gaze fell on my mother's empty throne. "It seems to me that you lack certain . . . assistance you enjoyed then. How will you keep what you hold, with Salena gone and the Tala in possession of the heir to *her* power?"

6

The great hall reverberated with the hush of utter shock and apprehension. No one dared move, lest they draw Uorsin's mighty rage upon themselves.

Old Erich—not so stooped, icy-blue eyes glittering with challenge—faced the High King without fear. Did he have a death wish? Had Hugh's loss so unbalanced him?

" 'Tis treason to speak those names in this noble hall," Uorsin replied, as if musing over a riddle. "What game do you play with me, my old enemy? Surely you don't believe this bear has lost his teeth."

"Don't I?" Erich returned calmly. "I see no bites taken out of our enemy. Instead my people and yours lick their wounds this winter. We looked to the High King for the protection he promised, and what did we receive? Nothing. Only war with demons who seek to destroy us. You promised us bounty greater than Annfwn's, and what do we see? The borders to paradise locked against us and our people starving at the gates. You made a vassal kingdom of noble Avonlidgh. You've made a cripple of her. Which kingdom is next, I wonder?"

More of the other kings had ranged themselves behind Erich,

rebellion in their faces. This was what Andi had seen. People fighting over her. Death and destruction. All those burned-out farms we'd seen. There would be more of that. Uorsin's peace would fail. The White Monk caught my eye, pulling the cowl back a bit, so the bright light of the marble hall illuminated the twisting shadows of scars on his face. His eerie gaze seemed to carry a message.

Peace is an expensive commodity.

"What do you mean, the borders of Annfwn are closed to us? What superstitious nonsense is this?" This from the Aerron ambassador.

Old Erich fixed her with a sharp eye. "Not superstition, Lady Laurenne. Her Majesty and the High King's heir, Princess Ursula herself, confirmed the truth of this."

I nearly groaned aloud and even caught Ursula rolling her eyes up in a grimace, a rare break in her composure. She was spared a reply—to any of the shouted questions—by the sheer cacophony of the response. Even Derodotur seemed at a loss to control the situation.

I stood, and everyone gaped at me, their demands for information falling into a confused jumble of murmurs. I was tired and suddenly starving. Having no idea what I should say next, I quickly descended the steps, so as not to be taller than Uorsin for longer than necessary, compounding my already unforgiveable breach of etiquette. To make up for it—though, judging by the astonished insult contorting Uorsin's face, nothing could—I sank into a deep and respectful curtsy. "Forgive me, Father. I know you'll think me weak, and indeed my frail woman's body begs for rest at this moment, lest I endanger my child, but I must honor my vow to my late husband."

Once I could have worked up pretty tears to sway him, but no. I'd never wept out of true sorrow in my life, and now that I had reason, I couldn't. Instead I gazed up at my King and father with wide eyes. The color of pansies, he'd always said.

"I took a vow and I mean to keep it. Please don't be angry, but

I fell in love with Hugh because I knew he was the only man"—
my voice broke suddenly—"the only one who came close to your
honor and integrity in my estimation. Hugh would have wanted
his son born at Windroven, like his fathers before him. I cannot
fail his memory."

Uorsin visibly softened and gestured at me to rise. Erich as-
sisted me himself, blue gaze assessing me. I wasn't sure if I'd
helped or hindered whatever game he played—or which I should
try to do. If only Glorianna would speak to me! I felt truly ill and
pressed a hand to my lips. Might as well make it clear to all. "I
fear for my child. For this babe who will be the hope of lasting
peace in the Twelve Kingdoms, if I can't be at Windroven, near
the poor, entombed body of Prince Hugh, who was the best of us
all. Glorianna keep him."

High Priest Kir echoed my prayer, stepping forward to sketch
Glorianna's circle in the air. "Let us all pray," he intoned, "for the
passing of Prince Hugh and his reception into Glorianna's loving
arms."

Even Uorsin bowed his head then, murmuring along with the
prayer. He seemed genuinely grieved, and I wondered what to believe. Still, he emerged from the moment with a different look
about him. No less angry, but more his usual kingly self. Perhaps
my invocation of Glorianna had enabled Her to reach out to him,
to soothe his destructive rage. He nodded at me, as if answering
my thought.

"You have always been loyal and selfless, my Amelia. Fine,
then—have the babe at Windroven, but then he shall come here,
to be raised by me and to rule as High King from this throne. I
have decided. Go rest yourself and the burden you carry. King
Erich, attend me in my study and we shall discuss this in private."

I did not mind at all being essentially sent to my rooms. Ursula
fell into step beside me, but I ignored her. We didn't speak until

we reached the rooms I'd been assigned. My childhood chambers had been refurbished after my wedding. Still I'd expected to return to the rooms I'd shared with Hugh those fateful few nights we'd stayed until the Tala attacked.

Instead, they showed me to my mother's old suite.

Marin bustled in, finding a space to brew her teas for me. As always, anticipating my need. Ursula stayed beside me in the doorway, equally astonished, I think. The rooms had been cleaned but otherwise were much the same. So far as I could tell—I'd been in here only a few times, when the three of us snuck in to poke around, to learn what we could of our mother.

Until Uorsin had found us out and ordered them locked and sealed.

"Did you know about this?" I asked Ursula under my breath.

"No. I would have warned you."

"It was my idea," Lady Zevondeth cackled out behind us, making us both jump like the guilty girls we'd been so long ago. "I informed the chatelaine that these rooms should be prepared for you, Princess Amelia. As a widow and the future Queen of Avonlidgh, no others are worthy of your rank. Let it never be said that Ordnung does not follow proper etiquette. Especially for our own."

"Until our father finds out," Ursula observed in a dry tone.

"I'll handle Uorsin," Zevondeth said, painfully hobbling the circuit of the outer room, examining the few artifacts of our mother that remained. Like Andi, our mother had never been much for books—something I knew because Ursula used to tease Andi so about it—but there the shelves held a surprising number of them. Zevondeth pulled a chair up to the newly kindled fire and bade a serving girl to build the blaze hotter and to give her an extra lap blanket. Oh, and to bring her tea. Then she cocked her head at us, milky eyes finding us unerringly. "Come, come, girls. We have things to discuss and I don't want to miss my regular afternoon nap."

Obediently, as if we *were* still girls and attending her for lessons in manners and elocution, we settled ourselves in chairs near her, Ursula perching on the edge of one to accommodate her sword. Zevondeth scowled at her.

"It's unladylike to wear a sword in the first place, Miss Ursula—much less indoors, and with a gown."

Ursula smiled, affection in it that surprised me. "I cannot wear pants in court and I cannot appear as less than any of the men or I lose their respect. This is my compromise. If you have another that meets the same criteria, I'll entertain it."

Zevondeth snorted. "By the sound of it, losing the men's respect is the least of your worries. Uorsin barely stopped short of disinheriting you entirely."

Ursula lightly brushed the jewel in the hilt of her sword. That was her other reason for wearing it all the time, I knew. It was her talisman, that jewel that had belonged to Salena. Ursula thought I didn't know, but bratty little sisters have ways of finding out such things. I'd kept the secret, biding my time until I could use it against her. Then I grew up and the moment never came.

Or had it?

"He'll come around." Ursula spoke reflectively, almost more to herself than to Zevondeth. "This is a difficult time—losing Andi to the Tala, the implications that she and Annfwn might be forever beyond his reach, on top of the crop failures and various forms of unrest. The advent of this new, male heir came at exactly the right moment for him to seize upon this as the road to a better era."

"Uorsin never did get over Salena's providing him with only girls," Zevondeth agreed. "In you, Amelia, he sees his chance to thwart her machinations."

"What do you mean?" Her redemption, surely, not her machinations? "No woman can control the sex of her babe."

"Can't she?" Zevondeth laughed that cackling sound that put my small hairs on end. Marin handed me her special tea and a plate of thin toasts with fruit spread. "Salena was no ordinary woman; make no mistake of that, little Ami."

"You speak of power that belongs to Glorianna alone—not to any human. Or demon."

"I speak of what Andromeda is learning, following in her mother's very powerful footsteps. Watch that you're not left in the dust."

"I wish for nothing more to do with her. Except justice." The tea scalded my tongue and I almost welcomed the burn. Everyone saw me as worthless, powerless. And here Zevondeth was talking like Andi was so wonderful when she was nothing more than a murderess and traitor. "She killed Hugh."

"Did she?" Zevondeth cast a white-eyeballed glance in Ursula's direction, and to my surprise, Ursula fidgeted. Was that . . . guilt? The sour scent of it drifted through the air.

"What aren't you two telling me?" I demanded, setting the plate aside. Then I snagged one of the toasts anyway, so ravenous for food, I couldn't resist.

"Is Ami's babe truly a boy?" Ursula asked. She wasn't avoiding the subject, however. I could see that much. She seemed to need the answer.

"Why? Did you have other intelligence?" Zevondeth smiled, the sweet old granny no one would ever mistake her for.

I snorted. "Andi seems to think she's some sort of prophetess now—she told Ursula that I was pregnant with a girl."

Ursula focused her keen gaze on me, raising her hawklike brows at me gobbling more of the toast. Glorianna help me—if I wasn't puking, I was eating.

"A little fact she knew before you did, I might point out."

"What else did Andromeda tell you?"

"We didn't have much time to talk," Ursula hedged.

"Ami, dear, would you send your midwife and ladies away?"

I nearly refused Zevondeth her demand, though we both pretended it was a request. In truth, however, the old woman scared me. Some things you never outgrow.

After the ladies withdrew, Ursula stood and moved away from the fire. Always more comfortable moving, she paced the chamber as she spoke. "She showed me the border to Annfwn and bade me—"

"Fancy name for a dismal place," I remarked. "It just means the Wild Lands. It's not even a real word."

"It means 'paradise,' in the old language." Zevondeth folded her hands over the top of her cane. "Make no mistake, Princess— Uorsin's appetite for the place has never diminished, though Salena led him away from it. And a man does not hunger for the undesirable."

"Well, it *sounds* dismal." They ignored me, as if I hadn't spoken.

"She bade me to try to cross the border," Ursula continued.

"And?" Zevondeth licked her brittle old lips. "What happened when you tried?"

Ursula shrugged, holding up her palms in bewilderment. "I could not."

"But the Tala could."

"Yes."

Zevondeth thumped her cane on the floor, face flushed with triumph. "That's my girl. She's truly taken the reins of her mother's power, then."

"I wouldn't have believed such a thing was possible if I hadn't experienced it myself," Ursula said.

"Well, I don't believe it." I poured myself more tea, to give myself something to do. All of this was absurd. "Need I remind you that she's a traitor and a murderess? Our mother would disown her if she could."

Zevondeth reached over and patted my knee. "You have been through much, young Amelia, and you are distraught."

"That doesn't mean I've lost my wits!" I looked accusingly at Ursula. "Surely you don't expect us to believe such a wild tale."

Ursula tucked her hands behind her back, spreading her legs into a solid stance—all wrong for the way she was dressed. She regarded me gravely. "I do expect you to believe it. It is the truth, whether the High King wishes it to be so or not."

I snorted, sipping the much cooler tea. I was not so emptyheaded, and I knew things they did not. "He'll find a way. If not him, King Erich will. We *will* have justice. It's Glorianna's will that we reclaim Annfwn for Her. A goddess is far more powerful than some Tala trickster."

Neither said anything, and I looked up to find them exchanging a speaking look. "What? It's true."

"Are you speaking as Glorianna's avatar?" Ursula's lips twitched.

"Do you mock me?" I set down the teacup. How I could feel the sting of such a thing, while the great, unanswered, and unshed weight of my grief crushed everything else, I didn't know.

"Well, let's see. She appeared to you in a vision when you were five, saying that you should have a new pony. And was it when you were eight that she said you should eat only pastries and sweets?" She ran a thumb over the cabochon jewel. "Don't you think you're a bit old for this—and the circumstances particularly dire for your little games?"

Games? So like her, to forever treat me like a child. I was a woman grown, a queen, and I would assume my rightful place as Glorianna's avatar. "Yes. I am speaking as the avatar of the goddess, as everyone but you acknowledges me to be! High Priest Kir himself said that—"

She barked out a laugh and scrubbed her hands through her hair, clearly having forgotten the pins, which fell to the floor. "I should have known better than to give him access to you. You need to learn not to listen to every bit of flattery lobbed in your direction."

"I'm not an idiot."

"No, you just behave like one."

I stood, automatically smoothing my skirts. "As these are my rooms, I think you both should leave."

"Sit yourself down and hear your sister out," Zevondeth snapped, shocking me. "You always were a willful thing, and the way Uorsin spoiled you made it worse. Tell me what else Andi said."

Tears pricked my eyes and I thought I might weep at last. But no. Unable to do anything else, I sat, feeling small and miserable and unloved.

"She also said to find the dolls our mother made for us," Ursula continued in an even tone.

"Clearly forgetting that our mother died birthing me, so there was never one for me, no matter what Ursula thinks."

A small stillness settled into the room. Ursula stared hard at Zevondeth, who actually looked uncomfortable. And much older. "She also said that you knew the truth and would tell us."

"And did she tell you the price of such information?" Zevondeth's opaque gaze rested on the gnarled hands folded on her cane.

"She did not mention, no."

"However," I inserted, "she did mention that she thought I should, in addition to this wild-goose chase after a mythical doll, send my infant daughter to her." I laughed, and the hysterical edge to it scratched my throat. Neither of them seemed to find it funny—just watched me with that pitying concerned look everyone seemed to have for me these days. Be nice to the poor, delusional, and grieving princess, whose life is already over before it fully began. "What kind of a fool does she think I am?" I spat out. "Maybe I should go to paradisiacal 'Annfwn' and let her plunge her dagger into *my* breast. At least she'd have to look me in the eye instead of sneaking around to kill everyone I love behind my back!"

"Did Zevondeth call you overwrought?" Ursula demanded. "Because you're behaving like a crazy woman."

"You're protecting her," I hissed, my fingers curving into claws and digging into my gown. "Giving me nice stories about how my dead mother left me some toy when we all know perfectly well she left me nothing!" I'd forgotten which of them I was talking about, but it didn't matter. They'd all left me, even my beloved Hugh.

Had he loved me at all?

"Call the midwife for her." Zevondeth creaked to her feet, leaning heavily on the cane. "Tell her the Princess needs something to calm her nerves, lest she do the baby ill."

I wanted to protest, even as Ursula moved to do her bidding, as if she were one of the servants. But I felt overwhelmingly tired—and there the nausea rose again. If only I could shed tears as easily as I brought up the contents of my stomach.

"Come, Amelia." Ursula was at my elbow, urging me to rise. I hadn't noticed her return. "Come lie down and rest. We can talk more later. Isn't that right, Lady Zevondeth?" I heard the command in Ursula's voice and knew she wouldn't stop until we'd gone over and over our mother's death. I, for one, didn't want to know. Had never wanted to.

"I don't feel good," I protested, sounding whiny and weak, even to myself. How I detested this new me. Ugly and ill and . . . maybe crazy.

"I know, honey." Ursula wrapped an arm around my waist and led me into the bedroom. "I'm sorry I was cruel to you. Rest now."

"You only care about the babe," I complained, but I settled onto the bed where she showed me, my body crying out with relief to offer up its exhaustion.

"That's never true. Look at me, Amelia." Ursula clasped my hand in hers and stared fiercely at me. Her eyes looked almost silver, ringed by a darker gray border. "Never believe that. You and I are together in this. Andi is beyond our reach for the time being, but you and I are sisters. First and foremost. Now and forever. I love you, Amelia, with all the power of my heart."

"Andi loved me once." Sleep was surging up to drag me under. I couldn't hold my eyes open.

"She loves you still. All will be well."

"Do you believe that, too?"

"Yes." Ursula's conviction cut through my fog. "It has to be."

7

When I awoke, the winter night had fallen hard and the lanterns were lit. Marin sat in a chair nearby, knitting needles flashing as always, catching the red-gold glints from the fireplace.

As had become my recent habit upon awakening, I took a mental assessment of my body, waiting to see if I needed to reach for the nearby basin.

Surprisingly, I didn't. I felt energized and more clearheaded than earlier. I hadn't handled that well, but Ursula and Lady Zevondeth shouldn't have ambushed me that way. If I was to be taken seriously as Glorianna's avatar, I needed to have a better strategy.

"I'm thinking you'll be hungry, Princess," Marin said in a quiet tone, the click of her needles soothing and unceasing in their rhythm.

"Yes." I was. Of course.

"Good. I took the liberty of asking that dinner be sent up to your rooms, so that you could lie abed quietly tonight. I sent word that you require this time to rest and recover from your journey.

Of course, if you prefer to join the court in the feasting hall, I can call your ladies. There's still time."

Once I would have insisted on going. What, and miss all the fun? Now I seized upon the excuse gratefully. Growing another human being apparently took more work than it appeared.

"I think I'll do that. Stay in. And I am starving. What's for dinner?"

"I asked for a number of things for you to try. You're getting to the stage where the child will tell you what it needs. The best way to discover that is to smell and taste. What you crave will be the right thing."

She set her knitting aside and helped me mound the pillows so I could sit up comfortably. It felt like being mothered might have, and her concern touched me. Marin, at least, cared for how I felt.

"Thank you for being so good to me."

She clucked at me, a mother hen calling her chicks. "I have a stake in the child you carry, too, Princess. I'm not above making it clear that you should be treated with the utmost care. I'd like to see him or her born strong and well—and at Windroven, as is meant."

"You don't believe the babe will be a boy?"

"It matters not to me. All children are equal in Glorianna's eyes."

"Too bad Glorianna has no teachings for pregnant women—I have no idea what I'm doing."

"Ah, but She does, Princess."

"I've never heard any." Shouldn't I know everything about Glorianna?

"That's because Her priests are less interested in the goddess as a mother. But in the old tales and the small chapels, where Glorianna's children worship Her in the quiet places, they pass along other stories."

"Will you tell me one?"

"Yes, Princess. While we wait for your supper to arrive, I'll tell you the tale of Glorianna and the birth of Her first daughter." She sat back in her chair, taking up her knitting and setting the rhythm of it before she began.

"Long ago, when all the gods and goddesses walked the earth, and lived in Annfwn together, none lacked for anything. The sun shone warm each day. The rains fell and soaked the earth. The fruits and vegetables grew jewel bright and the fish swam in the warm waters of the Onyx Ocean.

"Glorianna took a new lover. He was a beautiful human man, with all the strength and radiance of the rising sun. She loved him for his red-gold hair, like the light of dawn, for the bronzed noon-day strength of his body, for the twilight blue of his eyes and the midnight smokiness of his lust for Her.

"Though it was frowned upon to dally with human beings—for they are fragile in their short lives and their hearts are easily broken—Glorianna could not resist this young man. Her sisters, Moranu and Danu, understood and helped in Their ways. Night after night, She returned to his bed and Moranu's moon smiled upon them, lighting their lovemaking. When they played on the beach and swam in the Onyx Ocean, Danu's sun warmed them, never burning.

"In time, as such things happen, Glorianna's womb quick-ened. The other gods and goddesses mocked Her, for the babe could never be immortal. It would be forever a half-breed, be-longing to neither race, forever doomed to be neither fully one thing nor the other.

"But Glorianna didn't care. She loved her unborn child—per-haps even more so because it carried the human blood that made Her lover all She so admired in him. So She went to Her sisters.

"Danu cautioned Her that the others would seek to kill the child, out of spite and jealousy, to show they could. Danu offered Her spotless integrity and Her bright blade to guard the child. Glorianna accepted with gratitude.

"Moranu said that the child would need special gifts, in order to survive the trials ahead, so She offered the tricks of the night, the magic of the shadows. Glorianna accepted that gift, also.

"Glorianna, however, had no gift to give Her child, save the nourishment of Her own body. She knew that, once the child was separated from Her, that She would no longer be able to protect the infant from the world, as mortal babes require.

"So She went to the human women and asked them for their advice. They were awed by Her unearthly beauty, but they soon grew accustomed to Her. They showed Her their ways, how to nurse the child, how to introduce the soft foods, to chew the meats. As She learned from them, Glorianna wondered how to repay them. She wanted to offer the women a gift, such as Her sisters offered Her. Something that would guard and protect their human babes.

"She saw how they spun coarse thread from the animals they kept—the goats and horses—and how they labored at their looms, to make clothing to protect their mortal bodies from the elements. But weaving required the bright light of day. Glorianna's radiance comes from the between times. She is in the soft, rising dawn and in the falling dusk of brilliant sunset. Her gift, She thought, should be for those times. For when men and women sat together quietly with their children, to tell stories.

"So Glorianna took a rib from either side and shaped them into long needles. She touched the goats and gave them soft underdown and coaxed the rabbits from the hills with sweet clover. She spun the first yarn, soft and sweet as sunrise, then gave it the bright colors of sunset. Giving these things to the women, She showed them how to knit the yarn together, to make soft blankets for their babes while they sat together, sharing stories.

"And that is how we came to knit. Also why the luckiest needles are made of the bone of someone who loves you."

"Surely that last isn't true," I burst out.

Marin winked at me, her needles flying in their steady dance. I peered at them, trying to discern what they were made of.

"What happened to them?"

"To who, Princess?"

"Well, I know other stories of Glorianna, but what about Her lover? What was his name? And what became of the daughter? Did She have other daughters? You said the birth of Her first daughter."

Marin considered, and it occurred to me that we were doing as Glorianna had wanted us to do, sitting in the evening and sharing stories and time together.

"Can I learn to knit?" I asked impulsively. I knew how to embroider and other such elegant needlework, but now I wanted nothing more than to knit a blanket for my babe—son or daughter. Something soft and bright to wrap my child in.

"The stories never give the man's name," Marin said. "There's another tale, of how Glorianna's lover died, as mortals must, and how She grieved for him. In the madness of Her grief, She nearly destroyed the world. I always wondered if it was the same man."

Everyone knew that story. It was often held up as the example of Glorianna's ascendant power and how Moranu and Danu followed Her bidding, lashing the tides and scorching the earth as She demanded.

I understood that story better than I ever had. I'd always kind of puzzled over it, the tales of Glorianna's grief. How could She have treated the world and Her people so badly, when She was the goddess of love? It never made sense, and, especially as a girl, I'd wanted Her to get over it and go back to being benevolent.

But . . . now I comprehended on a visceral level how She'd felt. There was no choice about it, no getting over anything. Grieving is like being ill. Just as my body had taken control, flinging me to my knees with the wretched sicks, it seemed this terrible mourning had all my thoughts and feelings in a death grip around my throat, choking the life from my body.

The way the cliffs had beckoned to me, I still felt that siren call to end this pain and fling myself into numbing death. If I'd had Glorianna's power, I, too, would have wanted to take the world with me.

"Knitting might be good for you," Marin broke into my dark thoughts, nodding at me placidly when I started at her voice. "It will occupy your hands and give you a sense of peace."

She didn't have to say that I sorely needed some kind of peace.

"I should mention, though, that the reason you never learned before is because the fine ladies have long frowned on the art. Fit only for coarser hands and thicker yarns."

"But you'll teach me anyway—can I make something for the baby?"

"We'll start you with something simple and you can work up to a more complicated piece." The midwife chuckled to herself. "Though if Her Highness Queen Amelia takes up the art, she may yet start a new fashion."

"I'm not queen yet."

"Give it time, ducks. Give it time."

The next day, I made my way to Glorianna's Temple. It stood right outside Castle Ordnung itself, but still well within the walls of the keep, so I could leave my ladies behind. Though most of them had taken advantage of our visit home to be with their families and other friends. I didn't blame them—being in my circle these days sorely lacked the social whirl they'd always enjoyed. Of course, they, too, had abandoned me.

For the moment, however, I didn't mind. I needed to speak further with High Priest Kir about Glorianna's mission to recover Annfwn, so I could be prepared to put it to the High King in a clear way, without an opportunity for Ursula to poke holes in me with her verbal sword.

When I found the High Priest, his countenance brightened at my arrival and he strode away from a group of underpriests he'd been apparently lecturing. They all bowed deeply to me, scraping the pink tiles with their shaven brows, as if I were Glorianna Herself. They murmured a chant I hadn't heard before, something lovely and musical.

"Your Highness." Kir beamed at me. "You are as lovely as the dawn. It is easy to see how Glorianna's hand rests upon you."

You need to learn not to listen to every bit of flattery lobbed in your direction. I banished Ursula's nasty voice from my mind.

The White Monk lurked behind him, as he always seemed to do. He did not chant along with the others, it seemed.

"What is that prayer?" I asked.

"Why, it's yours, Your Highness." Kir smoothed his immaculate robe. "I composed it myself, to honor you and your son, who shall sit upon the High Throne and lead us all into Annfwn. Under his leadership, we shall reclaim paradise and, along with it, your birthright."

"What if the babe is a girl? And why not reclaim it under my leadership?"

Kir laughed. Then stopped himself as he realized I hadn't spoken in jest. "The child will be a boy. All the portents confirm that truth. As Glorianna lays Her trust in Her priests, She has determined that your son will lead."

"But Glorianna's first child was a daughter and the goddess loved her."

"Your Highness, I assure you, there was no such daughter."

"But I heard the tale of how she gave us knitting."

Kir looked aghast and, with extreme unctuous courtesy, silently urged me away from the still chanting priests. "Princess Amelia, I beg you to have a care which tales you listen to. There are many that purport to be of Glorianna but are not. They are heresies that can only lead to sorrow and misinformation."

The White Monk trailed behind us, silent as always. But I had the feeling that he listened to us intently. Kir seemed to make the mistake, as many did, of thinking the silent also don't listen. In Andi's case, that was often true. Not so for everyone.

"You must tell me where you heard such blasphemy," Kir

went on, an impassioned flush high on his cheeks, "and I shall see to it that the poor, misguided soul receives proper instruction."

"Blasphemy?" I echoed, aghast. Surely had Glorianna not wanted me to hear that story, She would have warned me somehow. A sense of wrongness should have alerted me. But it had felt so good, so right, tucked under the covers, listening to Marin's story. Knitting couldn't be blasphemous, could it?

"Oh, yes." Kir looked gravely concerned. "Be wary of those tempting you from Her path, Your Highness. Especially in these turbulent times."

"Oh?"

"Yes. The dark forces rise up against Glorianna's champions. You have already been tested—far beyond what any fair young damsel should be expected to bear. We grieve with you, Princess. The people of the Twelve Kingdoms feel your pain."

My heart flooded with emotion to hear this. I wasn't alone. They shared this terrible time with me. It meant everything.

"There are demons lurking among us, however," Kir broke into my thoughts.

Inadvertently, my gaze flew to the White Monk. He did not raise his bowed head, but he cocked it, ever so slightly. As if he might be laughing at me. How dare he? I was a Princess of the Realm, daughter of the High King, and future Queen of Avonlidgh. Not to mention Glorianna's avatar upon this earth. He should be kissing the hem of my gown.

"Princess Amelia, do you heed my words?"

"Yes." At least I thought so. Demons and lurking. Sharing my pain. Oh, Hugh.

"They seek to divert you from your holy mission, Your Highness. By telling tales to distract you, so you won't hear Glorianna's voice."

My breakfast turned over in my stomach. Had I already failed as Glorianna's avatar by listening to Marin's stories?

"As your spiritual guide, I feel I must warn you. I cannot put it strongly enough, Princess Amelia. Whoever is whispering such tales in your ear is turning your mind and heart away from Glorianna and the purity of the path She's laid out for you."

I wished that Hugh were here. I'd likely spend the rest of my life—however long that might be—wishing for that. He'd know what to do. I chewed my lip against the rising sick. I should have put one of Marin's mints in my pocket. Surely Marin was no demon, seeking to sway me from fulfilling Glorianna's plans for me?

"Who was it, Your Highness?" Kir's voice dropped to an urgent whisper. "At least give me a name, so I can investigate."

My mind warred with my heart. I turned my eyes to Glorianna's rose window, this the greatest of the three, here in Her stronghold, the High Temple. Surely no harm would come to Marin, should I say so. If she had told me the story in all innocence, then all would be well. If she'd spoken due to some demonic influence, then Kir would help her be free of it.

"My midwife, Marin." I said it quietly, so none other could overhear.

Kir relaxed and cast a reverent gaze to the heavens, murmuring the standard phrase thanking Glorianna for Her benevolent protection. Instead of echoing it, I found myself watching the White Monk. He wasn't praying, either, but stayed still, a snake coiled in the grass.

"She told me the tale last night. She meant to comfort me."

Kir's nostrils fluttered, his lips pinched, and he made the sign of Glorianna over my belly. "Glorianna grant us peace," he murmured. "I shall see to this, Your Highness. You did right to tell me."

I wanted to feel I did right.

"High Priest Kir!" One of Uorsin's valets approached with urgent footsteps. "The High King calls for your attendance immediately. Your Highness," he said to me, bowing belatedly, but the naked admiration in his gaze did much to bring up my spirits.

"Of course. At once!" Kir dashed out—with priestly dignity, but with clear excitement—after a flurry of excuses and promises.

I watched after him. He hadn't answered any of my questions. I wasn't even sure what I, as Glorianna's avatar and head of Her mission here in the Twelve Kingdoms, was meant to do to lead us into Annfwn. Besides gestate.

Surely I should be doing something.

"At a loss, Princess?" An amused voice hissed the question in my ear.

8

Startled, I turned. Then stepped back. The White Monk stood close enough that I saw his face clearly, despite the shadows of the cowl. His features were harsh but not misshapen. A strong nose with a high bridge dominated his face, sharp lined like his jaw. The spider legs of scars crawled over one cheek, a cicatrix of long-ago pain. As if he carried on his skin all the ugliness of the hurt inside me.

Though a jagged bolt of scar tissue cut through one eyebrow, his eye orbits were clear and open, pristine settings for the unearthly burning green of his gaze.

"What happened to you?" I asked, before I thought.

He smiled. Not nicely, because his upper lip snagged in the movement, making it into a snarl, like a wild beast curling its snout at an unwelcome odor.

"What happened to *you?*" he countered.

"I . . . I don't understand what you mean."

"Giving up your poor commoner of a midwife so easily. She'll suffer because of your disloyalty. She who sought only to help you."

I mastered the roiling sickness. "How dare you speak to me so? I know full well the measure of loyalty. Do you?"

"As a matter of fact, no." He laughed, a dry, whispering sound. "So I recognize its viciously opposite cousin when I see it."

"I'm the High King's daughter. I'll protect my midwife. No harm shall come to her."

"Are you sure, Princess?"

"Who are you?" I demanded.

"You asked that before."

"And you didn't answer."

"No? Perhaps you're not asking the right question."

"You cannot naysay me. I'll report you to High Priest Kir. No—I shall have you dragged before the High King to answer for yourself."

He shook his head, clucking his tongue as one might at an errant kitten. "Always running to Daddy. What power of your own do you possess, Princess?"

The way he said my title sounded like an insult, and I wanted to tell him to stop calling me that. Which was ridiculous, of course.

"I have enough power to have you beheaded on the spot. Or cast out of Glorianna's temple and turned out into the countryside with a brand declaring that none shall give you succor. I could ruin you in countless small ways. And you discount my power so glibly."

He tilted his head and I knew for certain that it meant he laughed at me. The cynical amusement, floating on the sweet scent of ripe grapes, altered the creases in his coarse face, and his eyes sparkled, glints of sunlight on stream water.

"The power to destroy is easily come by. Anyone can destroy."

"I can create, too."

He gestured at my belly. "That? Any female who spreads her legs can do that. It takes no special skill or ability. Nature did it for you."

I gasped, my palm oddly itching to slap him, though such a thing would be scandalously beneath my dignity.

"Are males any different? They cast their seed upon the wind, careless of whether it falls on fertile soil."

"Yes."

"Yes, what?"

He edged closer, turning so he blocked the chanting priests. "Yes, men are different. They're worse. Women at least must bear the burden of their choices, then are bound to nurture the child, if there's any humanity in them. Men can walk away and leave their carelessly cast seed to take root or die. They leave behind them a trail of uncared-for life."

I didn't know what to say. Never had I heard someone speak such words.

"This is why Glorianna and Her sisters are the ones who remained, to care for us. The male gods abandoned their mortal charges without a backward glance," he added.

"There are male gods?"

"Other cultures still worship them. We know better."

"Have you heard the tale of Glorianna's daughter, then?" Why the question plagued me so, I didn't know.

"I have. Shall I expect you to give me up to the High Priest also?"

I smiled up at him, gazing through my lashes. "Not if you'll tell me what became of her."

His gaze flickered over my face, not quite with that gleam of hatred, but without admiration. "You wield your beauty like a blunt-force weapon, did you know that?"

I blinked at him, fisting my hands in my skirts so I wouldn't reach up to touch my face, to feel what he saw there that seemed so brutal to him.

"Even when you don't mean to, you manipulate anyone who looks at you with the way you widen your eyes and moisten your lips." He studied me, as if I were a butterfly on a pin. We'd had a tutor with cases of insects on little displays, that we might learn their names. He'd looked like that, interested and without concern for their small lives.

I wanted to flee. But I didn't want him to know he frightened me.

"Why do you talk to me if you dislike me so?" My voice came out in a whisper, and I bit my lower lip, afraid I'd say more. I hadn't meant to ask that.

He lifted an eyebrow, the one interrupted by the scar that looked a bit like a lightning bolt. "Shall I compose a poem to your perfect pearly teeth and how they worry at the full rose petal of your lip? Perhaps that would make you more comfortable."

"I never asked for poems."

"But it's what you know."

"From what I hear of you, all you know is service to Glorianna, White Monk. Though I notice you're not so silent with me."

He barked out a bit of a laugh, unpleasant, like the cawing of a raven. "Don't believe everything you're told, Princess. You understand nothing about me."

"Then you tell me. You evade every question."

Shaking his head, he pulled the cowl into place, once again shadowing his features. "No—you haven't earned the right to my story. You'd have to do more than flutter your lashes for that."

Outrage flooded me. "Surely you're not suggesting—"

"Relax, Your Highness. I'm not even remotely interested."

Ah, that made sense. "I understand many of Glorianna's priests are lovers of other men."

"You would prefer that explanation, wouldn't you? No, I value my neck more than that. A dalliance with you would hardly be worth it. Even were I attracted." Those green eyes flicked over me again, with more than a little disdain.

Left with my outrage and nothing to do with it, I cast about for a reply. Every man wanted to bed me, and some women, too. I could read it in them, like the warmth from a fire, even the ones who were too polite to show it. I'd navigated my world by these stars, the desire and admiration. Even the troubadours who sang songs they wrote for me and then retired for the night with some brawny soldier—they coveted me for my beauty, too. As if I were an object of art.

"I believe it's time for me to go," I finally said.

"Fleeing an uncomfortable conversation? Doesn't speak well of your fortitude."

"You know nothing about me!" I flung his words back at him and caught, perhaps, a twitch of a smile. "You taunt me and answer none of my questions. Why in Glorianna's name would I stay? You bore me."

He made a tsking sound. "Ah, Princess. That's not true. You're fascinated, if only by the conversation. Else you would have flounced off long ago."

"I do not flounce."

"On the contrary, you have a most practiced and seductive flounce. I imagine it earns all sorts of attention and concessions."

"You watch me quite closely, then, for a person who hates me."

"I have my reasons."

"And they are?"

"Private."

He hadn't denied hating me, and though I shouldn't care, it pricked me like the thorns on wild roses, small and slim, dug deeply into the skin. Nobody hated me. I was beautiful.

I opened my mouth to announce that I was leaving, recalled I'd said that once already, so turned to go.

"Glorianna's daughter did survive. With her mortal blood, she eventually died, of course. But she lived a very long and full life. Her name was Talifa."

I looked over my shoulder at him. "I never heard of her."

He shrugged, his shoulders making sharp points against the robe. "You wouldn't have. She was erased from the official canon of Glorianna's teachings. 'Tis heresy to speak of her."

"And yet you speak her name in Glorianna's very temple."

"Heresy according to priests. Once again, I notice that Glorianna does not strike me down."

"That's the second time you've said such a thing. You must be quite confident."

His teeth flashed in the depths of the cowl. Not really a smile. "Or driven to other extremes. You pay close attention to my words, for a person who hates me."

"I never said I hated you."

"You did, actually—but without realizing it."

I rubbed a finger between my brows, smoothing away the frown. "How do you know of this Talifa, then?"

"Because she is the mother of the White Monks order."

"Oh." I felt a bit deflated. Some part of me felt attached to her, as if she might have a special meaning for me. Likely it was only that the story had tugged at my heart, the way Glorianna had sought out knowledge so She could cherish and raise Her mortal child. When I was little, before I knew better, I sometimes grew angry at my mother for dying. I'd childishly thought that if she'd been more careful, she could have lived and been my mother for real.

After I grew up, I understood that she hadn't been able to help dying. Women often died in childbirth. Still, every once in a while, a slice of that remembered anger welled up in me.

"Talifa lives on in your blood, Princess." The White Monk said it with what I would have called gentleness from a less callous man.

That caught me short, the knot of tears in my throat cramping in fierce response.

"How can that be?"

"Because she became the Queen of the Tala—the people named for her—as your mother was after her. You are not only Glorianna's avatar, as all seem to wish you to believe. You are Her descendant."

My gaze flew up to the rose window. Glorianna's descendant? Though I'd been compared to the goddess, even called a goddess from time to time, it had never occurred to me to see myself that way. I carried divine blood, and the thought made me giddy. And overwhelmed.

"I am no goddess." I found myself fluttering.

He laughed, raven voiced, threading his hands inside his sleeves, as if he restrained himself from something. "No, Princess, you are no goddess. Not even close."

Insulted rage followed that, and my face heated, the skin of my cheeks stretching with the pressure. Bastard to tease me and lead me on, then expose me as fishing for praise. I didn't understand myself anymore. I seemed to be tossed on a stormy sea of emotion, riding the wave of one only to crash into the nadir of the next.

"Did I make you angry?" He murmured the words, taunting. "What will you do now?"

"What I do or do not do is none of your concern! Why do you follow me about, only to express your disdain? I want to do right by my people, my child, my goddess, and, most of all, by Hugh's memory!" The pain spiked with his name and the realization that, in all this torturous conversation, I hadn't thought of him once. My words ended on a near screech, the songbird's scream of pain to his harsh corvid's call. The background chanting stumbled, losing its cadence, then sputtered into silence.

My breath pushed in and out, hoarse and unpretty in the sudden quiet. The knot of grief that lodged at the base of my throat swelled and groaned with urgency, turning into a spinning sphere.

Now I'll cry.

I didn't even care who witnessed it. Even this horrible priest who seemed to delight in tormenting me. I wanted the tears gone, to release this dreadful lock that kept me confined.

But no.

The pressure grew, until I staggered a little with it. Then one of his hands cupped my elbow, decorously over my sleeve, barely touching, but still grounding me. His other hovered near my cheek, as if he might cup it. And I would turn my face into his hand, taking comfort in the caress. His gaze burned into mine, fierce in that craggy face I could see again clearly, he was so close.

"Have you wept?" He asked the question no one else had, seeing more than anyone else could.

I shook my head. "I can't."

He nodded, as if that made perfect sense. "Sometimes the grief is too large."

"Yes."

He opened his mouth to say something more, his eyes softer than I'd ever seen them, pooling with some kind of compassion. Then he firmed his lips, so the scar whitened, and he stepped away, releasing my elbow and shattering the moment so thoroughly I wondered if we'd shared anything or if I'd imagined it.

"I shall not keep you longer." His tone was formal, as was the bow that followed.

Once again, I turned to leave, swimming through the confusion that darkened my mind, more than half expecting him to call me back again. But he didn't, so I straightened my spine and moved slowly—not that I had ever flounced in my life—from the cool rose-tinted shadows of the temple, out into the bright, white-stone light of Ordnung.

9

Unsettled and at loose ends, I wandered through the courtyard. It felt as if I'd been away forever, not just a few months.
Drifts of filthy snow filled the corners, where it had been pushed
aside and piled up, to keep the stones free for all the business of
Ordnung. This close to the mountains, the winter snows fell deep
and lasted the season.

The grief felt like this—shoved into the corners of my heart by
daily concerns, where it didn't melt, but froze there, accumulat-
ing dirt in the shadows. Spring would take care of this stuff, but
nothing could warm the unused corners of my soul. Perhaps
Glorianna could, but as much as I tried to pray and welcome Her
voice into my heart, She remained silent.

A group of young soldiers drilled at one end of the yard. Several looked my way, losing their focus. The instructor—a woman
I hadn't seen before—rapped one on the helmet, a ringing blow
like a bell. "Keep your head with your big sword, not the little
one, young cock," she barked. "Or you won't survive your first
conflict and will never tup another pretty maid again." She
glanced at me then and looked chagrined, even afraid, when she

saw who it was. "Apologies, Your Highness. No offense meant. I only saw the gown and—"

I nodded and moved past as quickly as I could.

This was who I'd been, once upon a time. Strolling about in my pretty gowns, being admired by the young soldiers with Andi, who was usually hoping to avoid her responsibilities and lessons, using me as cover to escape to the stables.

Just as she'd used me to escape into a world where she turned her back on us.

With her on my mind and the stables ahead, I made my way there. They smelled of wood, hay, and warm horses—and Andi. Her ladies used to despair of ridding her of the horsey smell for court, but the scent memory made me smile. Stable hands bowed and slipped out of my way as I followed the path to the stall where Fiona, Andi's horse, had lived. It suddenly occurred to me that it might be empty. Uorsin had threatened to kill Fiona if he had any reason to doubt Andi's loyalty. Surely she'd proven that.

But it filled me with awful dread, to imagine the gorgeous steed screaming and burning on a pyre, no matter what Andi had done to us all. Sorry I'd come, I started to reverse, then convinced myself Fiona would be there. Perhaps I'd take her with me to Windroven. She was a pretty, well-trained mare. Andi owed me that much.

But the box stall stood aching empty. Fiona was gone.

"Looking for something?"

Ursula emerged from the next stall, where her riding horse was stabled. Her fierce war stallion lived in another wing, where he wouldn't bother the mares. I waved at the empty space where Fiona should have been. "He killed her after all."

Ursula studied the space, as if Fiona might have been misplaced. The straw bedding lay fresh and clean; the trough held nothing. Her brows pulled together in thought, and I nearly told her she shouldn't do that, but I knew she wouldn't care for such things.

"What?" I finally said, irritated with her delay. "You know something."

She cast a measuring look over me, gaze lingering on the gown I'd dug out of my old premarriage wardrobe. It still fit perfectly. "You don't like it when I bring up Andi. Are you sure you want to hear it?"

"Just tell me if our father . . . burned the horse." Why I had to know, I wasn't sure. It sounded disloyal to suggest it. "I really thought he only threatened to. Not that he would."

She returned her gaze to the stall, arms folded, leathers dusty from whatever she'd been doing. "I wasn't sure, either. Before . . . I never would have considered it. Now . . . I'm not sure."

Such an admission of uncertainty from Ursula made me uncomfortable, so I pushed past it. "So he did? Or you don't know?"

"Andi was riding Fiona when I saw her." She didn't add more, saving me the mention of where and what had happened there.

"How is that possible? Fiona was here the whole time."

Ursula shrugged, then picked at a flaw in the leather of her sleeve. "I suspect King Rayfe arranged to spirit her away."

"That Tala demon! Did he want to use Andi's horse as leverage against her? Why would he need to—she made a vow to be his wife, and Andi wouldn't go back on that." Or maybe she would, since I clearly didn't know my sister at all.

"True." Ursula's lips curved and she shook her head absently. Then she brushed off her hands and ran her fingers through her short-cropped hair, stretching her spine. "I think he did it out of love, Ami."

"Love?"

"You say it as if you don't know the meaning of the word. Yes, I think he wanted her to be happy and rescuing Fiona was a gesture of his regard for Andi."

"But how would he have known?"

"One doesn't have to be around Andi for very long to know what matters most to her."

Which wasn't me.

"I saw them together, Ami," Ursula added in a gentle tone. "I could see they loved each other even before Andi said so."

I sighed out a long breath, the empty stall so compelling somehow. Like the big hole Andi had left in my world. "I suppose that's it, then."

Ursula didn't have to ask what I meant. We understood each other at least that much. "If you asked to see her, she would. You could go to Annfwn. Or send for her. There's very little she wouldn't do for you. Especially . . ." She trailed off, searching for the right words.

"Especially after what she did."

"Yes."

"I'm not sure what to think anymore. Nothing makes sense."

"Perhaps it will eventually. Give it time, Ami."

"Everybody keeps telling me that." Bitterness filled my voice and I didn't try to rein it in.

"That's because time is the only thing that will heal your wounds. Nothing we can say or do for you will make a difference. We know that, though it's painful to see how much you're hurting."

"I haven't cried for him." Now that I'd told it to the White Monk it seemed easier to say.

"You will."

"I don't know." Deliberately I tossed my hair over my shoulder, a shadow of my flirtatious ways. "Maybe I'm just that shallow. As frivolous and spoiled as you think me."

"I don't think that. I was angry when I said it and I'm sorry."

"I don't see why you'd be mad at me."

"I'm not. That's the thing." The faint scent of guilt soured the sweet, warm smells of hay and horses. Her gray eyes seemed full of something unspoken. Abruptly she made a fist and slammed the fat part of it against the wooden beam, below the plaque with Fiona's name made in flowers. A horse whinnied and shuffled a few stalls down. "I have to go. Command performance with the King. Wish me luck."

"Do you—" I hesitated. "Would you want me to come with you?"

I'd surprised her. Enough that she had to swallow her reflexive refusal and reconsider me. It irritated me a little, that it hadn't occurred to her to bring me along for moral support or advice, even—but then, I hadn't expected to offer.

Still, if I was to be Queen of Avonlidgh and Glorianna's avatar, then I needed to face some of the more difficult decisions. More than which dress to wear. In fact, I was a little sorry I'd chosen this delicate violet lace. It did lovely things for my eyes, but next to Ursula's fighting leathers, I'd look like a silly flower.

"Yes," Ursula decided. "I would. Thank you for offering. It means a great deal to me."

I nodded, the knot in my throat hard. "We are sisters, as Glorianna and Danu are sisters. We should help each other."

"And Moranu." Ursula cocked her head at me. I looked away, brushing a stray strand of hay from my skirts.

"Do you plan to change for the meeting?"

"No," Ursula replied, striding out of the stables as I hop-skipped to keep up without planting a silk slipper in a horse leaving. "I'm not going to impress Uorsin by wearing a fancy outfit. And I feel more confident in my leathers. Battle ready." Her thin lips twisted in a wry grimace.

"Are you . . . afraid of what he'll say?" I hesitated to ask it, but it seemed I should.

Ursula's hand dropped to her sword, her thumb passing over the topaz cabochon jewel. "Am I afraid? Fear is a funny thing. When people are trying to kill you on the battlefield, there isn't much time to be afraid. Beforehand—if you know it's coming, which a lot of times you don't—it's mainly nerves. Anticipation. It's afterwards, when I remember their faces, the brush of the steel that barely missed taking off my head, that's when I feel the fear."

"So right now, it's nerves?"

She slid a sideways look down at me. "Maybe some." She sighed. "But I also ask myself, what's the worst that can happen?"

I shivered. "Don't say that. It's bad luck."

🌹 🌹 🌹

Only our father and the ever-faithful Derodotur waited in Uorsin's private study. The High King wore his crown, however, which was probably not a good sign, as much as it irritated him to have it on. He raised bristling eyebrows and leveled a cold glare on Ursula.

"What are you doing here, Amelia? You don't belong in this meeting."

"Hello, Father!" I swept around the desk—dammit, that was a bit of a flounce—and kissed him on the cheek. "I haven't seen much of you, so I tagged along behind Ursula. You don't mind, do you?"

He patted my cheek affectionately. "It's always a delight to see you, Ami. How does my grandson come along?"

I kept my smile and laid a hand on my still-flat belly. "Gradually."

He made a hmphing sound. "Summer is a long ways off."

"I don't believe the process can be hastened," I teased him.

Instead of chuckling, he glowered at me. "You make light, but these are dire times. We need that boy to secure the succession."

I waved at Ursula, standing at parade attention, watching my little scene with interest. "There's our succession. Besides, I'm sure you'll live *forever*."

Uorsin slammed a fist on the table, making me flinch—though Derodotur and Ursula barely seemed to notice. They were used to this, then. "Don't you coddle me, Daughter! It's become absolutely clear that I cannot leave my kingdom in your weak hands." He spoke to Ursula now. "You lost me both Annfwn and a daughter. I feel sure a son would have done better. *I* would have done better."

"Then why didn't you go?" Ursula put the question plainly, seeming unruffled. "I've wondered that time and again."

"Because I trusted you," he shot at her.

Ursula shook her head. "That's not the reason. I know better than that."

Uorsin sat back in his heavy chair, an expression of utter disbelief on his face. "You dare to contradict me?"

"Yes. In this small circle, I do, as I never would elsewhere. You have, and always will have, my complete and utter loyalty. You are a great king, the glue that forms the peace that holds the Twelve Kingdoms together. Without you, we are lost."

He grunted, pleased, though he didn't want to admit it. Ursula dealt with him well. Better than I did.

"High King Uorsin cannot cross into Annfwn—he made a blood vow." Derodotur dropped the information as if casually noting the weather. Uorsin's visage flooded with rage. Derodotur faced him with ineffable calm. "They need to understand, both as your heirs and as their mother's daughters."

A blood vow? To whom? But it did explain so much. What in the Twelve Kingdoms had he traded for such a stricture?

"In exchange for Salena's help in the Great War?" Ursula had that look as when she played chess with him and had executed a strategic move. She thought so much faster than I did. Perhaps Father was right—I didn't belong in this meeting.

"All this time, I left them alone, until those upstart Tala infected my daughter's mind, making her betray us all. *She* could have been our key into Annfwn. You were to bring her here, in chains or dead if necessary—do you care to explain your failure?"

I bit one knuckle to keep from gasping at that. Ursula flicked an unreadable glance at me.

"The guerrilla tactics they used made our regiments easy targets for their attacks, as I understand was also true at the Siege of Windroven. Once we were deep in the hills and forests, the landscape became their ally and our enemy. We could not pursue effectively, for their speed and ability to hide outmatched us. There

seems to be only one entrance to Annfwn—through Odfell's
Pass—but the way is steep, narrow, and treacherous."

"Obstacles only."

Ursula inclined her head. "Just so. But the kicker was the
magic. It's true. None can cross the border—it's like a glass wall."

Uorsin tapped thick fingers on the desk and snorted. "Nonsense."

"What magics did Salena use that secured your victories?" Ursula retorted.

"They may have sealed off that border once, but it can't be
anymore. Once your mother left Annfwn, she made it that if any
of them left, they could not get back in. Obviously, they crossed
out and took Andi back in with them. Therefore, the border is
open."

"That was when they lacked Salena to work the magic." Ursula's gray eyes unfocused, as if she replayed the scene in her
head. "Now they have Andi."

"I find it difficult to believe that my least worthy daughter
wields so much power." But Uorsin's eyes strayed to the window,
and I thought I caught the wintery shiver of fear deep in his heart,
a rime of frost on the walls shadowed from the sun. "Besides, I am
not without resources. The Twelve Kingdoms are not the entire
world and the Tala are not the only monsters in it."

"High King Uorsin." Ursula's frost of unease tinged the air.
"Surely you're not considering—"

"What I do or don't consider is not the business of anyone
here. I am the High King and I alone decide! And I *will* have
Annfwn, one way or another."

"How? Andi—and Annfwn—are lost forever. We must move
forward without them."

Uorsin turned to her, the ice of his fear balling into meaty rage.
"This is your great lack, daughter. Why you cannot be my heir.
You are too easily cowed. You have a woman's softness, a female
need to give up in the face of adversity. If you cannot take Annfwn, then you will never hold the Twelve Kingdoms."

"Is that a challenge, Your Highness?"

"It's a command." Uorsin held up both hands palm up. "You may believe I hold the Twelve in the palms of my hands, cradling them like a benevolent father. It's time you face the truth of it." He curled his fingers into fists, until the knuckles whitened. "This—*this*—is how you hold the lands together. They may struggle to escape as we speak, but they cannot. Will you break the grip that holds our peace?"

"Erich?" Ursula asked.

"Of course." Uorsin dropped his hands to the desk and stood, leaning on it so that he and Ursula were within striking distance of each other, Derodotur and I flanking them like decorative bookends. Derodotur caught my eye with a subtle half smile, as if he thought it, too. "Erich thinks to snap his leash. He sees me as weakened by this."

"And the others?"

"Aerron, Elcinea, and Nemeth follow along, like starving vultures thinking to pick over the corpses."

"But not Duranor? That surprises me."

"Not openly. Stefan thinks to lull me with his dancing attendance and protestations of loyalty."

"He's waiting. Waiting to see how far the others get. Then he'll choose sides—or wait for us to falter in fighting each other and swoop in to take the throne for himself."

"Just so." Uorsin nodded. They'd clicked into their old ways, so much alike. Andi and I had never been able to follow their strategy debates. Uorsin and his firstborn had always been that way, as if they thought with the same mind.

She'd made him forget, I realized. Somehow Ursula had become his right arm again, without him being aware. If I were smart, I'd step in, to secure the High Throne for my son or daughter. For Avonlidgh and Hugh. Glorianna wanted Annfwn, and here, *this*, was my opportunity to act. She'd guided me here, to be present for this moment, so I could advise the High King and be the one to lead the Twelve Kingdoms into the peace and bounty that was our destiny.

"Annfwn should be ours," I blurted. Ursula's and Uorsin's heads swiveled toward me, at identical angles. Derodotur stared between them, a slight figure, adding up numbers in his head. I'd just changed the equation. "Now is the time for us to move. Glorianna wills it so."

Uorsin chuckled, but laughing at me. "And do you propose to waltz up to the border and ask for it, like you asked for that pony? Didn't Glorianna will that also?"

My lips trembled with the hurt, but I firmed them, pressing them together as I'd seen Ursula do. It helped. Maybe I'd made up a few tales in the past. I had changed. If I needed to prove myself as Glorianna's avatar, so be it. "If Andi had it in her blood to handle this magic border, then I might, also. But I have Glorianna on my side. Annfwn is the answer to everything—we can feed our people, appease Erich, and avenge Hugh."

"What do you propose to do, Amelia?" Ursula posed it as a question, but her voice contained a warning. I ignored it.

"I will go to Annfwn and prove that I can cross this border."

"And then what?"

I had no idea. Drag Andi back, kicking and screaming? Kill her?

"Glorianna will guide me."

Uorsin frowned in thought. "Should you travel in your delicate condition, though?" He worried for the babe more than for me—and I smelled his fresh hope, his bright interest. I could be more than the pretty, affectionate daughter. I would succeed where Ursula had failed. Risking a glance at her, I found her eyes grave, nearly sad. Did she mourn for her own lost throne or for Andi's demise?

Either way, in the flush of the moment, I didn't care.

"Ursula dragged me all the way here, didn't she? I can travel to Annfwn and play spy. Then I'll be at Windroven in plenty of time to grow heavy and have my lying-in."

10

"No." Uorsin sat heavily, gaze wandering to my midsection. It was getting old quickly, people looking at only that part of me. "We cannot risk my heir. You may travel to Windroven and there only."

"But, Father!" The protest burst out of me. I'd been so sure that I could give him what he wanted most. It was a mistake, because his brow knotted, the sense of thunder booming through the room.

"Argue and you will be confined to Ordnung until the child is safely birthed!"

"An excellent call, Your Highness," Derodotur inserted himself deftly, distracting the King's anger.

"Do you imagine I need your approval?" Uorsin glared at the slight man who'd been with him before even our mother.

"I think you're most wise to see that sending Princess Amelia back to Windroven will demonstrate confidence in the peace and stability of the realm. Avonlidgh must be loyal, if you trust them with the safekeeping of your daughter and heir."

"Am I still heir in the interim?" Ursula inquired, in the same tone that she might ask whether we thought it might snow tonight.

Uorsin shuffled a scroll on his desk to the side. "I have no choice there, do I?"

"Well, you could make Amelia regent for the impending heir," Ursula pointed out. "Though, hmm." She tapped a finger on her chin, ostentatiously thoughtful. "That could be problematic if Old Erich passes or cedes the crown of Avonlidgh to her. Then she'd be Queen and regent of the Twelve Kingdoms. Likely the High Throne would indeed move from Ordnung then."

Uorsin's head swiveled and he fixed an impatient—and betrayed—look on me. As if I'd already done what Ursula suggested. She met my gaze over his head. Not smug, but with the confidence of a fighter who knows she's stronger.

"You are heir until the babe is born." Uorsin unrolled the scroll and scrawled a note on it. "At that point, *I* shall be regent and raise the boy myself. At Ordnung." He looked to me for my curtsy of acquiescence and I gave it.

"But"—he pointed a finger at me—"you would do well to speak to Old Erich. Calm him down. Ensure his loyalty to my throne. I shall hold you personally responsible for his actions— and those of his rebellious cohort."

How in Glorianna's name could I possibly do that? I'd sunk myself, for sure. Ursula watched me process it with a serene expression, though I thought she must be dancing inside at outmaneuvering my pitiful efforts.

"Yes, High King," I said, curtsying again. Nothing else I could do. I missed Hugh with a sharp pang and a stab of anger. If he hadn't died, I would never have left Windroven or tried to play these games. Already I'd failed my son and Glorianna's cause.

"Run along, Ami, and plan your departure. I want Erich out of my court and away from easy access to his would-be allies. You can at least be useful there. Ursula, you stay. We have more to discuss."

Dismissed, I hurried down the hall. It was ever this way—me sent from the room while the grown-ups discussed the important things. My face felt hot and I gripped the fabric of my skirts, to keep from tripping on the lacy hem, yes, but also to keep my hands from shaking.

My few ladies who remained at Ordnung looked up from their sewing projects, startled, when I rushed into the rooms. Dulcinor put down the fabric she had been embroidering with Glorianna roses and came to me. "Your Highness! Is aught amiss? Is it the babe? I'll get you a cool cloth for your forehead, though you know it's impossible to get the maids to bring truly cold water here. I tell them, 'Fetch it directly from the deep well and don't dawdle on the way by the fire,' but it never seems to penetrate their thick heads. Truly I don't know why—"

"I'm taking a nap," I interrupted her. A memory of Andi pretending to throttle Dulcinor behind her back flashed through my mind and I split out a slice of my fury for her and her betrayal. "We leave for Windroven tomorrow. All of you—go do whatever it is you do to get us ready to leave."

"Ladies Raylea and Abaigeal are still visiting their families and—"

"Then send them a message. Or they can catch up. High King's command." The words tasted bitter in my mouth, and my ladies exchanged speculative looks. Careless of me. They'd all think *I* was in disfavor. I'd have to be sure to cozy up to the King tonight, to make it clear that I was still his favorite. I knew how to do that much. Smile. Be lovely and sweet. Precious princess. My only talent and worth.

"Where is Marin?" I asked. Her usual rocker was empty and her knitting bag nowhere in sight.

"I haven't seen her, Your Highness," Dulcinor answered. "Though, you know, I find her commoner ways are not exactly the thing—"

"Somebody find her for me. Tell her I need tea."

They fluttered about, gathering up their needlework, too savvy to discuss our sudden departure yet. No, they'd wait to gossip about me once they were out of earshot. That's how I'd always done it.

Once they'd left me to blessed silence, I prowled my mother's rooms, restless and with no idea how to console myself. I'd always taken comfort and pleasure in the company of my ladies, but now I wanted only to be alone. Or in Marin's restful presence. Andi always said that's why she preferred to ride, to get away from the castle and all the chattering people, and I'd never understood.

I saw them together. I could see they loved each other before Andi said so. Ursula's words trickled through my head. How could that be so? Love was what Hugh and I had shared—something noble, pure, and good. Surely she couldn't love such a beast. Likewise, a soulless demon like Rayfe couldn't possibly feel the tenderer emotions. But the way she'd looked during the siege returned to me. Little expressions, vague deflections. She'd asked Hugh relentlessly about a gift Rayfe kept trying to send her.

And she hadn't talked to me about it. Not really.

I'd thought she hated the enemy as much as we did. That traitorous blood must have been turning her even then. Our mother's blood. That mark that made her different and foul. I needed to understand what it all meant. Then I'd know what to do, how to think and feel. Surely if I could piece the puzzle together, I wouldn't be so storm tossed. I wanted my old serenity again.

I wanted Hugh back.

I could see they loved each other. That was *my* true love that Andi slaughtered and took for herself. It made sense—as if true love was a jewel to be shared among the three of us. I'd had it and Andi had been jealous. I remembered well the way she'd gazed on Hugh, how she'd flirted with him. Then she killed him and took the love for herself.

With a screech of rage, I pulled a set of books from the shelf and flung them to the floor. Their pages rustled like bat wings in the caves under Windroven and they lay in a gratifyingly scattered chaotic pattern. But they didn't hold the answers I sought. No, only one person knew Andi's secrets. Ones about our mother, I felt sure.

I needed that stupid doll. Another thing that Andi had that I didn't. If it truly existed, which I doubted. I searched the room, looking for things that might have stayed during the long years since my mother's death. But very little seemed to be actually hers. Ursula once said that our father had burned Salena's things after her death.

I could understand that desire. For surely he'd loved her and grieved over her loss.

Going to the door, I opened it to find the page stationed outside. He beamed at me, an angelic little boy, and I ruffled his hair, slipping into the role of the most beautiful princess easily. Happily he ran off to do his errand for me.

I went back to pulling books off the shelves, letting them fall where they might. When Dafne arrived, she gasped at the disarray and I felt briefly guilty. But I shouldn't. They were only books, and I should be more important.

"I need your help."

"Certainly, Princess!" She hastened to the books, smoothing their crumpled pages and stacking them carefully.

"Not those. They don't matter."

She obeyed, leaving them reluctantly. And that White Monk said I had no power. He didn't know what power was. Andi had left her little puppet of a librarian under my hand and I would treat her as I liked.

For the moment, however, sugar would get me further with her. I would make Dafne into my friend. Then she'd *want* to tell me all of Andi's silly secrets. The ones she should have told me, her baby sister, first.

So I smiled at Dafne and rushed over to pick up some of the books. "I'm sorry! I didn't mean it. I was looking for something and I confess I became most distraught—I don't understand what's wrong with me." If I could have worked up a single, lovely tear, I would have.

She fell for it, anyway, laying a gentle hand over mine. "You rest, Princess Amelia. I'll get the books straightened up. It's perfectly understandable. You've been through so much, and all the women say that the babe growing in you makes everything feel ever so much more."

Was that true? The sensation of being dashed from one emotion to the next came from the child? I'd have to ask Marin. Who should have been here by now. Surely the White Monk had been overstating and Kir would simply have spoken with her. Perhaps detained her for prayers. I tamped down the worry and gave Dafne my most appealing smile, the one that melted any heart.

"Will you help me find something?"

"Of course, Princess. What is it?"

"Do you remember the doll Andi had? She brought it with her to Windroven."

"That your mother made? Yes. I packed it for her to take to Annfwn when she married King Rayfe."

"She sent me a message." I wrung my fingers together, looking sorrowful, my eyes wide for best appeal. "That she thinks our mother made me one, too. I keep thinking that if I could only *find* it, that somehow . . ." I broke off, faking a little sob, surprised to find that it felt quite real.

"Don't you worry, Princess." Dafne clutched a stack of books to her breast, face earnest with sympathy. It made me wish that she actually was my friend and cared about me. "There are trunks stored from that era. I'll look for it."

"Oh, thank you! But . . . we leave tomorrow. Will there be time?"

Dafne's brow knitted in thought. Did no one ever tell these girls about wrinkles? "I'm not certain. That's not long to look."

"But you'll *try*? I can't leave without knowing!" That may have overplayed it, as my temper came through. Too much anger, not enough pitifulness. Dafne gazed at me with a carefully blank expression that nevertheless saw right through me.

"Perhaps some of your ladies could help me search. That would—"

"No!" I realized I'd clenched my fists and had to relax my hands. Where *was* Marin and that thrice-damned tea? "I, ah, don't want anyone else to know." The excuse sounded as weak as my trailing words, but Dafne nodded as if it made sense. I suppose it was true. Had my sisters been born with the ability to be secretive and devious? I seemed to lack all skill at it.

"Then I suppose you must help me." Dafne stacked the books with neat precision.

"Me?"

She revealed nothing, but I smelled her amusement. "Yes. Unless you trust another to send in your place?"

For some odd reason, I thought of the White Monk. Absurd idea. He seemed to hold me in the greatest contempt. Why in the Twelve Kingdoms would I ever think to trust him with such an errand? Not that I trusted Dafne. No, that was true power—knowing that you held someone's future in your grip, so they could not betray you. Ever so much more reliable.

"Fine." I started for the door, but Dafne didn't move. "Aren't you coming? I don't know the way."

She gestured at my lavender lace gown. "You might want to change your dress. It's likely to be dusty."

"I don't care."

"And there are spiders—they might crawl into the lace and nest there."

My skin crawled and I shuddered. Her lips twitched, ever so slightly. She was laughing at me. Well, I would get her back. "My ladies are not here, so you'll have to help me change, then."

She didn't seem bothered by the command, and followed me into my chambers. The variety of gowns available did seem to take her aback, however. And that I didn't have even some fighting-practice clothes to wear instead, as apparently Perfect Andi had done.

I'd never been in the castle stores. Why would I have been? The rooms fed one into the other, dark and more than a little dank. Freezing, too, though I wouldn't admit to Dafne that she'd been right to insist I don several extra layers. Up in my fire-warmed rooms, the heavy fabrics had seemed suffocating—and too bulky for my slim figure.

She consulted a sort of map and I peered over her shoulder, trying to make sense of the notations. To my irritation, she didn't explain, just nodded to herself and set off down a corridor at a brisk pace. Really, she lacked all sense of decorum and deference for my position. I opened my mouth to reprimand her but realized she might refuse to help me look if I did. So instead I trailed behind, skipping a little to catch up, nearly crashing into her when she popped out of rooms I'd been about to follow her into.

"Did your little map not tell you the correct location?" I demanded after the third mistake. Nice to know that the perfect librarian wasn't above misreading notes.

Dafne grimaced and shook a sticky cobweb off her hand. "These trunks were saved despite the High King's command. They couldn't exactly be listed as what they were on the official inventory."

"What? You disobeyed the High King?" My heart fluttered—with shock or the illicit thrill, I wasn't sure.

"Not me, precisely, but those entrusted with preserving the history and relics of the Twelve Kingdoms, yes." She studied me. "Have I made a mistake in trusting you, Princess Amelia? I thought your desire for this object your mother left you outweighed the danger of looking for it."

I hadn't realized this quest would be dangerous, but she'd assumed I'd known. Because, of course, anyone who'd thought it through would have. Ursula would have known that searching out Salena's things would be considered a traitorous act by Uorsin.

"This is why you wanted me to come along. So I couldn't claim you acted without my knowledge."

She smiled, thin lipped and without humor. "It pays to cover one's back in such things, yes."

"You don't trust me."

"Did you expect I would?"

"You trust Andi."

She tilted her head. Inclined it. The gesture spoke worlds, reminding me that she'd refused to tell me Andi's secrets.

"Fine." I used my frostiest tone, but she only raised her brows.

"In or out, Amelia?" She used my name in a serious tone, speaking to me as a person, not a princess or a queen. Before, I might not have recognized it. The White Monk called me by my name, too, in a similar tone—as if they somehow sought to catch my attention in a different way. Not the pretty petted princess, but *me*.

"I need to do this."

She nodded, crisply accepting my word, then gestured into the dark room. "Wait a moment and I'll get a lantern. There are none in here."

I stepped into the dark cellar alcove, which held several wooden trunks. Through the musty damp, the scent of spicy forests warmed the air. And—I fancied I smelled my mother. Absurd, since our lives had not overlapped outside the womb. I had no idea how she smelled. My abdomen burned, the small star of life there flickering, and I laid a hand over my unborn child. We would know each other, I promised in my heart.

Dafne returned with a glass lantern that sliced through the dimness and hung it on an overhead hook. I turned to the nearest trunk.

"Not that one," she corrected. "This one."

It was small. Not even the size of the least of my clothing trunks. "And the others?"

"There is only the one for Salena's things. She was not given to collecting material possessions."

My fingers itched to open it, but I stalled, a vague fear of the unknown holding me back.

"Did you know her?"

"A little, yes. She was kind to me."

I waited for the anger, the hot sting of jealousy. Oddly, I didn't feel those things. I didn't even feel the hard, spiny lump that locked all my tears inside. For the first time in ages, calmness settled through me, as with one of Marin's teas. I closed my eyes and imagined I felt my mother's hand on my cheek, the scent of her skin and the drape of her hair, backlit by the fire. It felt like memory but had to be a lie, since she'd never lived to hold me.

She said you knew the truth and would tell us.

"I was always told she died birthing me." I sank to the floor in front of the trunk. A fat black spider skittered into the shadows. Dafne hadn't lied about that. What other knowledge might she have?

"That's what we all were told."

"But you don't believe it." While Dafne considered how to respond, I studied the lid of the chest. Carved with a scene and inlaid with a shimmering white bone material, it showed a cliff overlooking a pristine shore. Even this had been hers. I knew it in my gut. It should have been ours. But for Dafne and her ilk, this would have been destroyed. Not out of grief, as I'd first thought. No—Uorsin had acted out of spite. The certainty filled me, as if Salena herself whispered in my ear.

"She had been secluded for her lying-in. The pregnancy had been hard on her, so we were told. Even Ursula and little Andi visited rarely. I was but a girl myself—with no status—so I hadn't seen her for several full moons. When the word came that she'd died in childbirth, but that you'd survived, they showed you to the court. I remember it well."

Her voice took on a reverent hush. "You were so beautiful, even as a newborn, not wrinkled and squalling, but luminous, like a perfect pearl, your eyes the same blue as now, and you even had your red-gold hair. It seemed a miracle to us all, that out of such dark news such a perfect child emerged."

Glorianna's avatar. Salena's redemption.

"Some whispered that you were no newborn because you seemed to be, instead, weeks old." She took a breath to say more. Stopped herself.

She didn't need to. Even I could decipher the implications. "Traitorous words to go with a traitorous activity."

"Just so. I won't say more."

Weeks. I may have been alive for weeks with my mother, who'd held me and nursed me and then died mysteriously. And my father had ordered her things destroyed.

How many other things didn't I know? Taking a deep breath, I fitted my fingers under the old wooden lip and opened the chest.

11

It was barely half-full. A few gowns. Some scrolls. Several smaller boxes.

But it smelled of *her*.

Abruptly I wished I'd thought to ask Ursula to come along, so she, too, could breathe in the essence of our long-gone mother. But another part of me—the selfish part still stinging from her outmaneuvering me—loved it. She had the cabochon topaz. This would be mine and mine alone.

"Do you smell that?" My voice sounded reverent. I added a mental prayer to Glorianna, for leading me here. The gratitude made up for the bit of spitefulness.

"It's the wood of the chest. That kind preserves the contents from insects and other kinds of decay."

I shook my head. "No. Not that. It smells like my mother."

With careful touches, I lifted a cloak out of the chest. Simple black and very worn, lined with some sort of fur I didn't recognize. I wanted to bury my face in it, but the other things called to me, so I folded it into my lap.

Eagerly, I reached for a box, holding my breath, hoping to see the doll inside. Seashells. Dull grays and tans. One had a pretty polished pink interior, but the rest were boring and unlovely. Why had she kept them?

There were scrolls, too. I started to open one and Dafne made a little noise and laid her hand on mine. I'd forgotten she was there. She wore soft gloves.

"Carefully, Princess." Her voice came hushed, as soft as her touch. She eased the scroll from my grip. "These are so old they could tear if not handled properly. Even the oils from your fingers could harm them."

"Nonsense." But I let her have them. They weren't what I wanted anyway. Dafne would be sure to tell me if they said anything important.

I pawed through the rest of it, checking each box, thinking at any moment my doll would be revealed. Far too soon my fingers scraped the bottom of the chest. Disappointment as bitter as the bile I'd puked up that morning lurked at the base of my tongue.

"It's not here."

"It appears not," Dafne replied, gentle. "I'm sorry."

I shrugged, the taste balling up into that familiar knot. Back again, my old friend. "Likely it never existed. It was only a tale to put me off." As with so many.

"Did you ask Lady Zevondeth?"

I stood up and watched as Dafne carefully repacked the trunk. Such an orderly person. I had never felt that desire, to put things away neatly. "We discussed it in front of her. She didn't say anything. Why?"

"She's a canny old woman. She might not say unless you ask directly—and offer something in return."

And did she tell you the price of such information?

"What kind of something?"

"It's difficult to say." Dafne was hedging. The scent of Andi's secrets quivered under her words.

"Don't you think it's rude to have more loyalty to Andi than to me?" I'd wanted to sound imperious, but the words came out petulant. Exactly how I felt. "Worse! It's betrayal! She's a murderer, a traitor to the crown, and you're covering for her."

She stripped off the gloves, having already wrapped the scrolls in a soft cloth. Her sharp movements conveyed the irritation she otherwise wouldn't dare express. When did everyone start hating me?

"I'm helping you out of loyalty to Andi, because she's my friend and because she asked me to. However, Your Highness, you do make the job exceedingly difficult."

I cringed, opened my mouth to apologize, and found the words locked around that same knot. Nobody understood me. Only Hugh ever had and . . . I was tired of thinking about it.

Tired of myself.

"Thank you for your assistance, Lady Dafne. I want to take this trunk with me to Windroven. Do you think that could be arranged?"

She nodded, measuring it with her gaze. "Good idea. It would likely be safer there. I'll take care of it."

I acknowledged her, feeling stiff, resisting the urge to thank her again. Not asking her why she liked Andi so much better than me.

"And, ah, you'll return with us to Windroven?"

"If you'll have me, Princess, I will. There is nothing for me at Ordnung and I like Windroven."

"It has its own kind of old and wild beauty, don't you think?" The words came out in a rush, some of the frozen feeling thawing at her answering smile.

"Yes. I do. I would offer to come with you to see Lady Zevondeth, but I think she'll talk more freely without me there."

She was likely right, but I felt a bit bereft anyway. Reaching into the trunk, I took one of the smaller seashells and put it in my pocket.

"For luck," I said. "Or something like that."

"I'd do the same thing, Princess, if I found something of my mother's to have as a talisman."

"But everything from your home is gone?"

"Yes. Destroyed with Castle Columba and ground to dust before the High King built Ordnung on its foundations. I was lucky I survived."

My father had done that. In the name of peace, of building the Twelve Kingdoms into the solid, strong whole we enjoyed today. But how awful.

Impulsively I took out another shell and gave it to her. "Then have this. You said she was kind to you. Perhaps this can be something of a substitute."

Her pretty brown eyes filled with tears, and she took it, pressing it to her heart. "Thank you."

"Will you still say it's difficult dealing with me?"

She laughed. "You do have your ways of making up for it."

There. I wasn't completely awful.

🌹 🌹 🌹

Lady Zevondeth's chambers blazed hotter than one of Glorianna's greenhouses—and smelled far worse. Sweet, but also rotten. Her maidservant admitted me and led the way to a chaise piled with pillows where the old woman reclined as if she were the queen and I the supplicant.

Her milk-white eyes tracked me across the room, not seeming blind at all. It made the hairs on the nape of my neck stand up.

"Welcome, sweet Princess. I wondered when you'd come to me."

I should have changed into my lighter gown, if only because it would have been cooler. Already sweat rolled down my back, tickling my skin until the gathered fabric around my hips soaked it up.

"You expected my visit?" Ursula would no doubt play this better, but I tried to be cagey.

Zevondeth chuckled, an unpleasant, croaking sound. "You want that doll, don't you?"

"Do you know where it is?"

"It may be that I do."

"If that's so, then you should give it to me. It's meant to be mine. You have no right to keep it from me."

"Don't I? You never missed it before. Could be I had my reasons."

"Such as? And I didn't miss it, because you deliberately concealed its existence from me."

"When you get to my age, child, you may also find that you have kept so many secrets that it's simply easier to lock them all away than reveal them piecemeal."

"Somebody said I'd have to ask you the right questions."

"Lady Dafne is a clever woman. You do well to listen to her."

"I didn't say it was her."

"You didn't need to."

She lapsed into silence, thoughtfully sipping her tea, then adjusting a golden velvet coverlet with fringe and tassels higher up on her breast. I supposed I was to ask my question, but hadn't I already? I thought back over our conversation.

"May I have my doll?"

Her head bobbed, maybe in drowsiness. But then she spoke. "What will you give me in return?"

"It belongs to me by right—I shouldn't have to purchase it from you."

"Ah, but it belongs to me in fact. You shan't bully me out of this, young Amelia, as the King attempted to do. You won't find it without my help. It's well hidden."

"My father?" I felt stupid. Of course she meant Uorsin. "He wanted it?"

"He wanted everything of Salena's. Everything she had with her when—at the end."

I sat on a tufted hassock near her feet, my thighs suddenly watery. "What happened . . . at the end?"

"Another question? And yet you have offered me nothing."

"Fine. What do you want?"

"Your firstborn." She answered me with certain immediacy, the deadly blade of her wish catching me as surely as Ursula's swift sword. My breath clogged behind that knot of tears, all bound up with the other ugly emotions that stuck to it, accreting like a dirty snowball rolling across the muddy courtyard.

But I stood almost immediately. "Good night, Lady Zevondeth. I would wish you well, but I don't."

Her croaking laugh followed me. "So the fragile flower has a spine, after all. Come back, little Ami. I didn't mean it."

I hesitated. "That wasn't funny."

"It wasn't a joke."

"You said you didn't mean it."

"I didn't. I said it to you, not in jest, but in warning."

"Warning that you'll take my child if you can?"

"That others will."

Despite the hothouse heat, a chill washed through me. "Who—the Tala?"

Zevondeth shook her head, but it might have been the palsy. Her blind eyes focused on nothing. "You will understand, when the time comes."

I wanted to ask what she meant, but we still hadn't agreed on a price. "If not my firstborn, then what will you take as payment?"

She smiled, cracked lips moving to show one unlovely brown tooth, alone in the gaps. "Blood."

Yuck. "Why?"

"Never you mind that. It's my price. Yay or nay?"

"How much blood?"

"You're not so silly. Even Andi didn't ask that."

"You took Andi's blood, too?"

Zevondeth pointed her chin at the mantel, where three crystal vials rested, two empty, one filled with dark fluid. "There. The same from you."

"And the third is for Ursula's?"

"Not yet. In time."

"What game do you play?"

"Not mine. I've lived beyond my years to finish this game for another."

"Salena."

"Get the vial."

With my body between her and the set of vials—just in case she *could* see—I touched the vial with Andi's blood, the middle one. Unaccountably, despite the blazing fire that seemed it could set my skirts on fire from sheer proximity, the vial was as cold as mountain water. And seemed fixed in place. It had occurred to me to take it, but it wouldn't be moved.

"Only yours, Ami. The others are not for you."

My skin prickling with foreboding, I took the vial to the right of Andi's. It came easily in my hand. Mine.

Zevondeth took it from me without fumbling in the slightest, set it in her lap, and then, quick as a snake, gripped my wrist. I forced myself not to yank my hand away and stared off over her head, at the velvet-curtained walls of her chambers. The pain came fast and nauseating, my blood oozed hot over my skin.

"You'd best sit, dear. No fainting allowed." She laughed, the croak turning into a hoarse, bone-deep cough.

I sank onto a tufted hassock, sucking on my bleeding finger, my mouth full of salt and fear.

When I managed to look at her again, the vial had disappeared, likely secreted somewhere in all those blankets.

"What will you do with it?" I whispered the question. I'm not sure why.

She whispered, "It's a secret." And she winked at me. "If you're not too proud, kneel down on those tiles before the fireplace. The ones with the deer mosaic."

I mentally groaned at approaching that blaze again. The hair all along my scalp seemed to be soaked with sweat. I'd have to wash it before dinner tonight, and it would take ages to dry. Once that would have been enough to ruin my day.

No more.

I followed her instructions and knelt by the tiles. They showed deer chased by curious half men, half wolves. I didn't want to know.

"In the one with the swan, lay your bloodied finger over the image of the woman in the woods."

I had to squeeze the finger she'd sliced, to make the blood well up again, then found the image she spoke of. The woman in the woods stood as a silhouette among shadows, dark hair flowing, her face obscured. Setting my finger on her, for a moment I smelled my mother again. The scent of forests and love. The tile gave way, shifting under my touch as if the mortar had dissolved.

Digging my nails into the sides, I managed to lever it up, showing a space beneath. In the cavity lay the pieces of a doll. Two legs and an arm were attached to a sack body dressed in pink silk. Another arm, a rose sewed to the nubby palm, sat nearby. I rummaged around in the niche but found nothing more.

"The head is missing."

Zevondeth sighed. "Yes."

"Where is it?"

"She'd sent for something to complete it. I recall her mentioning something along those lines, but I didn't pay close attention. Had I known what was coming, I might have done so."

"Before I was born?"

"After, Amelia."

So it was true. She'd been alive after I'd been born. The twin halves of sorrow and joy cleaved me. Breathing in and out over the change in my world, I tried to assimilate what that meant.

"What happened to her?"

"Replace the tile and seal it. Then come here. And stoke up the fire while you're there."

I slid the piece into place and rubbed my still-bleeding finger over the shadow woman, watching the edges this time. The mortar re-formed, matching the rest even to the soot stains, as if it had never come and gone at all.

Magic.

"I can do magic?" I asked the old lady when I returned to my perch. *So there, Andi!*

But Zevondeth snorted. "There's a difference between activating a set spell and working magic yourself. Your blood is the key. It opens many doors for you, if you but know where to look for them."

"Like the border to Annfwn."

"Think you to go there?"

"If I'm the only one who can, then I owe it to my King, my kingdom, my son—the future High King—and Glorianna to bring the traitor back and deliver Annfwn to the people of the Twelve Kingdoms." My tone sounded suitably ringing with purpose.

Far from being impressed by my noble intentions—or even fearful for the heir I carried—she laughed at me. "You have all of Uorsin's bold ambition and none of Salena's keen and strategic caution."

Stung, I fiddled with the doll. Such an ugly thing, made of some prickly cloth, without artfulness. It smelled bad, like old animal hair. Even when I pressed the dismembered arm up against the ragged shoulder, it looked monstrous in its decapitated state. The silly pink dress seemed to be a cruel joke. "I could also find the rest of this doll, maybe. Andi would help me. She told me to come."

"Which is it, child?" Zevondeth's voice gentled, became kinder. "Do you wish to punish your sister or visit her?"

"I don't—I just don't know." I nearly hurled the doll across the room. "I'm so angry at her. How could she murder Hugh. How?"

Zevondeth stared sightlessly over my shoulder. "If you go, be sure that you ask the right question."

"I'm tired of riddles."

"Then you've given up the game before it's barely begun."

"This isn't a game. This is my *life*."

She shrugged, settling into the blankets. "To the goddesses, there is no difference."

"Glorianna would not toy with us. She loves us."

"Ah, but what is toying to you may be an expression of love from Her. They are not the same as we are. The concerns of our mortal lives can't compare to Their long view of the world."

"I don't understand what you mean."

"Then ask a question you will understand the answer to. Start simple and work your way up to the more complicated ones."

Another person had said something along those lines recently—who was it? Ah, Marin with the knitting. Maybe she'd start teaching me tonight, before the feast. She'd be waiting in my rooms when I returned. My ladies would have found her, wherever she'd wandered off to.

"What happened to my mother?"

Zevondeth opened her mouth, throwing her head back as when she made that cackling laugh, but only a long breath rattled out of her. For a panicked moment, I thought she'd died. But she blinked open her milky eyes and stared at the ceiling.

"As if that's not complicated to answer."

"I deserve to know."

"You should count yourself lucky not to get everything you deserve."

"The worst has already happened. My one true love died. I didn't deserve that."

"And who are you to know? It's always been so with you—you claim the pride of being Glorianna's avatar, but you don't truly give yourself over to Her will."

She fell silent. The nearby brazier of red-gold coals snapped and sizzled quietly. I smoothed the doll's gown where my sweaty fingers had pressed creases into the old silk. When she seemed to be planning to say nothing more, I risked an inquiring glance at the old woman. She appeared to be sleeping, her breath rattling wet in her nose.

"Lady Zevondeth?"

She snorted, choked a little, and jerked those milky white eyes open. "You're still here? Go."

"But—"

"No. No more." With a palsied hand, she wiped tears from her face.

"I still don't understand why she died, though!"

"It's not given to us to understand everything," she snapped, snatching up a little bell and ringing it so loudly for the maid that my ears hurt. "Perhaps you should seek your answers elsewhere. Leave an old woman be—quit your pestering."

Standing, I gathered the pieces of the doll in a fold of my skirt. I didn't want my sweat to mar it any more. Dafne had said finger oils would harm the scrolls, which I acted as if I didn't care about, but what might sweaty hands do? Zevondeth irritably asked the maid for another blanket and the girl scuttled off with the speed of the well intimidated.

I seized the chance. "But it was put about that she died birthing me and you knew that wasn't true."

"Not such a silly goose," Zevondeth muttered, picking at her coverlets, eyes closed.

"So who told you not to speak otherwise?"

"You're out of questions, Princess, though that's a fine one."

"I'll give you something else. More blood?"

"You have nothing more I want. Go on with you."

"You clearly loved my mother. I just wonder why you never told anyone the truth!"

She cracked one eye open and fixed it on me. "I'm still alive, aren't I?" She let it close again and snuggled in. "Some things are worth dying for. Some worth living for. Salena taught me that. Go learn your own lessons."

12

$\approx$

I prayed to Glorianna in the quiet of my bedchamber. Marin had not reappeared and I felt queasy—both from the lack of her soothing tea and from the growing worry that something had happened to her. The White Monk had implied as much, hadn't he? That I'd put Marin in danger by revealing that she had told me that story.

My head felt muddled, swirling from all the conversations I'd had through the day. Kir, the White Monk, Ursula, the audience in the High King's study, and the surreal episode with Lady Zevondeth. I'd opened my window, to better view the sunset while I said my prayers, inviting Glorianna's illuminating light into my heart. The cool evening air felt delicious against my overheated skin. Not long ago I thought I'd never unfreeze; now I thought I might never stop sweating. It would be better if I could remove the heavy winter gown, but I'd need help with that and couldn't bear anyone else's company at the moment.

I drew another of Glorianna's circles in the air around the setting sun, whispering thanks for the sealing of the day and beseeching Her to rise again in the morning. The tip of my cut finger stung as the air moved over it, and impulsively, I departed from the prescribed prayers.

"Please send me guidance, Glorianna." The rays barely warmed my face, but Her light shone with fierce glory. "I am lost. I have no idea what I'm meant to do. Every step I take seems to be the wrong one. I thought You wanted me to go to Annfwn, to begin claiming it for You, but I've already failed at that. The same way I've failed at everything. Nothing has been right since Hugh died, and I"—I had to pause to silence the hiccups of my faltering breath—"I feel I'm failing. That I truly am worth nothing. I think that maybe my mother died to protect me, and what if I'm not worthy of that? What if—"

"Your Highness?" One of my ladies—a quiet girl from Castle Avonlidgh who had no one to visit at Ordnung—peeked around my chamber door. "I'm so sorry to disturb your prayer, but High Priest Kir requests an audience with you."

"I'm not dressed for visitors. And I need to prepare for the feast tonight."

"I told the High Priest as much. He indicated that they would meditate and wait upon your convenience."

My brows rose in surprise and I stifled the movement, so as not to crinkle my forehead. "The High Priest chooses to wait on me? And is that White Monk with him?"

She nodded, her soft blue eyes wide with anxiety. Torn between obeying her future Queen and the High Priest of her goddess's temple—that couldn't be easy. "He asked for my utmost discretion and obedience, in the name of Glorianna."

"All right then, Ilsa. Set up my bath. Tell them I'll be out as soon as I'm dressed and ready. Warn him that it will be some time, as I must wash my hair. If Kir prefers, I can speak with him at the feast."

"I suggested that, in lieu of disturbing you. He seems most insistent on speaking in private."

Curious, as we'd spoken just this morning. "Has Marin arrived?"
"No, Your Highness. No one seems to be able to find her."

I didn't rush through bathing, but I didn't take my time, either. I needed to start being smarter, watching my words. The guilt ate at me that I might have indeed endangered Marin. Had Kir done something to her, as the White Monk obliquely warned he might? And why wait on a private audience? I could think of only one reason not to wait for the feast, or for them not to leave and return later—because Kir did not wish to increase the chances of his being seen coming and going.

Finally, I emerged, my semidamp hair artfully coiled and braided by Lady Ilsa, a heretofore unknown talent of hers she seemed happy to employ. I'd donned a purple gown with green trim for Hugh's memorial feast—a nod toward Avonlidgh's traditional colors, but festive enough to satisfy the High King's directive that this be a celebration. As if he commanded our hearts as well as our actions. The disloyal thought surprised me.

High Priest Kir waited for me in the formal outer chambers. The White Monk sat on the window seat, apparently praying, though the last of the winter sunset had long left the sky. Salena had sat in that same spot, I remembered Ursula saying once, forever staring off into the Wild Lands. Was that a sign from Glorianna?

"Princess Amelia"—Kir stood and bowed elaborately—"you are lovelier than the sunrise. You do honor to Glorianna with your bright beauty."

The White Monk did not look over at us, his cowled profile indicating he stared out the window. Something told me, however, that he listened to every word. *Any female who spreads her legs can do that. It takes no special skill or ability.*

"I'd like to think I honor Glorianna with my thoughts and actions, as well."

He scratched his nose. "Well, that is certainly something worth aspiring to, Princess. Perhaps with prayer and study—and a holy mission."

"Oh?" I settled myself into a chair carved with roses and padded with pink satin cushions. With an odd certainty, it occurred to me that my mother would have hated it. Surely it was never here when she occupied these rooms.

"I understand you proposed to the High King that you travel to Annfwn."

How could he possibly know that? Ursula would neither confirm nor deny something like that, so I simply waited for him to continue, my face smooth and blank.

When I didn't respond, annoyance flitted over Kir's face. "I have reason to believe that King Erich and his allies would support such a venture."

"I have not spoken to Erich since yesterday," I said in an agreeable tone. Courteous small talk worked well for this, for being discreet. I needed to know if Kir had done something to Marin—it wouldn't do to make him too irritated with me.

"He is careful of the High King's displeasure."

"As are we all," I reminded him.

"Naturally. Though, in this instance, King Uorsin wishes greatly to achieve the mission you proposed. Only his natural fatherly concern for you prevents him from taking advantage of your special entrée to Annfwn."

"That and the well-being of his unborn grandchild and heir."

"That should not be an issue if you're properly protected and guided."

A shiver of excitement ran through me. I could go to Annfwn after all! There I could take my revenge on Andi. Once I'd returned triumphant, Uorsin would see that his worry had been for naught.

"I had a visitation from Glorianna." Kir spoke in urgent tones, as if he thought I needed convincing. "She gives Her blessing for this holy mission. She directed me to tell you that you must follow Her will in this."

That bothered me. Why hadn't Glorianna spoken to me Herself? I pressed away the frown between my eyebrows.

"Your impulse to offer to go to Annfwn came from Her. That is how Glorianna moves—by guiding your thoughts and feelings. When you spoke, that was Glorianna speaking through you."

"Truly?" I asked, before I could stop myself. That would make so much more sense—if Glorianna was sending me some of these strange ideas and enormous emotions.

Kir nodded solemnly and made the circle of Glorianna over me. "You are, as yet, an impure vessel. As you meditate and study, you will learn to discard your own muddied thoughts and feelings and allow Glorianna's will to move through you. You will become her perfect avatar, her perfect servant—doing only as Glorianna wishes."

Once, when I was a little girl, a troupe of performers had performed for the court. They'd asked for volunteers from the serving staff and then dressed the valets and maids in fine costumes. The performers stood behind the dressed-up servants, who were tied to them with ropes at waist, wrists, and ankles. The servants had scarves in their mouths so they couldn't speak; instead, the performers moved them about and said things for them. They acted out scenes, which made everyone laugh—most of all Uorsin—but I hadn't liked it.

I felt like one of those people.

As if he sensed my uncertainty, Kir laced his fingers together and leaned forward. "Do not doubt, Your Highness. You received divine inspiration. Honor that. Honor *Her*."

"I do," I breathed, opening my eyes wide and moistening my lips. "What would I do without your wise guidance, High Priest Kir?"

He beamed at me and seemed not to hear the muffled cough from the White Monk. "Then you accept this holy mission?"

"Yes!" I drew Glorianna's circle in the air, let my hand falter. "Oh . . . but my midwife cannot be found. I couldn't possibly travel without her support."

He waved a languid hand, gaze hard. "The commoner has received succor in Glorianna's Temple. I could not allow her to continue with such wayward ideas, for the sake of her own salvation and accord with the goddess."

"Then I shall have to stay here."

It satisfied me, to see the High Priest momentarily gape at me. "But, Princess, Glorianna specifically desires that you—"

"I don't care!" I put on my finest pout. "I need Marin. I can't possibly take on a long journey without her. I couldn't possibly risk my child that way."

"We shall find another midwife to travel with you," he soothed, looking more than a little frantic at my tantrum. And here I'd barely wound up.

"No!" I wailed, adding the drama. I stood and paced the room, throwing up my hands to the skies. "She is the *onliest* one who has been able to treat me. Glorianna sent her to me. I know that in my heart." For emphasis I pounded my fist against my breastbone.

"I can't see how that's true, with her heretical ways," Kir made the mistake of snapping at me.

I buried my face in my hands, sobbing. The artifice made the thorny ball in my throat spin, digging in painfully. Oh for tears, even manufactured ones. "Who better to help her than Glorianna's own avatar? I feel I was meant to take her under my wing, to lead her to the truth."

"Princess Amelia, I, that is, we, while we believe that you are, indeed, the hand of the goddess, you are not trained as our priests are."

I wailed into my palms as if my heart broke into a million pieces. "I shall stay here and learn from them. I *must* have Marin to tend me or I fear I shall lose the babe! I'll talk to my father. He'll understand."

"No!" Kir coughed, stopping what he'd been about to say. I peeked at him through my fingers. My dramatics had brought me to the other side of him, and, over his shoulder, I saw that the White Monk had risen from the window seat, hands tucked into draping sleeves, cowl pulled back, a strangely victorious light gleaming in his apple-green eyes. "Princess, Glorianna needs you to go and—"

"I shall go with Her Highness." The White Monk's words broke into our scene. Kir physically startled, because he'd not seen what I'd seen.

"I shall accompany Her Highness and take the midwife's education upon myself. I see that this must be why Glorianna called upon me to journey with you at this time. It is the perfect solution." He intoned a prayer, drawing Glorianna's circle, and Kir was compelled to follow along.

"I shall think upon it, but this might be the best solution," Kir reluctantly agreed.

"I am not without martial skill," the White Monk told him, "so I shall be of double benefit to our holy mission."

I studied him with an eye for that surprising disclosure. The White Monk, though tallish, lacked Hugh's broad shoulders and the physique that had allowed him to wield his heavy sword so well. Though Ursula could best most fighters, even those who outweighed her, as so many did, given her long, lean frame. She always said that cleverness, agility, and speed could win out over brute strength, if the fighter trained in those aspects enough. *If they can beat you with strength, don't let the match become a contest of strength.* Andi used to mimic her saying that, especially when she returned from fighting practice with a new bruise.

One of those bits of advice that sounded much easier in theory than it was in practice.

It applied to my situation. I was not the strategist Ursula was or all full of special witchy magic as it turned out Andi possessed. So I shouldn't get into those contests. Unfortunately my only talents lay in being beautiful, and no one held contests for that. I suspected I could throw only so many temper tantrums before they lost potency.

Maybe being Glorianna's living, dancing doll was all I had to offer. That and being mother of the next High King. Both of those things came from others, though. Still not me.

What power of your own do you possess?

"Will that be agreeable to you, Princess Amelia?" Kir startled me from my thoughts. The White Monk observed me with a cynical expression, his eyes mocking me, as if he'd followed my train of thought, that I understood I was as without power and worth as he'd accused me of being. No, it wasn't agreeable. I didn't want him around me with his hateful glares and taunting remarks. But I'd won my chance to find my purpose, to serve Glorianna and the High King both.

"I accept the mission." I declared, hoping I sounded noble and self-sacrificing. "And the subpriest may accompany me, so long as he doesn't make a nuisance of himself." That should put him in his place. That mouth, cruelly bisected by the scar, twisted in a wry imitation of a smile. He seemed uncowed but pulled his cowl over his forehead so I could no longer see his face.

"I shall speak with King Erich, then." Kir straightened his robes.

"No. I shall." I moved to the door and called my ladies to attend me, effectively ending our private meeting. "It's so good of you, High Priest Kir, to have offered my midwife the many benefits of Glorianna's Temple. I'll wait here for her immediate return, so she can tell me all about what she's learned."

Kir's stiff bow transmitted his intense displeasure, but he murmured agreement. The White Monk inclined his cowl in my direction; a flash of his eyes seemed to hold . . . surely not approval? Then the men were gone and my ladies were fussing over me that I'd be late for the feast. But I waited for Marin's return.

It was the right thing to do.

13

⚜

We left Ordnung with far less fanfare than our arrival had garnered. Neither my father nor my sister saw us off, sending the excuse that they were deep in strategy meetings. Ursula was likely still angry with me. Not that I cared.

I didn't mind a bit not having to discuss anything further. We both knew where we stood.

If it pained me a little that Uorsin didn't come to say good-bye, well, he was the High King, after all. After I succeeded in penetrating Annfwn, then he'd see me in a different light.

The caravan ostentatiously set off for Windroven. No one had yet told me the plan, which rankled somewhat. After all, we embarked on *my* holy mission. But when I'd spoken with Old Erich at the feast—discreetly, I thought—he'd acted vaguer than usual and told me only that he looked forward to my riding in his coach in the morning.

At first I nearly protested, because his old coach bounced something awful. It had been the one he'd used in the Great War and had never been intended for comfort. Not the opulently cushioned carriage Hugh had commissioned for one of my bridal gifts. Even as I opened my mouth, though, I caught on. Clever of Erich to make sure we'd speak privately.

The four of us jounced along, even on the perfectly planed and level road that led out of Ordnung. King Erich muttered about too much wine and appeared to settle in for a nap. Marin knitted furiously, still not speaking to me except to inquire after my well-being. The White Monk stayed true to his order and said nothing, simply sat with his cowled head bowed. Dafne should have ridden with us—at least she talked to me and usually had interesting things to say.

I really didn't see what the point had been of me riding with Erich if we weren't going to confer on the mission. If there would be a mission, as we were going entirely in the wrong direction. Perhaps I'd misread him and he'd simply wanted my company, as he'd said.

Well into midmorning, I sighed, thoroughly bored.

As if this had been a signal, the caravan turned off the main thoroughfare and onto a side road. Soldiers, ladies, and servants milled about. I made a move to exit the coach, if only to relieve my sore bottom for a bit, when Erich's head snapped up and he fixed me with his aging summer-blue eyes, an older echo of Hugh's, like when the sky seems to get worn-out and pale in the afternoon.

"So, my brave heart-daughter, you propose to cross into Annfwn."

"Yes, my king," I answered, sounding brave and noble, indeed. Marin cast me a black look.

"Are you certain you will be able to undertake what may be an arduous journey?"

Couldn't be more arduous than riding in this disaster of a coach.

"I'll be fine—my midwife assures me the babe is strong and healthy, as am I. There will be no risk." We hadn't actually discussed it, but there really hadn't been an opportunity. She glowered at me but didn't disagree.

Erich cleared his throat, an old man's too-loud coughing har-rumph, then gave me a kindly smile. "I meant more, my dear, if you're certain you'll be up to riding or perhaps even hiking, as it may be necessary."

"Oh! Um . . ." *Ride? Hike?* Belatedly I remembered what Ursula had said about the way into Annfwn. The narrow trail. The attacks along the way.

The White Monk raised his head slightly, so his smirking travesty of a smile clearly showed. He seemed to be daring me to back out. Awful, awful man. Ursula would have been prepared for this. Okay, if pretending was my talent . . .

"Of course! I love to ride, and long walks, too."

"Good, good." Erich nodded with his words, though I thought I heard a muffled snort from the not-so-silent White Monk. "We would not risk you, were not the situation so dire. We must ascertain if you can indeed enter Annfwn. That is all your mission entails—attempt to cross the border and test to see whether the others in your party can or cannot—then return to Avonlidgh."

I pushed my finger against the knot between my eyebrows. "But I should do more than that. I planned to—"

"What?" Erich barked it, sounding like the great general he'd once been. "Confront your sister, the traitor? Drag her to Ordnung by the hair? How do you propose to do that—lure her with tea cakes and a chance to play dolls?"

The reference to dolls jerked me out of my building sulk. Did he know about my personal quest to complete the doll? No. I could read in his face that he didn't—he was simply needling me about my silly feminine ways. Erich had always been distantly kind to me, treating me with offhanded affection, much more keenly interested in what advantage I brought to Avonlidgh than anything else.

Hugh, though—he'd sometimes called his father a despot and a tyrant. I'd always laughed, kissed him, and said none could compete with my bear of a father. Hugh would agree and recount how he'd rescued me from my lonely imprisonment at Ordnung, always embellishing the tale until I giggled so helplessly he could kiss me as much as he liked.

Maybe if we'd had more time together, we would have gotten to those stories. But I hadn't liked when Hugh turned somber, as he often did when he spoke of his father, so I'd always teased and distracted him. Now, facing Erich's contempt, I wished I'd paid more attention.

The regrets seemed to be piling up lately.

He reached over and patted my hand. "There, I've frightened you. I'm sorry, but you need to be more wary. You may remember Queen Andromeda as your childhood playmate, but she has changed. She has become fully Tala, a witch with possibly greater power than Salena even had, and look what she accomplished." He shook his head.

"What did she accomplish?" I asked the question timidly, certain he wouldn't answer, but he cocked a bushy brow at me.

"Uorsin loves to spin the tale to his own advantage, doesn't he? You'd do well to remember that, daughter of the man who did not bother to say farewell. Did you never wonder why High King Uorsin succeeded in uniting the Twelve Kingdoms where countless others failed?"

Others like Erich himself, I suddenly realized. I shook my head. I hadn't ever wondered. Uorsin won the Great War because he was Uorsin, hero, conqueror, and a king for the ages. So said all the songs and stories.

Erich laughed, a harsh sound not unlike Lady Zevondeth's cackle, as if their ability to laugh had dried up with age and bitterness. "Ah, that is ever Uorsin's talent—he plays the part and no one ever wonders how he came by it in the first place. Somehow he enlisted Salena of the Tala to his cause. He made a bargain with her—the same bargain that resulted in your sister being promised to them, more fool Uorsin for agreeing to *those* terms— and Salena won the Great War for him."

"How?" My question fell into the center of the coach, sitting there heavily while they all three regarded me with varying degrees of astonishment for my ignorance.

"Magic, Princess Amelia," Erich intoned. "Black, dark, and bloody magic. Shape-shifting and the bending of hearts and minds. None were safe. None shall be while the Tala remain a free people."

A soft sigh as the White Monk turned his gaze out the window.

"It seems that sister of yours has inherited that legacy," Erich continued. "Had I realized she could, we would have stopped her ever marrying Rayfe. We were fools."

"We tried to stop it," I pointed out. "The entire Siege at Windroven was all about preventing that marriage, but—"

Erich was shaking his head at me. "No, you pretty idiot. Not with the siege. The siege was doomed and my empty-headed son too full of noble heroism to see it. It was a waste of Avonlidgh's great people."

"Hugh died trying to retrieve Andi!" I cried, determined to defend him. Hugh had never been stupid. Full of grand and good intentions perhaps, but he'd been smart and strong and he'd tried to save Andi because he knew I loved her.

"I believe, Princess," the White Monk spoke, still gazing out the coach window at the busy people, his cowl in profile, "that King Erich is attempting to make you understand that the simplest, most direct method of preventing the Tala from accessing your sister and the power she holds would have been to kill her."

"You overstep yourself, Priest." Erich pointed at the coach door. "Both of you, out. I will speak privately with my heart-daughter."

The White Monk bowed, apparently with solemn respect, but a scent of cynicism like pine sap ran beneath it that Old Erich seemed unaware of. Marin scrambled out after him, giving Glorianna's priest a wide berth and moving with a speed that spoke of her gratitude to escape.

Erich stared at me as they left. When the door clicked, he leaned over, hands on his knees. I shrank into the hard seat.

"Could you do it?" Erich demanded of me. "Do you hate her

enough for what she did to Hugh, to her own sister, to cut her throat, to plunge the knife in her breast before she used her magic on you?"

"Wait . . . what?" My gorge rose and I pressed a hand to my belly, covering the babe.

"No, you couldn't." King Erich said it as a condemnation of my character. "So you will follow orders. Attempt a border crossing only. Do *not* make contact. Once we verify the information that you can cross, you will turn around and return to Avonlidgh for your lying-in. We will use the time to make plans and assemble our allies."

"Allies?" Did he mean Aerron, Duranor, and the others, as Ursula suspected?

"I am not without resources." Erich coughed again, a dark, rattling sound. "Consider this a test of your loyalty, heart-daughter. And a test of your strength and determination. Cross the border. Return. If you follow orders exactly and no word of any of this leaks to those at Ordnung, then, once you have safely divested yourself of my heir, you will have your opportunity for revenge. Do you understand?"

"I'm not sure." In truth, I wasn't entirely clear, but this conversation had been illuminating. Playing the silly airhead did encourage people to spell things out. "What if Glorianna asks more of me?"

The old king huffed with impatience. "I will guide you. If you can cross that thrice-damned magical border, we will return in force and you will escort my army over it. I will do what Uorsin could not: Annfwn will be mine. With Annfwn's rich resources, Avonlidgh will reign supreme. Your son, my blood, will follow me as High King—in Avonlidgh, as it should have been all along. Your traitorous sister will be thrown at your feet, with no way to defend herself. You will do as you wish with her then."

"Oh."

"It will be a cold revenge, but all the more satisfying for that." The mad light in Erich's eyes transformed into that grandfatherly twinkle that no longer deceived me. "Won't that be a fine moment, Princess? She robbed you of so much. You will have everything of hers. This shall be your reward—*if* you perform perfectly. Everything you want shall be yours."

I couldn't swallow past the ball in my throat. Was this what I wanted? I no longer knew. If I'd ever known. Still I nodded and smiled, though my lips trembled with some unnamed emotion and my jaw clenched. "I shall strive to do my very best."

"Do that." Erich reached over and patted my knee again, his hand sliding farther up my thigh. Fortunately, I could feel nothing through my cloak and heavy gown, but I wanted to draw away. "Your loyalty to Hugh does you great credit. No doubt he is looking down from Glorianna's arms, full of pride and love."

I nodded again, one of those puppet people, my chin jerking up and down. I wanted to yell at him that he didn't get to tell me how Hugh felt about me, whether he watched me. Hugh was *mine*, and I remembered more and more the comments he'd made about his father, how he'd hated him. He'd asked for Windroven because he didn't want us living at Castle Avonlidgh. As Erich's hand moved with greasy familiarity on my thigh, I understood why. Hugh had been protecting me. He'd just never told me so.

"I'll do this, King Erich. I'll make Hugh—and you—so proud."

"See that you do. I can be a kind man, Amelia. Kinder than Uorsin. Show me that you belong to Avonlidgh and I shall make you Queen of Annfwn and you shall rule through your son. You will have more power than you ever dreamed of." His breath washed sour over my face, and my stomach, so settled until now, turned over ominously. "Reach out and take the power I offer you."

"It wouldn't really be mine." I swallowed against the sick. "It would be only borrowed from you and my son." Just as I'd borrowed power from Hugh. Even he had treated me as something to be protected. A beautiful ninny who couldn't be told the cold truth.

"Such is the way of the world for women. But you have your ways of pleasing men." His hard hand caressed my cheek. I turned my face away, struggling to master the nausea as it rose with violent urgency.

"No, beautiful Amelia." He grasped my chin in a firm grip and made me face him. "Don't be shy."

"I'm going to be sick!" I squeaked, pressing my lips together as fast upon the words as I could, blindly groping for the door handle.

Erich looked horrified and jerked back. He was quick enough to avoid most of it, but his boots were not so lucky. A veteran of far worse gore, he merely looked disgusted. Embarrassed, but also with a teensy feeling of retribution, I wiped my mouth with the cloth Marin had pressed into my hand before she exited.

"I apologize, King Erich." The smell of my puke filled the coach and I thrust open the door, lest the odor make me barf again. "I'll send a servant to clean it up straightaway."

Outside the coach, the White Monk leaned against a tree, hands folded into his sleeves, only his scarred mouth visible beneath the cowl. Still, it curved in a more genuine smile than I'd yet seen from him.

"Well done, Princess," he said. "Very well done. I shall check upon our traveling companions."

I glanced at the coach. The White Monk should have been too far away to hear anything. How had he known?

Our small party waited in an abandoned barn while Erich's caravan pulled out again, bound for Avonlidgh. Marin, of course, knitted, having long since made sure my stomach had settled. I was learning not to confuse her solicitude for my health with actual caring for me. Her anger brewed, chilly and implacable. If I addressed her on any topic other than my pregnancy, she acted as if she didn't hear.

The White Monk sat meditating, apart from Erich's soldiers from Castle Avonlidgh. Wearing full armor and Avonlidgh's colors, they played some sort of game of chance that involved carved tokens of animals. They laughed and talked quietly among themselves, their lieutenant alternately watching them and me.

A hard-skinned, stone-eyed man, Lieutenant Graves seemed entirely without humor or joy. He seemed to expect any of us to attack him, keeping his hand around the hilt of his sword, more attached to it than even Ursula was to hers.

I hadn't talked with Erich again—just as well. His seneschal introduced me to Lieutenant Graves, who treated me with militarily precise etiquette and not a glimmer of flirtation. He vowed that he and his men would protect me and deliver me safely to Avonlidgh. "In and out, Your Highness. A quick reconnaissance where no one gets hurt and we'll be on the road home in a sevenday." Then he returned to the circle of his men and his constant vigilance.

Finally, the scout—a young redheaded man scarcely older than myself, who they all called Skunk, for no apparent reason—returned with the all clear.

"The caravan is well under way and all of Uorsin's spies have stayed with it." He winced when Graves knocked him on the side of the head.

"Mind your manners around Her Highness," Graves told him.

Skunk bowed and then bowed again, face flushing brighter than his hair. "My apologies, Your Grace—Graciousness. I mean, your Great Highness, um . . ."

Graves sighed heavily and told Skunk to eat and rest. "We'll head out in an hour. Your Highness; you'll want to change your clothes shortly."

"My clothes?" I looked down at my skirts, but all was fine. My aim had been excellent, with none of my sick on my hem.

"Did you plan on riding the back way through the mountains and the Wild Lands dressed like the Fairy Princess of Avonlidgh?" The White Monk smirked at me. The soldiers shuffled their feet and looked uncomfortable at his attitude.

"Perhaps you should take another vow of silence," I suggested. "I feel sure that's what Glorianna wants most from you."

"You, too, priest, should show appropriate respect for Her Highness, the future Queen of Avonlidgh." Graves frowned at the White Monk and I sent a sweet smile from behind Graves's back.

"Of course, Lieutenant," the White Monk replied agreeably with a bow to Graves's authority. "Though we are all equal in Glorianna's eyes."

"Sadly, we live in the real world, not the bower of Glorianna's arms," Graves rebuked him. "But I'm given to understand you offer your physical protection for Her Highness, to supplement that of my men."

"Yes, I do."

Graves surveyed the man's white robes with barely contained contempt. "Forgive me if I think we won't plan to rely on you, Priest."

"You might be surprised," the White Monk replied in a mild tone.

"Oh, yes?" Graves set his sword aside, stripped off his chest plate. "We have some time to kill. Let's see what you can do."

The men had already scrambled to create a clear space, anticipating what Graves planned.

"Hand to hand?" The White Monk stood, obliquely glancing in my direction.

"If there's a man under those robes, yes." Graves, now bare chested, flexed his arms, his pecs bulging. He had to outweigh the White Monk by at least half again. "Unless you'd prefer to take on someone more your size—Skunk, perhaps?"

The men grinned at one another and Skunk swallowed the soup he'd been drinking, wiping off his mouth and nodding with a grin. The other soldiers surreptitiously exchanged a few of the tokens they'd been gambling with, a couple of them casting snickering glances in the priest's direction.

The White Monk looked tense, his shoulders a creased line under the robe. He seemed to be debating, the quiet current of his deliberations like the scent of rosemary. He glanced my way again, then came to a visible decision, pushing back the cowl from his scarred face. The lieutenant's granite face showed little reaction, beyond the scrutiny in his stone-dead eyes. The White Monk pointed at him.

"I'll fight you."

14

I nearly protested. Then stopped myself, wondering why in the Twelve Kingdoms I cared what happened to the White Monk. It was his business what he chose to do. Should he be injured fighting the much larger man, it mattered not to me. It hadn't been my idea for the White Monk to come along anyway.

Still, sourceless worry curled through my gut.

The White Monk worked the ties of his robe, undoing the fastening at his neck, then releasing the frogs down the front. His green eyes flashed toward me and I averted my gaze, not sure why I'd been staring. Curiosity, most likely. I would soon see if his body showed the same scars as his face.

The other soldiers had gathered into a murmuring knot, trading tokens and arguing quietly, a pack of dogs growling at one another. Graves ignored them, taking the match seriously, despite his earlier mocking. It had taken him slightly aback, that the White Monk agreed to fight him. He watched the priest remove his robes, his gaze assessing in the way fighters did. Measuring their opponents before engaging. The play of interest and speculation on his remote face finally tipped me over the edge, and I had to look again.

As I'd suspected, the White Monk did not boast the brawny physique Graves did, nor did he have the smooth, golden muscularity Hugh had. No, the White Monk's body looked as lean and sharp as the line of a whip. He wore only tight-fitting black pants, his torso and feet bare. Sparse dark hairs dusted his arms and lower calves, curling and wiry. The tight muscles of his chest were partially obscured by thicker hair that formed a triangle, arrowing down his midline and disappearing beneath the waist of his pants.

More though, layers of scars, striped and jagged, showed pale through the hair, distorting the spare lines of his body. He bared his teeth at me, that glitter of hatred in his eyes, and pivoted slowly, as if for my inspection. His back was worse—a corruption of scars, layers of pain, ugliness, and horror.

"I hadn't realized Glorianna's temple exacted such a price," Graves commented, a new measure of respect in his voice.

The White Monk looked away from me—in relief or reluctance?—and acknowledged Graves with a nod, then shrugged elaborately, treating the horrific scarring as trivial. "The follies and deserts of a misspent youth. Hand to hand—no weapons?"

Graves agreed, though it seemed he was more interested in the test now, no longer sneering at the man he'd treated as a worthless burden. In a blur of movement, the White Monk darted in and out again. It seemed he'd only been testing Graves's speed, but the lieutenant thoughtfully rubbed his lower back. "Nice hit, White Monk, but do try to spare some of my organs for this trip. I do have a duty to perform."

The White Monk tossed off a two-fingered salute. "I'll try, but you know I don't dare let this become a contest of strength."

Ursula's adage, out of his mouth. It seemed Glorianna must be telling me something, speaking through these others.

The men had reengaged. Graves attempted to lock the White Monk in his massive grip, to use that strength. But the White Monk slipped away easily. Just as those muscular military arms seemed sure to trap him, he danced free with uncanny speed, folding and feinting, lithe as a weasel and equally difficult to lay hands on. Graves grunted and wheezed out laughing gasps of pain at blows I never saw land. Finally he called a halt, bending to rest his hands on his knees while he caught his breath, great chest billowing as he drew in air.

The White Monk stood nearby, sheened with sweat but otherwise seeming unharmed. He accepted the congratulations of the other soldiers with grace. If a thread of irony ran beneath his easy smile, they didn't seem to notice. Skunk, it appeared, had been the only one to bet on the White Monk, a broad grin splitting his face as he pocketed the double handful of animal tokens.

The White Monk caught me watching and raised his eyebrows, cynical, and swept a hand at his scarred body, as if inviting me to be disgusted.

"Few men could survive that sort of whipping," Marin said quietly.

I started, surprised as much that she voluntarily spoke to me as that she stood so near. "Is that what caused his scars—even on his face?"

The White Monk was donning his robe and boots again, the soldiers easily joking with him.

Marin shook her head. "Not all of them, Princess." The way she said my title made it sound like not a compliment. As if I were a silly frivolous thing who didn't understand what causes which kinds of scars. Which, in truth, I didn't. My own skin was flawless. Even Hugh had only a few minor scars, from various nicks, he'd said, as thin as the sharp blades that had caused them. "No, those scars come from lashings and beatings over days and weeks. Wounds on top of wounds."

"And the ones that look kind of . . . melted?"

"Burns," Marin replied, short and to the point. "Bad ones. Fatal ones, to my humble eye."

"Yet they weren't, because here he stands."

"Indeed he does. The mystery is not that he does, but how he managed it." She snorted, eyeing me with an unfriendly look. "It was a risk that he let you see so much. That he let any of them see. Do you mean to betray him, too?"

My stomach clutched a little and I couldn't meet her gaze. "I didn't mean to. It was a careless mistake."

She hmm'd to herself. "That's almost worse, Princess. That you hurt the people around you because you don't give a thought to them."

Miserably, I nodded. She really shouldn't talk to me this way, but I deserved the rebuke.

"You can't be doing that, Amelia," she said, not unkindly. "You're still young and more naïve than most, but you can't be careless with the power you wield."

"I don't have any power," I protested. "I'm like one of those animal tokens the soldiers gamble with, traded from person to person."

Pursing her lips thoughtfully, she acknowledged the point. "But they gamble with those tokens because they represent something more—they have a certain unique value they hope will bring them wealth and power. Unlike those wooden pieces, you have a heart and a mind and a goddess-blessed soul. You have agency of your own. You can decide not to be traded. To possess your own power."

"I don't know what it is." I felt queasy.

"Then find out." She handed me a mint. "You're not a stupid girl, just careless and foolish. Unfortunately you're also the daughter of the High King in turbulent times. That makes you dangerous. As for yon priest"—she jerked her chin at the White Monk, who watched us curiously, though Skunk seemed to be telling him some long story—"a man only gets those sorts of scars for two reasons: battle and prison. He's too young to have fought in the Great War, and those scars are too old for the recent conflicts. That leaves only one possibility. I'll get your riding clothes so you can change. It must be nigh time to leave." She bustled off, leaving me to my unsettled thoughts.

The White Monk was a criminal.

I don't know where they found the "riding clothes" for me, but they certainly hadn't been tailored for me. Really, I never wore pants. On the rare occasions when I'd ridden with Andi, I'd donned split skirts, which looked much prettier. Now the coarse material chafed my inner thighs, rubbing between my skin and the saddle. I fretted about the unsightly rash I'd get, though I wasn't going to complain to anyone. It bothered me, this insight that Hugh had seen me as someone to coddle. We'd loved each other so much—surely he, at least, had seen me as more than a pretty face?

A test of your strength and determination. I would pass this test and show them all what I was made of. I could be my father's daughter as much as Ursula.

We rode through the woods, looping around through the hills behind Ordnung, the long way, staying off the main trails, which made for slow going. Midday had passed while we hid in the barn, and now the afternoon lengthened into long shadows. The soft layer of snow muffled the horses' steps, and we moved more or less silently, as Graves had insisted—looking most pointedly at me.

I hoped we'd stop at twilight, but Glorianna's sun went beyond the overcast horizon without a prayer of acknowledgment. I whispered one to myself, making a discreet circle in the air, and caught the cynical green of the White Monk watching me. Some priest of Glorianna he was. If he was truly any priest at all.

More likely, with his criminal mind, he'd scammed his way into being Kir's assistant, using the cover of the sect he'd supposedly come from. When we returned, I should report him to at least the High Priest, if not Uorsin, despite Marin's warning. It was only right, and what loyalty did I owe this monk? There was no release from prison under Uorsin's rule. He did not believe that those sorts of people changed. From time to time, various groups had come to plea for clemency for some prisoner or other, citing good behavior or unfair imprisonment. The High King had never conceded once, and Glorianna's temple concurred.

If there was to be forgiveness, Glorianna would be the one to give it. Anything less than death was clemency to Uorsin, and he made no bones about it.

Marin had to have known I'd put together that much. I might be naïve, but I knew this basic truth of life in the Twelve Kingdoms, even if I'd never known a real criminal before. Our lasting peace rested on this foundation. Justice was swift, sure, and irreversible. No one was released from prison.

The White Monk, therefore, had escaped.

What puzzled me most was that Graves and the other soldiers had to know this. It explained the speculation on Graves's face as he watched the priest divest himself of his robes. Nothing, however, accounted for the risk the White Monk had taken by revealing himself that way—or why the soldiers had done nothing about it. More, why they now treated him with a certain respect that bordered on reverence, as if he were some sort of hero.

I was missing something—which wasn't unusual, especially lately—but it niggled at me, distracting enough that I could mostly ignore the growing ache in my hips and the burning pain of the once-perfect skin of my inner thighs. Perhaps it was fair turnabout, that my skin should suffer, too.

Night fell, heavy clouds obscuring the sky so no moonlight or starlight lit our way. We climbed the foothills in a single file, my steed in the center of the lineup with its nose in the tail of the horse Marin rode. The White Monk followed directly behind me, soldiers sandwiching us between. Below in the valley, the lights of Ordnung shone through the darkness, a beacon of civilization. Despite the warm cloak I'd been given, I shivered with the longing to be tucked inside my suite of rooms there.

So many things had been decided for me, like the cloak and what clothes I'd wear. I supposed they normally were, as my ladies and maids took care of me and packed for excursions. But they knew to include what I liked and would probably want. If I'd realized I'd be bundled along, I would have found a way to bring the doll pieces too. Instead they were in one of my trunks, bound for Windroven without me. Stupid oversight. How was I to find the missing head without the matching body?

I fretted over the error. This wasn't the mission I'd had in mind at all. Somehow it had become entirely what Erich wanted and nothing of mine. Still, I wouldn't fail.

Unless I fell out of the saddle first.

Hopefully we'd camp soon. Maybe after we climbed this trail.

We topped the hill, but my hopes were dashed when we re-formed into a loose knot, the soldiers making a circle around us. The disappointment brought all my discomforts crashing in. I was cold and tired and I thought my legs might fall off. I might have whimpered a little, because the White Monk, who never strayed far from me, on the pretense that he planned to defend me, rode close enough that our knees bumped.

"Problem, Princess?" he asked. Always with that mocking tone in his voice, though he kept his voice low, as we'd been instructed.

"I'm fine," I replied tightly, clenching my jaw so my teeth wouldn't chatter. *I would not complain. I would not complain.*

"You'll likely have to tell Graves that you need to rest. He's used to this kind of thing and to being with other soldiers who are, too. Not pampered royalty who never ride except for pleasure."

"I'm not complaining."

"No, you aren't." He sounded reflective, maybe even puzzled. "You're not being stubborn, are you?"

I laughed, trying to make it sound lighthearted and merry, which is hard to do quietly, much less when you're ready to scream from pain. "While being stubborn might be counted among my many character flaws, I believe no one has ever accused me of being stubborn for the right reasons."

"Have you ever ridden astride before?"

"I know how." His silence accused me of prevaricating. I blew out a breath. "But I rarely ever did. I always rode sidesaddle because"—I felt so frivolous—"it looked nicer."

Above the quiet snow crunching of the horse's hooves, I heard a scraping sound and realized the White Monk scratched his bristled chin. "This is the first day of at least three or maybe even four—and that's on the way in. If you ride beyond your ability to recover, then we'll have to wait for you to do so. Might add another day or three, with everyone waiting on you."

"I'll be fine," I repeated. "I can do this."

"I didn't expect grit from you," he finally said, after a long, thoughtful silence. It may have been the first thing he'd ever said to me that wasn't couched as a taunt. Then he kicked his horse into a trot, becoming one of the many shadows around me. I stewed, knowing he'd gone to tell Graves that the fragile princess couldn't handle the mission—on the first day.

After a few minutes, he returned. "We can't stop here—it's not secure yet—but there's a cabin ahead. Can you make it maybe another hour?"

"Of course. I didn't ask to stop."

He laughed a little, under his breath. "Glorianna save us all if you do become Queen."

I didn't dignify that with an answer. Besides, I suddenly wasn't sure I could make it another hour. I felt moisture making my pants stick to the skin along my legs, and the fear seized me that I might be losing the baby. The thought struck through my heart with dreadful worry, and I placed my right hand over my belly, trying to feel for that flutter of life. I wanted to ask Marin how I'd know, but it wasn't safe to stop here. If I was miscarrying, then it had already happened and stopping now would change nothing.

Instead I wrapped myself in silent prayers to Glorianna, beseeching Her to save my child, not to let the babe die. I should offer Her my lifelong service, but wasn't I Her servant already? And I'd promise to be a better person, but I wasn't sure how to do that. All I could think to tell Her was that if my baby died, I wasn't sure how I'd survive it. The thorny ball of unshed tears in my throat grew thick with mucus and misery, edging out all else, until I only chanted *please please please* over and over in the depths of my mind.

"Ami!" The White Monk stood at my stirrup, his hand closed around my booted ankle, shaking it. By his tone, I guessed it wasn't the first time he'd addressed me. I peered blearily at him. We'd stopped, obviously, and he and I were behind a small stable, his horse shuffling beside me.

"Where are we?"

"The cabin I told you about. Graves and his men will bunk inside. You need to stay in the stable, or you'll be recognized." He sounded apologetic. "Marin is inside making it comfortable. It's not much, but it's warm. Can you dismount?"

"Of course. I told you I'm fine."

I went to sling my leg over and the rough pants tore against my skin, both sticky and with searing pain. My hip grabbed and I sobbed a little.

"Here, here. Shh." The White Monk spoke soothingly. "Take it slowly. I'm going to put my hand on your hip to help, okay?"

I nodded, unable to speak.

"Trust me. Let me lower you. Move slowly and I'll lift you down."

I did as he coached, creaking my leg over the horse's rump and letting him put his hands on me to lower me to the ground. Only Hugh had ever touched me so intimately, but I was beyond caring in that moment.

"Brace yourself on my shoulders. Can you stand?"

I faced him, pressed up against his body, my arms in a choke hold around his neck. "Of course," I answered, though I couldn't feel my feet. I let go.

"Whoops!" His breath whuffed out as he caught me before I crumpled to the ground. In another moment he'd lifted me, carrying me against his chest in the strong cradle of his arms. "Fortunately you're only a bit of a thing."

He kicked open the stable door with his foot, startling Marin, who was spreading blankets on a pile of straw. "She's done in," he said by way of explanation, kneeling down to lower me to the straw.

"Oh, Marin!" I grabbed her hand and started kind a kind of hiccupping dry weeping that seemed to be all that was left to me. "I've lost the baby!"

"Now, now, Princess, calm yourself. Let's see to you here."

"I'm . . . I'm all wet down there. And it hurts. I hurt so bad, Marin."

The White Monk moved away with a cough.

"Don't you go anywhere," Marin ordered him in a sharp voice. "Bring a brazier of coals closer to the Princess and fetch me another lantern."

"I should see to the horses," he protested, but he obeyed, setting the warm brazier near my head and the lantern by my waist.

"The princess is more important."

"Graves said we're not to use her title—in case we're overheard."

"Amelia is more important, then. Here, love, let me see to these trousers. Monk, turn your back and hold her hand. The cloth is stuck to her skin and I'm going to have to use my knife to cut it away. This might hurt, sweetling."

The White Monk did as she said, wrapping his big hands around one of mine. He still had on his winter cloak, but he'd pushed aside the hood along with the monk's cowl, the white a snowy lining against the dark wool. His unsettling gaze focused on mine, and he smiled his lopsided smile.

"You're an idiot, you know."

"Graves is the idiot," Marin muttered. "Risking the P— Amelia this way. I'm practically stove up from that ride and I've been on horses all my life."

I hissed when she peeled the sticky cloth away from my skin, my flesh going with it by the feel.

"Blisters," she pronounced. "The babe is fine. You wore your poor skin raw."

Thank Glorianna. I sent Her a fervent prayer of gratitude.

"How bad is it?" the White Monk asked, gaze never leaving mine. He squeezed my hand.

"Bad enough. She's chafed from ankle to crotch. Worst part is where she sat on the saddle. Looks as if she rubbed blisters, popped 'em, and rubbed more."

I gasped when warm water touched my skin, fiercely stinging, then soothing. The White Monk let go with one hand to smooth my hair from my forehead, the look in his face strangely admiring, even affectionate.

"More than one man would be in tears by now. You're some woman, Ami."

"It's not me."

"What isn't?"

"I'd be crying like a baby if I could. I told you—I can't."

"Ah, that's right. You will."

"No. I think that part of me died with Hugh," I surprised myself by telling him. "I'm only half a person, scarred and lame and messed up like you, only you can't tell it by looking at me."

Too late I realized how that sounded—and Marin clucked reprovingly—but the White Monk only cocked his head and regarded me seriously. "You're not crippled," he said. "Not like me. Yes, you'll always carry some of that grief, but you're not scarred. Your wounds are fresh, still open and bleeding freely. The scars happen later and only if you don't heal right. You have far too much vivaciousness and vitality not to heal right. Too much life."

It might have been the first time anyone had given me a compliment that wasn't about my looks. I wasn't sure what to say. But he saved me from answering.

"You'll live to weep again someday, Ami. The grief will lessen its horrible grip and you'll know it has when the tears return. That's when you'll feel you're a human being again and not some distorted monster."

"How . . . how do you understand so much?"

He smiled ruefully, the scar yanking his lip to the side. "That's how I felt. How I still feel some days."

"But you said it would pass."

"For you, it will."

"Why not for you?" I insisted, strangely committed to wanting him happy all of a sudden.

"For some of us it's too late. The scar tissue is too thick. It's covered over and corrupted even our souls—we'll never be whole again." He let go my hand. "I'll go take care of the horses."

15

~~~~

Marin didn't say anything, only worked on spreading on a healing cream that felt like paradise, then wrapping my thighs with soft bandages.

"I didn't mean to be cruel to him," I told her, feeling I needed to explain. "I was really trying not to."

"Sometimes it's not about you," she said, more than a little terse. The she blew out a breath and patted the outside of my leg. "It's a difficult lesson to learn, but often how people behave is all about their own wounds and has nothing to do with what you do or don't say."

"Oh." I turned that over, but my mind was muddy with exhaustion. "I'm so glad the baby is okay. Maybe this mission was a bad idea."

"I can't speak my mind without doubting my king, but this venture could have benefited from better planning." She sniffed and wiped her nose, which was red from the cold. When she said "my king," I knew she meant Erich and not Uorsin.

"Well, we were already here—the way was so close." And I'd wanted to go. Had pushed for it. Glorianna willed it, but I wasn't going to say that to Marin, especially as she seemed less angry with me finally.

"I suppose that's true, but there's no never mind. You can't possibly ride again tomorrow. There won't be a mission now."

That woke me up. "I'll be fine in the morning," I insisted.

She gave me an incredulous look. "Shall I unwrap these bandages and show you how your poor legs look? I'd tear into you for being such a fool if I didn't know you did this partly because of what I said to you, to prove yourself to us. You're blistered as badly as someone burned in a fire. The disruption of the tissue goes deep. We'll be fighting infection as it is."

I'd never really been hurt before, so I didn't realize how bad it was. She'd said the White Monk's scars came from burns. "Will it leave scars?" I levered myself up to see, but my slim thighs were wrapped in the bandages, the white of the cotton nearly the same as my skin. Strangely, I kind of hoped there would be a mark, an unexpected longing for some sort of permanence.

"Not if I can help it," Marin declared, as if I'd questioned her abilities. She handed me some tea that had been steeping and covered me with several blankets. "Drink this and sleep. We'll make decisions tomorrow."

🌹 🌹 🌹

Come morning, I was not fine. I lay there, sweating with fever, while Marin and the White Monk argued over me.

"Graves says we cannot stay here!" the White Monk insisted, all semblance of the diffident priest gone. "The family already wonders who slept in the stable. Amelia will be discovered and that will go very badly for us all."

"Not so badly as the Prin—Amelia losing the child or her own life!" Marin snapped, nearly nose to nose with him. Her broad figure would have eclipsed his, had he not been so much taller, bending over to skewer her with that apple-green gaze.

"She's not safe either way. Better to go."

"Go where? We should take her down to Ordnung."

"And say what? 'Oops, look who we found in the forest. Sorry'?"

"Does it even matter?" Marin gestured to me under my pile of blankets. "Look at her! We have no choice."

He did look at me, a muscle in his scarred cheek jumping with anger. Then his gaze softened and he dropped down beside me, once again smoothing my hair from my forehead. "Here we are, debating this as if you're not even here. What do you say, brave girl?"

I didn't feel brave at the moment. In fact, facing my father's rage at my disobedience was the last thing I felt up to doing. Had Andi felt this way? All of a sudden, I understood how she did it. Not kill Hugh, but defy our father. It's not always a huge decision, like you wake up one day and know what you must do. Instead it kind of happens by accident, because you're just fumbling along, trying to do the best thing.

"I don't want to go back," I told him. "I'm so sorry I screwed this up, but I want to complete my mission. I need to do this."

He nodded. Was that approval in his eyes—and why did it matter to me what he thought? It mattered, though, that he'd asked for, and apparently would abide by, my decision.

"Well, you can't, missy," Marin said. "You can't sit on a horse and we have no other way to carry you through the snow.

"I can help her."

At first I thought the White Monk meant that he would carry me, as he'd done the night before, but that would be impossible, even as strong as he was.

"How?" Marin oozed cynicism.

"Leave us for a bit."

"Absolutely not." She folded her arms over her substantial bosom. "I cannot possibly leave Amelia alone with you, even if you are a priest of Glorianna."

Neither of us spoke the rest—that he'd likely lied about that. Glorianna's church didn't accept escaped prisoners.

"Do you worry I'll impregnate her with my bastard seed?" he tossed at her with impatience.

"That's not the point."

He ignored her and spoke only to me. "Do you trust me, Ami?"

I searched those odd eyes. They were the bright spot in his angular, corrugated face. As with the lighthouses on the craggy coast near Windroven, beacons cutting through the storms and fog. I shouldn't trust him, this criminal who'd lied about who he was— probably for this very reason, to insinuate himself into my company. It seemed clear that had been his agenda all along. What remained obscure was why.

And yet, he'd been bare-hearted honest with me in a way no one else ever had. He never fawned over me or praised my beauty. Sometimes I thought those flashes of hatred were because of how I looked or acted—but they were sincere, gut reactions.

I did trust him.

"If I agree, will we go on to Annfwn?"

The scar across his lip tugged and twitched up into his half smile. "Yes. Yes, we absolutely will."

"Then yes."

"I don't like this," Marin grumped.

"You don't have to, old woman," the White Monk said over his shoulder. "Go away. You can stand outside the door, in case she cries rape."

"Why can't I stay? I won't be in the way."

He just stood and regarded her. I had a sense of the implacable stare-down he gave her because the stalwart Marin shook her head in disgust and left, grabbing her cloak and muttering about how she should never have left home. The White Monk moved a heavy grain bucket in front of the door and returned to me.

"What are you going to do?" I ventured, my fingers curling into the blankets up under my chin. It did unsettle me, to be

alone with him. Really, the only man I'd ever been alone with before was Hugh.

The White Monk raised his eyebrows, punctuating the expression with a sardonic twist of his lips. "Magic."

I remembered how my blood had unsealed, then resealed the
tile. "Okay," I answered, which wasn't what he expected.

"I'm going to have to raise your skirts and undo the bandages." He regarded me steadily, waiting for me to object. But I'd
figured as much when I agreed.

"Help me sit up, then. I want to see."

He did, mounding a blanket behind me so I leaned comfortably against the stable wall. I kept the blankets over my lap and
pulled up the hem of the nightgown I'd changed into. The White
Monk averted his gaze while I bunched the cloth and some of the
blanket over my crotch, for what little modesty I could salvage.
Fortunately my flesh there only felt bruised and sore. The worst
damage was where my thighs had rubbed against the saddle, the
coarse cloth of my borrowed pants acting as sandpaper between,
from the rounds just above my knees up to the fullest swells before where my legs hollowed out again to meet the pelvis.

He knelt between my spread legs and my face grew hot. He
touched me with impersonal fingers, though, unwrapping the
bandages with gentle care, commenting that we'd want to reuse
them, to give me some protection. The innermost layer came
away wet with yellow fluid and spots of blood.

"Dear Glorianna," I whispered at the sight of it. My flesh
looked like a raw side of meat, the skin ragged at the edges. Even
I didn't understand how I'd kept riding.

"Pain is funny that way." The White Monk finished unwrapping the other leg. "After a while, you don't feel it. Especially
once you've decided you can't do anything to stop it."

I wanted to ask if he spoke from experience, but of course
he did.

"This might sting, quite a bit. You can't cry out. Do you want
something to bite down on?"

"Can I try to see if I can do without?"

He shook his head, laughing a little under his breath. "Of course you want to try. I thought I'd gotten this pretty, pampered princess and she turns out to be a badger in disguise."

Oddly this pleased me, though I knew it shouldn't. Badgers were well-known for their irascible tempers and fierce claws. He flexed his fingers, rubbed his hands together, and laid his hand over the weeping corroded expanse of my inner thigh.

It did hurt, and I clamped my teeth together over my cry of pain. His gaze flicked up to my face, assessed, then returned to focus on my wounds. Heat flowed from him to me, little lightning bolts of fire pricking my skin and making my leg jump. I couldn't hold it still, and with his free hand, he clamped down on my calf, pinning my splayed-open leg to the floor.

I understood he needed to do that, but something about the way he knelt between my spread thighs, holding me open for him, reminded me of those intimate dark nights with Hugh. My woman's parts heated, all wrong in this moment, but I found myself pulsing with longing to be touched again. Touched the way Hugh had touched me, what I'd never have again.

The White Monk's gaze returned to my face, a thread of something dark beneath, and I wondered if he sensed how I felt. The thrilling vibrations of the magic ran up and down my leg, coiling deep into my sex. I had to restrain a moan.

At least the pain was gone.

I stared at him, our eyes locked, and I shuddered under his hands. His lips parted and I thought he might kiss me.

"Other side," he said.

Bemused, I looked down at my leg. The skin looked pink and tender but was whole again.

"Praise Glorianna," I breathed.

"Glorianna has nothing to do with this. Healing is not Her provenance."

"All things under the sun are Glorianna's provenance," I reminded him.

He laughed that under-the-breath chuckle. "We are not under the sun, are we?"

Well, only because we were inside. "Who, then?" I challenged him, gasping a little as he arranged my still-injured thigh to his liking, pinning my knee down in advance this time and sending a surge of longing through my intimate folds, hidden away from sight.

He took a breath, seeming to need to calm himself. Then he looked at me, and that current of *something* ran stronger, pulsing through him. "Her dark sister, Moranu," he answered—her name sounding like a prayer—and put his hot hand on my wound.

I threw back my head, straining not to make a sound. The pain spiraled through the desire until I couldn't tell them apart. I came undone under his touch, my breath coming hard and fast. When he took his hand away, I managed to focus on his face. Sweat rolled in beads down his face, tracking sideways over one scar. He panted, too, as if he'd run a race. The skin on that leg gleamed pristine again, if terribly pink.

"How does it feel?" he asked, gaze riveted on my thighs.

"It doesn't hurt."

"Good. It will be tender still, but that's the best we can do." Cutting away the fouled part of the bandages, he rewrapped my thighs and I concentrated on not squirming. A hungry, dark part of me wanted to press my sex against his hand, as an animal would, wanting only in the moment, thinking nothing of the future or what was right or appropriate. I hoped he wasn't aware of it. Then a thought occurred to me.

"Is this why you had Marin leave?"

"I didn't want her to see exactly what I'd do, yes." He didn't look at me. "Surely you know how the folk of the Twelve Kingdoms feel about magic."

"I mean—you knew how I'd react."

His eyes found mine. They looked like molten glass. "You're never quite what I expect, Ami."

He set to work on the other bandage, the unspoken words uncomfortable between us.

"I didn't expect it, either," I confessed to him, unwilling to leave it unsaid. "But then I—no other man has been so close to me, down there, this way."

I sensed more than saw that he raised his eyebrows. "Don't tell me you're a virgin. Even Glorianna doesn't work that way."

I blushed, sorry I'd pursued the conversation, wishing I could close my legs. "No. No—I mean . . ." I sighed. "You understand how it works, I'm sure. Hugh didn't have to be so close to me, like that."

He stopped, his hand still half on the bandage, fingertips brushing the skin in the hollow of my inner thigh, stroking me a little, though I thought he didn't realize it. That hot, dark thing in him ran strong, and he smelled of sweet smoke. *This is how lust looks.* He swallowed visibly, his lean and bristled throat moving with it. "Did your husband never sit between your thighs like this, hold your knees open and place his mouth on you?"

"Glorianna no!"

My face flamed hot. My ladies had sometimes giggled over such things, but I thought they were mad stories. Jokes. But the White Monk wasn't joking.

Embarrassment found refuge in offended outrage, and I jerked away, standing and pulling my nightgown into place. "I grant that you didn't know Prince Hugh, but he was a fine, noble man who *loved* me. He would never have treated me like a . . ." I floundered, grasping for the right word. *Trollop. Whore. Slut.* All so ugly.

"Like a real woman," the White Monk finished, as if that were the only possible, natural ending to my sentence.

Where were my clothes? I hated that his words echoed some of my disloyal thoughts, that Hugh had treated me as a precious doll and not . . . *like a real woman.* "That is *not* what I meant!"

"Perhaps not, but only because you haven't experienced what

is real. What truly passes between a man and a woman when they're not spinning sugar-coated fantasies for each other."

"And what do you know of it?" I flung at him. "You're consecrated to Glorianna's service." Too late it came back to me that he was a fraud, a criminal masquerading as a priest. The words hung between us, a challenge.

He inclined his head. "Do you imagine that all of Glorianna's priests remain faithful only to her?"

"Do you suggest that any real priest of Glorianna's would dare fail her?"

Shaking his head, he pulled the pale cowl around his face, hiding the scars, which seemed even deeper now, crevasses of shadow, the green as dim as stagnant water. "Just when I start to find you interesting, I am reminded what a fool you are."

"I don't care if you find me interesting," I snapped.

"Nor should you." He seemed inexpressibly weary. "But I crave a boon from you, Princess. Will you promise me that you won't tell anyone what I did for you here?"

For a heated moment I thought he meant how I reacted to his touch. But no.

"The healing? Why didn't you make it contingent on keeping your secret?"

He kept his head bowed. "Because I would have done it for you, regardless."

"Why?"

"Why indeed?" The smoky scent froze brittle at the edges. "I'll send in Marin with your clothes."

Graves and his men did not comment on the delay. I wasn't sure what Marin and the White Monk, my team of minders and defenders, had said to them. We met the soldiers in the woods, well away from the cabin, the three of us from the stable having gone the long way around, sneaking out the back.

We rode along three abreast, Marin on my left and the White Monk to my right, the soldiers leading the way and bringing up the rear. I held a string of yarn in my right hand that trailed between me and the White Monk, tied around his wrist. He'd handed it to me after he helped me mount.

"Yank this if anything happens." He mounted his own horse, making sure there was some slack in the yarn. "But do me a favor and try not to wake me if you don't have to."

"Wake you?" I echoed, sounding like an idiot. "Do you plan to sleep?"

"No planning about it." His voice sounded rough, rocks grinding together. "Sleep will grab me by the throat and take me under at any moment. I can't promise I'll awake in time if we're— should anything happen."

If we're attacked, I thought he meant to say. "Did you not sleep last night?"

"Magic exacts a price. Never forget that." *Princess.* He didn't add the mocking title on the end, but I heard it there anyway. "And clasp the horse with your knees, hold yourself tight to it, so you don't bounce around so much."

"What about your steed—what if he stops? Or tries to wander?"

The White Monk patted his horse's neck with affection. "Least of my worries. We have an understanding."

True to his word, he soon fell into a deep sleep. We rode for hours, cutting through the woods, following what Graves called deer trails. Amazingly, my legs felt good, tingly but not painful. I wore several pairs of silk trousers under a top pair of wool, which made for a lovely cushion. The magic still zinged through me— flowing down to my ankles and up through my hips, a healing, energizing stream.

I practiced squeezing my thighs as I pressed against the saddle. This had the side effect of bringing my woman's mound hard against the leather, rubbing me in the same way Hugh's body had. Instead of abating, the desire continued to simmer in me. Likely an ongoing effect of the magic. I'd certainly never daydreamed about being intimate with a man before. At least not like this, in such a nonromantic way. The thoughts bubbling up in my mind weren't of sweet kisses and whispered love poems.

No.

Instead . . . instead this fantasy kept building in my head of the White Monk and his strong, heated grip on my skin. I imagined him tossing me to the stable floor, tearing my clothes away, and pinning me with his weight. Those penetrating eyes would flay me with their ferocity and he would put his mouth on me, devouring me as a wild animal might.

I thrust the images away, appalled at myself, and concentrated on a cycle of prayers to Glorianna. But the fantasies simply roared in again, and I found myself grinding against the saddle, imagining the White Monk ravishing me with hard hands and ravenous mouth.

They were my own thoughts, and no one—certainly never *he*—would know. But Glorianna saw me, and Hugh, looking down and protecting me from above—he would see how quickly I turned from his memory and indulged in prurient longings for the most inappropriate of men.

He would never have imagined it of me.

And that bothered me, too. Why hadn't Hugh seen me as a real woman? It made me angry, enough that I dreamed up the conversation where I'd demand that he explain himself to me. But he was dead and gone, which only made me angrier, which then faded into guilt.

We stopped at a hunter's shelter for the midday meal. The White Monk never stirred, despite the relative commotion among the men of dismounting and discussion of whose job it was this time to dispense rations. Marin heaved herself down and trudged into the woods to answer the call of nature.

Uncertain if I should wake him, I nevertheless thought the White Monk probably needed to eat. I wound the yarn around my hand, giving it a gentle tug.

He didn't move, head bowed, face hidden away. I pulled harder.

Still nothing.

Some defender he'd be. With increasing irritation, I gave the yarn a hard yank.

He exploded into action. In a blur of movement, he'd thrust back the hood and cowl, a long blade in his hand, scarred face set in harsh lines as he took in the situation in a moment—and settled a black scowl on me.

"Explain yourself," he demanded.

"I thought"—I clamped my teeth together to keep them from clacking together, he'd frightened me that much—"you might want to eat."

His gaze assessed me with something barely short of contempt. "Did I say to wake me if there was a picnic?"

"Fine." I tossed the yarn at him. "Stay here, then."

I swung off my horse and tramped through the snow to the little shelter, feeling as if I could eat a side of beef.

"You're moving very nicely, Ami," he called after me, once again his taunting self. My face heated as I remembered how intimately he'd seen me. He could never know of those horrible, tempting fantasies that plagued me so.

16

We stopped well after dark, sleeping in an abandoned cabin. Graves built a fire, though the White Monk argued against it, saying the Tala might detect our approach.

"There's not a soul lives out here," Graves scoffed. "We're in the depth of the Wild Lands. We'll be at Odfell's Pass come midday tomorrow."

We slept all in one room that night, Marin putting her bulk between me and the men, as if they might molest me otherwise. The White Monk lay between me and the door, like a faithful dog protecting me from intruders in the night. I avoided him and we hadn't exchanged further words. It was surely my own imagination that I felt something more than that silly string of yarn thrummed between us, the lowest strings of a harp, sounding an inaudible vibration long after the chord faded away.

I'd never experienced anything quite like it. A strange and mysterious thing, magic was. I wanted to ask the White Monk so many questions—why could he do magic? where did he learn?—but I had promised not to reveal his secret. In my heart, anyway, since he hadn't stuck around to hear the actual words.

And I really did want to be better about how I treated people.

He'd done me an enormous service. I owed him at least my silence.

The next day, he seemed replenished. We still didn't speak, but we had nothing to discuss. That is, not that could be spoken of with the others about. Mount, ride. The landscape grew steeper, with great boulders and very tall, straight trees. They formed infinite pillars into the distance, the evergreen canopy high above, and it hurt my eyes the way they seemed to fold into one another and multiply.

As the morning progressed, a feeling of uneasiness nibbled at me, then began taking greater bites of the peace of mind I tried to maintain. Shadowy shapes seemed to move in the corner of my eye, then vanished when I looked directly. The hair prickled on the nape of my neck, tingling as the White Monk's magic had.

Sometimes snow sifted down from the branches and the wood creaked when a hand of wind fisted through the limbs high against the wintery sky. It seemed other things moved there, too. Wrong things. My memory flashed onto those strange oily creatures that had invaded Ordnung when the Tala attacked and came after Andi. I tried to get a better look, but they were like the childhood monsters that disappeared when you lit a candle.

"What do you see?" the White Monk asked, riding close, speaking for my ears only.

He said it in a serious tone, not as if I were being a silly girl, but as if I might see something he didn't. Still, I hesitated to say anything. "I . . . I'm not sure."

"Don't think. Describe."

That helped. "Shadows? Like a cloud when it crosses the sun, that kind of chill when it touches my skin. Flashes of . . . something out of a nightmare. Like the kind you have when you're a kid and it's mainly that you don't quite understand what it is you're afraid of." I shivered.

He only nodded and pushed aside the hood and cowl, head bare to the cold while he studied the landscape. "I can't feel it," he said finally. "I thought I might."

I opened my mouth to ask what he meant, but his horse sprang ahead into a trot until the White Monk reached Graves. They halted our procession, Graves squinting up at the trees and then back at me. They fell into a discussion, heads close so none of the rest of us could hear. Finally Graves shook his head and we moved forward again. The path grew steeper and narrowed, so we rode two abreast, Marin falling behind us.

The White Monk rode at my side, looking grim, his blade drawn, resting on his thigh. "Do you have a dagger?" he asked in a conversational tone.

"Me? Glorianna, no. I'd likely prick myself as anyone else." He didn't say anything to my standard joke. I suppose it wasn't funny to a man like him. "Why, what's going on?"

"Graves is a bold soldier, but he was a poor choice for this. He wasn't part of the Siege at Windroven, nor the last attempt at Odfell's Pass. Neither he nor his men mixed with Ursula's Hawks on the journey from Avonlidgh, so he knows nothing of what they encountered. Fools." His frustration filled the air, grit from a whetting stone.

"But you did?"

He laughed, under his breath and without sound. "I do my research."

"And what did you find out?"

"To take the unseen seriously. And that the Tala aren't the same as humans."

Oh. "Is that who you think I'm seeing?"

He lifted one shoulder. "I wish I knew. If we could combine my knowledge with your senses, we might get somewhere." Absurdly, given how much tension he radiated, he grinned at me, that scar hitching the lip on one side, eyes bright. He looked . . . happy, of all things. "Guess we'll have to figure it out as we go, huh?"

I didn't know how to reply to that. Such an odd man, that this was fun for him.

"But you expect them to attack—that's what you told Graves."

"I think they're aware we're here, and we have the advantage because you can sense them. We should use that advantage."

"Maybe we should go back."

"Is that what you want to do?"

No. Even though fear nibbled at the edges of my mind, I didn't want to give up, just because I saw some shadows. They hadn't made any overt threats. Besides, Andi had invited me.

She didn't invite the rest of them, though. Only me.

"Why can I see them?"

He sighed out a long breath of a person practicing patience. "It's in your blood, Ami. Your sister is the witch queen of the Tala—did you think you had nothing of that in you?"

I had thought that. Until Lady Zevondeth showed me how to work the spell by using my blood. Maybe that's why she wanted to keep our blood in her little vials. Like keeping keys that fit certain locks. "I can't work magic," I reasoned, thinking it through, "but my mother's blood gives me certain access, a kind of sensitivity."

"Yes. That's right."

"So why did you think you would?"

"What do you mean?" He seemed to be surveying the woods, but I sensed the evasion, a shifting silver thread.

"You said you hoped you'd feel it." The realization dawned on me. "Are you—is that why you can do what you do?"

I'd tried to be oblique, but he flicked me an irritated, burning glance, then returned his attention to the woods and shadows. "If I were, if I could live in paradise, why would I be living this life of exile in the Twelve Kingdoms?"

"I don't understand why everyone thinks Annfwn is so wonderful. If it's really paradise, why haven't I heard more about it?"

"Consider your upbringing."

"How so?"

"You were raised in a bubble. Your father, far more than most parents, controlled what you knew of the world—as who he is, he had total control of your world, and made sure you only knew what he wanted you to, until you married and left home. After that . . ."

"What?"

"You went from one bubble to another."

"You talk about me as if I'm some hothouse rose." I meant to score a point, but he considered that thoughtfully.

"An apt analogy. Beautiful. Precious. Protected. Meant only to be touched and seen by a privileged few."

Like Hugh had treated me, too. And worthless outside of that. He didn't say it, but I smelled the weedy accusation beneath. It rankled, but I couldn't argue with it. We fell silent. Snow began to fall, as if forming from the fog between the trees, fat flakes that landed on my horse's hide and lay quivering before melting into nothing.

With a whoosh, a clump of snow landed off to the side and I started, my nerves twanging. The conversation, though uncomfortable, had been at least distracting.

"So what didn't my father want me to know?"

The White Monk glanced my way, a quick assessment, and went along. "Only you can be the judge of that, but consider who he is. He placed his seat—the High Throne that was the trophy of his Great War—at the back door to Annfwn, as close as he could get to it without violating his pledge to your mother. Between his forces and the landscape, no one goes in or out of Annfwn without his knowledge. He cut it off from the rest of the kingdoms. If he couldn't have it, no one would."

It made a weird sense. I remembered minstrels thrown out of court for singing the "wrong" songs. I was framing my next question when something that wasn't the wind soughed through the trees, strumming my nerves so they sang in response.

The soldiers ahead halted. We were against a steep wall on one side, a drop-off on the other, and the curve of the path kept us from seeing where Graves led the group.

Odd grunting noises floated down, disturbing in their formlessness.

The White Monk slid off his horse, holding a silencing finger to his lips, and gestured to Marin to go back down the trail. The soldier next to her shook his head—but obeyed the rule of silence—and pointed emphatically to show his desire to go forward. His fellows agreed, showing their impatience to help in the restless stamping of their horses' hooves, an urgent cadence pressing them forward.

But we blocked their way.

The White Monk held up his hands in a gesture for me to dismount. So pressed together were we on the narrow trail that it forced our bodies into contact. Despite my tense nerves—or maybe because of them—that frenzied desire for him, complete with dark fantasies, leapt through me. I stepped away as fast as possible, but took the hand he held out, following him past the horses, smashing myself against the snowy stones to ease past the soldiers' mounts.

We reached the clear space just past them and the White Monk pressed his blade into my hand. "Use it if you have to," he said. Moving fast, he returned to our horses and, as near as I could see, moved his ahead of mine, nodding for Marin to slide hers behind his, pressed tight against the cliff wall. She'd been too stout to slide past as we had.

Freed, the soldiers trotted past in single file. Too fast, and perilously close to the cliff's edge, for one horse's hoof slid off the uneven rocks, unbalancing them both. For a heart-stopping moment, they hung there, teetering on the brink. Then, with twin shrieks of terror, they fell together, horse and soldier, plummeting down to the far canyon below.

I cried out with them, taking an involuntary step forward, as if I could somehow catch them. The White Monk clamped me against him, hand over my mouth. I sobbed, tearlessly, of course. He pressed his cheek against mine. Not in remonstration, I realized, but in mute sympathy. Dampness made them slide together and I looked at him to see silent tears running down his face.

Marin had her hands clamped over her eyes, as if she, too, wished she could unsee what had just occurred.

The White Monk released me and urged us down the trail to a place where we would be less likely to be knocked off into the crevasse.

We waited. I opened my mouth once to ask what the plan was, but the White Monk made that gesture of silence again. I didn't see why. By his own estimation, the Tala already knew we were here. We'd been talking until the attack, so it made no sense for us not to talk at all now.

Still, I followed along. *Do you trust me?* he'd asked, and for no good reason, I did.

After a while, the White Monk stood and, taking his blade from me and motioning for us to stay put, crept up the trail again. I nearly protested. We hadn't heard any sounds, not even those odd, soft grunts, for quite some time. He returned fairly quickly.

"They're all gone," he told us without preamble, crouching in front of me, "even the horses. You need to make a decision."

"What does 'gone' mean? Dead? Did they all go over the edge of the cliff, too?"

He shook his head. "Vanished. The snow is scuffed, but there's no sign of the men or the horses. No bodies. Just gone."

I assimilated that, feeling the weight of things. "You think we should go back."

"Is that what you want to do?" His unnatural eyes were intent but deliberately neutral. I couldn't read what he thought was the right decision. But I smelled his anxiety, his driving desire to go forward, as hot as midsummer sunshine. "This is your mission. You're the one who was invited."

"Then why did you spirit me away from the fight? Maybe the Tala wouldn't have . . . done what they did, if they'd seen me with the soldiers."

He blew out a breath and studied his gloved hands, knotted between his knees. "I don't think it works that way."

"How does it work?"

"I think we're dealing with the equivalent of . . . guard dogs, if you will. They respond to certain cues. Smarter than dogs, but not exactly rational beings you can reason with, either."

"How do you know so much?"

He gave me a wry look through his unkempt brows. "Let's say I've studied a lot."

"So the princess will be allowed to pass, but no one else—is that how it works?" Marin nodded. "Then, if you go on, I'll head down the trail to the last cabin and wait for you there."

"Can you do that?" I kind of gaped at her. I didn't think I could walk that far, and going by myself would be daunting.

"I've done that much and more, missy," she answered, not un-kindly. "I'd rather do that than be scooped off the mountainside by yon magical guard dogs."

"We could all go back." The White Monk regarded me with that neutral expression. "There's no shame in a retreat when fac-ing unfavorable odds."

I didn't like that he'd laid the decision so firmly in my hands. He was doing it on purpose, too. Making me take responsibility. Testing my resolve? Taking me seriously.

"I want to go on. If you think my invitation will protect me— after all, I have the babe to think of—then I'll continue." I didn't like the idea of going alone, but I couldn't place him in jeopardy, either. That's how a good queen would decide, wasn't it? "You and Marin can go to the cabin and wait for me there."

He laughed, that soundless, under-the-breath one. "You're not going alone. I'll be with you every step of the way."

"But what if they come after you?"

"I can take care of myself." And his eyes glittered again, with that odd joy I'd glimpsed before. He *wanted* to come with me. More than he cared for his continued safety. This was why he'd wormed his way into being my priest confessor and bodyguard. He wanted to see Annfwn.

He gave his pack to Marin. Now I understood why he kept it tied to his back instead of his horse, as the rest of us had. A rush of relief poured through me that I hadn't had the doll with me after all. It would be vanished with my horse, who was maybe broken at the bottom of a ravine. I hated to think of that fate for her. She'd been a good steed and the guilt ate at me that I might have brought her to her death.

We said good-bye to Marin, watching her steady, surefooted march down the trail. Then we headed up. This time I led the way, the White Monk at my back, by unspoken agreement. If I was the key to passage, then I should be in front.

When we reached the place where the soldier and horse had gone over, I couldn't help but look, more than a little afraid of what I'd see, but unable to stop the horrid desire to find out. The White Monk put his hand on my arm. "Don't look," he said in my ear.

"Did . . . did they all go over?" I had to know.

"No. Only the pair we saw, I think. I have no idea where the others are."

Of course, he had looked. Even though he'd shed the tears I'd wanted to at their sudden, wrenching demise, he'd had the stomach to see. Nevertheless, I was glad he'd stopped me, even if it meant I lacked his courage.

We continued around the bend to where Graves and the other men had been attacked. The trail widened into a clearing here, and a vast circle of disrupted snow bore silent witness to the strange battle that had occurred. Mud scuffed up from beneath stained the snow in patches, but no blood.

Still, something about the clearing felt odd. I stared around it, trying to discern why my nerves hummed and my grief, always in the background like a faithful hunting dog, descended, leaden and impenetrable in the corners of my vision.

"What is it?"

"I don't know," I answered. "Something."

He waited patiently. I wandered through the clearing. No strange shadows prowled the perimeter, validating the White Monk's theory that my presence gave us passage. Not sure what I was looking for, I spotted a clear patch that held, of all things, a spot of green. Bright, acid green, like the White Monk's eyes when he was most amused—or most hateful.

Kicked-up snow mounded around it, but now melted, sliding off and making a damp, muddy ring. A patch of grass, incongruous in the frozen landscape, with a flower inside. A forget-me-not, but larger than it should be, the vivid summer-sky blue of Hugh's eyes.

My heart clutched, the painful ball in my throat spinning. The White Monk crouched beside me. "What do you see?"

"I think—" My voice croaked and broke. I swallowed down the cursed ball of thorns. "I think this is where Hugh died."

"I don't see anything—just snow."

"It's like a little hothouse. Living grass and a forget-me-not, but the biggest, most beautiful one I've ever seen. It's not possible that it's here."

His breath sighed out. "Then this is a memorial. An eternal blossom. Created and preserved by magic."

I nodded, unable to say more.

"Only one person that I know of could do such a thing—and would want to."

Andi. I tried to conjure up that image I'd nursed, of her fierce and corrupted joy as she plunged the knife into Hugh's breast. Instead I saw her here, planting this blossom and making a little dome of eternal summer around it. I pulled off my glove and reached in, my hand passing into the moist warmth, the petals velvety and vibrantly alive.

I said a prayer, wordless, a formless burst of love, sorrow, gratitude, and remorse.

When I drew my hand away, the cold stung my skin, a reminder of what was real.

"May I try?"

I wasn't sure why he asked my permission, but I nodded. The White Monk yanked off his glove and reached out as I had, but his fingers stopped in midair, as if encountering glass. He ran his hand over it, forming an invisible dome in the air.

"As the border will be," I breathed out the revelation.

He seemed disappointed, a tinge of bitterness in the air. Then he took my hand and searched my face. "Will you try something with me?" The simplicity of the question belied the deep, emotional earnestness in his gaze. This mattered greatly to him.

"Yes."

His scarred lip twitched into a smile and he opened his mouth to say something, then shook his head and tugged off my glove, gently, finger by finger. With a rush, the fantasy of him ripping off my clothes hit me again, and I had to bite my lip against it—and to stave off the black guilt that followed. Here I knelt at the spot where Hugh had given up his life only months before, possessed by this insane lust for another man. If the White Monk knew, he gave no clue, but he did cradle my naked hand in his, our skin touching in some deep communication. With our fingers laced together, he lowered our hands toward the blossom.

Seamlessly our hands slid inside, penetrating the perfect slice of summer together.

"I see it!" He turned his head and grinned at me, a smile so broad even the scar didn't distort it, the greatest expression of pure happiness I'd ever seen on him. It made the thorns inside me prick with envy.

Nothing could ever make me that happy again.

17

As if he sensed my shift in mood, his smile dimmed. Suddenly I was sorry to have ruined the moment for him. I created a smile, the party one that usually charmed everyone, but it was too late. Besides, he always seemed to see through me. He pulled our hands out and handed me my glove.

"Do you want some time here?"

Ever considerate of me and my hair shirt of grief.

"No." I stood, pulling on my glove and adjusting my cloak. I couldn't explain my irrational anger at Hugh. At Andi for first killing him and then making this memorial, as if that changed anything at all. But I could walk away for now. "Let's move on. Surely the border isn't far from here."

It wasn't. We'd barely gone the distance it would take to cross Ordnung's great courtyard before the snow, which had been growing thin, melted completely into mud. Ahead, the same tall evergreen trees marched on in their great columns, but beneath, on the forest floor, grass and riotous wildflowers grew in a rampant tapestry of color.

Paradise.

With a breath of wonder, I reached down and plucked a scarlet blossom. It was exotic and fragrant, unlike anything I'd ever seen.

"Princess?"

I looked back, and the White Monk stood an arm's length away, as if stopped by a wall, his gaze unfocused into the distance.

"Ami!" he called, with greater urgency.

"Right here," I said, but he didn't seem to hear me. I went to him and the near panic in his face changed to relief. He seemed about to embrace me in a rush of emotion but stopped himself. "Couldn't you see me?"

"No. It was as if you disappeared. Like you vanished into that blizzard." He gestured at the summer landscape beyond.

"You see a blizzard there?"

"You don't?"

"No." I felt a bit of the happiness that I'd longed for only a few minutes before seep into my limbs, like a draught of good wine, warming and relaxing, diffusing the anger. "I see paradise."

🌹 🌹 🌹

We practiced with the barrier for a bit. The White Monk said he didn't wish to leave any important bits of himself behind. Turned out it was much more difficult to move two bodies in tandem than it had been our interlaced hands. When our bodies grew too far apart, say, where our forearms diverged due to the angle of our elbows, he'd begin to feel a burning, repellent sensation.

He tried tossing a rock through, but it ricocheted. The same happened when I tried. But I could carry that rock over. Wryly, he remarked that it would be best if I could carry him over, but I could never lift his weight. With rapt wonder, we watched as a flock of birds flew through.

"If only we hadn't lost the horses," he sighed. "I bet that would have worked."

"You don't have to go through, do you? I could go in and, um, look around a little." Really, according to my assignment, we could leave. We knew I could cross the border. I sincerely doubted that I could bring Erich's—or Uorsin's—armies across, but that was a problem for another day. Something to think about later.

The White Monk stood, hands fisted on his lean hips, staring down at the snow as if it might give him the answers he sought. He looked up at me when I suggested he stay behind, the green dimmed, the bitter grit of frustration and disappointment in the air. He wanted this. There could be no doubt of that.

"What if you carry me?" I blurted out.

"We could try that."

We both knew that the alternative would be for us to somehow plaster ourselves together. He came close to me and paused, oddly diffident in that moment, though he'd carried me before. Seeming unsure how to touch me, he stroked a hand down my back, barely touching.

"Ready?"

I stood on tiptoe and wound my arms around his neck, laying my cheek against his, rough with his scruffy beard and the ridged scars. He felt good. Hard and warm. I pushed the fantasies aside. "Like you did before. It's fine."

He bent his knees, scooping me up with easy strength. I pressed my face into his neck, as if the skin-to-skin contact would help, but shamelessly indulging myself, breathing in his scent, campfire smoke and man. He smelled nothing like Hugh had, and that helped immeasurably. I'd missed being touched. So, so much. This small thing meant nothing. Here and gone.

Taking a deep breath, he curled me tighter against his chest and stepped up to the barrier. Moving slowly, head bent tight over mine, he eased through. Under my ear, his heart pounded, echoing through his body, a drumbeat of fear—and wild excitement.

With a sensation of a bubble popping, we emerged into full summer. The White Monk looked around in unbelieving amazement, then down at me, the radiance of his joy as palpable as the welcoming sunshine. He let me down, then tossed his head back, whooping with a full-throated cry of celebration, much like a wolf baying at the full moon.

A laugh escaped me, released from its barbed prison by his sheer exuberance. He snapped his gaze down to me.

Then seized my face in his big hands and kissed me.

Shock held me still for a blink, and then all that yearning, that bottled-up longing, surged up to meet him. I opened my mouth, giving in to the hard, seductive strength of his. Just as in my lurid fantasies, he wasn't gentle or sweet or reverent. He didn't treat me like some fragile doll to be protected. He devoured me, drinking me in, and my entire body melted into a hot stream for him to consume.

He broke away from me and I staggered, momentarily unanchored and bewildered.

Moving away a few steps, eyes wild and panicked, he bent over, resting hands on knees and panting. I took a step toward him and he held up one hand, forbidding me to come closer.

Too hot—from the sun, nothing more—I busied myself with removing my winter outer garments, neatly folding the heavy cloak, my gloves and scarf. Already chagrined and more than a little humiliated by my response, I decided he'd already seen plenty of me, and it hardly mattered now, so I stripped off a few layers of pants and shirts, so I wore only a few light silk ones. They still covered me modestly enough to please Lady Zevondeth, but after wearing so many layers, I felt nearly naked.

When I finished, I found the White Monk regarding me with a deliberately opaque expression, one I recognized from early in our acquaintance.

"Forgive me my trespass, Princess." He bowed, formal and deep. "I was overcome by the moment and forgot who you are. Inexcusable of me, nevertheless."

Not exactly what a girl wants to hear from the man who just kissed her with more passion than she knew existed in the world. Tempted to fling myself against him and pound my fists against his chest, I nearly yelled that I wanted him to be overcome by me. By *me* and not the stupid moment.

But that was the old Ami. I ran a hand over my messily braided, likely knotted, and days-oily hair. I wore this odd assortment of patchwork garments and likely smelled to Glorianna's bower and beyond. Of course he wasn't overcome by me. Even at my best, the beauty that had always been my glory seemed to disgust and repel him.

He'd "forgotten" who I was. I supposed that was the only way he'd forget whatever it was that made him hate me so.

"We'll forget it ever happened." I tried to make it a crisp order from the offended but forgiving royal personage, but my voice sounded dull. What was wrong with me?

He lost the impassive expression and held out a hand toward me. "Ami—"

"Ami."

The other voice overlapped his, an eerie almost echo. Andi.

I turned and there she stood, smiling tentatively at me. My first impulse—born of long habit—sent me running toward her, for one of our gleeful, squealing hugs. But that was before, and I managed to yank myself up short before she, too, could reject me.

No, I rejected *her*! She had murdered Hugh. I hated her. I didn't care about her guilt in planting that flower.

And she looked so amazingly beautiful. Had she always been this way? She looked . . . taller somehow. Her hair, which had always seemed a muddy brown mix somewhere between my red-gold and Ursula's deep auburn, now seemed a deeper, richer color, the crimson-black of banked coals. Her gray eyes, not cloudy anymore, were the color of thunderheads, shimmering full of ominous power, large in her face and fringed with thick, dark lashes.

Worse, that *thing*, that strange prickle she'd always had, loomed large in the air, the static charge of lightning about to strike. And when she tipped her head to the side to study me, an oddly animal movement, a kind of unearthly light shimmered over the gray in her eyes.

"I'm glad you came," she ventured, her smile fading.

"I'm not here because you said to come," I said with defiance.

"All right." She considered me, gaze flicking to the White Monk, who was, at long last, living up to his reputation of silence. "Why are you here?"

To begin the process of invading your country and destroying you. To wrest from you the one legacy my mother left to me. To defeat Moranu and win Annfwn for Glorianna. To see if paradise is real.

All of these answers stuck in my throat with the rest of my grief, rage, and uncertainty—and an odd longing. It was mixed up somehow with the plaguing desire for the White Monk and the hurt that he didn't want me, that no one loved me, that Hugh hadn't even seen me for myself and the jealousy that Andi had a real home, where I . . . I didn't somehow.

She nodded, as if I had said something. "Are you ready to hear my apology, perhaps?"

"No!" I flung it at her. "There is no apologizing for what you did. You destroyed Hugh and thus may as well have plunged the knife in my breast yourself. You killed me, too."

She continued nodding, her gorgeous witchy eyes filling with tears that then poured down her face with enviable ease. "I understand."

"Why did you do it? *How* could you do it?" Without realizing, I'd been moving closer to her, drawn by our old connection. I missed her as much as I hated her as much as I loved her as much as I wanted to destroy her and everything she cared about.

She twisted her hands together, weeping still. "It was a horrible, terrible accident. If I had the power, I would change it. As it is, I go back over and over that moment, wishing that I could make it so it never happened. But I can't."

"You're not so powerful, then," I sneered at her.

She shook her head, long, thick hair roping over her shoulders, gleaming and vibrant. "No one has the power over death. No one should, much as we might long for it."

"Easy for you to say."

"No." Her gaze cleared and sharpened, though the tears still fell. "Never think it's easy."

"You have everything and I have nothing." My voice cracked, pain oozing through my heart. A comforting hand touched the small of my back, rested there. I looked up and the White Monk stood right behind me.

"You're not real," he said to Andi, surprising me.

She tilted her head, that movement like a predator seeing potential prey, and wiped her face clear of tears, assessing him with keen interest.

"Who are you?"

"Queen Andromeda." He bowed. "I am the White Monk."

"That's a title, not a name," she observed.

"That's what I keep saying," I muttered. "What do you mean she's not real?"

"Try touching her."

I reached out to touch her sleeve, a gorgeous, filmy aqua that reminded me of the summer ocean at Windroven. My hand passed through it as easily as it had the magical barriers.

She smiled, rueful. "It's true, I'm not physically here. I'm sort of—making an image of myself from far away. When I sensed you cross the barrier, it would have taken me too long to reach you physically. I wanted to be here to greet you."

"You've been watching me?"

"Only since you crossed the border."

"The first time."

She smoothed her expression and gave me a slight nod, studiously not looking at the White Monk. She'd seen, then. She'd seen him kiss me and how I'd responded. My cheeks burned, the skin tight and hot. So much for my impassioned righteousness over losing Hugh.

"I don't judge, Ami," she said with gentle forgiveness that only fueled my embarrassed anger. "It's good for people to move on, to live life. We have only a short time—"

"Spare me your philosophy, murderer," I snarled.

She flinched. Some buried part of me was sorry. Still, rage felt better than being naïve and pitiful.

"I want you to know that I'll never send my child to you. Never! More, I *will* find a way to destroy you. You won't benefit from your ill deeds. Glorianna seeks justice. Annfwn belongs to her, and I am her avatar!" I finished on a triumphant shout, but Andi seemed only confused.

"And this is what you journeyed here for? To tell me these things?"

It seemed stupid, put that way.

Well, and I wanted to see if I could cross into Annfwn. I didn't expect to run into you. Couldn't say that.

"Annfwn will always be here for you, Ami. For you and your blood. This is your legacy, too. You and your daughter."

Her and the "daughter" thing. I couldn't answer, grinding my teeth over the desire to tell her to keep her trumped-up prophecies, generosity, and our mother's legacy. That I didn't want it. *Oh, but I did . . .*

"But you"—she studied the White Monk again—"you should not have been able to cross."

He slid the hand up my back to rest on my shoulder. "Princess Amelia's ability brought me over with her."

"No." Andi sounded very sure of herself, imperious. "It doesn't work that way."

"I beg your pardon, Your Highness, but that's what happened." The White Monk spoke the respectful words, as he did with me, but he didn't mean them any more than he did with me. Was he such an outlaw that he kneeled to no one?

She narrowed her eyes, looking through him. "You're Tala part-blood. Not enough to cross on your own, but enough that Ami's blood could add to yours, to bring you over."

"My father—he was Tala and always seeking a way to return. He'd been separated from his warrior brethren during the Great

War, making his way west. Then he met my mother. He stayed
with her, but she said he never forgot Annfwn."

"Where was this?"

"In Nebeltfens—about as far from Annfwn as you can get and
still be in the Twelve."

"Did he find his way back?"

Grief flowed through the air, redolent of stagnant anger. "No.
The village priest accused him of being a demon, and they . . .
burned him alive."

The horror of it choked me. I reached out to touch his arm,
but he yanked it away, wanting none of my comfort. Andi, though,
his gaze was glued to her, telling *her* what he wouldn't tell me in
all those times we spoke.

"How old were you?" Andi sounded genuinely sorrowful
for him.

"Thirteen. I tried to save him, but . . ."

"You could not."

"No. No one could, least of all a skinny half-breed boy terri-
fied they'd turn on him next." Bitterness now. Self-hatred. The
ground grew boggy with the swampy scent of it.

"So you came instead. Since he never could."

"Yes. I've tried before, but I could never cross on my own."

That startled me. He'd acted as if he'd never seen the border
before. He'd played me. Probably all of it, taunting and teasing
me, the healing and the touching, even that kiss—all to get me to
do what he really wanted. My nails dug into my palms painfully.

Andi seemed to fall into deep thought. "I shall have to discuss
the implications of this with Rayfe."

"Must be nice to have a husband who's alive to talk to." The
snipe escaped me, and I regretted it. I seemed to be trapped in
the role of petulant baby sister, sounding like she'd taken my toy
instead of the center of my world. Instead I wanted to be Ursula,
swinging my sword to kill them both.

Andi sighed. "You say you're not ready to hear this, Ami, but

I'm going to say it. I'll say it as many times as it needs to be said."
She held out her hands, palms up. "I made so many choices to try
to save others during that horrible time, and I ended up destroying the life of a good man who wanted only to protect me and ir-
reversibly damaging one of the people I love most in the world,
depriving my niece of a father. I cannot make it up to you. All I
can offer is my remorse. I will regret what happened until the end
of my days and likely beyond. I rue it, now and forever. I offer you
my apology, Amelia, from the bottom of my heart and soul and
mind."

Something glittered in the air around us, as if something magical had occurred. But I felt no different. This changed nothing.
They were words. Nothing more.

"I don't forgive you."

"I don't ask for it. I don't seek pardon for my actions. They are
done and I cannot take them back."

"You could return to Ordnung and face justice for your actions. That would show true remorse for your sins. And your betrayal of your family and your kingdom."

"I can't." She said it in the tone of someone who'd weighed
that very thing and made a hard decision. "That might be the easier path for me, but I have people depending on me. I can't speak
of it to you, but I must stay in Annfwn. This is all I can offer, pal-
try as it is."

"It's not enough."

"No. Nothing ever will be."

"And yet you seek to take more from me."

Andi was already shaking her head before I finished. "Not
take. Give. You could be happy here. Ami—I wish you could see
it. Annfwn is like . . . no other place."

I gestured to the summery forest. "I see it. Okay, it's warm
when it shouldn't be, but it will be the same at Ordnung or Windroven come summer. So far I'm unimpressed by this so-called
paradise."

She smiled, laughing at my ignorance. "This is but the gateway. A sort of . . . buffer zone. Come with me, if only for a day. There is so much more. People dream their entire lives of having what Annfwn offers. It could be yours, too. And your daughter's."

"I'm not interested."

The White Monk brushed his hand over my back again, and I glanced at him. His face showed that longing he'd had before, that desperate hope. He wanted to see it. More than he wanted anything else in the world. It ran bright and strong in him. *Well, welcome to longing for what you can't have.* He hadn't cared for my feelings. I didn't care for his.

"We have people waiting for us. People depend on me, too. We must return."

Andi inclined her head but seemed saddened. Then she held out a hand to the White Monk. "And you? I regret that you could not cross without Ami, but the fact that you could cross at all means you belong here. You are welcome to stay. Perhaps find your father's family, as I found my mother's."

18

I stepped away from him. Away from the surging, fierce, and triumphant joy that saturated the ground, firming and steadying it. All this time he'd dogged me just to get this. And now he'd walk away without a backward glance, leaving me as they all did. Who cared about stupid, pretty little Ami?

Then the joy dimmed. He looked at me, but I refused to meet his gaze.

"Thank you, Queen Andromeda. What you offer is all I ever wanted. But I must go with the Princess. I could not abandon her."

"Sure you could," I said in a bright tone. *After all, everyone else does.* "I don't need you."

"Regardless, I will stay with you."

I finally spun on him. "I can walk down a hill by myself."

"Are you sure?" He mocked me. "You weren't so great at riding a horse."

A funny sound—Andi snorting with laughter—interrupted my furious rebuttal. For the first time, I recognized the old Andi in that odd, unattractive laugh of hers. Our nurse had despaired of ever getting her over it and simply urged her never to laugh at court functions. She pointed a finger at me even as she covered her nose and mouth with the other hand.

"What?" I demanded, further enraged that she was laughing at me, yet again.

"You've met your match, Miss Ami." She tried to stop laughing and snorted again. "I never thought I'd see the day."

"Hugh was my perfect match! My one true love. He"—I flung a hand at the White Monk—"is a low-life former convict, without royal blood, who means nothing to me."

He froze, face going impassive, eyes congealing in that apple-green hatred. "Just so," he agreed in a cold tone. The ground had frozen and he bowed formally to me. "I shall await you on the other side of the border, Your Highness. I presume I can exit on my own, Queen Andromeda?"

Andi nodded. "Yes. Easier for me to do that way. If you ever wish to return, do this. Test the border and wait. I'll remember you and send someone to bring you over. We'll figure out a way to manage this. Also—if you meet other part-bloods or stranded warriors who cannot cross, tell them we're working on bringing them home, too. My solemn promise as Queen of Annfwn."

Others? So there were other Tala out in the Twelve Kingdoms. Did Kir know?

The White Monk took a few steps, then knelt at her feet, bowing his head. "Thank you, my queen." He spoke with a heartfelt reverence that burned in my gut. How I hated them both.

"This is a traitorous conversation," I declared.

They both looked at me as if they'd forgotten I was there.

"Do you believe High King Uorsin wishes there to be Tala hiding among the people of the Twelve Kingdoms?" Andi asked me in a reasonable tone.

"Of course not. He's issued an edict that they be killed on sight." I bit down on my words, realizing suddenly that the law applied to the White Monk, too. He was twice dead—for escaping prison and for his dirtied blood. He rose from his ridiculous obeisance, bowed to Andi, and strode back for our crossing place in rigid, angry strides. I refused to watch him go.

"And you?" Andi turned on me. "Ursula?"

It took me a moment to understand what she meant. "We are not Tala."

"You're as much as the White Monk is—more so, actually. Same as I am."

"I am *not* like you. You're the one who bears the mark. Ursula and I escaped the taint."

She laced her fingers together. "It doesn't work that way. The mark only means that I have our mother's magic. Please listen to this, Ami—you will breed true, because our mother's blood was so strong, and for other reasons I can't tell you. Your daughter also bears the mark."

My hand covered my belly. "I carry a son. I have no daughter."

She tilted her head in that uncanny way again, looking into me somehow. "Your daughter bears the mark. She grows strong, already full of magic."

"Nonsense."

"Have you noticed anything unusual?"

"Like barfing my brains out every morning or if someone boils fish?"

She wrinkled her nose. "I'm sorry. That must be awful."

"Save your sympathy." I felt brittle. I'd wanted her with me, to say exactly that, and now here she was. Who knew it would be so hard to keep hating her?

Taking one of the long skeins of her glossy hair, she thoughtfully wound it around her fingers. "I mean more—do you sense things you never did before? Maybe heightened perceptions in some way?"

"I saw . . . things. In the woods. On the way here."

"Staymachs," she answered in an absent tone. "They won't hurt you."

"They hurt the soldiers escorting me. Killed them and the horses."

Her dark brows winged up. "Oh! Oh, no—not unless the men resisted too fiercely. And never the horses. They were all likely relocated."

"What?" How was that possible without us seeing?

"Taken somewhere else."

"I know what 'relocated' means."

"Sorry—it's a new program. We've been retraining the stay-machs to lead interlopers away instead of killing them outright, whenever possible. But they always would have let the horses free. The Tala love horses." She smiled, a secret, loving curve of her mouth, and I recalled what Ursula had said, about Rayfe rescuing Andi's mare. How had he done that?

"I don't see how that's physically possible. We were right down the hill and didn't see them."

"Oh, well." She looked chagrined and waved her hands in the air. "Magic. It takes some getting used to."

"I've seen staymachs, at the Battle of Ordnung, remember? They're not very big."

"They change shape," she assured me, as if promising the sky was really blue.

An awkward silence fell between us, as we both acknowledged what a strange conversation this was. The great, unbridgeable distance between us. "Do you?" I asked into the space. "Change shape?"

"Yes, Ami, I do." She looked very grave. "That's part of what the mark means. Your daughter will be able to shape-shift, too. That's why you have to bring her here, before she becomes a woman. I might not be able to help her after that. It very well could mean life or death for her."

"You survived."

"I was lucky."

She looked bleak, and those years came back to me. Awkward, invisible Andi. My daughter would never be that way. She'd take after me and I would teach her what I knew. Except there would be no daughter; I was having a son. I mentally shook myself for falling into Andi's witchy wiles.

"More than that"—Andi drifted closer, the sunlight clearly streaming through her image, her gray eyes turbulent—"if she never learns, she'll be forever a shadow of who she could become, half a person."

For some of us it's too late—we'll never be whole again. I shivered. "Like the White Monk." I murmured it to myself, but Andi nodded, sympathy for the man she'd barely met stark on her face.

"Maybe if he'd come to us as a young man, the shamans could have helped him. Now it's too late. He can never be whole."

"He's perfectly vital and strong," I snapped without thinking. "You don't know him."

"Forgive me—I was speaking more in a metaphorical sense. I meant no offense to your lover."

My face flooded hot, guilt and shame pounding at the inside of my skin. "He is *not* my lover, Andi! What kind of person do you think I am?"

She regarded me with clear, wise eyes. "I think you're a young, flesh-and-blood woman with her entire life ahead of her. Happiness is not thick on the ground—gather it when you may."

Thick on the ground—curious that she put it that way. "Sometimes . . ." I hesitated over the words. "I mean, since I've been pregnant, I've been feeling emotions. My midwife says that's part of it, but . . . it's as if emotions have a smell. Or I feel them, under my feet. I realize that sounds like I'm being silly and I'm just—"

"It's not silly," Andi interrupted my building babble. "The gift comes from your daughter, and it's a powerful ability. Even our mother did not possess such a talent. I'm so happy your daughter will have that as her legacy."

"Once she's born, I'll lose it?"

"I don't know. Most likely. I'm sorry."

I shrugged, trying to act as if it didn't bother me at all. "Why should I have anything? Our mother left nothing else for me."

"Did Ursula tell you about the dolls?"

My laugh came out as a bitter snort, not unlike Andi's, but without the comedy. "Oh, yes. How about that? Zevondeth had mine, only it's missing a head. Too bad for me."

"Oh, Ami . . ." Her face crumpled, and she wrung her hands together. "That can't be right. Are you sure?"

"That my doll doesn't have a head? Yes—that kind of detail is kind of hard to miss. Stop feeling sorry for me. I've been fine without it."

"That can't be right," she repeated to herself. "It must be somewhere. She wouldn't have—"

"Well, she did. She was waiting for something to be sent and she died before it arrived. Story of my life." I couldn't match Ursula's hard demeanor, but I carried off the not-caring attitude pretty well.

"Sent? Sent from Annfwn?" Andi's face cleared. "Of course! I wonder what happened? I'll look for it. I'll find it and send it to you. But you might not need it."

"A headless doll isn't much of a thing."

"What I needed was inside the body. Look there. But I'll also see what I can find among her things here."

That rankled. "Don't bother. It's not important."

"But it is." That in her big-sister tone. "You'll need it in the days ahead. If not you, then your daughter will."

"I'm not having a daughter!" I was sick of this game. "Zevondeth says the babe is a boy and the High King has declared him as his heir."

Andi positively faded at that news, her face whitening under the golden tan, trees visible through her image. "What? That's terrible news! How is Ursula?" She twisted her fingers together in that weaving motion, her gaze focused on something only she could see. "Moranu curse Uorsin and his cruel ways."

"He's not cruel," I protested. "My son will be High King. That will be a fitting legacy for Hugh."

Her attention returned to me. "I would ask what's happened

to you, but I suppose I know. Still, you never used to be mean. Of the three of us, you were the most loving, and now—"

"Maybe I'm growing up. It's a hard world. As you said, happiness is not thick on the ground. I'll stop distressing you with my presence."

"Come back anytime." She said it to my back as I walked away. "My love goes with you, Sister, always."

I snatched up my things and stalked back over the border, where the White Monk sat by a small campfire, warming himself, naked blade on the snow at his side, waiting for me.

His head snapped up as I emerged, and the cold hit me like a fist of ice. Stupid not to get re-dressed before crossing, except that the dramatic exit was worth it. The White Monk didn't comment when I stalked up to the fire and hastily layered up again. Nor did he say anything—or move—when I finished and stood there expectantly.

"Well?" I finally prompted. "I'm ready. Let's go."

He cast an eye at the sky overhead. The snowflakes fell thick and heavy from the darkening clouds. "It's almost nightfall, there's no moon, and the weather is treacherous. It would be suicide to descend tonight." He'd returned to his formal, neutral mode. No warmth about him. None of that smoky sense of desire that so intoxicated me.

It had been so sunny in Annfwn, I'd forgotten. As if the eternal summer made even the sunlight last longer, though it seemed to be early evening in both places. Here, that time meant winter dark.

"But we don't have blankets to sleep in. Or any shelter."

"True. We'll freeze to death if we stay here."

"So we die either way?"

"Well, there is one warm place to spend the night." The White Monk raised his brows at me.

Of course. "So this is your plan to get me to take you back into Annfwn. Clever."

He didn't respond. He didn't need to, as it had been foolish of me to say. He could have stayed in the first place.

"Fine." Torture that I'd have to let him carry me again. "But I forbid you from any touch other than necessary, understand?"

He scattered the burning branches with a stick, scuffing snow over the embers with his boots, scarred mouth in a grimace. "Believe me, *Princess*, I'm not the least tempted to touch you in any way."

"Good." I waited for him to finish, the cold still in my bones. "You might have mentioned this plan before I got all these winter clothes on again."

"I didn't want to overstep my bounds, Princess. Seeing as how I'm just a low-life former convict and not fit to be in your exalted presence." He sheathed the blade with a snap that made me jump. Only then did I smell his anger. Like hot blood splashed on the snow beneath my feet. But a rage so old it had frozen over, a scar tissue of ice. He scooped me up without meeting my eyes, staring into the distance and the blizzard that went on forever for him. With perfect faith, he strode without faltering, straight into the paradise long denied him.

And that I denied him still.

He could come back, though. Once he'd delivered me to safety, Andi would let him in and he could be rid of me and the rest of the Twelve Kingdoms. Good riddance.

I was ready to tell him to put me down, but he dumped me unceremoniously on my feet the moment we crossed. Score one for him. He stalked away, ripping off his outer layers with fast jerks, surveying the landscape.

Andi—or her image—was gone. Still, I felt a prickling, a sense of her in the ground. Feeling self-conscious, I said out loud, "Andi, we're here again because we need to spend the night so we won't freeze. I, um, hope you don't mind. We'll stay near here and be gone in the morning."

No answer, only a chorus of evening birds with a fluid, heartbreaking song I'd never heard.

"I don't want to talk to you again," I added, for good measure. "I hope you'll respect that."

Once again, I divested myself of all the winter gear. It would have been so much easier to make this plan to stay the night inside Annfwn earlier. In my heart of hearts, however, I knew it was my fault.

I walked over to where the White Monk studied several branching paths. "I didn't mean to call you a low-life former convict." It wasn't exactly an apology—after all, it was true—but I honestly hadn't meant to blurt it out that way.

"You meant it, all right," he commented without any emotion in his voice. "I think this path."

"Why can't we stay here?" At least the logistics gave us something to discuss that wasn't treacherous ground.

He glanced down at me, eyes full of contempt. "We have no food or water. It would be as unwise to venture down the mountain in the morning without strengthening ourselves as it would be to go now."

Oh.

"I suppose you imagined that servants would appear from nothing and bring you dinner?" Full of scorn, he turned his back on me.

I hadn't thought about where food would come from. Even after all I'd experienced on this journey, I behaved like a spoiled princess, that person clearly reflected in his gaze.

No wonder he detested me so.

No wonder everyone did.

And yet, I felt like a hind trapped by a pack of hunting dogs; no matter the reprimands everyone flung at me, I couldn't seem to change anything. They nipped bites out of me, but I couldn't seem to stop being who I was.

How did a person change?

We started down the path the White Monk chose, me trotting behind to keep up with his long strides. Just another puppet, following along because I didn't have enough sense to know we needed to find food, or a warm place to sleep. This was supposed to be my holy mission, and I'd been useless or a hindrance or annoying people. No power of my own, once again. Nothing useful to offer. Even the one thing I'd been able to contribute—crossing the barrier—came from an accident of birth.

My whole life seemed to be an accident of birth, in fact.

Even this new ability to detect emotions was only borrowed, as was my time in Annfwn. And I'd been wasting them, going in my own circles. Maybe a person changed by breaking out of the circle. I looked around me, hoping for a sign.

In a glen to the left, dappled with golden light, a deer stood on the trail running through it. Her fur gleamed a glorious red-gold. She could have stepped out of my thoughts, the image of the hind—only this one looked free and powerful. No dogs chased her. She moved down another trail. Looked at me. The White Monk's ferocious strides carried him off through the trees.

This was something I would never do, follow a random deer in the forest. A good place to start.

"Hey, Monk!"

He stopped, shoulders tense, and turned with the infinite patience of a man about to lose his temper entirely. "Yes, Your Highness?"

I pointed to the hind, who took several significant steps down the path and looked back at us expectantly. "I think we should go that way."

His gaze flicked to the deer and then to me. "Now you're an expert in omens in Annfwn?"

I wouldn't let him ruffle me but stuck close to my conviction. "This *is* my mission. You came along for the ride and I understand why you wanted to—though you might have told me. I'm going this way. You can follow me or not."

19

I turned away from him and went after the deer. After a bit, I heard the White Monk follow me, his fuming gaze palpable on my back, his anger like roasting meat. How long would he stay angry?

Not that it bothered me. We would part ways, as we were meant to.

The rest had been nothing but a fantasy.

I found that I could be okay with that. With the deer a vision of grace ahead of me, the birdsong, the sweet redolence of the exotic flowers, studding the emerald forest floor like the richest jewels, the gentle evening sun—it all worked on me, sending a feeling of peace into my heart. Even the iron fist of thorns lodged in my breast dissolved a little. My hurt, anger, and self-reproach thinned at the edges and cooled along with the violet sky above.

Like a gift, the trees gave way to a great clearing, a bowl holding a perfectly calm lake that mirrored the sky. All around, the verdant forest spread thick over the hills and I felt I could see it clearly for the first time.

On a moss-covered bank lay a blanket and a basket, along with a copper flagon, beads of sweat showing that whatever was inside would be cool. With a little coo of delight, I ran to the basket and opened it up. Inside was a feast—fruits, pastries, cheeses, some cold meats. I popped a grape into my mouth. It burst on my tongue like a melting, sugary snowflake. We'd had them once, when a delegation from Elcinea brought them to court. Those had been kept on ice for part of the journey, but they'd shriveled some on the way after it melted, the Elcineans said. I'd thought they were miraculous. After I gobbled all of my share, Ursula and Andi gave me most of theirs, too, I'd loved them so much.

Now I understood how grapes should be. Just like this.

And Andi had remembered. Indulging me now as then. Both gestures made out of love. Maybe those meant more, the small actions, than the poems and protestations.

I plucked another, ready to savor it, when the White Monk knocked it out of my hand.

"Ami! Don't eat that stuff."

"Why not?" Clutching the bunch of grapes to my breast, I put distance between us.

"It could be poisoned."

"I thought this was paradise."

His jaw muscles clenched. "A euphemism. That doesn't make it perfect."

I deliberately put the basket between us. "I think you're mad that invisible servants *did* show up and provide me with dinner." Slowly and deliberately, I placed another grape on my tongue and crunched it, letting the pure sweetness of it fill my mouth. "Mmm . . . delicious."

His gaze seemed to be riveted to my mouth. The hatred had faded from his eyes, and I smelled that dark, smoky current. Not so oblivious to me, perhaps. It helped to know what this meant, my borrowed gift.

"You're being foolish. It's my job to protect you," he ground out through clenched teeth.

"Can't protect a fool from her own choices, can you?" I shrugged cheerfully, spreading my arms wide. Oh, yes, he looked at my breasts as they bounced, even if he immediately yanked his gaze out to the lake. Feeling much better, I sat and emptied the picnic basket. "You can wait and see if I die. Meanwhile, I'm starving."

I poured some of the water into a thoughtfully provided cup and drank deep. It tasted like the snow at the top of the mountains looked. Making myself a plate of the food, I soaked in the gorgeous scenery. If this was only the buffer area, what was the rest of Annfwn like? Feeling happier than I had in forever, I devoured the food, wordlessly passing a bunch of the grapes to the White Monk when he grudgingly sat. Without further comment, he ate them and the other offerings. Guess he'd decided I would have died by now if they were poisoned.

He repacked the leftovers in the basket and set it aside. Sated and sleepy, I decided I'd better brush my hair, lest I fall asleep soon. Rummaging in my cloak pocket, I pulled out the brush, then unbraided my hair and starting counting strokes. A bright moon had risen, the lake reflecting the light with silver-violet serenity.

"You brought a hairbrush?" the White Monk asked, breaking the long silence.

"In my cloak, yes."

"You don't have a dagger to defend yourself with, but you keep your hairbrush on you at all times."

"Yes. And you're making me lose count."

"Count?"

I stopped at twenty, an easy number to remember. "One hundred strokes, every night. Well, usually. I missed the last couple of nights."

"Unbelievable."

"If I were Ursula and hopped up to practice moves with the dagger you think I should carry around, you wouldn't be so incredulous."

"That's different." He sounded as grumpy as ever.

"Is it? I will never be Ursula. Maybe I need to learn to use what I'm good at—like I have a different kind of weapon."

He heaved out a breath, reclining on the blanket to watch me. It was frankly a relief to have him relax a little.

"Your beauty is not a weapon, Ami."

And at least he wasn't hurling titles at me like rocks.

"Don't say that."

"Why not?"

I pointed the brush at him. "Because it's all I have. Didn't you point that out to me first? I have no power of my own, only what I can borrow or steal from someone else. I certainly don't have smarts to offer. How I look is my best tool. Perhaps I'm coming to terms with that."

He fell silent, so I resumed brushing, the rhythm of the count like one of Glorianna's prayer cycles.

"I didn't mean it that way," he finally said.

"No?"

"I think you have many talents. You're unbelievably strong-willed, courageous, sensitive, passionate . . ."

He trailed off after the last word, leaving it to hum between us. Something he hadn't meant to say. It made me smile, and he shifted, looking away.

"I don't think that counts as an ability."

"It does," he countered immediately. "You have no idea how many people in the world lack that ability, to love life and live it. Even now, when you've been kicked in the worst way, over and over, you revel in everything. Look at you—brushing your hair, laughing at me. And the way you ate those grapes . . ."

The dark current of desire deepened, and I breathed it in. Infinitely preferable to that stagnant hatred and scorn.

"What about the way I ate the grapes?" I teased him.

"Never mind." He growled the words, but I could feel that he wasn't angry, not anymore.

"Okay, let's try this. Why did you say those things to me if you didn't mean them?"

"I wanted to . . ." He heaved out a lungful of impatience. "To get through to you. To get you to really see what was going on around you."

Aha. "Why?"

He didn't answer. I tipped my head sideways, brushing up in the reverse direction, from the bottom over the top of my head. In the sapphire dusk, his eyes gleamed without color. Not saying. Okay, then.

"I guess we all say things we don't mean sometimes."

He nodded, with a rigid jerk of his chin.

"Look." I set the brush aside and leaned on the blanket on one elbow, propping my head on my hand. "I apologize for what I said. I'm thoughtless and I blurt things out when I'm angry, which I was. Andi and I . . ." I sighed and rolled onto my back, staring up into the sky. Stars were beginning to prick the darkening sky, glittering with prismatic brilliance. "I don't know how to handle anything anymore. But I am sorry that I hurt your feelings. You're right—I meant what I said, but I didn't say it to wound you."

Seeming as if he couldn't help himself, the ground growing soft and warm beneath me, the scent of wood smoke and grapes in the air, the White Monk edged closer. Picking up a long tendril of my hair, he rolled it through his fingers.

"You didn't wound me," he said, sand soft. "You're right—it was all true. Of course you were angry at the insinuation that I would be your lover. It's an absurd thought."

How did a person change? Maybe by doing things they wouldn't normally do.

"No, it's not," I told him. "That's the thing. It's not absurd at all."

My breath held tight in my chest. *Happiness doesn't grow thick on the ground.* This might be my chance. If not now, when? We weren't even in the Twelve Kingdoms, so it seemed that none of those rules applied. And I wanted this. Wanted to know how it felt to be with at least one other man. One who saw me as something more than a fragile prize to be protected. I'd been trying to seduce him, I realized, luring him in.

And he said beauty didn't count as a talent.

He wound the lock of my hair around his finger, studying it as if it held all the answers. "You would take a criminal—a demon part-blood—to your bed?"

"We're not in a bed," I answered lightly. My breasts felt tight and hot, my nipples pushing against the silk. I wanted him to touch me. Hard. I wanted to feel something again, some of that passion he thought I possessed.

He laughed under his breath without humor. "That's not really the point, is it? You and I both know I'm not fit to touch even this much of you."

"You touched me before, far more than this."

"That was different."

"You healed me—and slept for a day and a night to pay the price for it. I owe you."

"You were my ticket here. I think you realize now how I tricked you."

"And yet you're willing to leave, to see me to safety."

"I might be a low-life criminal, but I'm not one to abandon my duty," he growled. My skin warmed, heat pooling between my legs. I liked him this way, a little impatient and rough.

I stretched my arms up over my head, letting my back arch, aware of how the movement drew his gaze, the air and ground thick with his wanting. With our intertwined desire. "I didn't thank you, for healing me. What kind of boon can a poor princess offer a man like you for her rescue from dire straits?"

He stilled, my hair wound so many times around his finger that I felt it pulling against my scalp. At last it was sinking in.

"You can't mean it," he said, in a rough whisper.

"It's not as if you can get me pregnant." This felt wild. Totally unlike me. Not the pretty princess. I wanted this. "Tonight, can't I just be Ami? And you can be just . . ."

I waited for him to fill in the space.

"Ash." The name fit neatly into the quiet spot.

"Ash," I repeated, tucking his name away like the gift it was. "Ash, I want you."

He groaned a little, lifting his eyes to my face. I waited while he lifted a hand and held it near my cheek. It hovered there, shaking a little. "I was wrong," he gritted out. "You wield your beauty like the finest blade. So sharp you cut me to ribbons before I knew it." Still without touching my skin, he drew his hand down my center, floating barely out of reach. I held still, praying for him to touch me.

"You are so damn beautiful, Ami, looking at you is like staring into the sun. I'm afraid I'll come away burned and blinded."

"Then close your eyes," I urged him. "Don't look. But, Ash, please. I want you."

He did close his eyes, shuddering, the musk from our desire wrapping around us like down-filled quilts. Then, in a quicksilver movement, he straddled me, pinning my wrists over my head, craggy face close to mine.

"Last chance to back out." He said it like a demand. My blood heated to boiling. This would happen.

"I don't want to back out."

His grip tightened on me. "It won't be gentle. I'm no nobleman to courteously and reverently make love. If you don't say no, I'm going to fuck you, Ami. Do you understand what I mean?"

I shuddered, trembling with a lust so fierce I thought it might tear me apart if he didn't do as he promised.

"I understand." I lifted my hips, brushing his hard member with my belly.

He lowered his head, lips a breath from mine, my wrists still held in his implacable grip. I wanted to thrash against it but didn't want to frighten him away.

"Say it one more time," he commanded. "Three is the magic number."

"Ash," I breathed. "I want you."

His mouth clamped on mine, as if he devoured the words from my lips along with the breath that spoke them. The kiss crashed through me, breaking me apart, making me wild. Now I did writhe against him, opening my mouth and letting him plunder it as my fantasies had promised he'd do.

Giving myself over, I cried and whimpered, urging him on by rubbing my body against him wherever I could. He pulled away from the kiss and I followed him, trying to chase the fiery feeling of his mouth. Nipping me on the lower lip, he told me to behave, then sat up, knees still straddling my hips.

"Don't move." He released my wrists and I curled my fingers into fists to obey. Moving slowly—tortuously so—he trailed a finger down my throat and down over the silk, between my breasts. "From the first moment I saw you, I dreamed of this moment. They warned me that your beauty is like a drug. That once a man beholds you, he won't think straight again. But I thought I'd be immune. No such luck."

"Is that why you hate me?" I whispered, my nipples so hard, so desperate for him to touch, that my head spun with it, as if I'd drunk too much wine.

He was shaking his head. "I don't hate you, Ami." Winding his fingers in the silk of my shirt, he pulled the fabric tight. "I hated how much I wanted this."

His face contorted with a passion that rocked me to my core, he tore open the shirt. Involuntarily I cried out, my back bowing as the silk pulled me up, the moonlight revealing my naked breasts.

With an incoherent groan, he cupped them in his big hands, the calluses rough on my tender skin. He handled me with rough strength, as I'd somehow known he would, the pleasure nearly painful, except that it transported me so. Unable to stay still, I clutched his shoulders, my fingers curling into the light shirt he'd worn under the leathers. He didn't object, just slid his hands under my back to lift my breasts to his mouth. With hot swipes of his tongue and nipping bites, he covered every inch, as if starving for the taste of my skin.

I reveled in it. My breasts had grown so taut, so sensitive and full to bursting lately, that this teasing torment only served to ease that tension. When his avid mouth fastened on my nipple and sucked hard, the lightning bolt bifurcated, shooting to my groin and mind at once, pouring out of my mouth in a scream of ecstasy.

His hands dug into the muscles of my back, holding me while I thrashed in his arms, his lips and teeth clamped on my breast. The intense wave left me and he resumed licking and kissing, transferring attentions between my breasts, while my head draped down and the world turned upside down.

"I need you naked," he muttered, standing and drawing me to my feet. I stood on the velvet, lust-filled grass, swaying and bemused, while he stripped the silks from my body. The moon, nearly full, rose high and platinum bright. With greater care, Ash unwound the bandages from my thighs, then tossed those on top of the pile of my discarded, shredded clothing.

Kneeling before me, he sat on his heels, eyes a dark gleam in the night, staring at me like a predator stalking a deer. Even with Hugh, I'd never stood fully naked this way. Self-conscious, I shrugged the cape of my long hair around me, the silky ends tickling my bottom and upper thighs.

"No." His tone crawled harsh over my skin, making the fine hairs stand on end. "I may have only this one chance. You gave yourself to me and I want it all. Gather your hair and hold it on top of your head so I can see you."

A fine trembling took me, my skin both hot and chilled. Winding my hair into a loose bundle, I raised it the way he wanted, needing both hands to hold all of it. His breath shuddered in and out, in satisfaction and a kind of physical torment. He stood and walked around me, trailing a hand down my spine and then drifting over one globe of my bottom. I waited in a state of mindless anticipation, my skin singing to his least caress, the hot, aching flesh between my legs craving more, more, more.

He dropped down in front of me again, knees wide, still fully dressed. Grasping my ankles, he moved my feet a little apart. Then he slid one hand up my calf, over the inside of my knee and up to my inner thigh. My breath came in little pants and I watched, riveted by the sight.

Caressing the newly healed skin there, he flicked a sly glance up at me, teeth showing in a rare open grin that nevertheless looked more feral than joyful, he drew his finger higher, stopping only where my thighs met.

"Is your skin sensitive here?" he asked in that gravelly whisper.

I nodded, biting back a moan at his feathery strokes.

"Maybe I should check. Spread your legs more, so I can see."

My face hot and nipples aching ferociously, I eased my thighs apart a bit more. He followed the gap with only the one finger, leaning in close, his breath hot on my skin.

"More," he demanded.

Biting my lip against the terrible tension, I gave him what he wanted, the night air cool on the hot tissues of my sex. With excruciating slowness, he dragged the tip of his finger over the round of my thigh, skidding on the slick moisture that had wicked down.

"What's this?" Adding more fingers, he dabbled in the wetness. "Are you so hot for me, then? Already primed and ready for fucking, Ami?"

Wildly embarrassed, I tried to close my thighs and pull away, dropping my hair.

The hand between my legs clamped onto my slick thigh, preventing me, and his other hand held me from behind, a vise on my bottom. Rocking on my feet, I grabbed his shoulders to steady myself, to find him staring up at me, harsh face fierce in the moonlight.

"No, you don't. There's no escaping me." He flattened the hand between my thighs, using my own moisture to glide it back and forth, inching it up so the edge of his knuckle just brushed my slick nether lips. I moaned at the aching pleasure. "That's it, my treasure, never be ashamed. This is a gift. No one else will see. I'll protect you and pleasure you and it will be our secret. You can be anyone with me."

20

The murmuring words flooded through me, opening doors I hadn't known were closed. Or maybe I had known—and knowing it led me here. His hard hand pushed higher and I opened for him again, longing for more than the brushing, teasing tickles on my lips. I wanted—no, *needed*—more.

"Harder," I whispered, and he laughed that soundless, dry laugh.

"It will be, Princess. Don't you worry." But his fingertips barely parted the lips of my womanhood, taunting me. I pushed down into his hand and he drew the touch away, tsking at me. "So impatient. All right, then. Lie back on the blanket."

With relief I did, holding up my arms to receive him. At last.

He stood over me, looking and thinking. Or just looking. Then he kneeled down and straddled me on all fours, his loose shirttail brushing my belly, hands on either side of my head. With a sweetness he hadn't shown before, he kissed me, slow and gentle, laving the sensitive insides of my lips with his tongue. I held on to his shirt, then tried to push it open, to feel his skin beneath. With an iron grip, he clamped my wrist and drew my hand away.

"No."

"I want to touch you," I protested.

"Not a subject for debate. Stretch your arms over your head and keep them there or I'll tie them that way."

Breathless, I obeyed, my blood hot, staring up at the sky, dense with stars except for the bright hole made by the moon. He crawled down my body, dropping kisses and little bites here and there, humming when I leapt to the caress. Reaching my feet, he took my ankles in his hands again.

"Do you remember what I said to you in the stable?"

I nodded, unable to speak.

"I've thought of doing nothing else since then." He pushed my ankles apart, opening me to his gaze. I squirmed, vividly aware that he saw everything of me. More than even I had. He placed my feet on his shoulders, the muscles there firm against my arches. My breath nearly sobbed out of me.

He feathered his fingers down my inner thighs and then cupped my bottom, lifting me to his mouth as he'd done with my breasts.

Tension racked me, making me shudder. "I'm afraid," I whimpered, though that wasn't the right word.

"Never be afraid of me." The breath carrying his words fluttered over my exposed and sensitive flesh, and I clutched the grass above my head for some kind of anchor. He waited for me to calm myself. "Tell me you want this."

I nodded, only it was more of a thrashing of my head from side to side. My world was coming apart.

"Not enough, Ami." His bruising grip dug into my bottom, and he sounded angry. I knew, though, by the ravenous energy prickling up from the ground, that it was something else. "Tell me yes or I stop."

I was a glass vessel, overfull and ready to shatter. There was only one answer to give.

"Yes."

And his mouth was on me. Hot. Hungry. Full of teeth and lips, tongue penetrating me. My hips bucked wildly and he held me tight, growling in his throat as he devoured me. The sky broke into kaleidoscoping colors, whirling and flashing in the backs of my eyes. My heart pounded, rattling against my ribs, and I cried out, a long wailing song of something beyond pleasure. Mind shattering, I broke apart, suspended in space, tethered to the world only by his hands and mouth.

I didn't think I'd fainted, but I became aware of him licking me, not ferocious as before, but with a gentleness that roused me, desire prickling up from my toes. My knees were draped over his shoulders, my hips pressed to the blanket as he pressed me down. He took the kernel of keenest pleasure between his teeth, flicking with his tongue, then sucking hard.

Moaning a protest, I pushed against his head. He ignored me. The tension mounted more, making me shift restlessly. I wound my fingers in his curly hair, pulling. No longer sure which way I wanted to move him.

"Hands," he growled, "or I will tie them. Don't think I won't."

Chastened, I dropped my hands to my sides, clawing my fingers into the blanket. "Ash . . ." My throat scratched, swallowing his name. I cleared it and tried again, trying to keep the thought as his mouth worked me, driving me to that mindless plain. "Ash—I don't think I can do any more."

He laughed, dry and breathless, and pressed a sloppy kiss on my inner thigh. "Oh, yes, you can. I'm not done with you, yet. Not by a long stretch."

Pushing my knees apart, he stared down at me, then slid a long, coarse finger inside, curling it up, so I convulsed, gasping. "Oh, yes," he said, all smug male, "you have plenty left." He added another finger, pumping them in and out of me, gaze on my face as the deeper pleasure took over. His thumb pressed down on the upper kernel and I thrashed at the double-layered sensation.

I whimpered again, this time when he withdrew his hand, and he patted my flank. "Shh . . . only for a moment." His clothing rustled; then he settled himself between my thighs, his manhood pressing against my opening. Bracing myself, I waited for him to thrust in. But he stopped there, just barely inside me, arms straight, holding himself above me. Unbidden, I remembered Hugh, how he'd done this, his skin warm against mine. With a pang of guilt, I missed him.

"Look at me," Ash urged.

I opened my eyes, his face close above mine. He kissed me. Withdrew.

"Is this how you did it before?" he asked.

I nodded, uncertain what he meant. This wasn't going how I'd expected. He still waited. "Isn't there pretty much just one way to do it?" I whispered, utterly self-conscious to be discussing it. How horribly naïve was I? I turned my face to the side, waiting for his laughter.

Instead, he took my earlobe in his teeth and stroked the hard ridge of manhood against me, gliding easily against my slickness—and I moaned at the dual sensations, losing my embarrassment immediately.

"I mean," he murmured into my ear, "face to face this way."

"Oh!" The heat burned in my face. "Yes. Like this—Glorianna's way."

Now he did laugh, a huff of breath across my cheek. "I have to know what you were thinking."

"Oh, no. I was only confused a little."

He settled his hips deeper, pressing barely into me and stopping, sweeping a long line of kisses down my throat. I lifted my hips, beseeching. But no.

"I must know, Ami. You had such an odd look on your face. What did you think I meant?"

"It doesn't matter," I urged him. "Just do it."

"Like this?" He pressed into me and I caught my breath, waiting for the stroke inside me, but he pulled out again.

"Oh, please!" I cried out before I knew it.

"Then tell me."

"I can't."

"You trust me with this, but not your thoughts?"

"I don't have the words."

"Try," he coaxed, sounding ever so amused. The playfulness, so unlike his usual demeanor, curlicued through his thick passion, shimmering streams of bubbles in wine.

"After. Afterwards I'll tell you."

"Now. Or you'll try to squirm out of it." He lowered his weight, pinning me down as if to illustrate. "Tell me, sweet Ami."

I closed my eyes, glad of the shadows that should hide my red face. "I thought that there was another way than the man putting his . . . part inside of my . . . area."

To his credit, he didn't laugh. "Ah, I see." He pushed his manhood into me and I whimpered. "This part?"

"Yes."

"And this area?"

"Ash!" I let go of the blanket and seized his hips, trying to pull him inside of me. "Yes, already! I *told* you I didn't have the words."

"I know. I'm sorry for teasing you. I only . . ."

He trailed off and I paid attention to his expression, wondering why his mood changed, a whiff of desolation creeping through. I lifted my hands and framed his face. Turnabout.

"Tell me."

He sighed and leaned his forehead against mine. "I realize this is only for tonight, but . . . I have to know that you remember this is me. That you're not . . . dreaming of a ghost."

He'd known somehow, that I'd drifted, before. The expression on his pitted face seemed stark, the naked hope and fear of the wounded animal. His skin, all the uneven lines and scars, made me realize, more than anything, that this was *him*. And I knew what to do.

"Then take off your shirt. Get as naked as I am." I told him. "Let me see and touch *you*."

Sitting up, he looked at me, splayed before him, and hesitated. "I have scars. Lots of them."

"I've seen—remember?"

"Touching is different. Most girls—other women, I mean—are repelled. It's not pretty."

"I've had pretty. Now I want you."

He stilled at that, fingers flexing on his shirt, and for a moment I thought I'd blurted out the wrong thing again. But no—he laughed, soundlessly, and shrugged out of the shirt. Tossing it aside, he pulled off his boots, stood, and pushed the narrow black pants down his legs. His manhood stood out straight from his body and I found myself staring, aware I'd never seen Hugh this way either.

So much we hadn't done with each other. But, though the thought made me sad, no ball of iron thorns followed it; my throat didn't seize with grief. We'd thought we'd have all our lives and lost all those years in an instant. Over time, we would have come to know each other better. Maybe Hugh had treated me as he thought I wanted him to. Glorianna knew that I'd never said otherwise. I'd been delighted to be petted and cosseted. It wasn't his fault that we hadn't had the chance to grow up some. If I had learned nothing else, I knew that—time could be cut short.

"Show me one of the other ways," I told Ash, standing up and boldly putting my hand on his . . . what? "And what do I call this?"

"Cock," he answered. "There are as many names as stars in the sky, but that will do."

Keep your head with your big sword, not the little one, young cock. The drill instructor had said that to the soldier in the yard and now I understood her subsequent apology.

Ash's hands settled on my hips, under the fall of my hair, and he pushed his cock through the circle of my hand so the furry hairs of his chest tickled my nipples. That part of him, his cock, wasn't rough or scarred, but felt smooth and velvety. Tender, even.

"You can do it harder than that."

I liked harder. I tightened my grip and he gasped, the cock

flexing in my hand. He pulled away from me and took my hands in his. Lying back on the blanket, he drew me over him, positioning me so I straddled him. Lifting his cock in one hand, he pointed it up and moved me by the hips so the tip was just inside me.

"I want to do it," I said.

"Then do it," he nearly growled.

Wrapping my fingers around it again, I savored the sweet texture of his skin there, so hot, with muscular hardness beneath.

"Can I put my mouth on you, as you did to me?" I was more wondering out loud, but he clapped his hands over his eyes, grinding the heels into the sockets, making a horrible groaning noise.

"You will be the death of me."

"I just wondered."

"No." He dropped his hands to my hips and sank clawed fingers in. "Not now."

"Why not?"

"Because you look like the goddess of sex sitting over me, your juices dripping down my cock, and I can't hold off a moment more." With a burst of speed and strength, he pulled my hips down and flexed his body, driving up and into me.

I rode him like a steed, plunging up and down, the excruciating pleasure arrowing through my pelvis and up through the top of my head.

Throwing back my head, I laughed, straight to the moon. I felt like the goddess of sex. Ash sat up, following the arch of my body and winding his hands in the length of my streaming hair, making me bend backward while his mouth plundered my breasts and that fierce *cock* drove up, pinioning me with such sharp thrusts that I convulsed.

Over and over, my whole body spasmed and I dug my nails into the wiry muscles of his shoulders, the ridges left by the lash like a puzzle to be reassembled. With a last cry, I collapsed, falling backward into the pull of his grip on my hair.

He followed me, barely allowing a breath of distance between our slick skins. My knees bent under me, my spine still arched by his merciless grip, I became the horse he rode, pounding into me with all the ferocity I'd fantasized about. My body screamed with it.

I did, too. Lost in a world of such extremity that I knew nothing but his flesh in mine.

With a final shout of what sounded like victory, he slammed home, grinding hard and pushing my straining hips wide. I split apart, sundered by him.

Lost to the night.

🌹 🌹 🌹

But morning found me anyway.

Rosy fingers of Glorianna's dawn rippled over the sky, turning it and the lake the perfect pink her priests strove to re-create. I sat up to see better, wincing at the intense ache between my thighs. I'd been wrapped up in the blanket, as securely as if it were a bandage and all my skin abraded.

Ash sat nearby, fully dressed, long arms wrapped around his knees.

And brooding.

"Good morning." I worked a hand free to tuck my hair behind my ears. It was curling madly, tangled, and no doubt standing out around my head like a bonfire leaping out of control. Out of habit, I looked around for my brush, wherever I'd tossed it last night.

"Looking for this?" Ash's voice sounded more full of rocks than usual. Maybe broken glass mixed in. Pain and regret salted the soil. I sighed for that and held out my hand.

"Yes, thank you."

He shook his head, more at some thought than at me, but didn't hand it to me. Instead he came to sit behind me and gently worked the snarled mess from under the blanket. I froze, uncertain if he intended what I thought. Tentatively, he drew the brush through it. Far too gently.

"You can do it harder than that," I teased him and was rewarded by his sharp intake of breath at the reminder of how I'd worked him with my hand. My body warmed at the memory.

"I don't want to hurt you." He sounded funny. Smelled guilty.

"You've groomed horses, right?" I kept my voice light. "Imagine this is a tail."

"I never did enjoy getting mule kicked," he observed wryly, which was better. More, he dug in a bit harder. Still not quite enough.

I held my hand over my shoulder for the brush. "Here, let me."

"No," he snapped, and I flinched a little at the frustration in his tone. He drew in and blew out a long and deliberate breath. "I want to do this for you. To make things up to you."

"Even my hair has been mussed once or twice," I told him, mild and even. "I survived."

He tugged harder and I braced myself, being careful not to show any twinge.

"Not that." The brush snagged, then got wrapped up. He cursed, but his tugging got him nowhere. I turned, working my other arm free of the blanket, and took over. In a few moments, the brush came free and I set to teasing out the rest of the tangles. He watched me, bemused. "How do you do that so easily?"

"Lots and lots of practice. See, you have to start at the ends, this way."

"Last night you brushed from the top down.

"It wasn't all knotted up then." I smiled, because he still looked unhappy. "And I didn't know you were watching that closely."

"I'm always watching you, Ami." His gaze wandered over me, unwillingly, I thought. "It's as if I can't look away."

"Should I apologize for that?" I hadn't forgotten how he'd said that he hated wanting me. Like a poison.

His gaze flicked to mine, haunted. "No. I should apologize to you. Once you've . . . tidied yourself—you can bathe in the lake—I'll heal you. I can do that much at least."

"I don't need healing." I paused in the brushing, surprised. "My thighs are fine."

"Not that!" In an excess of impatience, he yanked the blanket down, baring my bosom. "Look at yourself. Look at what I did to you."

Shocked and rather overwhelmed, I took in the sight of my breasts, blooming with bruises, scraped here and there. On the high, round curve of one, a set of teeth marks showed dark red amid a flowering patch of yellow.

"You look as if a wild animal has been at you." The bitter roil of disgust poured out of him and into the ground, sour with self-loathing. "You should see the rest."

"Okay." I tossed the brush aside and stood, dropping the blanket entirely. He cursed under his breath, but—true to his words—seemed unable to look away. My hips ached and the fiery burn on my thighs turned out to be some sort of rash. I fingered it, finding it was composed of hundreds of tiny scrapes.

"From my beard stubble." The words grumble out of him. "Go bathe so I can heal the damage I did."

"I don't want healing. But I will bathe." Snagging the brush again, I strode naked down to the lake, savoring the feel of my bruised body as I moved. *You look as if a wild animal has been at you.* That's how it felt, too.

I loved it. The new me.

But I let him stew anyway. I hadn't changed *that* much.

21

When I returned, still naked, because I liked the way he stared at me, the scent of his desire percolated up through the rest. He'd packed up our few things and had laid out a shirt and pants for me that had survived his mauling, mainly because I hadn't been wearing them.

His gaze crawled over me, full of the lust I loved from him, threaded through with guilt and anxiety. Enough of that. I tossed back my hair and fisted my hands on my hips.

"Skip the apologies," I said.

His mouth thinned. "No apology is sufficient, Princess Amelia, I—"

"Glorianna save me!" I burst out, thoroughly annoyed with him, and he gaped at me. Enough that I laughed. As I'd laughed last night, howling at the moon, while he drove his cock into me and neither one of us worried about small things like bruises and being royalty or a convict. "Ash—I don't want your apologies because I'm not sorry. I'm not fragile and I don't want to be treated like some hothouse rose whose petals might crumple. I enjoyed last night and I'm not letting you remove a single bruise or scrape. They're . . . trophies." Evidence of emotion that showed on my skin finally. Not like those seeping, bleeding wounds inside that no one saw.

"I'm only sorry," I continued in the face of his silence, "that I fell asleep so early.

"You flat passed out, Ami." He was back to angry. Far better than that oily guilt.

"Mmm, yes. And slept harder than I have . . ." Since I heard Hugh had died. "In forever. I don't mind that. But I wanted to try my mouth on your cock and find out how that feels, too."

He made a choking sound and rubbed his forehead.

"What? Am I not supposed to use the words now?"

"It's not that." A muscle in his jaw clenched and he seemed to be grinding his teeth. "Why don't you put your clothes on?"

"Why? Am I so ugly that you can't bear to look upon me?"

"It's not that." He stared over my shoulder, at the lake or nothing at all. I tossed my hair over my shoulder, and sure enough, his gaze dragged unwillingly to my breasts and down the rest of my body. I sauntered toward him and he took a step back, holding up his palms, as if to ward me off. "Stay away, Ami. Get dressed."

I kissed the center of one palm and he yanked it away as if I'd burned him. Taking advantage, I slipped close and began unfastening the buttons of his shirt. More than one way to get inside a man's guard. If this was indeed my weapon, I planned to learn to wield it well.

"Stop that." He gripped my wrists, holding them tight in place. But it lacked the force of his usual demands. And the smoky scent of his desire thickened.

Deliberately I pressed against him, testing, my naked belly brushing against the upthrust line of his cock straining against his pants. "It won't take that long, will it?" I looked up at him through my lashes, swaying against him. "You feel ready to me."

He groaned, casting his gaze up to the sky. "This was the worst mistake I ever made. If I could take back what happened last night, I would."

Cold washed through me, a blizzard taking all the sweet warmth of our combined desire with it, leaving the air sterile, without life.

"Ah." Shame found me, and I was embarrassed to be naked. "Good to know that, Monk."

I pulled away, but he held me, grip strong on my wrists. The emotions bleeding out of him tasted muddy, swirling with doubt, longing, self-hatred, jealousy, and an under-riding current of help-lessness that made the ground shift like sand beneath me.

"It's not what you think." He searched my face, the scars deepening on his. "I didn't mean what I said."

"You meant it, all right." I said it with all the flat coolness he'd used to deflate me with those words the day before. And it worked equally well on him. He relaxed his hold and let me slip away. "I'll get dressed and we can go."

"Ami . . ."

I yanked on the pants and buttoned up the shirt, then tightly braided my hair and tied it off with a strip of the torn silk. It suited my mood, to have it out of my way. Gathering my things, I cast one long look at the beautiful place. No longer sure how I felt about anything at all, I nevertheless appreciated that Andi had offered me this sanctuary. It no longer seemed so impossible that my daughter would want to come here. Maybe I would come with her.

As if in answer, a bit of life turned inside me, a little starburst of someone else there. I laid my hand over my belly and turned my gaze farther west.

"Thank you, Andi," I whispered. I almost told her that I would return. Or that I might. In the end, I left it at that, trusting that she heard me.

I flicked a glance at the White Monk, who stood nearby, fists clenched around the straps of the pack he wore. He'd retreated behind that implacable and stern mask, eyes like cloudy glass.

"I'm ready to go," I said and headed into the larger world.

This time I bundled up again before crossing the border, but winter still hit me with an unexpected blow. Without pausing, the White Monk clomped through the snow, breaking a trail for me. When we passed the altar for Hugh, the flower as verdant as Annfwn itself, I drew Glorianna's circle in the air and spoke the benediction for the dead. My body ached in delicious ways from being with another man, and yet I felt no guilt.

I almost thought Hugh would approve of the woman I was becoming. The one he never had a chance to get to know. And I would never know what kind of man he would have become. That was the greatest tragedy.

"Do you want to stop, Princess?" the White Monk inquired, formal and solicitous of his charge.

"No. You may proceed."

He'd drawn the double cowl deep over his face, so I felt the glitter of apple green more than saw it. He didn't much appreciate me turning the distance on him.

Still, this would be better. We could not be together as lovers outside of that bubble of paradise, no more than Hugh's forget-me-not could survive more than a moment outside the magic dome. Even if I built a hothouse to hide ourselves away in, the glass would eventually shatter and we'd be exposed to the cruel elements of our world.

No. The High King's daughter and the future Queen of Avonlidgh could not associate with an escaped convict and Tala partblood. We both knew it. For the first time I felt the bite of duty. This was what came of claiming my own power—responsibility. Our reality wasn't something I could pout or tantrum away.

Ash would be better off returning to Annfwn—his true desire, regardless—and making a life for himself there. I would keep his secrets. For myself, I would forge ahead, playing my role in the fate of Annfwn and the Twelve Kingdoms. It wasn't the happily ever after I'd envisioned when Hugh and I wed, but it could be a good life. An important one.

And maybe I would find other men to enjoy.

I owed the White Monk that much. If my power lay there, then I would apply myself to the study of it. If Glorianna was the goddess of love, then perhaps she was also the goddess of sex. I could take as many lovers as I wished and none would gainsay me. As long as they were no threat to the thrones, I could dally with anyone. Girls, too, as some of my ladies amused themselves that way.

Perhaps I'd lost my chance at true love, but I could have happiness, thick on the ground or not.

The descent went quickly, especially as we walked without speaking, each absorbed in our own thoughts. I sensed the stay-machs moving through the foliage, but their flitting shadows no longer frightened me. The White Monk was frankly brooding, judging by the taint he left in the footsteps I followed in. The farther we got from Annfwn, however, the less I sensed his feelings. Maybe a whiff in the air now and then, but barely in the earth at all after a while, as if the soil outside Annfwn lacked something, like desert sand that held no water.

It troubled me, this sensation that the very ground of the Twelve Kingdoms was somehow failing. Was this why the crops and livestock were doing poorly? Maybe our answer lay not in conquering Annfwn for Glorianna, but in restoring some kind of vital magic to the rest of the Twelve Kingdoms. I started to send a prayer to Glorianna for guidance and paused in midthought. Maybe she had already guided me and I needed to listen better.

When we reached the bottom of the narrow trail, where it widened again and our troop of guards had ridden three abreast so easily, the White Monk still stalked ahead of me, stiff gaited and seething. Needing to answer the call of nature, I ducked off the trail and went behind a bush. I didn't tarry overlong, but before I caught up with him, he was charging up the trail, blade drawn, cowl thrown back and eyes bright with panic.

His relief washed over me like the breeze off the mirrored lake in Annfwn, then crackled and crumbled into the ash he was named for under the heat of his rage.

"I understand," he gritted out. "You seek your revenge by toying with me. By testing me. Well played, Your Highness."

"Why in Glorianna's name would I want revenge?" I replied, honestly dumfounded. "I had to pee."

He winced, making me smile. Okay, maybe that had been playing him a bit. But it was fun, too.

"I apologize," he ground out, "for hurting your feelings. I—"

"You didn't." I cut him off right there. "I'm fine. It's too bad you regret what happened, but I don't."

Sheathing his blade, he refused to look at me. *Like staring into the sun.* I rolled my eyes, and the memory of Andi doing that so many times, and being elbowed by Ursula for it, hit me with fond nostalgia. In that moment, I knew I didn't hate her anymore. Maybe I'd never really managed to. It felt good. As if a heavy burden had been lifted.

"Are you laughing at me?" He sounded astonished, a draft of wounded male pride wafting low to the ground.

"You know, I never thought I'd be in the position to say this to someone else, but not everything is about you."

His jaw worked as he chewed over that. Finally he inclined his head. "Your point, Highness."

"What will be my prize?" I asked archly.

"I believe, since we failed to set terms, that the lady decides." He gave me a short bow and waited.

"Tell me about how you learned to heal, why you went to prison, and how you got the scars on your face."

He stilled. A deer about to flee into the forest. "A severe price—and three things, not one."

"Tell me they're not connected and I'll trim it to one."

A huff of that soundless laugh. "Adding to your armory of secrets to use against me, then."

"Ash." I laid a hand on his chest, his heart booming underneath my touch, the hunted animal showing in his eyes. "I want to understand you. That's all."

He laid his hand over mine and quirked his mouth, not quite a smile with the scar pulling it sideways, then stepped back and pulled the cowl deep around his face, as if to keep me from seeing him. "As you wish, Princess. But we should keep going."

I fell into step beside him.

"You heard me tell part of the story—my father burned to death by the priest of Glorianna."

I shivered, not from the cold. "Yes. I'm sorry. I didn't know they had the latitude to do that."

"Latitude?" His breath puffed out in a cloud. "By whose charge? The High King declared that the Tala don't exist; therefore, we could not be spoken of by anyone with allegiance to his government. Even if we can find our way to Annfwn, we can't cross without a certain mysterious percentage of blood—unless we're lucky enough to have assistance.

"So, thanks to Salena, we were scattered across the Twelve Kingdoms, fighting her war, and then left to interbreed with and hide ourselves among the mossbacks."

"Mossbacks?"

He turned his head and gave me his twist of a smile. "Non-Tala—because you can't shape-shift."

"Can you shape-shift?" Such a thing had never occurred to me, despite everything.

"No. Not all Tala can."

"Then it's hardly a fair thing to call us," I pointed out.

"You can take it up with the committee."

"Okay, fine. Keep going."

"As for the latitude you speak of, High Priest Kir has long cultivated a belief among Glorianna's chapels and priests that there are demons cloaked like wolves among sheep. Priests who rout them out and send proof of a kill are richly rewarded."

My mouth was dry, my lips cold. "What kind of proof?"

"Blood."

"How does Kir tell Tala blood from another's?"

"Something I also want to know."

"Which is why you insinuated yourself into his company?"

"One reason. But that's not one of the stories you asked for." He waited and I stayed silent so he'd continue. He took in a long breath and tipped his head to look at the sky. "So here's a juicy secret for your arsenal—I killed the priest and retrieved my father's blood."

We walked in silence while I assimilated that. I sent a prayer to Glorianna, expecting a sense of horror and outrage that he'd killed one of her priests, but nothing came. Except a rush of admiration for the lost and wounded thirteen-year-old boy who'd avenged his father.

"Go on," I said. Apparently that was enough for him.

"Of course, I bungled it. I destroyed the blood, but they caught me and sent me to prison. I was not . . . a good prisoner."

Which explained the lashings.

"I was so full of rage. Most days I felt more like a wild animal than a boy or a man. As if some beast was trying to claw its way out of me, shredding my humanity in the process." He shook his head, the cowl moving back and forth. "What the prison guards didn't destroy of my heart, the beast did."

"Because you couldn't . . . change into the beast?"

"Probably. Some think so. My father tried to teach me, before he died. For years. But we had to work in secret because my mother—rightly so, it turned out—feared we'd be discovered. Besides . . ." He paused, gathered himself to admit it. "I never could."

"Andi told me—she said something similar. That my daughter would need to come to Annfwn, to learn her magic, or it could tear her apart. I wonder if that's what she means."

"If you want to learn from my tale, I'd take that advice seriously."

I mulled that over, letting him collect his thoughts, willing the smell of old failure away.

"Fortunately"—his voice held deep irony for the word—"the prison teemed with Tala part-bloods. They taught me how to use my heritage to fight and win. When I hadn't run afoul of the guards—which happened regularly—and thus was recovering from yet another lashing, I built my strength and speed. There wasn't much else to do with ourselves.

"We staged matches, which the guards encouraged, placing bets and pitting us one against the other. I liked winning, so I got better at it. Some of the others taught me how, though the inner beast couldn't come out, I could use it to be even stronger and faster."

He paused and I gathered that some of those lessons had been harsh ones.

"One old Tala man, though, who'd been in the prison and fought in the Great War—he recognized how the magic was killing me from the inside out. He caught me when I was down from a bad beating and couldn't fight him off. He taught me to channel the beast. I couldn't change my own flesh into something else, but I could heal myself to some extent and others even more so. I practiced on the other prisoners—the ones that let me—and learned something of compassion along with it. By then I was twenty-three."

I wanted to touch him then but felt I couldn't. Ten years locked in that prison when he should have been growing up, learning to be a man.

"He was the one who told me the way to Annfwn. And he told me about you." Ash looked over at me then, gaze bright before he looked away. "You were but twelve years old then, younger than I was when I went to that place, and they sang songs about you that made it even into our hellhole."

I flushed, beyond uncomfortable, but he seemed to enjoy my discomfort, because he pressed on.

"You want to understand me, Princess? Imagine a prisoner, beaten, starved, more animal than man, living among other animals, discovering compassion for the first time in my life, finding that maybe I could do more than kill and destroy—and hearing about you."

"You hated me," I whispered, puffing the words into the cold air.

"I hated you," he confirmed. "Living in your white palace with your father the High King, showered in jewels and dresses, favored by Glorianna—Her living avatar, they said—beautiful and perfect with the world at your feet."

"I don't blame you." How many others had felt that way? And I'd never given any of them a thought. Had never known they existed so I could. Living in a crystal bubble, indeed.

"I loved you, too." He spoke it as a confession, not looking at me still. "Obviously not *you*, the person. But the idea of you. I used to dream that I'd escape and track you down. That I'd kidnap you from your pretty palace, throw you over my shoulder, and . . ."

"Ravage me?" I couldn't help the humor in my voice. "And look at you now."

"It isn't funny, Amelia." His voice was tight with self-loathing. "It took me a long time to become a different person than that. That wounded boy—he's gone. Buried under scar tissue. He didn't even know what he really wanted."

"And yet, he found a way to have it." I pointed out, feeling merciless.

"It's not the same."

He'd dug in his heels, but I knew that this lay at the core of his regret. As if his younger self had somehow managed to break free and steal me away, raping me in the wilderness. Though we both knew the truth of how it had gone between us.

"Tell me the rest. Your escape and the scars."

"You assume I escaped?"

"I know there are no pardons."

He was quiet a moment. "How long have you known that?"

I shrugged a little. "It wasn't part of my world, but I suppose I've always known that, on some level. But Marin told me, when she told me what the scars meant."

"The ones on my face?"

"The lash marks. She said the ones on your face are from burns."
I said it matter-of-factly, the only way I could think of to show him
I didn't care about them.

"I see. I escaped because a man I healed was capable of gratitude. He killed three guards to set me free, knowing they'd exe-
cute him for it."

"He gave his life because you saved it? That makes no sense."

"I know. He said that it was the only thing anyone had ever
done for him out of the goodness of their heart and he didn't
want to live long enough to forget the feeling."

"Glorianna save us," I breathed.

"She had nothing to do with it."

I almost argued but decided to wait. Perhaps meditate on the
matter. "After you escaped, then?"

"Prisoners are branded, with an emblem on their chests and
on their cheeks—did you know that part?"

"No." My stomach, which had been behaving so well, turned
over. Farmers branded their animals in springtime in Mohraya,
and sometimes the flower-scented breezes also carried the smell
of burned flesh and the panicked cries of young creatures. "I've
never seen one, I think."

He laughed, soundlessly. "You wouldn't. It's the surest way to
be recaptured and sent to the nearest prison. So the first night I
was free, I cut mine off with a knife I stole from a farmhouse. I
also took an oil lantern, a loaf of bread, and a chunk of cured
jerky." He recited the list as if he were enumerating his sins. I
imagined he repeated them to himself, in the sealed-over recesses
of his mind, those scarred places he claimed no longer capable of
tender feeling.

"I was worried that the placement of the scars would be too
obvious. So I doused them with oil from the lantern and . . ."

"Oh, stop!" I held up a hand, trying to master the image, then
lost it and turned away, puking into the snow. He held me, brac-

ing my forehead with his hand. Not revolted by it. Of course, he'd seen much worse than my sick.

"I'm sorry, Ami," he whispered, gravelly. "I didn't think."

"No." I kicked snow over my puke and grabbed some fresh to rinse my mouth before facing him. "It's not your fault. I'm weak stomached these days and the thought of you . . ." Truly his scars had never bothered me much, I'd been so tortured by what lurked in his pained gaze. But now I couldn't look away. Compelled, I pulled off my glove and reached up to touch the rippling scars. He flinched, then held still, wariness in the air, and then something else. I glimpsed him then, that young man Ash thought had died. He looked at me with such love and longing, I could barely breathe.

His eyes locked with mine, Ash slowly turned his head and pressed his roughened lips against my palm.

A shout in the distance had us both shading our eyes to look out over the glittering snow. Graves and the other soldiers trotted toward us over the meadow, waving and calling out in relieved joy. They were fine—and even had our horses—exactly as Andi had promised.

22

"At last," Ash spoke with pained irony, pulling away, "rescue arrives."

"Thank you for telling me your story."

He regarded me with a twist of a smile, already sealing himself off again. "You're the only one I've ever told."

"I'll keep your secrets."

"Not that it matters. Do as you wish—I don't expect you to protect me."

I put my hand on Ash's cloaked arm. "Nor do I plan to, even if I thought you needed it. But I want you to finish your quest. Graves and the others can see me safely to Windroven."

He looked down at my gloved hand on his arm, still unwilling to see the face, that so troubled him. "What are you saying?"

"I'm telling you to go. Back up the hill and across the border. Your destiny awaits in Annfwn. You deserve the chance to take it."

"Princess Amelia!" Graves called out, clearly having forgotten his earlier cautions. Though it hardly mattered anymore. "Are you all right? Were you harmed in any way?"

"I'm fine, Commander," I said, stepping away from Ash and drawing myself up. "We have been concerned for you."

"It was the damnedest thing." He shook his head and Skunk grimaced in agreement. "We were climbing that path, thinking you were right behind us, and then we seemed to be going downhill. We found ourselves in the next drainage over, with no path behind us and none of you in sight. It's taken all night and most of the day to make our way around."

Sliding off his horse and sinking to one knee, Graves yanked off his helm and bowed his head. "I failed you, Your Highness. As a soldier derelict in his duty, I accept whatever punishment you deem right and just. I only ask that you allow us to try again to reach the border. After that, should you wish to have me executed, I'll at least die knowing I completed my mission."

"You weren't derelict, Commander." I placed my hand on his bent head. "You faced a cunning enemy who simply waged the battle on a different field. Now rise."

I stepped back and nearly trod on Ash's toes, he stood so close behind me. Ignoring him, I said, "Besides, the White Monk and I reached the border."

The air around me stilled, tense and waiting.

"And the mission?" Graves asked, carefully.

I shook my head. "Neither of us could even see where it was. The rumors are true. No one can enter Annfwn. It's as if it fell off the map."

"Sad news, indeed, Your Highness."

"Yes. I propose to leave the White Monk here, to keep an eye on the border in Glorianna's name. He can stay at yon cabin through the winter. My midwife is taking shelter there."

I looked up at Ash over my shoulder, his transparent gaze at last meeting mine. "You'll indulge me in this request, White Monk, yes?"

He wavered, uncertain. That turbulent mix of emotions tumbled around us. I stared him down, willing him to take the opportunity.

"As you wish, Princess." He inclined his head. "Tomorrow I will watch you ride away without me."

I gave him a court smile, full of benevolent pleasure, but a bitter taste of regret lingered in my mouth.

Marin greeted us at the cabin as if we'd only been out for a short pleasure jaunt. Of course she couldn't know all that had transpired, but her unflappability made for a welcome homecoming.

The soldiers cooked a stew and we sat around the fire, exchanging more of our stories. The only deaths had been the horse and soldier who went over the cliff, which only one of the men had witnessed and seemed to remember only vaguely.

That disturbed me, in a forlorn way, but Graves's insistent questions about our experience wouldn't let me dwell on it. Fortunately Ash stepped in to elaborate on my thin story, inventing a convenient cave where we sheltered for the night before trying to find the impassable border once more. He never wavered from my tale, that neither of us could pass through, even when we thought we might have come close to it, for which I was grateful.

Though he carefully avoided looking at me, the bit of silent collusion gave me a cozy sense of companionship with him. Even if we never saw each other again, at least we would forever share these secrets. His and mine, tied together.

Something private for me to hold on to, like my mother's treasure chest. Perhaps I'd sew something out of the silk scraps I'd saved from the night before. A memento.

I meditated on it while I brushed my hair and Ash—and the other soldiers—pretended not to watch. Here in the remote cabin on frozen ground, he didn't fill my senses as he had in Annfwn, but I knew enough of *him* to separate his desire from the idle lust of the others. His had a certain bittersweet flavor to it.

I needed just one more taste—and I had no intention of ever again missing out on something because I hadn't asked for it.

As everyone settled into their blankets for the night, I announced that I needed to answer the call of nature, yet again. Sometimes being with child offers convenient excuses. As I knew he would, Ash ignored the groans of the other soldiers and said he'd go with me, for protection.

The others were happy enough to leave us to it, though Marin gave me the side eye. As with Andi, though, she didn't judge. Of course, she liked Ash. More than she did me, when it came down to it. Somehow the thought didn't sting as much as it once had.

We donned the layers of our cold-weather gear once more and went out into the night.

Above, the same nearly full moon that had shined on us the night before ducked in and out of tattered clouds. Only a few stars pricked the sky, with pale white gleams.

"Why do even the stars look different here?"

Crunching through the snow beside me, Ash shrugged his shoulders. "Why should I know?"

We reached the ring of trees and he pointed to a pile of fallen logs. When Ash led me toward the semiprivate screening, I tipped back the hood of my cloak, letting my hair spill free. A glint from the shadows of his cowl confirmed that my gambit worked. I had his attention. Taking his hand, I tugged him along with me.

"What are you up to, Princess?" He tried to sound stern and genuinely confused, but the way his desire thickened the space between us told me all I needed. He'd lost that calloused membrane of anger that he'd used to wedge us apart, and before he could raise his guard, I slipped inside.

"I'm cold. Can I get under your cloak?" I had already parted the folds and burrowed inside by the time he broke through the shock and tried to refuse me. Then my hand found that hard ridge of his cock that never seemed confused about how it felt, and I had his pants open.

"Ami!" He gasped, a harsh whisper. I stripped off my glove

and wrapped my fingers around his length, hot in contrast to the cold night. He made a strangled sound and then buried his hands in the long fall of my hair. "You can't—oh, Moranu."

Because I'd found him with my mouth. He felt as velvety as I'd imagined and I ran my tongue over his smooth flesh, savoring the sensation. Not sure what to do, for surely his techniques wouldn't work in reverse, we were so differently shaped, I followed instinct, letting his intensifying desire guide me.

It seemed to work, because his fingers tightened with brutal strength in my hair, pulling on my scalp. He caused me pain only when he lost his caution, and this was how I wanted him. Just like this. Harder. Bucking his hips and clinging to me as if he were dying.

With a low growl, he tore himself free of my mouth and pushed me to all fours in the snow. He shoved up my skirts—which I'd changed into with expressly this in mind—and groaned to find me naked beneath. Then reached around to cover my mouth with his hand and plunged into me.

He took me as he had at the end the night before, with ruthless strength and wild abandon. Pressing low over my spine, one hand clamping my hip into place, he pounded into me, hot breath in my ear. Coming at me from behind, the pleasure worked me in a different way, and I bit down on the meaty part of his hand because I couldn't stand not to.

And then I shattered, dissolving under his thrusts, sobbing into the palm of his hand. His body went rigid and he moaned through clenched teeth—so it sounded. Flexing my one bare hand in the snow, I made myself stay awake and alert, enjoying the way he milked himself in and out of me, those last few finishing shudders of his muscles and the way the bitterness of his longing smoothed into sweet satisfaction, if only for a few moments.

"Don't move," he whispered in my ear, and I shivered in delight at the gravelly command, then in earnest as the cold air hit my naked bottom when he pulled away. A tearing sound and then a woolen cloth, scraping my thighs and spread tissues, tenderly wiping away the fluids of our union. He must have done this for me the previous night, before he wrapped me up in the blankets. The thought moved me.

He helped me up and, not looking at me, cleaned himself with a fistful of snow before the cloth, then fastened his pants. "You might do the same," he said, almost as if speaking to himself, "or they might smell it on you."

"Let them."

His hands stilled. "It's a reckless game you play, Princess. Unfortunately I will be the one to pay the forfeit."

Winding up my hair, I tucked it behind my neck and pulled up my hood. "You will be beyond anyone's reach tomorrow. And this was no game for me."

"What is it, then?" His strained voice reached across the gap between us. Nothing of him showed but his cloaked silhouette. But my body still throbbed from his touch and that was enough. It would have to be.

"I wanted more. Something to remember you by."

"You didn't have enough already?" He sounded wry, a hint of bitter flavor in the air.

"Stop that," I snapped, still quiet but with the same demanding force he used. It took him by surprise, the bitterness popping like a soap bubble. "No. I didn't have enough. I'm starting to learn that we maybe never do. That things and people and pleasures can be yanked away from us at any moment, but it's not because we had enough. I wanted you while I could have you.

"Also, I wanted something *here*. Look at the sky, the moon, the stars—even they seem less beautiful. It's not fair that Annfwn keeps all the magic. I understand you regret our time together, but I needed to know that you still wanted me regardless, outside the sway of paradise. We likely will never meet again. I didn't want to leave it the way we did."

"Ami . . ." He trailed off, sounded defeated.

"It's okay. You don't need to explain. I'm all right with this."

In a breath, he closed the space between us, gripping my arms and staring fiercely down into my face from the depth of his hood. "You don't understand," he ground out.

"Then explain," I answered gently. "Tell me, Ash."

"I don't regret knowing you. Being with you, touching your skin, and drowning in that insane passion burning in you—I feel as if I've been immolated."

"Burned to ash?"

"Yes." He laughed soundlessly, under his breath. "That's what happens when you stare into the sun."

"I'm sorry," I whispered.

"No." He was shaking his head, slowly, from side to side, eyes fixed on mine. "Never be sorry for this. I'm not."

"But you said—"

"I lied."

I absorbed that. "Why?"

"Why does anyone lie, Ami? To hide the truth."

"And what is the truth, Ash?"

"I'll give you one. The most important truth. That you own me, body and soul. I'm helpless to resist you. My only freedom will be to stay far, far away."

"Annfwn is far, far away."

"Yes."

"Then go." I'd said it earlier today, but this felt more final. "I have no wish to burn a man alive, much less you. Go, if you have to."

"I think I have to."

"I understand that."

"You're different now," he observed, hands relaxing and flexing on my arms in an almost caress. "I'm not quite sure how to define it."

"Good. I wanted to change. I didn't like who I was."

"I liked you." He searched my face, his longing as quenching as water in my parched mouth. "I always will."

"No matter who I become?"

"You will always be my sun."

"Will you kiss me good-bye?"

Instead of replying, with an urgent gasp of breath, he released my arms, knifed his hands inside my hood, and wound his fingers in my hair. Clasping my skull, he held me tight and plundered my mouth with his. It was less a kiss than a devouring, and I held on to his wrists, though I couldn't have fallen over if I tried. I opened my mouth to him and let him take whatever he felt safe to have of me.

When he let me go and turned away, I didn't mind. I would let him go, too.

It was how things had to be.

My internal voice said so, and I was learning to listen to her.

23

I didn't see Ash again. When I awoke in the morning—because Marin finally shook me, telling me everyone was ready to leave and I could sleep the day away after we reached Windroven— he'd gone hunting to supplement the provisions we'd leave in the cabin for him. Or so Graves said.

Instead I pictured him hiking up the long trail and knocking on the door Andi had promised would be opened for him. The image made me happy, so I kept it in my mind and embroidered it as we rode through the stark Wild Lands. Finally I made myself finish it and tuck it away in my mental treasure chest, alongside the sweet memories of Hugh. My touchstones of happiness. My forget-me-nots. Short-lived and hard won.

And all the more precious for it.

The trip back seemed uneventful, even boring, compared to the way in. Graves—mainly due to Skunk's excellent scouting skills—deftly avoided the patrols from Ordnung. There were fewer than the men expected, in fact, as if Uorsin's forces were engaged elsewhere. Once we finished our long circuit around the castle itself and made our way to the high road, it became clear that tensions had only risen during our short time away.

Various squads and patrols passed us with alarming frequency, and we were all glad of the decision to disguise me further, as I surely would have been recognized and Uorsin would discover I'd not returned to Avonlidgh, as I'd been told to do. Marin found me a plain gown, apron, and kerchief to wear over my signature hair, tightly braided away and smudged with dirt. Introduced as the midwife's apprentice to the inquiring patrols, I kept my eyes cast down and earned no more than a few leers and usually a complete lack of interest.

I discovered an unexpected freedom then, in being someone and somewhere no one thought I would be. It seemed that even the sun can be ignored, lacking the proper setting and legendary status.

You will always be my sun.

It helped, knowing I would burn in Ash's heart that way, tucked away in his memory box, also. I liked it, too, being this girl who wasn't worth much notice. The kind of girl who might have heard songs of me and who I would never have known existed. It felt like another step toward being someone I liked better.

As if our positions had indeed reversed, Marin had thawed toward me and resumed her motherly care. We spent more time together, the only two women in this group of military men who preferred one another's company. Enough so that I finally screwed up my courage to ask what had happened to her in Glorianna's temple.

She didn't answer at first, and I thought she wasn't going to. Staring between her stolid mare's ears, she fell into thought.

"It's over and done with. I know you didn't intend it. No need to dwell," she finally said.

"But there *is* a need," I insisted, keeping my tone apprentice humble. "I'm expected to assume a role in that . . . system. Taking a person and keeping her hostage a day and a night hardly seems something Glorianna would condone."

Marin laughed, a short, impatient laugh that reminded me of

Ash. "Think you that Glorianna and Her temple are one and the same?"

I always had thought so, but it seemed that had been one of my many naïve ideas.

"What the goddess intends and what mortals do with Her representation on our earth are two different things. Being part of Glorianna's temple is not about the goddess for all who claim to serve Her."

I mulled that over. "What is it about, then?"

Her fingers twitched and I knew she missed her knitting. "The High King, praise his name, has invested Glorianna's temple with a great deal of power. There are those drawn to that. If you wish to make changes, look for those who most benefit from access to that power."

She wouldn't say more and, really, she didn't need to. I'd been blind not to see it before, how Kir sought to control me and solidify his power in the temple. He'd removed Marin not to cleanse her soul but to eliminate her from influencing me. Taking me for the fool I'd assuredly been, he'd manipulated me, quite successfully.

At some point in my journey, my eyes had opened and I saw the world more clearly. Perhaps my crystal bubble had shattered.

Best of all, Marin had relented and was teaching me to knit. While the men played their games of chance at the inn tables in the evening, Marin taught me how to judge yarn and the simple stitches that looped together, row after row, each one adding to the next so they made something greater than themselves. Though my work looked pitifully askew, it meant more than I expected to be able to make a thing. To take bits of fleece and turn them into something useful.

Seeing us, other women would bring their knitting, too. Sometimes they traded yarn, telling tales of the flowers they'd gathered to dye it, or taught each other new stitches. Only a girl to them, perhaps a silly one, to be just learning what their daughters had been doing since they could grasp the needles, I disappeared into their conversations.

They knew far more than my ladies had, with their idle chatter about the court dalliances and prettiest gowns. Or perhaps that had been my influence and the ladies had kept to topics that pleased me. But around Ami, the midwife's apprentice, the common women spoke with insight and intelligence about the undercurrents in the Twelve Kingdoms. They, some of them who'd fought alongside their men in the Great War, worried for their sons and daughters.

It seemed that the High King—spoken of with more fear than reverence—had called in all of Mohraya's trained soldiers and, worse, had taken a tithe of all apprentices from every practice, from the strength-focused blacksmiths and glassblowers down to the softest arts.

Duranor had sent its due to Ordnung, but no more, not even when word of the additional tithe went out. Avonlidgh and Elcinea hadn't sent even that much, if the tales could be believed, and the remaining kingdoms were rumored to be cutting off trade and recruiting heavily from their own populations. Information, however, grew thin with the passing days. The High King had proclaimed that, to ensure peace of mind for all citizens, all court minstrels should stick to "happy" songs, and the traveling minstrels should find a sponsor, stay in one place, and do likewise.

Several seemed to have gone missing.

Rumors were, there would be more tithing to come. The worst stories spoke of press-gangs sweeping through outlying villages and taking all the able-bodied young people unfortunate enough to be out and about.

"Best watch out for yon missy, there." One of the women angled her chin at me while she advised Marin. "She's weak and clearly no fighter, but that doesn't seem to matter to the recruiters. They want warm bodies, they do, and none cares so much how long they'll be able to keep themselves alive."

The tales became more lively once we crossed into Avonlidgh.

For the first time on the journey—one that took much longer without Ursula's charging-bull style of travel and without the right-of-way royalty commands—a minstrel played in the inn's common room. No one in our party commented on it, though Graves and his men knew about the High King's edict as well as I did. Never had it been more clear to me that their loyalty belonged utterly to King Erich.

"I don't care for the way times are changing," an older woman clucked over her knitting, her foreboding an odd contrast to the silly nonsense reel the minstrel sang. He kept to that part of the new law, at least.

"We can't afford to give more to Uorsin's vendetta against the Tala," another agreed. "All of my neighbors along the High Road? Burned out—and by Uorsin's troops, too. He cares naught for Avonlidgh."

"Never has." Another nodded along, needles clacking with her anger. "We pay our taxes and tithes, and what do we get? The hope of Avonlidgh, slaughtered in the midst of nowhere."

Several paused and drew Glorianna's circles, murmuring a prayer for Hugh. The moment made my heart burn in my chest with all those tears I still hadn't shed. At this point, it seemed I never would. Hugh's people remembered him fondly, and I clung to that solace.

"There's the Princess, though—and the heir," one mused.

The first one paused in her knitting to take a draught of wine. "*That* one. She's her father's creature—mark my words."

"I hear she's still at Ordnung and will hand over Hugh's babe to the High King. Avonlidgh has lost all. She'd never have the spine to defy him."

"Even if she did, she never loved Avonlidgh. Did you ever hear of her learning anything of us, visiting any other place but Windroven?"

"The poor thing was still on her honeymoon."

"Ach, she's naught but a pretty face. If only Prince Hugh had kept his head and married the eldest as he ought to—none of this would have happened. Mark my words."

"King Rayfe would never have shown up to demand his due?" a middle-aged pregnant woman scoffed. "I'm not so old as you and even I understand that was part of Salena's price for handing us over to Uorsin."

"I can't speak to that, but I do know that Princess Ursula is the best of those two. *She* wouldn't have pranced about Windroven having picnics while her people suffered. At the least she would have been out fighting, shoulder to shoulder."

"I hear Princess Amelia isn't at Ordnung, but returned to Castle Avonlidgh with Old Erich."

"Old Erich," cackled another woman. "He's a clever fox. Perhaps he'll keep yon pretty princess under lock and key until he extracts the babe."

"After that, it hardly matters what happens to Hugh's fancy piece of ass. She's worth nothing to us."

"Erich has a way of dealing with those who aren't useful. He's not so old he's lost his mean edge."

"I almost feel sorry for the Princess," the pregnant woman said. "Surely she has no idea the danger she's in."

The old woman snorted and quaffed her wine. "I wouldn't waste your sympathy on her. She'd have none for you. She doesn't even know we exist."

"Besides, she'll have enough troubles just birthing that child, if you take my meaning."

They all nodded wisely, and questions burned in my throat. What did they understand that I didn't?

"Didn't you say you're a midwife?" The pregnant woman eyed Marin. "What say you about the Princess's babe?"

"What's to say?" Marin huffed, eyes on her knitting. "She's a woman as any other. Women grow and birth babes all the time, bless Glorianna."

The old woman, who I'd decided I greatly disliked, even if she wouldn't have said any of this to my face, barked out a laugh, then wiped wine spittle from her chin. "Nooo, she ain't! She's no human woman. She's half-animal, half-demon like her sister. No matter which kingdom wrestles the babe from her womb, the child will be no one's heir. It's an abomination against Glorianna and we'll be lucky if it doesn't pop out of her cursed cunt with horns and covered in fur!"

As happens in crowds, it seems, her vile words reached a peak right as the minstrel finished his tune and the background conversation lulled.

"Barbara!" one of her cronies hissed. "You mind your mouth. There are strangers among us and impressionable young ears. Perhaps you should take your apprentice away, midwife?"

"She's heard worse," Marin replied mildly, unconcerned as ever.

"Bah!" The garrulous woman poured more wine from the pitcher. "And if yon young missy is too missish"—and here she snorted wetly at her own joke—"to hear the truth, then she can retire to her lonely bed. What say you, missy? Are you a virgin yet, or have you enjoyed what a great, strong cock can do for you?"

My face heated and they all laughed, happy to have a diversion, and began teasing me about how long my young man could last and if my jaw grew sore or his did. I almost wished Marin would have taken the chance to spirit me out of there, but I also understood that this was one of her ongoing lessons—mixed, perhaps, with a bit of payback for what I'd put her through with Kir. I let my blushes speak for me and kept the lid on my box of memories tightly closed.

They were for me, and me alone. At least I understood the jokes now.

"You ladies seem to be having a fine evening," a lovely tenor voice flowed over us. The minstrel stood there with his lap harp, smiling in a charming way. "Can I add to your frivolity with a bit of song?"

His gaze passed over us, then returned to me, lingering. Hastily I frowned at my knitting, resisting the urge to press the furrows away. Marin had pointed out that I looked less like the paintings of me when I scowled, so I tried to do that if anyone gazed too long. And fervently hoped the lines wouldn't truly linger as my nurse had so often warned.

"Yes, boy." The old woman's eyes seemed glued to his trousers. "Sing to us of the Great War. 'The Wolf Song.' "

He grinned easily. "And lose my head to the High King's executioner? You'd have to tip me well indeed, my lady."

She hmphed in irritation. "I know well the innkeeper is paying your wage. I have no intention of lining your greedy pockets, too."

"Forgive my lack of enthusiasm, then," he returned with such smooth courtesy that she only grunted.

"I'll have a tune." Marin rummaged in her pocket for a coin. "Sing us one about the Princess, our future queen."

Several others, including the pregnant one, agreed with enthusiasm. As if they thought to make up for their uncharitable conversation with renewed patriotism.

"That I can do," he agreed. "The High King famously dotes upon his youngest, you know." He sat, straddling a stool, and set the keys on his harp. "I saw her once, on a visit to the court at Ordnung."

Glorianna save me. Why in the Twelve Kingdoms had Marin encouraged him to stay? Surely he'd recognize me.

"Did you?" One lady who'd been quiet so far perked up. "Surely the tales exaggerate—she can't be as lovely as they claim. All that nonsense about sunrises and birdsong."

"Oh, but she is." He grinned and winked at her. The man seemed to have his smile honed into a fine art—or a deadly weapon—he wielded it with such skill. "Of course, she doesn't look like light or sound like a bird, but there's something about her that makes one think of those things. Something ethereal . . . and unmistakable."

I felt his gaze on me again and wished I'd been able to knit something larger than a hankie to hide behind. A kind of crooked one at that. It was supposed to become a baby blanket, so Marin assured me was possible, but I imagined he'd be on the High King's throne before I managed to put that many rows together.

"More"—he plucked a few chords—"she has a loving heart. It shows in her words and deeds. Always a smile for those who serve her and a kind word for the least around her."

Marin snorted and rubbed her nose. I wanted to kick her. It was her fault we were subjected to this.

"It seemed every man—and more than a few women—fell a little bit in love with her. Not only for the alabaster curve of her cheek, or the violet glory of her eyes, but for the way she embodies love. As with Glorianna herself."

"No one has violet eyes," one woman protested. "They're just blue."

"Not so, my fine lady"—he played softly, a harmony I didn't recognize—"they're true violet, like a pansy. I'd know them anywhere.

I kept my violet eyes locked on my knitting. Impossible that he could see the color in the dim tavern. No one had commented on them in ages.

Fortunately, he launched into the song.

> *Look not for the maid of roses,*
> *She of the violet and cream.*
> *Dusted away are her sunrises,*
> *Gold burned into gleam.*
>
> *Turn around and see.*
> *Turn around and look for yourself.*
> *Gone is the girl of your youth.*
> *Gone away into the sea.*
>
> *Where have you gone, my lovely one?*
> *What made you leave us behind?*

Sunrises fall into sunsets
True love is buried in snow.

Turn around and see.
Turn around and look for yourself.
Gone is the maiden of roses.
Swallowed up into the sea.

The final haunting notes faded away and I became aware that I'd stopped knitting and the point of one needle pressed painfully into my palm. My ears rang with a sense of foreboding, a wordless warning.

"I've never heard that song before," the old lady grumped.

"It's new," he answered easily.

"What does that mean, that she's gone?" The pregnant lady sounded unhappy. "Are you saying she's dead? Drowned? Surely we would have heard."

"It's a metaphor, Suze," another answered. "It means she's no longer a maid because she's becoming a mother. Maiden, mother, crone. That's the succession of a woman's life."

The older woman had fallen into a drunken sleep, chin propped on her ample bosom and knitting forgotten in her lap. They all looked at her and away again.

"Who wants to become the crone?" one whispered, and they all fell into a fit of giggles.

"The crone is also the wise woman," Marin asserted. "She who's gained the knowledge of experience and has honed her skills in the world."

"Certainly a finer way to look at it," the minstrel agreed, standing. "I shall bid you ladies good evening."

24

In the morning, as we saddled up, the minstrel appeared again, leading his horse and giving me a saucy wink I caught even with my eyes averted. His dark hair shone with red glints in the sun and his eyes seemed to be an unusually sharp silvery blue.

"What is he doing here?" I hissed under my breath at Marin. She managed to shrug while looking as if she only struggled to stuff something into her saddlebag. Graves hailed the minstrel, clapping his shoulder.

"This is Wyle. Likely you all heard him in the tavern last night. He's offered to entertain us on the way to Castle Avonlidgh in exchange for protection from the various wild animals along the way," Graves announced. He made a wry face, making it clear that they, too, had heard the tales of the Mohrayan press-gangs.

I gritted my teeth against the urge to protest. And to question our direction. We were meant to be bound for Windroven. As we traveled, I fretted over it. The gossip had been only that—idle talk and tale spinning. But I had been alone in that carriage with Erich, felt his lecherous grip on my thigh, and knew quite well what went on in the unclean crevices of his mind. I hadn't been practiced enough then to interpret what I sensed, but now I knew how to label that scent.

The ladies knew how these things went. To control the babe, Erich needed to control me. I would never make it to Windroven. It occurred to me, as I retraced the conversations in my mind, that he'd always said I'd return to Avonlidgh. I had assumed Windroven, not Castle Avonlidgh, his seat.

A very foolish assumption.

At first opportunity, I rode up next to Skunk. Wyle and Graves seemed to be great buddies already, laughing and joking with each other. Graves didn't much care to talk with me, and besides, a girl of my apparent station wouldn't approach him anyway. In this kind of circumstance, my disguise grated on me and provided no succor or amusement. What I wanted most was to command that we go straight to Windroven.

And for Graves to knock that nosy minstrel over the head and leave him in the borrow ditch.

"Why did Graves say we're bound for Castle Avonlidgh?" I asked Skunk casually, so anyone eavesdropping would think we discussed the weather.

Skunk's shoulders slumped a little. "Commander said you wouldn't be happy. King's orders. We're to report in."

"Castle Avonlidgh is nearly on the Duranor border." I said it mainly so they'd understand I wasn't completely ignorant. "It's not exactly on the way. And with everything going on . . ."

"I know." Skunk dropped his voice. "But I have no more power than you do. Graves is fixed on this."

His words hit home with a prickle up my spine. I'd become so accustomed to my new persona that I'd nearly forgotten that they all served me. Not the reverse. It was one thing to learn humility—and I had—it was entirely another to give up my power. *My* power and might, that came from me.

That came from people knowing who I was.

Accident of birth or not, that was mine. Another weapon I needed to learn to wield.

I laid the seeds at lunchtime, pretending that I wasn't hungry and pleading fatigue. When we resumed riding in the midafternoon, I watched the signs for a good-sized town, preferably one I recognized. Graves preferred to stop at the roadside inns, where we'd blend with other travelers more easily. As if in answer to a prayer, the sign, when I spotted it, was perfect.

When we were barely short of Lianore, serendipitously the home of one of my ladies, Giseleigh, and thus the seat of one of Avonlidgh's nobles, I began clutching my stomach and groaning.

Graves called a halt and Marin tended to me with several teas, eyes narrowed. The men, naturally, gave us plenty of room, so when she asked me what game I was up to—good thing I didn't have to fool her—no one overheard us.

"Do we have much coin?" I asked her.

"*We* meaning, do *I*?" she returned archly. "For, to be sure, Graves was entrusted with the funds to convey you safely about."

Daughter of the High King, Princess of the Realm, future Queen of Avonlidgh, and not a penny in my pocket. Richly ironic. And ridiculously careless of me. Holding my belly and whispering prayers of protection to Glorianna for the babe, lest she take me seriously and truly put the child in danger, I told Marin my plan.

"I'll help you, Princess." She pretended to feel my forehead. "To be sure and it will be good to have you in your rightful place. You have rank and duty to uphold, and your people deserve to see you for yourself as you pass among them."

"I understand that's what you wanted me to see, but . . . Marin, they hate me." I felt a little broken and pitiful about that. All this time I'd thought I was so loved and really no one cared for me. Except in unexpected places.

"They don't know you," Marin returned. "And you're going to fix that."

She rose and went to Graves, gesturing to me. He frowned, shaking his head as he had at the pass. Stubborn man. I groaned and drew up my knees, trying to look pale and miserable. Finally he came over and knelt beside me.

"The midwife wants to take you to the Lianore manse," he said, "but I feel this is unwise. Can you make it to the inn?"

"Maybe." I tried to look brave. "Hopefully I won't lose the babe if I try."

He looked as stricken as I'd hoped. "What of the minstrel? He'd never believe we'd deviate for a lowly maid."

I nearly broke character, wanting to smack him for his blindness. For a smart and stalwart soldier, he had some remarkably narrow views. "He knows perfectly well who I am. He recognized me at the inn last night, which is, no doubt, why he weaseled his way into your company. Take me to Lianore manse so Marin can get the supplies she needs to ensure my health and that of your next king."

I thought I'd maybe laid it on a little thick, but Graves, if nothing else, was a trained soldier, and he responded viscerally to the sting of command in my voice. In fact, he nearly saluted me, barely stopping himself.

In no time, Skunk had been sent to the manse, returning with a carriage for Marin and her "sick apprentice." Lady Giseleigh, Gilly to her friends, had often spoken of her mother Lady Lianore's soft heart. Glorianna surely smiled on my plan, opening a rose-petal-strewn path to this opportunity.

Though they took me to the servants' quarters when we arrived, I was given a private room, which was exceptionally large and well furnished. I made a mental note to review Windroven's facilities. I should do no less for my people than Lady Lianore did.

As I'd hoped, the lady herself paid me a visit. And, though I wouldn't have been able to pick her out of a crowd, she drew up short the moment she entered the room, gaping at me.

"Good Glorianna," she breathed. "You're not . . ."

Pulling off the kerchief, I gave up the appearance of illness and stood, taking Lady Lianore's hands. "Your reputation for giving succor to the least of Glorianna's daughters precedes you,

Duchess Lianore. I depended upon it, as I've been traveling incognito."

She clutched my hands, her skin cool with shock. "Princess! I mean, Your Highness, I—" Abruptly she tried to kneel, but I stopped her.

"I think we're past the formalities, Lady Lianore. Gilly has been a great friend to me and I fear I must ask you to be, also. Will you help me?"

"Anything!" she gasped. "Lianore is so honored by your presence. We are so small and out of the way, that—oh, the people would so love to have met you. I hate that we haven't properly received you."

"I have been on a long, strange journey, seeking to preserve the future of Avonlidgh and the rights of Hugh's child."

"Then it's true." She squeezed my hands. "I told everyone you would be loyal to Avonlidgh. Do you travel to Windroven, to have the babe there, as is the tradition?"

"I do. I vow to have Hugh's heir at Windroven." I decided to take the risk. "But some, among them soldiers in my retinue, seek to stop me. They intend for me to go to Castle Avonlidgh instead."

Her snapping brown eyes took on sharp indignation at that. "Canny Old Erich. I should not be surprised."

"I believe that the people of Avonlidgh will support me in my quest to go to Windroven—and stay there."

"Yes, they will." She drew herself up with pride. "I speak for Lianore and we support you. What can we do?"

❀ ❀ ❀

Ursula would likely have laughed at me, but sometimes a pretty new gown and a ball *are* the solution.

Lady Lianore—Veronica, she asked me to call her, though she refused to call me by my name—arranged for a bath, cosmetics, and her seamstress to alter a dress intended for Gilly. She even loaned me her own jewels, proclaiming that the people would expect no less.

Though we'd arrived in late afternoon, by the supper hour not only had Veronica dispatched a messenger to Castle Avonlidgh, where it turned out my entire retinue had been diverted, but she'd also arranged a grand feast and invited the pillars of the local community to attend.

Marin reported that Graves didn't like it but had been mollified by assurances that I enjoyed a deep and drugged sleep and that Lady Lianore had planned this entertainment for ages. Her valiantly loyal staff backed her tale seamlessly, and none had an inkling of the courier sent to Castle Avonlidgh.

So far as Erich would believe, I'd thrown a very typical tantrum and insisted on having *all* of my ladies about me for the journey to his side. By the time he knew different, I planned to be safely inside the walls of Windroven, which even Rayfe and all the might of the Tala had been unable to breach.

Hopefully Erich would recognize that and not put me and the strength of Windroven to the test. But if he did, I fully intended to lock him out until the babe was born. After that . . . well, I had months to come up with a plan.

First steps first.

My grand entrance went perfectly. After all the guests were seated, rumors buzzing about a delightful mystery guest, I stepped into the room, pausing in the scrolled doorway, flanked by flaming sconces.

I'd left my hair down. Newly clean and shining, it spilled in brilliant contrast to the pearly white gown. Diamonds sparkled at my ears, throat, and wrists. The cosmetics applied by Veronica's lady emphasized the violet in my eyes—I intended to layer on proof of who I was—and the court minstrels played one of the most famous of "my" songs.

Gratifyingly, the assembly gasped, their admiration and wonder flowing over me like the scent of jasmine on a summer night. Seated with the Lianore minstrels, Wyle tipped a wry salute at me, and Graves, face as red as an overheated teakettle, glowered at me from the soldiers' tables.

He and I would speak later, and he—and all his men—could make their choices then.

Lady Lianore introduced me, as if it were necessary, and the meal was delayed as each guest insisted on paying fealty, creating a line that lasted quite some time. Even Graves came up with Lianore's officers, his ire banked with ruthless discipline, as he bowed over my hand.

"You appear to be feeling much better, Your Highness," he said, with pointed courtesy.

"Yes, indeed." I smiled, ever the gracious monarch. "It seems Lianore manse was exactly the thing to restore me to myself."

He laughed, despite himself, and shook his head. "Well played, Your Highness. Well played, indeed."

🌹 🌹 🌹

The following morning, I summoned Graves and his men to my rooms. During the feast, Marin and Veronica's amazingly efficient housekeeper had arranged to move me and my meager belongings to the best suite. The master suite, in fact, as Veronica confided—when I objected—that she hadn't been able to bear to sleep in there since Lord Lianore died several years ago of an illness. They'd been married more than thirty years and she'd never been able to get over reaching for him during the night in the bed they'd shared.

Instead she kept it for special visitors, and she seemed genuinely delighted that she'd be able to say the Queen of Avonlidgh had slept there. She even planned to rename the suite for me, something I decided to simply not argue with.

It struck me, particularly when she took my hand and expressed her deep sympathy over Hugh's death, saying that she knew something of how it felt, that our marriages had been totally different—and thus our losses were, too. I'd loved Hugh with a fervent and innocent ferocity. A love I knew he returned. But we'd been so young and had so little time together. Already I felt older, changed in ways Hugh wouldn't have recognized. How would the years have treated us? Would we have grown closer and steadier, as Veronica and her husband had, or would we have grown bitter, sleeping in separate rooms, like my own parents?

Whoever had made that situation—my mother or my father, or the two of them mixing together—I had them both in me. I supposed it didn't matter, since fate had taken such an unexpected turn, setting my feet on this path that had already changed me from that sweet bride full of blushes and shyness. But I reflected on it while I waited for the soldiers.

Graves led the way into the sitting room, which was flooded with morning light. I sat strategically in the pool of it, wearing a gorgeous pink gown the seamstress must have stayed up all night to make for me. Roses of the exact same shade had been sent over from the local chapel of Glorianna, and they sat on a little table next to me. Graves had seen me dressed to the hilt the night before, but the other men hadn't, and they drew up short, hovering by the doorway, taking in my elaborately styled hair and regal demeanor.

Realizing who they dealt with now.

A pretty dress is far from important, but I'd been different women in the last weeks—the grieving widow, the miserably sick pregnant mother, the traveler through the winter mountains, the midwife's apprentice, even the naked and carefree lover in paradise—and it had become clear to me that these things mattered. Not that I couldn't be the future Queen of Avonlidh dressed in a plain dress and dingy apron, but working my presentation saved trouble.

The Lianoran guards retired to wait outside the room, closing the door behind them. Graves bowed, and the others, after wide-eyed awkwardness, followed suit. I let them all stew a little, remember how casually they'd come to treat me, the little apprentice midwife in their midst, and I drew out the silence so they'd understand well who had the power here.

Not them. Not Graves.

Me.

Finally, when all but Graves—who retained his granite stoicism—looked thoroughly unsettled, I spoke.

"I wish to express my gratitude to you all, for your excellent service in conveying me on our mission and safely home again. I've arranged with Lady Lianore for you all to receive a bonus from me, as an expression of my appreciation, and of Avonlidgh's."

As I expected, they all brightened at that. A treat instead of chastisement—always a pleasant surprise. Typically, however, Graves frowned. "While your generosity is most appreciated, Your Highness, we expected King Erich to complete the . . . payment for our efforts."

I plucked a rose from the vase, to hide my smile, and toyed with it. He thought to remind me who paid his bills. As if I'd forgotten.

"As to that, Commander, gentlemen, you have a choice to make. I am bound for Windroven. I would enjoy your continued companionship and protection en route. In return, I offer you the opportunity to become part of my elite personal guard. You all have demonstrated loyalty and bravery in the face of a variety of dangers. I would see that you were rewarded commensurate with your new status."

They gaped at me, with varying degrees of hope, confusion, and—in the case of Graves—outrage.

"You ask me to betray my charge?" Graves demanded, forgetting again who he spoke to. "I cannot be bought. Nor can my men!"

Judging by the consternation on their faces, some of them would argue with that.

I twirled the rose in my fingers, tilting my head and giving him a sweet smile worthy of Glorianna at Her most beneficent. "That's your prerogative. However, I feel I should remind you that *I* will be Queen of Avonlidgh, possibly sooner rather than later if Erich attempts to take my child. Oh, yes"—I nodded at their shock—"this shall be a frank conversation. I'm well aware of Erich's reasons for insisting you bring me to Castle Avonlidgh. I believe you may have heard the adage that no animal is more dangerous than a mother in defense of her cub. It seems to be true. I'm feeling particularly ruthless.

"I *will* go to Windroven. If you choose not to come with me, Lady Lianore invites you to enjoy her extended hospitality, though you might find the accommodations a bit severe." I gestured at the Lianoran guards in the hall. "Only until the current conflict is over, as I can't afford to have you running about telling tales."

"It seems we have no choice but to serve you or become prisoners," Graves gritted out.

I breathed in the perfect scent of the rose. "Well, there's always immediate execution, should you attempt to actively thwart my plans."

"If you have us executed, Erich will demand justice."

I shrugged a little. "He can demand all he likes. I don't answer to him."

Considering, Graves took in the guards, assessing them and his chances. The other men looked uncertain. Skunk even chewed his lip in anxiety over the outcome. They carried no weapons, but I knew well enough that they would not be easily defeated, even so.

"Tell me something, Lieutenant Graves"—I said it softly, waiting for him to meet my gaze—"when you realized our traveling companion was an escaped convict, why did you say nothing about it?"

Skunk looked guilty and two of the other men exchanged looks. Graves clenched his jaw, then relaxed it and shook his head, laughing softly. "I've seen some strange things these last weeks. You'd think I'd have learned not to take anything at face value." He squared his shoulders and folded his hands behind his back, a soldier facing review by a superior. "I figured a sheltered noble like you would never know what those scars meant. So I judged us safe in keeping it from you."

"And your duty to the laws of the Crown?"

He inclined his head. "You have me there, Your Highness. I chose not to report the man to the authorities. It was a personal decision."

"One that we supported." Skunk spoke for the first time, and the others nodded in agreement.

"Why?"

"Since we're being frank, Princess Amelia?" Graves's lips twitched with wry amusement. "The prisons are torture chambers. Men are incarcerated for the slightest reasons—often due to petty vendettas of corrupt officials—and then starved, beaten, used for slave labor, and worse. With no hope of redemption. A man like the Wh—our friend, who managed to escape and not only hide himself in plain sight, but thrive there? He deserved my admiration, not my betrayal."

I nodded, mostly to myself, pleased that it fell along the lines I'd thought through. "And I?" I asked him pointedly, with arched eyebrows.

"Each of the men must decide for themselves." Graves blew out a breath, making the decision, and knelt on one knee. "Glorianna forgive me for foreswearing my vow to King Erich, but I choose you, Princess Amelia, future queen and mother of my future king. I will take you to Windroven and defend you with my life."

Skunk immediately followed suit, echoing the words, but with a grin of sincerity. The others all agreed, also, but I made note of their level of enthusiasm. Two I decided to leave with Lady Lianore for "further arms training." I couldn't afford to make any mistakes.

My revolution had well and truly begun.

25

Like sieges, if done properly, revolutions are quite dull.
In some ways, I appeared to be no different than the pretty
Princess Amelia who'd thrown parties and dances at Windroven—only now I did them for the benefit of the people of Lianore
and the surrounding countryside. A great deal depended on King
Erich believing I had simply tired of not having a social life or my
proper attendants.

We put it about that I awaited the arrival of my retinue, because I simply refused to journey another moment without them.
Erich should believe all was well and that I meekly planned to
travel to Castle Avonlidgh. I even commissioned a gown for a ball
he meant to hold in my honor, as a letter from him indicated, in
terms alternating between impatient command and insincere flattery.

He looked forward to my *particular news* he wrote—or rather
his scribe did, as I had no doubt Erich did not possess such fine
handwriting—and to me sitting at his side for the glory of Avonlidgh. It made my skin crawl, and after a bit of internal debate, I
decided to show it to Veronica.

Her face confirmed my instincts, both in having her read it

and that his intentions toward me were not noble. She'd been loyal to my cause from the first moment—thank Glorianna for guiding me to Lianore—but now she turned fierce with it.

At every possible moment we entertained, providing daytime festivals for the commonfolk and rich evening festivities for the more select. Midwinter was dark and cold, with little to do for distraction. People turned out in droves to make merry. To ensure that everyone could enjoy a carefree time with their visiting future queen, Lady Lianore recruited extra troops so people would not fear the rumored robbers and press-gangs.

In truth, she was assembling an army for me.

Finally, to much trumpeting and tossing of forced daffodils, my entourage arrived. I received my ladies privately, and they embraced me with genuine affection. They cooed over my stomach, barely showing still, but emphasized by my clinging gown, as Veronica had wisely ascertained that my people would be moved to see evidence—and proof—that Avonlidgh's royal line would continue through me.

Because I'd asked her to, Dafne accompanied them, though she hung back, reserved. I could hardly blame her, as badly as I'd treated her.

Soon I dismissed Gilly to visit with her mother and the other ladies to rest and refresh themselves for the evening's welcome ball. Tonight would appear to be all about silly frivolity. With any luck, we'd be gone before Erich's people awoke from their hangovers. Hopefully my ladies truly would avail themselves of a nap this afternoon, because we'd be traveling all night.

"Dafne," I said, as soon as we were alone, "please tell me you brought my mother's trunk and didn't leave it at Castle Avonlidgh."

I hadn't been able to think of a way to get that message to her. Too many ways that it could be discovered and my simple plan shattered. If I had to, I'd sacrifice the trunk—and the doll—and make my way without them.

But Dafne smiled, as pleased with herself as if she'd gambled and won. "I did bring it. I thought sure you'd want it at Win-droven. Once we hole up there, it will be difficult to get anything out of King Erich."

I laughed. "I hope you're just very clever and no one else has so easily seen through me."

She cocked her head at me. "I didn't see through you so much as I know you're a much smarter woman than most give you credit for. The babe must be born at Windroven—and out of reach of both kings. For us, for Avonlidgh, and for the good of all the kingdoms—including the thirteenth."

"I hope that's true."

"I have something for you." Dafne pulled a small package out of her pocket and gave it to me.

Peeling off the decorative paper, I found a thin glass inside, bound with bright copper at the edges. Inside the glass—no, pressed between two pieces—was the dried rose I'd taken from Hugh's tomb. Tears pricked my eyes, and it seemed they might actually fall. Though I felt less choked by the knot that kept everything in, I still didn't weep. But I pressed the glass to my bosom, moved beyond words.

"You're welcome," Dafne said softly, without sarcasm. As if she understood what I hadn't said.

"I haven't been kind to you, and yet, you do this for me. Why?"

Dafne cocked her head a little, her cinnamon hair brushing her shoulders. "Because I thought it would please you. It seemed to be the right thing—that you should have some treasures to put in your own keepsake chest, for your daughter to look at someday and remember you by."

"You think the babe is a girl, too."

Dafne lifted one shoulder and let it fall. "Andi thinks so and that's enough for me."

"Can you keep a secret?"

"Aren't I already?"

True. "I saw Andi and talked with her."

Dafne's fine eyebrows arched with interest, and she tucked her hands in her skirt pockets. "Does that mean you've been in Annfwn?"

I looked around, though we were as private as before. "Yes. But barely inside. Please never tell anyone. Erich sent me to see if I could cross and take someone with me."

"He plans to invade." Dafne's tone was flat. "I suspected as much."

"It's like a mirror to people without the ability to cross. I lied and said I couldn't do it, that I wasn't even sure where it was."

"Did you?" Dafne grinned at me. "Look at you, Princess Amelia. I'm impressed."

"I'm still not certain why I did. Also, I was able to take someone with me."

Her eyes shone at that. A sweet scent of her longing tinged the air, fading roses at the end of summer. "Will that person keep your secret?"

"I believe so. It was Kir's assistant priest, the White Monk. I don't know if you met him."

"Ah, yes. We had some interesting conversations."

A little pang of envy hit me at that. Of course Ash would have liked talking to Dafne. He undoubtedly appreciated her contemplative nature and deep thoughts.

"Well, anyway, he stayed there, so we won't be seeing him again."

"Ah." Dafne nodded, the scent of longing winding between us. "Good for him."

"I should have given you the opportunity to come also." I spoke the words in a rush. "It was thoughtless of me not to. I didn't understand how badly you wanted to go there."

She regarded me with some surprise, her clever mind working. I realized she'd never said she wanted to go and that she calculated I must know some other way.

"Did you . . . discover new abilities in Annfwn, Princess?" she asked me in a very soft way, making it clear that she knew she crossed a line by prying.

I debated not answering. But I also thought someone else should know, for my daughter's sake. Marin wouldn't understand. Ash had judged her right in that. She wouldn't have liked to see him work magic.

"Not me." I laid a hand over my belly, rounder and curiously solid. "Andi said my daughter can sense emotions, and, while I carry her, I share the gift."

"I see."

"There's something else, Lady Dafne. Something I need you to know."

She nodded solemnly, pulling her hands from her pockets and folding them in front of her, as if in prayer.

"Andi said that . . . if anything goes amiss, my daughter may need to be taken to Annfwn. For her health and safety. I haven't decided what—if anything—I will or won't do, but if for some reason you see that she is having trouble . . . trouble of any kind, and I can't take her, will you . . . ?" I'd built up speed as I spoke, an odd sense of urgency driving me that abruptly vanished, leaving my words to trail off.

"Yes. I will. I will take her to Annfwn if you can't. I swear to find a way."

"Thank you," I breathed. I added a mental prayer of gratitude to Glorianna, too. "You've been a friend to me when I wasn't one to you. I'm trying to be better about that. If you're willing to continue as my companion, I promise to do my best by you—and get you into Annfwn if I can."

"I appreciate that, Princess. I don't mind hitching my wagon to your star." She grinned at me.

I smiled back. "After all, I *will* be Queen of Avonlidgh someday."

"And a fine one, too, I think, Princess."

"Thank you. Coming from you that means a great deal. Now, I plan to nap and advise you to do the same. We have a long night ahead."

🌹 🌹 🌹

Our "escape" to Windroven was not dramatic. We kept it quiet and dressed up to please the eye.

Gilly organized the other ladies—with the exception of Lady Dulcinor, who we decided couldn't be trusted to keep her mouth shut and so would have to stay behind—having them excuse themselves singly or in groups from the ball. Veronica had arranged for so many invitations that, with the influx of Erich's people, the manse overflowed. The night turned out surprisingly mild, so people strolled and even danced in the gardens, where bonfires were lit and braziers of coals tucked under benches for cozy companions.

Even when I slipped out of the party claiming drowsiness, no one seemed to take note; they were having such a fine time. Marin met me in the servant's room I'd stayed in the first night, and I changed into my apprentice dress, dusting my hair again.

A group of Veronica's finest guards—all men and women who'd volunteered to relocate to Windroven—awaited me by the stables and we went off into the night.

When I popped into the public eye again, it was a full day later, at a popular inn on the main road, well after the fork that led to Castle Avonlidgh. With my ladies about me, all of us dressed in our finest, we took over one end of the dining hall. Wyle played and sang every song about me he knew, and we talked openly—even gaily—about the journey to Windroven.

As they heard, people streamed in, offering toasts and good wishes for Avonlidgh's heir—along with their unmitigated joy that the babe would be born at Windroven.

After that, we traveled in full sight of the people, stopping often to visit at the various towns, villages, and chapels. I'd learned my lesson and did my best to convey to everyone I met my loyalty to Avonlidgh. Glorianna bless Veronica. I would have to dig deep into Windroven's treasury to reimburse her, for she'd provided bags of coins and tokens for me to distribute.

I stopped at every chapel of Glorianna, to pray and give my blessing as Her avatar, receiving armloads of roses in return, which I then gave to children along the way. We rode on horseback in the winter sunshine, under clear blue skies, singing songs and laughing, sharing our joy with all we encountered.

Moranu's midwinter feast had passed while I traveled—unnoticed, as that celebration, too, had been outlawed—and gradually the days would grow longer and warmer again. After an early winter, the specter of press-gangs, and more war, all under the shadow of Hugh's death, the people of Avonlidgh seemed more than ready to celebrate. Birth and rebirth. Glorianna was the goddess of spring and I was Glorianna in their eyes. I tried to do Her justice.

By the time word would have reached Erich, we were so in the public eye, with such a groundswell of joyful support—indeed, more than a few people had joined our entourage, making the journey with us to Windroven, as a kind of pilgrimage—he couldn't divert me without causing a civil war.

It was the most public escape possible. Ursula would be proud.

🌹 🌹 🌹

We arrived at Windroven in triumph. Jubilant people lined the winding road up to the castle itself, despite the strong breeze off the ocean, tossing roses and rose petals. My heart lifted to smell the salt and joy in the air and to see the cliffs rising over the glittering waves. It even gave me a feeling of comfort, to know Hugh lay nearby again, in the tombs overlooking the surf.

Our child would be born here, as was good and right. Ursula had done the best thing at the time, making me come away. Now I had returned knowing more about myself and my world. Seeing Windroven with more experienced eyes.

I was home.

It seemed that Glorianna smiled upon me, because within a day of my homecoming, the unusually fine weather collapsed under the onslaught of a Mornai storm. They blew in off the ocean, full of moisture and, upon meeting the colder winds from the Northern Wastes, turned into heavy-bellied storms that dumped man-sized drifts of snow over all the land.

If Erich had planned to come after me, the storm neatly prevented that.

We settled in to wait it out, spending the evenings by the fire while I worked on knitting something large enough to be a baby blanket and Dafne read to us. I asked mainly for mythology—tales of Glorianna, Danu, and Moranu—and anything that she could dig up that referenced the Tala, Annfwn, or the Great War.

Some of my ladies didn't care to hear these tales, particularly about the demon shape-shifters, and I gave them leave to spend their time elsewhere. But I didn't relent on what I needed to learn. If being one of my ladies wasn't the party it had been, then they'd best learn that sooner rather than later.

Soon the snow would melt, the roads would open, and I needed to be ready to act.

Through the next snowbound weeks, my belly grew along with a picture of our history. The way the tales had it, the crops and livestock had been failing since long before the Great War. One very interesting historian traced the beginnings of the war—which did not start with Uorsin, only ended with him—to the internecine struggles between neighboring kingdoms that usually left both conqueror and conquered in worse shape than before.

"It seems," I observed late one night to Marin and Dafne, after the other ladies had retired to their chambers, "that the concept of Annfwn being closed off isn't all that old. The tale you just read made Annfwn sound no different than the other kingdoms—and that magic occurred everywhere."

Marin hmphed but never lifted her gaze from her knitting. She'd been making swaddling clothes and nappies, it turned out, one after another until it seemed we'd have a mountain of them. When I complained that we'd never use them all, she actually laughed at me.

"It's true." Dafne set the book aside and swirled the brandy in her goblet, staring into it as if it might yield answers. "The very old tales make it sound as if magic was, if not commonplace, then pervasive. Over time it seems that the people outside Annfwn became . . . I can't think of the right term."

"Mossbacks," I supplied, squinting at my stitches. Surely I'd dropped one, Glorianna take it.

"Excuse me?" Dafne asked on a laugh. I looked up, and Marin had me fixed with a knowing eye.

"That's what Ash—the White Monk—said the Tala call us. Mossbacks, because we can't shift and, I think, anyway, because we seem so conservative to them."

"Very interesting." Dafne pressed her lips together, the scent of her amusement giving me a pang for the grapes we'd eaten in Annfwn.

And for Ash.

"This explains her great interest in the Tala all of a sudden," Marin muttered.

"Oh, stop it, you two," I grumbled at them. "He happened to mention it once. And I know perfectly well that you figured him for Tala part-blood early on. All this reading we've done confirms that the prisons contain overwhelming numbers of Tala prisoners of war and their by-blows. An escaped convict is much more likely to be Tala than not."

"They should have gone home, shouldn't they?" Marin shook her head. "I don't begrudge them that opportunity, but this isn't their land. They don't belong here."

"I wonder why Salena stomached that." I stared into the fire. "If she made this grand bargain, used her people, all to save Annfwn, why did she allow them to be stranded?"

"Because she couldn't help it," Dafne offered in a gentle voice. "They were part of the price."

"For what gain? If she wanted a daughter like her to hold the barrier strong, why not stay there and do it herself?"

"She was getting older and needed a successor?"

"That could be. But I have this idea that somehow Salena knew it wasn't working—this separation of the kingdoms. She had to know of the growing strife outside Annfwn, that somehow, by condensing all the magic there, they'd starved the rest of the land. And the starving animal will always come after the fat one, no matter how well protected."

Dafne cocked her head at me. "That's a fascinating idea. How did you arrive at that conclusion?"

"I think . . ." I realized I was blushing in pleasure. Had anyone ever said I had a fascinating idea before? "I've been trying to listen to what Glorianna is telling me. High Priest Kir"—I ignored Marin's snort of disgust—"thinks that Glorianna wants Annfwn. I think she wants Annfwn's magic shared with the rest of us. To bring the land back to what it should be."

"How do you propose to do that?" Dafne's eyes were bright with interest.

"I'm not sure." I caught Marin's gaze and held it. "But I do know that dealing with Kir is one of the first steps."

26

That night, instead of going to bed after I brushed my hair, I got out the doll again.

The partial doll, that is. With a sense of reverence, I unwrapped the cloth we'd stored her in and laid her on the desk I'd had moved into my private sitting room. Sometimes I went over the tales Dafne read aloud, to cement the details in my mind. As I stuffed myself with food and the babe grew, I fed my brain with information, letting that gestate, too.

That way, when the babe was born, we would both be strong and ready to act.

I set the unattached arm where it should be and studied her. It was prettier than I remembered Andi's being, from when I would stare at it on her high shelf and beg to play with it. She'd always said no and so I never saw it close up like this.

Instead of mine being dressed in pink silk, as I'd first thought, it turned out the dress made up the body. Taking Andi's advice, I'd made a slit in the back side of the doll and looked inside. Dried rose petals made up the interior, fragrantly crumbling to brown dust.

No magical motherly messages.

I'd gotten over being so angry about it, however. Something about those hours spent with Ash had released that burning resentment. Things weren't always fair. My mother hadn't meant to die and leave this unfinished any more than Hugh had meant to abandon me. Still, it niggled at me, this mystery that needed solving.

It had to be something to do with the missing head. I'd gone through everything in Salena's trunk. More than once. And, while the activity made a lovely way to while away a blustery afternoon, dreaming about who my mother had been, I still knew no more than I had.

No, that wasn't exactly true.

The more I assembled the pieces of the woman and queen she'd been, the more I understood the sacrifices she'd made. All for love of Annfwn. Or perhaps, for the world outside Annfwn, too. It would have pained her greatly to know of her people stranded outside the barrier. I knew that in my heart. Once Andi had been born, Salena would have wanted to take her to Annfwn. That seemed clear. Had they gone then, Salena could have opened the wall to her outcast warriors and raised at least Andi in the witchy ways she'd inherited.

But she hadn't. All because of me.

She'd had to wait another five years—to make sure I'd be strong, giving me the gift of health and time—and made sure I'd be born.

Even if she hadn't counted on her untimely death, it only made sense if I had a purpose, too.

My mother had foreseen something for me. A destiny as important as Andi's. Though I knew it to be small of me, I felt better knowing that. And she *had* left me the doll, carefully kept in the magical storage place. A message only for me.

I just had to figure out how to read it.

Eventually, the Mornai storms unclenched their fists and the snow stopped falling. Within days, the drifts began melting and people dug their way out. Before three days had passed, a messenger from Erich appeared on my doorstep much like the unpleasant beetles that plagued the kitchen staff the moment winter thawed.

I read his letter several times, more interested in what it did not say. Not that he'd mention my secret mission, but neither did he inquire about the babe, unless asking after my health counted. He of course invited me to visit Castle Avonlidgh, but also suggested that he might make the journey to Windroven for the "summer festivities."

Why he'd resorted to that euphemism, as if the birth of Avonlidgh's heir was some sort of state secret, I didn't understand.

He also indicated that High Priest Kir had wintered with them—quite the stroke of luck for me—and inquired after my spiritual progress. Taking that as a sign, I seized the opportunity and replied that I'd greatly love for Kir to visit, to provide much-needed guidance. I also made it clear that I'd failed in my "quest for Glorianna's service" and indicated a level of shame that sent me fleeing from the public eye. I invited him to officiate at the Spring Feast for Glorianna.

The trap laid, I waited for my prey to arrive.

I might not have my mother's talents for foresight and strategy, but I rather thought she'd have been proud.

Kir arrived a week before the spring equinox. Though the wind off the ocean blew chilly, the sun shone warm and welcoming. Setting my plan in motion, I made sure to welcome his arrival with appropriate grandeur, all the better to convince him of my continued fealty and admiration.

Flattering the flatterer.

All the priests within traveling distance met Kir at the base of the mountain, forming an honor guard to convey him up the hill. A brace of muscular young soldiers seated Kir on a traveling chair the size of a throne, draped in streamers of ribbons and roses, and hefted it to their shoulders, carrying him like a king. Or a god. Children dressed in shades of white to bright pink lined the road up the mountain, singing praise to Glorianna in their high, clear voices. They waved blossoming cherry-tree branches and pussy willows from the fens.

The people of Windroven turned out in force for the rest of the welcoming ceremony in the great inner courtyard of the castle. I should have predicted, but they were jubilant that the High Priest of Glorianna's Temple would officiate *their* spring festival, and they praised me for making it happen. Glorianna smiled upon the people of Avonlidgh again, they told one another, full of hope in new birth.

Kir lapped up the adoration as . . . well, as I once had. His narrow face cracked open with smiles, and I smelled the love of power filling him. It all seemed a little much to me, but I was glad to observe. The people conflated their love of Glorianna, and all the good, life-giving blessings she brought, with the High Priest.

I would have to be very careful how I destroyed him.

Receiving him on foot, so he could look down on me from his platform of youth and vigor, I also curtsied deeply, gazing up at him through my lashes. I wore a pink gown—of course—cut very low to display the upper curves of my breasts, which had grown quite large in my pregnancy. In contrast, my hair spilled loose like a maiden's. Only I knew of the heart of the much-wiser crone who lurked inside me.

The men lowered his chair and he rose, stepping down and taking my hands. Kir smelled giddily of candy and overeating, beaming at me with fatuous condescension. "Your Highness," he cooed, "I am witness to a miracle indeed, for, impossible though it may be, you are even more surpassingly beautiful than when last I saw you."

"Glorianna has favored us with your visit, High Priest." I said it breathlessly, gazing at him with more of that adoration he seemed to love so well. "I'm so grateful for your visit—I'm in dire need of your guidance."

He patted my hand, happy to be of fatherly assistance—and to direct me toward his cause. How I hadn't recognized the smell of ambition on him before, I didn't know. But what mattered was that I knew it now.

"Of course, my child. Shall we go to the chapel to pray?"

"Oh, no! I wouldn't presume. Besides, we have a feast prepared in your honor. There will be time enough for me to tell you of my visions from Glorianna, so you can interpret them for me."

My seed planted in his mind, I allowed Kir no time to question me further, but swept him into a grand banquet. I strung him along that way for the next several days, always keeping him busy with some entertainment or treat. All designed to puff him up and increase his sense of importance. At every opportunity, I flattered him, hanging on his every word and letting him believe that he, and he alone, could tell me how to interpret the visions. I'd insisted on waiting for the equinox, so Glorianna would smile upon whatever Kir told me I should do.

By the eve of Glorianna's Feast Day, I had Kir so burning with curiosity and so feverish to hear my mind so that he could use me to further his power that he nearly salivated when he looked upon me. Not with lust—at least not for my body—but with a desire as twisted as the ones his retinue whispered of to the Windroven servants. Taking a page from Veronica's book, I'd encouraged the staff to share what they knew with me. They channeled the information gleaned from Kir's people up through Marin and Dafne, ranging from some as prosaic as Kir's preferred wine, which I immediately sent for, to the horrible insinuations of Kir's predilection for very young boys, who were then sent off to the White Monks to be sealed in silence.

I thought of Ash then. That wasn't exactly true. I thought of him all the time. But I realized then that I'd never asked how he came to be one of the White Monks. Or if he'd simply assumed the disguise. Somehow I thought it had been more than cover.

Kir hadn't once inquired after his erstwhile assistant. I'd asked Graves and his men to stay out of sight, lest Kir remember them, and I'd made sure Kir and I had little time for conversation. Still, it irritated me, his lack of concern for Ash. I'd planned to say he'd disappeared and was presumed dead—to give Ash room either way, should he ever rejoin us in the world of moss-covered stones—but Kir never asked.

I lay in bed the night before solstice, awake late and staring at the pink rosettes frolicking on the canopy overhead. The window shutters were open a little to the spring breezes, but a fire crackled in the hearth to offset them. A deep loneliness ran through me, a cold, gray sorrow that chilled me. With a start, I realized that tomorrow would have been my first anniversary.

Hugh and I had married only a year ago.

It felt like a lifetime.

Running a hand over my belly, so oddly hard, I missed both men. Hugh and Ash. And with them came the empty spaces where Andi and Ursula should be. And the old mourning for my mother. Some of them were dead. Some so far away that they might as well be gone from this earth.

Restless, I rose and put on my robe. In my sitting room, the chair by the banked fire sat empty. No Ursula to pierce me with her knowing looks. Wandering into the hallway, I smiled at the guards who'd been playing cards but leapt to their feet to follow along behind me. "I'm only stretching my legs a little," I told them. "I thought I'd walk up to the turrets, taste the wind."

"Yes, Your Highness," one replied. "We followed behind Princess Andromeda often enough."

That's right. Andi had paced all over Windroven during the siege. As surely trapped within as the Tala had been trapped without. Not unlike the situation we found ourselves in now, but without the obvious armies. The siege had solved nothing. It had only caused more death and suffering.

"Which rooms were hers again? I think I'll go there instead."

They led me to the tower room I vaguely recalled Hugh saying he'd given her. He'd always been considerate that way, remembering people's preferences. He'd commented that Andi liked to be able to see a long way.

Though her room had been cleaned, no one else had occupied it since. That was clear from the few things left on the dresser—needle, thread, and ribbons—the ladies had used to dress her for the wedding. My loneliness throbbed a little with the wistful thought that I should have been with her, overseeing the preparations.

I'd acted badly at the wedding, refusing to stand up for her. I'd thought it was so wrong, such a travesty of fate.

Something gleamed at the rear of the dresser, gold and sparkling. Andi's rose of Glorianna pendant. The twin of mine, which lay far below, entombed with Hugh. I searched my memory and recalled the cloth-of-silver gown she'd worn—and Moranu's silver moon on her breast. Even then, she'd made her choice.

Just as I'd made mine.

I fastened the necklace around my throat and returned to my empty bed, feeling a little less alone.

🌹 🌹 🌹

Glorianna's Feast Day dawned brightly beautiful, dazzling and filled with all that spring should be. Kir officiated at the sunrise services with what seemed to be all of Avonlidgh gathered along the road and on the various ledges and pockets on the eastern face of the old volcano. The sun rose over the farmlands, the young crops flashing the bright green of Ash's eyes. A full-throated roar of celebration went up from the assembly, an atavistic joy in the life-giving warmth of all Glorianna brought to us.

Traditionally, after the morning services, the day was spent with family, or in quiet contemplation, until the evening feast, with dancing and festivities that would last well into the night.

I spent it cornering Kir. Honoring Glorianna's will in my own way.

We prayed in the chapel together, Kir offering me the pink wine of Glorianna's absolution from hands that seemed to me to be dripping with the blood of innocents. Then, his eagerness ill disguised, Kir led me to a private alcove and urged me to confess my visions to him.

Biting my lip and gazing at him, I pretended to a hesitation I didn't feel. Kir praised and petted me, and I let him for a while, giving him the illusion of control. Finally, I told him the visions started when I crossed into Annfwn.

"But, Your Highness, I understood that you couldn't even find the border," he said. I'd shocked him and he smelled of equal parts excited ambition and confused apprehension.

Before he could recover himself, I went on, only wishing I could dredge up a few tears for the occasion.

"I found the border and I was able to cross it."

"Then Princess Ursula lied."

I looked as sorrowful as I could. "I'm not sure what made Ursula say so. But, High Priest—I didn't know what to think—for Glorianna Herself descended from the heavens and spoke to us."

"Are you sure it wasn't Tala magic?"

"I know you'll be able to tell me if so. She said that it wasn't for me to claim Annfwn. That Her paradise belongs not to kings and queens. Not even to Her avatar. No, She said only Her priest could claim Annfwn. She bade me return home and tell you this news on Her feast day—that you, and only you, should be the one."

"Truly this is so?" Kir breathed, flooded with an almost perverse excitement. For the first time in weeks, my stomach turned, recoiling at the smell of it.

At least it helped me look miserable. "She said that as Her avatar, my job was only to give you the message and the means. I'm to fund your expedition."

"My expedition?"

"Yes. She said Annfwn awaits you and that when you cross

into paradise, it shall be yours and that the High Throne of the land shall belong to Her church, not rest in the hands of mere kings." I furrowed my brow at that, resisting the immediate urge to press the wrinkles away. "I don't really understand what She meant by that."

He patted my hand. "Don't you worry, Princess. I understand."

"My son will still inherit the High Throne, won't he?" I thought the whine in my voice might be a little much, but Kir only smiled harder, nearly manic with ambition. I'd stoked him into such a frenzy over the last few days that I feared he teetered on the brink of going mad with it.

Though it would only help my plans if he did.

"All will be as it should be, praise Glorianna."

"I'm so glad!" I gave him a trembling smile. "I hated to lie to King Erich, but She said to tell you in secret, and my allegiance to Her comes first. And She said that you had pursued Her sacred cause where the kings had not."

His lips curved in a secret smile of satisfaction. "You did exactly right, child. Did She say aught else?"

"She said that She would show you the way, but that you should go north, past the Phoenix River, and then in to Annfwn. There is a secret way in."

He blanched at that, and I worked not to hold my breath. That was nearly to the Northern Wastes. It would take him well into the summer or longer to get there.

"That's why I was to wait," I layered on the story, "because She feared your loyalty and obedience to Her would cause you to set out too early on your journey. But She said that She's spoken to you and given you signs, so you'd be expecting this." I paused, drumming up extra anxiety. "You did hear Her voice, didn't you?"

"Of course I did." He smiled, but I smelled his worry. "Really none of this is a surprise to me. I suspected your information would be this very thing."

"Praise Glorianna!" I favored him with my most brilliant smile. "I knew the White Monk must have lied."

Kir blinked. He had totally forgotten about Ash. "The White Monk? He was there?"

"Oh, yes. He crossed over with me and witnessed Her message, too. But he said that Glorianna meant any priest and that, since he was already in Annfwn, he would claim it. He ran off and left me there." I tried to look pitiful, though the building rage on Kir's face nearly made me laugh.

"That upstart! After all I did for him, elevating him to a position far beyond his station in life."

"Glorianna spoke again after he left . . ." I let that trail off, leading him to my bread crumbs.

"She knew he would try to usurp me!"

I nodded, eyes wide. "She said that you must stop him. That only you have the secret of the blood test."

He recoiled, stopped himself. "Whatever do you mean, Your Highness?"

"I don't know!" I pouted with a pretty tremble of my lips. "I told you I didn't understand it all. She said for you to leave it with me, so that I may carry on your sacred work while you claim Annfwn. To cleanse the land of the demons. Is that right?"

Kir relaxed, nodding knowingly. "Ah, yes. I can see that you are meant to serve me in this way."

Was he even listening to himself? I clenched my teeth against my ire, casting my eyes down so I wouldn't give the game away. At any moment he might reveal it to me.

"Do you swear to Glorianna never to reveal this to another living soul?" Kir intoned.

"I swear my loyalty to Glorianna and all that falls to Her under heaven." I held the pendant in one hand and drew Glorianna's circle with the other, praying that She would understand my lie of omission in Her service.

With great ceremony, Kir withdrew a packet of cloth from an inner pocket and unwrapped a small, round object. He cupped it in his hands, a sphere made from some kind of red-gold woven floss, a long, dangling tail. "In the presence of Tala blood," Kir said, gravely serious, "this turns deep red. It's a warning talisman. So that by this you may know them."

I took it, holding it gingerly, half afraid of what it would show about me, quickly wrapping it in the folds of my skirt. I should have worn gloves.

"Use it well, Princess. Soon the time will come when the land will indeed be entirely cleansed of their unwholesome presence. Until then, it's the one sure way to tell."

Nodding, I kept myself composed, dizzying excitement thrumming through me. I had no idea how Kir had laid hands on it. He clearly had no idea what it was, always holding it upside down. But I'd recognized it nearly immediately.

The missing head of my doll.

27

Once Kir departed, well funded and traveling in secret, I assumed the reins of Glorianna's church. It would be slow going, but balance would be restored. I'd depose Kir with his ostensible blessing. By the time he returned—if he returned, as I trusted to Glorianna to mete Her justice there—he would have no entry.

Working with a few local priests, I found some who abhorred the practice of ferreting out and burning part-bloods. Ruthlessly, I advanced them to positions of power and found "missions" for the others. Employing trumped-up visions of Glorianna's wishes as willfully as I'd done as a child, I invented a dire need for Glorianna's word in Kooncelund and the Isles of Remus.

In groups or one by one, I sent them off on quests, hopefully far away from any Tala.

I sewed the doll together, carefully attaching the head and the arm, even mending the seam up the back that I'd opened. Her hair had become a greasy rope over the years, from being gripped in Kir's hand. I nearly replaced it, then thought better of it, not knowing for sure where her magic lay. It served as a reminder of my own journey, from being a pawn directed by someone else, to becoming . . . maybe a whole person.

With no other message forthcoming, I took bringing the doll together as another kind of message and followed my other instincts. The world needed balance and cohesion. Flushing the poison from Glorianna's church was only the first step. If the bulk of us could not go to paradise, then perhaps we could bring something of magic back to the other twelve kingdoms.

Bringing the three goddesses back into balance also meant strengthening the presence of Moranu and Danu, so I sent invitations to those chapels. I wanted to be sure that Windroven and the surrounding areas, at least, observed Danu's midsummer festival, approaching with the same astonishing speed as the prodigious growth of my belly.

The priestess from Danu's small chapel in the mountains seemed taken aback by the attention, but also delighted to advise us on planning the proper rituals and presentation. Moranu's priestess, too, visited Windroven for a short time, though she seemed uncomfortable inside the walls and left quickly. Dafne caught me staring speculatively after the silver-haired priestess, and I smelled the secrets in the air.

"She looks so familiar," I said, inviting Dafne to confide in me.

She hesitated only a moment. "She helped Andi, when she was here and feeling ill from the effects of the Tala magic working on her."

"I'm glad she had someone to help her," I murmured, half to myself, though Dafne still stood there. I hated that I hadn't paid enough attention to Andi—and now could never make that time up to her. Would we always have recriminations between us?

Dafne put a hand on my arm. "Andi wanted to protect you the same way you wanted to protect her. It's the way of sisters."

I ripened along with the crops, growing as heavy and full as the stalks in the fields, their heads hanging with the weight of the fat seeds they bore. On Marin's advice, I took a lot of long walks, along the cliffs overlooking the tranquil summer sea, through the forests, alongside the fertile fields. Dafne or Gilly most usually accompanied me, along with one or two of Graves's squad, just in case.

In the evenings, I entertained. Because I had suitors again, Glorianna save me.

As if my festive return to Windroven had been a signal, princes and other noblemen from all the Twelve Kingdoms came to visit and pay court. Dafne and Gilly developed a game of tracking how many of my body parts they could praise without ever noting my swollen belly. Though I felt sorry for the men—after all, it's not easy to flirt with a woman so visibly pregnant with another man's child—I also had little patience for them.

Where before I met Hugh I'd loved spending time with the many handsome and charming men who paid suit to me at Ordnung, now I chafed at what felt like wasted time. Ursula had been this way, irritated with what she'd called false flattery and "romance as a spectator sport." I'd laughed at her then, and the irony didn't escape me that I now found myself in her shoes.

Because, like her, I never intended to marry.

But all of my advisers counseled me that I should give the appearance of being open to remarriage. The hopeful men came from all over, competing with one another for the opportunity to marry me, elevating not just their own status, but that of their home country as well. Some even hinted at alliances, aligning our countries to break clear of Uorsin's grip, stopping just short of outright treason. I pretended not to understand these, though I made careful note of who did the most hinting.

Perhaps I'd been an oblivious girl before and had only heard how much my suitors loved and admired *me*, but with this round, it became painfully clear that, more than anything, these men desired my power. They praised my beauty, of course, as always, but

I smelled their ambition, the stench of freshly slaughtered meat laced with the metallic tang of calculation. And, like that, it sickened me.

I sometimes had to grit my teeth to appear sweet and pleasant, to *not* scream in their faces that I knew how they really felt. My daughter's gift would be a difficult one to bear. There was nothing quite like hearing an apparently heartfelt declaration of undying love, looking into the warm and earnest eyes of a handsome man, while smelling his true intentions in the air, as if he'd passed the worst gas in your presence.

In truth, I missed Ash. All the time.

Which pissed me off even more, because I knew he didn't miss me. He was, no doubt, relieved to be away from me. He'd likely found some pretty Tala girl who didn't mind his scars and ate grapes for every meal in paradise. Meanwhile, I was lonely. My body hurt, I felt ungainly and awful, the heat of summer pressed down on me, and, more surrounded by people than ever, I wanted the one person I'd never see again.

Sometimes I'd glimpse a white robe, a lean man who moved with wolfish grace, but it was never the right man. They filled my court like worshipful flies, buzzing and flitting about. In a fit of pique, I almost ordered them all out, but Dafne's startled glance gave me pause and I managed to convert my words to a more benign request. She eyed me thoughtfully, likely guessing the source of my unhappiness.

But she never said anything about it.

"You need to think about who you want here for your lying-in," Dafne said to me one morning during our walk. The flowers of summer bloomed in riots of color, covering the cliffs in purple and yellow. Glorianna's midsummer feast would be on us in the next days and, shortly afterwards, the birth of my child. "Depending on the distance and their health," she continued, as I hadn't replied, "it could take some a month to travel. That means they would need to start planning soon."

"I don't want anyone here," I complained. "What, are we going to lay me out on a display table in the great hall so everyone can peer between my thighs to watch the bloody emergence of the child?"

She snorted out a laugh. "What an image. I imagine some would love if you did, but I think we can safely go with more privacy than that."

We walked in silence for a bit, Skunk following well behind. The ocean breeze whipped my skirts against my legs and tasted of fresh salt. Finally I sighed, caving as she knew I would. "I suppose they all think they should be present, to lay their claims."

"Yes. They will want to hear immediately if the babe is a boy or a girl."

"And then the games will begin in earnest."

"No doubt of that."

I imagined the scene, Uorsin and Erich—possibly all the other kings and queens—arrayed around my court, all eyes on my belly. *Childbirth as a spectator sport,* Ursula's wry voice offered in my head. And then, in my mind's eye, they transformed into starving wolves, fighting one another, tearing me and my daughter apart in the process.

"I don't want any of them present," I decided. "They don't need to be and we can't afford for civil war to start inside Windroven. My first responsibility is to protect my child, then the people of Windroven, then the people of Avonlidgh, then the remaining kingdoms."

"Even Annfwn?"

"Even so."

"As you wish, Princess," she agreed, maybe with some approval.

"Do you know who I really want to be there?" Besides Hugh, who, by rights, should have been there for all of this and would have loved to see his child come into the world. And aside from

Ash, who would maybe come if I asked. That would be selfish of me, though. He'd found his paradise and deserved to stay there.

"Who, Amelia?" Dafne coaxed. "This is your choice."

"My sisters. I want Ursula and Andi with me."

"Then you should write to them and ask."

"Having Ursula there would be the same as having the High King there."

"No, it wouldn't, and you know it. She wouldn't be there as the heir; she's your sister first."

I wasn't at all sure that was true. We hadn't communicated since I was at Ordnung. She was likely still angry at me. Considering how I'd behaved, I didn't blame her a bit. "If the babe is a boy, she won't be the heir anymore. Would I be asking for trouble?"

"Are you seriously wondering if Ursula would harm your child?" Dafne sounded sincerely incredulous. And well she should. Ursula might or might not be my sister first, but she wore her integrity like another suit of armor. She would never betray my trust.

"Andi won't be able to come. If she even wants to. She said there were reasons she couldn't leave Annfwn."

"You don't know that for sure. Ask."

☙ ☙ ☙

So I wrote them both. Sending a missive to Ursula seemed ridiculously easy compared to contacting Andi. If we wanted real peace in the future, we would need to open up communications between Annfwn and the other kingdoms. Even if we couldn't travel back and forth, it seemed we should at least be able to talk to one another. I didn't want to go the rest of my life not being able to communicate with Andi.

Finally I asked the priestess of Moranu for advice. She visited me in private, as I really couldn't walk or even ride out to her chapel in the woods. I felt as if the least untoward movement would make the strained skin of my belly pop open, like an over-ripe fruit bursting in the heat.

"I hope you don't mind if I keep my feet up," I said to her, by way of greeting, and gestured for her to sit. The silver-haired woman had a lovely scent about her, one that reminded me of Ash, like the forest at night.

She surveyed me with a bit of a smile where I reclined on a chaise, my feet bare and propped on a pile of pillows. "I do not mind, Your Highness. I remember well that final month of my pregnancies—it seemed they'd never end."

"You've had babies?" I was intrigued. The priests of Glorianna and the priestesses of Danu usually observed celibate lives.

"Five." She nodded. "All grown and leading their own lives with their own children."

"Do you miss them?" It was intrusive of me to ask, but I wondered so much about my own future, how my life would be.

She didn't seem to mind. "I lead a full life. And I see them from time to time."

"And their father . . ."

"Fathers." She grinned at my surprise. "The priestesses of Moranu traditionally do not marry, but take many lovers. She is the goddess of the night and the moon, after all. Sensual frolics in the dark please her greatly."

Her words brought to mind a vivid image of the nighttime frolicking Ash and I had engaged in, under Moranu's moon, and my face heated. She chuckled knowingly. "How can I be of service to you, Your Highness?"

"I am told you met my sister, Queen Andromeda of the Tala." I'd discovered bluntness worked well for me. It served when fancy politics did not. It also tended to elicit similar frankness from the person I spoke to, if I'd chosen well. Apparently I had.

"Yes. And King Rayfe as well. They met with each other in my chapel."

My head spun and I tipped it against the high back of the chaise. Though, in truth, I wasn't that surprised. "When?"

"During the siege," she answered easily.

"So you're saying she somehow sneaked out of Windroven to meet with our enemy."

"She sought to stop the war. King Rayfe would not—could not—give up the fight for her hand in marriage. She hated watching people—yours, hers, and the Tala—die in such a futile struggle."

"My kidnapping . . . she arranged it?"

"That I don't know, Your Highness."

A renewed sense of betrayal swirled around inside my heart. This. *This* was what they all were lying about. Andi had pretended to trade herself for me, but it had all been an elaborate ruse. Because she knew Hugh would never have given up the fight for anyone but me.

Because he'd loved me more than even his sworn word.

The tears balled up in my throat, choking me. I wiped sweat from my forehead instead, my pores at least shedding water.

The priestess waited quietly, as if she perceived my struggle and knew only I could find my way through it.

"How did King Rayfe know to come to you?" I focused on the real point of this conversation.

"The Tala look to Moranu in particular. Her chapels serve as way stations for them. As places of refuge, should they need it."

"So there *are* Tala nearby." I studied her as she firmed her lips against confirming that. The evergreen scent of the truth wafted through the air. "Don't worry—I don't intend to hunt them out. What I want is someone to take a letter to my sister."

"Certainly, Your Highness."

"Just like that? They'd have to pass by Ordnung, which can't be safe these days."

Her lips curved in a secretive smile. "There are other paths. Though I'll deny it, should you ever claim I said so."

Funny that I'd made that up for Kir's sake and it was true. Hopefully he wouldn't accidentally blunder his way into Annfwn after all. But no—Andi's barrier would prevent it.

Just in case, however, in my letter to her I hinted at an unexpected visitor who might be coming their way.

Ursula's procession climbed the winding road to Windroven, an easier journey for her this time, in the bright summer sun, and with a much smaller entourage. Really it looked to be only her special squadron. My letter had taken some time to reach her and she'd sent a reply from Branli, of all places. What she and her Hawks had been doing there piqued my curiosity no end—and made me nervous, as I'd sent Kir in that direction.

Some people turned out to witness her arrival and offer gifts of summer fruit and fresh cheese. They received the High King's heir with reserved welcome. Though some factions had felt the High King and King Erich should be present for my lying-in—mainly for the cachet of it all—most everyone else seemed just as glad not to deal with a major state visit.

They reached the top and Ursula's clear gray gaze found mine—then dropped to my burgeoning belly.

"Danu damn me—are you going to pop?" She gave me a cheeky grin with it and I rolled my eyes. The relief that she wasn't angry felt like a cork pulled, my fermented regret draining away.

"I certainly feel that way, so don't poke me or you might be sorry."

She looked less thin, but still harried, still tired, her cheekbones too sharp and her narrow lips colorless in her tanned face. But her smile for me was genuine and her love smelled as warm and comforting as baked bread. I breathed her in and mourned a little that I would lose this gift of knowing. It would have helped before this to know Ursula loved me, despite her hard-shelled ways.

"I'm so glad you came," I told her and took her hands in mine. Her fingers always seemed to be cold. "It means everything to me."

She squeezed my fingers in return. "I'm grateful you asked. Otherwise I would have had to barge in and boss you around again."

I laughed and linked my arm through hers, leading her inside and letting Dafne and Gilly settle the others. "And, tell me, how angry is our father that I told him not to come?"

"I don't know—we haven't spoken." She said it neutrally, but with a note of finality that meant she wouldn't discuss it further. "I could ask the same of King Erich."

"I don't know—we haven't spoken." I wrinkled my nose at her.

"If the kings show up on Windroven's threshold, will you really turn them away?"

"Truthfully, I have no idea. I thought I'd cross that bridge if and when it happened."

"They believe you will, which is enough."

"Do you think so?" We settled into chairs before the large windows that overlooked the ocean in my favorite private sitting room. Books lined the shelves, some that Dafne had salvaged from our visit to Ordnung, others that we'd been collecting here and there. Glorianna's chapels had yielded up some interesting finds.

"They must or they'd be here already," she observed. "You've been working the politics quite well—I'm impressed."

I laughed and poured some chilled white wine for us both. "I'd be offended at your surprise if I wasn't so flattered to have your approval."

"You never needed anyone's approval, Ami—or rather, everyone always loved you, so you knew you already had it."

"Oh, you have no idea." I shook my head a little for the needy girl I'd been even a short time ago. Who still drove me, but not so insistently. "So why were you in Branli?"

She raised her auburn eyebrows and sipped her wine. "Should I ask how you knew that?"

"Your messenger brought the letter personally. I asked after the weather at Ordnung and she said she didn't know but fall had come early to Branli."

"Indiscreet of her. And Branli is quite a bit farther to the north. Winter comes early there."

"I imagine she thought you would not keep secrets from your own sister."

Ursula smiled blandly. "She'd be wrong."

"Branli is also in the west and borders the Northern Wastes, as I recall."

"You always did have a good memory."

"Looking for another way into Annfwn, are you?"

She blinked innocent eyes at me. "I have no idea what you're talking about."

Disgruntled, I sat back in my chair, smelling nothing but wine and ocean air. Then dug out the pillow behind me and tossed it to the floor. "I invited Andi to be here, too."

That surprised her in truth. She set her mug down and leaned forward, elbows on her leather-clad bony knees. "And how did you get a message to her?"

I smiled prettily and batted my eyes. "Secret."

"Ha!" She barked out the laugh. "But I'm still not spilling mine."

"Your prerogative." Unhappy with my position, I reached for the pillow again and groaned a little at the stretch.

Ursula snagged it easily with her long arm and handed it to me, watching me with something like horror, though it didn't smell that way.

"I'm glad you're providing the heirs," she remarked, "because I am not *ever* doing that."

"It just looks bad right now. When you fall in love someday, you'll want to have his baby, I'm sure." I kind of trailed off then, remembering the jokes about Ursula and her sword, or that she must be a lover of other women. "Or hers," I added.

Ursula snorted. But then, she'd been hearing those rumors longer than I had. "Sure you should be so glib promising that?

I've heard that you've had all sorts of offers and haven't bit on a one."

"Hugh hasn't even been dead a year," I snapped at her. "I'm hardly going to dally with a new lover at this time. Besides the fact that I look like a three-days-dead bloated cow." I tucked away the thought that I'd already done more than dally with Ash, but nobody needed to know about that. In my mind, it still somehow didn't quite count as real.

"You look as radiant and perfect as Glorianna Herself," Ursula returned in a mild tone, "as I'm sure you know, since you've never had a shortage of mirrors."

"You're just annoyed that I suggested your true love might be female."

She laughed without humor. "If I got annoyed by that kind of hinting, I would be walking around pissed off nonstop. No way to live."

I felt a pang of sympathy at the desolate sound in her voice, the hollow scent of a long-buried misery. "I'm sorry."

"Don't be." She was back to brusque. "So no hunting for true love again for you yet?"

The pillow was poking into my spine, so I pulled it out again with a heartfelt sigh. "I don't think you get it more than once."

"What do you mean?" She wrinkled her forehead and I had to stop myself from telling her not to.

"True love. That's the 'true' part—you get one chance and that's it. Mine has come and gone. Maybe you have to be young and innocent for it to work. I'm okay with that."

"Truly." She even smelled astonished. "I'm amazed you think you won't find love again."

"This coming from the woman who has never so much as tripped over a guy—or *gal*," I had to insert, to needle her—"in her entire life?"

"We're not all built the same way, don't want the same things."

"Did you know the priestesses of Moranu don't marry, but instead take many lovers throughout their lives?"

"Interesting. I'd heard rumors of it. I think they keep it pretty quiet. Why—are you considering that?"

"Why not?"

"Because High King Uorsin would go into such a rage that he'd lock you in a tower for the rest of your life?"

"I'm a grown woman."

"And he's still your liege."

"Then he'd have to lock up all of Avonlidgh, too."

"Don't think he wouldn't, Ami." Ursula frowned at me in deadly earnest. "Tread carefully with him. Avonlidgh is one of the jewels in his crown. He'd lose Duranor first."

"I wasn't being serious," I replied irritably, shifting again in my chair.

"Do you ever sit still?"

"My back hurts. Don't criticize until you've been in my shoes, which are much larger, by the way, my feet are so damn swollen."

She looked alert. "Your back hurts? Isn't that a sign of labor?"

"How would you know? Besides, my back hurts all the time lately."

"I pay attention. Women talk—even women soldiers." She sent a maid for Marin and I grumbled about it. "Indulge me." She patted my hand. "I'm trying to be a good aunt."

"Auntie Essla. I can't wait to hear that."

Ursula gave me a funny look. "You haven't called me Essla since you were little."

I shrugged one shoulder but smiled to see that I'd touched her. I owed her that and more. "I might have figured out how to say your name right, but I'll never forget my big sister. Thank you for putting up with me."

She reached over and tugged a lock of my hair. "Always, Baby Girl."

28

To my satisfaction, Ursula was wrong. Marin said the birth wouldn't be long off, however. The days passed while all of us waited—them for me to go into labor and me for word from Andi.

Though it didn't come. Ursula knew I fretted over it and offered to send some of her scouts to look. I refused. Where would they go? Andi knew the way well enough. If she was coming—which she clearly wasn't—she would have been here already.

The day I went into labor was the day a squall from off the ocean hit Windroven with snarling fury, dashing itself against the stone walls. Marin set me up in my bedchamber—in the bed Hugh and I had shared, where we'd made this babe, when I thought that was how our whole lives would be—and I winced as the wind hit the shutters.

"Is this a bad omen?" I asked Marin.

"Tut, Princess," she answered with a brisk shake of her head. "Just the sisters having some fun, blowing off some steam."

Ursula had dragged in her favorite chair from my sitting room, reclining in it and propping her feet on the bed. Keeping me company. I'd asked my other ladies to wait elsewhere, so, while Marin went to assemble her supplies, it was just she and I.

"I'm sorry Andi didn't make it in time," she offered.

"I knew she wouldn't. She said she couldn't leave Annfwn. I just . . ." *Hoped.*

Ursula had gone as still as a cat with her eye on a helpless bird. "Oh?" Her tone was easy, friendly. Too neutral. "When exactly did she say that?"

I waved an irritable hand at her. "You told me that—when you talked to her. At the border."

"Uh-uh, Baby Sister." Her gray eyes glittered. "I know she didn't. Don't play your games with me. When did you talk to her?"

"Glorianna teach me to keep my mouth shut," I groaned, dropping my head on the pillows.

"If Glorianna had *that* much power, she'd have done it long before. I've certainly prayed hard enough for it."

"Very funny."

"Stop ducking the question and tell me."

"Tell me what you were doing in Branli," I retorted.

"This isn't a game of let's trade secrets. If you somehow managed to talk to Andi, then I . . ." Her mouth fell open and her feet hit the floor. "Good Danu—you went to Annfwn after all."

I folded my arms and glared at her.

She pointed a bony finger at me. "You did! You went straight from Ordnung, I'll bet. Who helped you? Had to be Erich. What is his plan, Ami? Does he hope to use you to invade Annfwn and use her as a lever against the High King?"

A contraction ran through me then and I concentrated on it, breathing into the pain as Marin had taught me. Ursula took my hand and held it, offering encouragement. And returned to badgering me as soon as it was over.

"I'm amazed at you. After you were *so* self-righteous about Andi being a traitor, and you openly defy the High King's command? What in the Twelve Kingdoms were you thinking?"

"I didn't openly defy him," I muttered.

"Danu take me," Ursula breathed. "I didn't think you had it in you."

"Well, it was really tough," I snapped at her. "I didn't get to change my gown five times a day, and you know how I live for that."

She only raised an eyebrow and looked amused.

"I had to find out for myself, okay? I had to look Andi in the eye and hear for myself what happened." As I said it, I realized that had truly been my reason to go. All the others had been convenient excuses to do that one thing. Though I'd needed to prove something to myself, too—that was clear in retrospect—and I'd done that, as well, hadn't I?

"And did you?" She seemed curiously tense. A different kind. The sharp scent of guilt wafted off of her. And the slippery smell of lies.

"She told me the same story you did," I replied evenly, watching her relax. Glorianna take them both. "Which means you're both lying to me."

Her tension tightened into wariness. "Why do you think that?"

I made an unladylike noise at her. "I can smell it on you. I don't understand why you two think I can't handle the truth."

"It's not that," she replied in a frank tone, her gray gaze serious. A sense of relief dulled the painful edges of my dread over what the truth might really be. At least she wasn't pretending anymore. It helped, too, in a personal and foolish way, that they weren't only protecting their delicate baby sister. "The full story doesn't change the reality of how Hugh died—or the tragedy of it. But it might change how you choose to act upon it. You, the Queen of Avonlidgh."

Another contraction took me, harder, more wrenching, and she held my hand. It struck me as funny, for no good reason, that though there were only two sisters here, the room was crowded with our public faces and the interests of everyone who wanted a stake in us and our lives.

"Tell me, then," I told her, when I could breathe, "while I'm just Ami and you're not Uorsin's heir. Pretend you're just my sister."

She gripped my hand with ferocity, nearly crushing the bones. "Don't you see, Ami? We are never only that. We're always our responsibilities. Otherwise Andi would be here. Otherwise you would have known the truth from the start. This is what we were born into—each one of us—and this is how we'll die."

"Do you ever hate her?" I panted a little, feeling as if I couldn't take a deep breath. "Salena? This was all her plan. As if she's some witch reaching from beyond the grave, making us dance the way she wanted." Like those performers had made the servants dance. I gritted my teeth at how horrible that had been.

"Yes." Ursula surprised me and nodded when I searched her face for the truth. "I wonder what kind of woman could have planned to use her daughters as weapons against her greatest enemy. Who married him. I think sometimes that she had no heart."

"And Andi has stepped into her shoes."

"We all have." Ursula looked grim. "Each one of us, in our way. And in our father's, continuing this thing they started long ago."

"It's not right." Something felt very tight inside me.

"No? Tell me, then, future Queen of Avonlidgh—what are your plans for this child? Shall we set him or her free, to grow up in ignorance, perhaps fostered with a nice sheepherding family in Noredna or some fruit growers in Elcinea?"

"I should." A contraction bit down with dull teeth and I gritted through it, keening. The wind howled outside, mocking me. "It would be a kinder life."

"I'm not sure anyone gets that."

"No." I tried to catch my breath and thought of Ash and his many scars, inside and out. With a deep pang, I wished for him to be there with me. It resonated, expanding out and suddenly snapping. Fluid gushed hot between my thighs.

Ursula jumped up. "Are you okay? You look . . . pale." She pulled the covers away and, hardened warrior that she was, still gasped. "Danu, you're all over blood. I'm fetching Marin.

"I'll tell you the truth later—we need to focus on getting your through this. Don't make me lose you, too." She looked so fierce, love and panic drenching the air in the room, that I had to smile.

"Yes. You *will* tell me the truth."

She stopped, hand on the door latch, head bowed. Then she nodded.

The rest of the day and much of the night flowed in and out of my memory like a badly knitted blanket made of different yarns. This one Ursula, alternately cajoling and browbeating me. The steady thread of Marin, saying all would be fine, though her face grew increasingly pinched with concern, the winter rime smell of fear tingeing the room. Dafne wove in at some point, coming and going, bringing me icy water from the deep wells, cinnamon sugar in her calm support.

Hugh was there, summer gold and blue, wrapping me in love, and I remember talking to him. Ursula tried to tell me he wasn't there, but Dafne shushed her. It comforted me to have him with me, as I felt my body weaken. Had he felt this way, too? The steady loss of blood and, with it, life.

As the hours passed, bringing despair and no babe, I wished desperately that I'd made Ash stay with me. I could have commanded it, and he owed me for giving him his greatest desire. He damn well should have come to Windroven to see me through this birth. He wouldn't let me die, no matter how much he hated my power over him.

I began pleading with him at some point, to help me. Saying that I was sorry for being cruel and vain and heartless.

But I didn't want to die. Surely Ash wouldn't want me dead.

I was dying, though. Perhaps my daughter with me. That broke my heart most of all.

Another hand on my brow, this one sparking warm with tingling magic, and I opened my eyes to see green ones gazing into mine—but lighter. Like the leaves of spring, like new apples. Like life.

"Ash?" I think I made no sound, but he nodded.

"It's all right, my sun, I'm here." His voice, gravel grinding together, sounded sweeter than one of Wyle's lullabies.

"I'm dying," I whispered, too weak to speak louder. "I know you hate me, but will you save my daughter? Take her to Annfwn for me."

"I won't let you die." He sounded angry. "I would have been here long since, but . . . never mind. You sleep. Remember the stable and your wounds then?"

"Yes. You healed me. And I wanted you so much I couldn't stand it."

"Shh. There are others here. I'm going to heal you as I did then."

"Don't let the others see you—it's not safe."

"Don't you worry. The babe will be fine and so will you."

"If you have to make a choice, save my daughter instead of me."

"Don't you worry," he repeated. "Sleep now."

I seized his wrist, surprised at my own strength. "Promise me."

He turned his hand, wound his fingers through mine, and dropped a kiss on the back of my hand. "I promise, my sun. But I won't let it come to that."

🌹 🌹 🌹

When I awoke, for a moment I thought I'd lost track of time. Ursula slept in the big chair next to my bed, snoring softly. Was she there to make sure I wouldn't go to the cliffs to dig out Hugh's body?

No, that was ages ago. Why was she here?

And then the babe in her arms cried a little and my breasts ached, dripping moisture. I reached out and must have made a sound, because Ursula's eyes flew open and she leapt to her feet, child still curled protectively against her, naked sword flashing in her other hand.

Dafne, on the other side of the fire, struggled blearily out of her chair. "What? What's wrong?"

"Nothing," Ursula reassured her. "She's awake."

They came to me, Dafne helping me to sit up and plumping pillows behind me. Ursula laid the infant in my arms with a proud smile. "Your son, Amelia. Strong and healthy. And hungry as a horse."

"A son?" I stared at him, uncertain.

"Yes. A *son*," she affirmed. "And he's perfect."

I opened my nightgown—fresh, white and not bloodstained, so they must have bathed and changed me—and he latched onto my breast with a ferocity that made me gasp, my nipple tender and sore. Ursula laughed softly. "We've been helping him nurse from you while you recovered, so he knows the way well. Marin said it would be better that way—for both of you."

"How long . . ."

"It's been four days since you went into labor," Dafne informed me. "Nearly two since he was born."

"I've been asleep for two days?" I echoed, horrified.

"You needed the rest," Dafne said, in the same soothing tone.

I looked around the room. "Where's my daughter?"

Ursula kept her face inscrutable, not a flicker of response, but Dafne looked away and bit her lip.

"Daughter?" Ursula shook her head and pointed at my son. "You had a boy. Just as Lady Zevondeth said you would. There he is. The next High King."

"I was supposed to have a daughter. Where is she?"

"Andi was wrong. So much for prophecy."

"No. That can't be right. Did I have both—a son and a daughter?"

"Ami, I don't understand what you—"

"Tell her." Dafne's voice didn't sound like her, nearly strident, shredded with emotion. "Tell her now or I will."

"Tell her what?" Ursula's voice rose, too, and she stood, hand going to the hilt of her resheathed blade.

"The truth about her daughter!" Dafne looked almost unhinged, her face distorted in the candlelight, and I realized she was crying, tears streaming down her cheeks.

"We agreed that—"

"No!" Dafne screeched. "I *never* agreed. Tell her the truth."

My heart splintering into wild, frenzied pieces while my son suckled happily, a red-gold fuzz of hair gleaming with the candlelight, I looked between them. "One of you tell me. Next words out of your mouth."

Ursula's shoulders sagged and she sat again. "Ami—" she started, and her voice cracked. She cleared her throat, struggling. It occurred to me that lately she'd been the bearer of all my bad news. "Your daughter was born, yes. Born first, in fact. But she didn't last the night. I'm sorry."

I swallowed that information, choked it down past that steadfast ball lodged in my throat, hoping it would stay there. The grief, the despair, the sheer soul-shattering unfairness of it all, ground together. And grew beyond control.

It would not stay down.

I pulled my son from my breast and wordlessly handed him to Dafne, who took him and soothed his protests.

The ball sprouted thorns, ripping its way down as it sank into my chest, stabbing hotter, with relentless ferocity. Then it unfurled, like a flower that had been tightly budded all this time, fertilized in grief and despair. It opened, tearing me apart inside, and all those tears I hadn't shed flew in all directions.

I wept like the surf, an endless surge of salt water dashing itself upon the shore. I cried until I had nothing left. Until I was an empty husk.

I cried until I disappeared.

29

Something nudged against my breast and I tried to push it away.

I was dead.

Why wouldn't they let me stay dead?

But the something rooted at me with demanding animal cries and then latched onto my nipple with painful determination. I pushed again at it, but my hand was trapped.

"Stop it, Amelia," came a stern voice.

I opened my eyes to sunshine so bright it hurt. Dafne sat cross-legged on the bed, my wrist pinned under one of her knees as she held a baby to my engorged breast.

No—not just any baby. My son. I blinked at her and everything flooded back, leaking out of my eyes. As if, now that I had started weeping again, I'd never stop.

"I know," she said, face somber, cinnamon eyes moist. "But your son needs you. *We* need you."

"Let me up."

With a dubious look, she moved her knee off my wrist, keeping a hand on the babe, lest I dash him to the floor like some maniacal creature.

I pushed myself up, my mind clearing like the crisp blue sky out the window. Pulling my son close, I found a better position for him. He wrapped a chubby fist in my snarled hair and stared at me with Hugh's summer-blue eyes. Something turned over in my heart.

Maybe I wasn't completely dead.

"How long was I asleep this time?"

Dafne shook her head infinitesimally. "Not that long. It's only midmorning and we . . . last talked in the middle of the night."

"Where's Marin? And Ursula?"

"Those are longer stories."

"Tell me everything. I can handle it now," I added, when she didn't answer right away.

"You were in labor all day and into the night, when the blood loss began to seriously worry Marin." Dafne got up and poured me some water, handing me a glass. "Which reminds me, you're to drink as much water as you can. You need to replenish, especially when nursing. You were feverish, hallucinating. Talking to people who weren't there. If Ursula could have used her sword on them, I think she would have." A ghost of a smile dusted her lips, but her eyes were haunted, echoing the harrowing ordeal.

"Finally Marin said that we had no choice but to cut the babe—babes—out, that the alternative was to wait until you had died and that was more dangerous. Ursula threatened to cut *her* throat first and they were arguing when this wildman burst into the room—drenched from the storm and demanding to see you."

"Ash," I breathed his name like a prayer. "I thought maybe I dreamed him."

"It seemed like a dream. Marin and I knew who he was, even without the monk's robe, but Ursula nearly killed him on the spot. Would have, too, if he wasn't so amazingly fast with that blade of his."

"They fought?"

She nodded, eyes wide. "Until Marin threw a bucket of well

water on them and told Ursula he was a friend and possibly the only hope of saving you."

The babe let go of my breast and started fussing at me. I switched him to my other breast, nodding at Dafne to continue.

"Ash made us all leave the room, which Ursula hated and Marin insisted she do. Frankly, I don't know how Marin convinced her. We three waited in the sitting room. He let Marin in, finally, but told us to stay outside. I thought it might kill Ursula. She doesn't wait well."

"No, she doesn't."

"Then Marin called us and Ash was out cold on the floor. You were sleeping, but looking as if you might live, and the babies"— her voice caught and she smoothed it—"both babies were squalling up a storm."

"Both." I looked down at my boy and he returned my gaze with solemnity, his disgruntlement gone.

"A boy and a girl, one fair-haired, one dark. We cleaned them up and Marin settled them into their cradles. Ursula had some of the footmen carry Ash to a guest room, to rest."

Good on Ursula.

"Where is Ash now?"

"Still sleeping. We're getting worried."

"He has to sleep, after healing." Still, I would have to check on him, when I could face the world again. "What happened then?"

"It was nigh on dawn by then, so Ursula said we'd wait to announce the births until after the sun rose. We were exhausted." It sounded like an apology. She paused, eyes shadowed as she stared at the memory.

"Tell me."

"We all fell asleep right here. Marin by the cradles, Ursula in the chair, and me on the floor. When we awoke—it could only have been a few hours—the girl babe had died." She lifted a shoulder, but a tear rolled down her cheek. "Just died in her sleep."

"Oh." Replete, the little boy had fallen asleep. So pink and healthy, with his round, soft cheeks. It didn't seem possible that his twin sister had died, just like that. But then, I hadn't believed Hugh was dead until I saw his corpse. "Did you see her?"

"Yes, of course."

"Tell me how she looked."

"Like him, only with black hair"—she gestured at the boy sleeping in my arms—"very much the same in size. She seemed just as healthy. But Marin said sometimes babies fail suddenly that way. And the labor was so long and difficult that—"

"No," I said, losing patience, "how did she look dead?"

"I—" She faltered, as she so rarely did.

"Don't be squeamish. Did she look like she was sleeping, for instance, and only when you touched her you knew, or—"

"She looked as if she'd shriveled," Ursula said from the doorway. "Like a fruit left too long in the sun, with the water dried away. Is that what you want to hear?"

She seemed more like a blade than ever. Angular, with her edge dulled by fatigue, guilt, and grief. Also, she had that look in her eye, as when she feared I'd throw myself from the cliffs.

I returned her bottomless stare evenly. She imagined that it hurt me to hear it, but she didn't know how little of my heart I had left. "Yes. It is. Thank you. I'd like to be alone now."

"Ami—"

"I won't do anything rash. Just, please, Essla." My voice broke over the rising tears. Maybe I had more heart to wound than I'd thought.

She flinched at me using the old pet name. "We'll be back in a little while."

Dafne took the baby from me and they both left without another word. I stared up at the roses on the canopy, pink promises of life everlasting from Glorianna. It all seemed so wrong. Could this be all? No daughter with the mark. I should have used the doll's head to check the boy. I still could.

Maybe Andi had been wrong and he would be the one. Something of all this needed to make sense.

Feeling surprisingly strong and healthy—no wonder Ash still slept, with that toll of saving my life—I untangled myself from the sheets and made my way to my desk. In the drawer where I kept her, the doll lay.

What I needed was inside the body. Look there.

I hadn't asked Andi what she'd needed, what she'd found. But I needed help now, if only to understand. Maybe I could change the course of things somehow. Hadn't Andi? Altered things for us all and now queen of her destiny. Taking the doll out and smoothing the red-gold floss of her grimy hair, I gently turned her over and picked apart the threads I'd placed there. In the back of my mind, it seemed my mother lingered, her scent blending with the dried-rose-petal stuffing, her own fingers sewing this doll. A last gift to me.

Nothing in there but the rose-petal stuffing. I dug it out gingerly and spread the petals—some whole, some no more than mauve dust—across the glossy wood of the desk. Some, it seemed, were darker than the others. With age or petal variation. Though the rose Dafne had pressed for me, preserved between the plates of glass and sitting on the desk, showed no such darkening. I picked out the darker ones, sliding them together like puzzle pieces.

Blood? Yes, they were stained with it. My mother's blood—it had to be.

Remembering how my blood had unlocked the spill in Zevondeth's chambers, I put all the darker petals into a cup and added cooling tea from the pot that had been left nearby. The dried flakes swirled, rusty red eddying up from their faded pink.

On impulse, before anyone could return to stop me, I drank it. If I didn't die of poisoning, Ursula would kill me.

I sat in the chair and prayed to Glorianna to appear, as I'd fancied She had when I was a girl.

Instead of the goddess, however, with her pink rays of light and tumbling roses, another woman took shape from the sunlight coming in the windows. Long, dark hair flowed around her like a cape, glinting with deep red reflections of the firelight. I thought she was Andi for a moment, her eyes the same stormy gray, but she was different. Older, more careworn.

"Mother?"

"An echo of her, yes. I am more of a message. A letter, if you will, that only you, my baby Amelia, can read. This is a little piece of myself that I carved away and left behind, once I knew I wouldn't be able to live to see you grow. That might be my greatest regret— and I have many—that you might not remember me at all."

"I remember," I said through my tears. "I always said I didn't, but I do. And I . . . saw you sometimes. I thought you were Glorianna."

My mother laughed, and in it were shades of both Ursula and Andi. "I don't think Glorianna would claim me. You did well to find the vial I left for you. I hope your sisters found theirs, as well."

I shook my head. "Andi found something. I had only blood-stained rose petals."

"You must help them find their own vials. There are things they need to know."

"Andi said it helped her, somehow, in Annfwn."

She sighed and closed her eyes as if in prayer. "I am so thankful she is there. I worried for her."

That stung. "Well, she's fine. I'm the one who's had a tragic life. You can't know."

She smiled then, with so much love it made me ache. "Ah, my lovely baby girl. You were born at dawn, you know, with all of the new day's perfect beauty and potential. Filled with love for the world. You have always been the most blessed."

"I don't feel blessed. First you died, then my husband, and now . . . I'm all alone." Except for my son. He would have to be enough.

"But you are," she insisted. "I planned to take all of you to Annfwn, but you carry the magic inside you. As will your daughter. You two, at least, will never know the pain of being closed away from paradise. That is your gift—one of unparalleled value."

"She died." I started weeping again, if I'd even stopped, and my mother drew close. She placed a ghostly hand over my heart, a cool shiver running through me at the touch.

"Weep not. Your daughter will live, twin to her brother. Look for the trick."

"What trick?"

"Childbirth nearly killed me, too. Every time." She spoke in a gentle voice that I would have found soothing in other circumstances. "I would never have wished this on you, if we didn't need these children so very much. The girl and the boy, to bring balance and knit the kingdoms. I had hoped that my third daughter could have her own life. But Ursula came first—I couldn't foresee how she'd be until much later—and then, once Andi was old enough for me to see her fate, I knew what your path would be.

"Both of your children will live. I want you to remember that, because it's important. Do you understand me? Look for the trick."

"No. Ursula wouldn't lie about that. Spare me your empty promises."

"They're not empty. Bleak at times, perhaps, but always real. You have the twin gifts of life and love. Use them. See through the trick." She flickered, became more transparent. Much as Andi's image had. "Good-bye, Amelia. Know that I love you, that part of me is always with you."

"Me, too," I told her. "I think of you, all the time. I always will. I wish you didn't have to go."

"I must. I already have." She smiled, and love warmed her gaze. "Trust in your heart, for it has no limits. You will always have love to give. You have always had mine. Know that I'm proud of you, my daughter of dawn's promise, my rising sun."

She faded completely and Ursula stood in her place, very like our mother, in a honed way. She frowned at me and I wondered if she'd heard me talking aloud. "You should be in bed."

"I feel fine, thank you." *Thanks to Ash.* And hopeful again, thanks to my mother.

Ursula was scowling at the debris littered across the desk. "Why did you tear the doll apart again?"

"Andi was right. There was a message, from Mother. I talked to her, Essla. Just now. She loves us. You need to find your doll."

"Okay, sure." She nodded and gave me a gentle smile. Indulging the crazy girl. Oh, well, she'd find it when she needed to, no doubt.

"I have a question for you—are you sure my daughter died?"

She sighed and looked down. "Please don't do this."

"It's important. How sure are you that was her?"

"What in Danu are you getting at, Ami? Of course it was her. I'm sorry for it, but your daughter died. I couldn't do a thing." She flexed her empty hands, staring at them. Not reaching for her sword hilt for once. Because none of her fighting skills had saved my daughter.

"You buried her?"

She nodded, shortly. "With her father. I thought—" Her steely eyes shone with tears. "I thought you'd want them to be together."

"And no one else knows—you kept it secret?" I stood and went into the bedroom, trusting that she'd follow, if only to keep an eye on me.

"I thought it best to keep it quiet. Let the people celebrate the boy's birth and not mourn what they never knew they lost. Of course, you can always announce her birth and death still if you—what are you doing?"

I arched my eyebrows at her and finished stripping off my nightclothes. "Getting dressed." I pulled the first gown I found over my head.

"You can't greet your people in that dress," Ursula snapped, then groaned. "Danu, we've traded bodies. I can't believe I just said that."

"I'm not."

"Yes, you are. If you feel good enough to get up, then you're up to dealing with the current chaos outside. Which, I might point out, I've been handling for you. You're welcome."

"Thank you." I turned around and made her help with my laces. With an impatient sigh, she did.

"Aren't you going to ask what's going on?"

"Let me guess. Messages went out to Uorsin and Erich, who have been waiting with full battalions at the ready and are moving into position to claim the baby. You likely feel conflicted because you're meant to command Uorsin's troops in his name, but your loyalty to me and your new nephew means you should marshal my troops to defend Windroven. However, this selfsame new nephew also means you lose your bid for the High Throne, so the obvious thing to do is to hand him over to Erich. Did I miss anything?"

She yanked on the final knot with a grunt. I'd likely have to get one of my ladies to cut the ribbons later, to win free of it. "I liked you better when all you cared about was gowns and dances."

"No, you didn't."

The annoyed set of her mouth uplifted in one corner. "At least you see what needs doing."

"Yes, though my priorities are different. I'm going to check on Ash and then I will see the child buried with Hugh. All else can wait."

She looked at me with that cautious sorrow she'd had in her eyes after Hugh died, when I had been out of my mind with grief. "Oh, Ami. You mustn't—"

"No, Ursula!" My voice lashed out with a strength and confidence I hadn't realized I'd gained. "*You* mustn't. I will see this child. I won't let you stop me."

"*Your* child," Ursula insisted. "It won't hurt less to pretend she isn't yours."

Love for her, working so hard to protect me, filled me to bursting. "I'm not sure what child you found in the cradle and entombed with Hugh, but she isn't my daughter."

"You're out of your mind." Ursula looked so devastated that I went to her and hugged her. After a stiff moment, she returned the embrace, so fierce and hard that I gasped.

"No. I'm not crazy. In fact, I have my head in exactly the right place. My daughter is alive. I don't even need to see what you buried to be certain."

"Then why put us all through such a dreadful thing?" Ursula demanded.

I smiled at her and went to the door. "To prove it to you."

Dafne stayed with the boy—I needed to decide on a name for him and my daughter—while Ursula took me to the room they'd stowed Ash in. It was far from the best levels, and we took the rear stairs to avoid anyone but the servants, who gave me startled bows and congratulations. Windroven bustled with jubilation. Ursula's instinct—as always—had been correct on that. News of the little princess's death would have only marred a much-needed celebration of birth and life.

But she shouldn't have lied to me. About anything. Before this was out, I would have the truth from her.

We descended to nearly the servants' quarters, reached one that sometimes doubled as a jail cell, complete with guards, and I raised my eyebrows at Ursula, who stalked, as stiff legged as a recalcitrant stallion, beside me.

"What?" she snapped, but sent the guards away. "The man is an escaped convict. He wears the brand, plain as day, even if he removed the brand from his face, however he managed that."

"He used a knife blade. Then spread lantern oil on his cheek and set it on fire, to cover the scar."

She hissed and slammed a hand on the door, to keep me from opening it. "You knew? And who in Danu is he to you, anyway?"

"He saved my life."

"If I didn't know that, I'd have packed him off to the nearest prison already."

"Just like that? With no trial or test of justice?"

"He's already had that or he wouldn't have been branded."

"Are you so certain of that, Sister?" I returned without anger. "Seems to me you're very sure of a number of things it's clear you're wrong about. Why not this?"

She clenched her jaw. "Fine. I won't say anything. Yet. But you're not acting like yourself."

"On the contrary. This is myself. I've only recently found out who that is."

She followed me into the room and I decided against trying to lock her out, as restlessly as she fingered her hilt. Spoiling for a fight she could win.

Ash lay on the narrow bed, thin and pale, the scars standing in stark relief to his sallow skin. I sat beside him, taking his hand in mine. It felt limp and damp, like old lettuce. I chewed my lip, worried. "Where is Marin? I need one of her restorative teas."

Ursula didn't answer right away, and I realized Dafne had never answered that question, either. I looked over my shoulder at my sister and she looked grim.

"Gone."

"Gone? You don't find that odd?"

"She went to join one of Glorianna's cloisters. To atone for what happened."

I laughed, the sound bursting out of me, which didn't help my campaign to make Ursula believe I hadn't lost my mind. "Did she *say* that?"

"No." Ursula waved an impatient hand. "She left a note."

"Convenient. Except that Marin bore no love for Glorianna's temple—and she can't write. She told stories because she never had schooling. Probably whoever took my daughter made Marin come along, to care for her."

Ursula's irritation morphed into shock, then something else. I let her mull over the implications and concentrated on Ash, gently patting his cheeks. He didn't move. I considered tying a piece of yarn around his wrist and yanking it, sure that would bring him instantly awake, so ingrained in him was that duty to protect me. Wherever it came from.

But I was loath to startle him so. *You have the twin gifts of life and love. Use them.* I leaned over and brushed my lips over his. Using my body to hide it from Ursula's view, I slid my hand over his cock and deepened the kiss. She made a sound of protest, but I paid her no mind.

Under my touch, Ash's body warmed and he groaned, mouth moving under mine and arms coming around me to pull me close while he kissed me like a drowning man gasping for air. I laughed, pulling away, and he yanked me back, holding me tighter, mouth devouring mine with his typical ferocity.

Until the tip of Ursula's blade prodded his neck.

He let me go, eyes traveling up the length of her sword. "Ah, the fearsome dragon protecting the fair princess."

Ursula smiled thinly, without humor. "Unhand my sister or I'll remove your hands."

"Leave him alone, Ursula. He's weak as a kitten."

"Gosh, thanks, but I'm not that bad off," he said in a dour tone, but his eyes glinted. "It's good to see you alive, too, Your Highness."

Ursula huffed out a breath, clearly incredulous at his attempt to show decorum.

He ignored her and picked up a long lock of my hair. "You haven't brushed your hair. What's wrong?"

"I need your help, Ash."

"I thought I already did that." His words were teasing, but faded when tears escaped my eyes. He thumbed them away with great gentleness. "You're crying. I thought you couldn't."

"I can. Now. It means something, I don't know what. But, Ash—we have to rescue my daughter."

He sat up with his preternatural speed, casting about for his clothes and weapons. "Who took her?"

"I don't kn—"

"*Nobody took her,*" Ursula gritted through her teeth. "Don't buy into this, convict. The Princess is beset with grief and unable to face reality. We all hate it, but the girl child died. It can't be good for her to indulge this twisted fantasy."

He assessed her with one sweep of his gaze and focused on me. "Did they show you the child's body?"

"No," I answered in relief while Ursula huffed out an exasperated breath. "That's all I'm asking for the moment. I want to see if it's her."

"Will you know?" he asked.

"Yes. I'm sure of it."

"How are you so certain?"

I slid my eyes over to Ursula's and held her gaze. "My mother told me."

"Let's go, then." Ash stood, pulling me up with him.

"Absolutely not." Ursula barred our way, her sword still drawn. "Just because you're both crazy doesn't mean I am."

Ash sized her up. "I could take you. I had you last time."

She lifted her lip in a sneer. "In your dreams. Besides, you have no weapon and I'm not in a generous mood."

Knowing full well Ash's hand-to-hand abilities, I stepped between them. "Stop this, Ursula. If I'm crazy with grief, what's the harm in this? We go to the tombs and see. Either way, the path from there is clear."

The steel in her eyes softened, the lines around them deep with sorrow. "Ami, I can't bear for you to go through that."

"Don't you see? You can't protect me from this sort of thing. I *have* to do this."

Her shoulders sagged. Another defeat. "Fine. Is there a back way?"

Of course there was. The castle at Windroven had been built into a defunct volcano ages ago. While part of it had been constructed of shaped and relocated stone, much of it—especially the deeper levels and tunnels—were the natural, labyrinthine passages formed by lava and the nearby ocean tides. During the siege, Andi had dragged me along on her restless "explorations," since she couldn't run off and ride for the first time in her life.

Coincidentally, one of these internal excursions led to my convenient capture, which it was clear she had set up. Born of a desperation I now understood.

I led them down the route the castle denizens used to reach the cliff walking paths. Not exactly secret, but not frequented by many, either. With Andi heavy in my thoughts—and my mind free to focus on next steps, now that I was getting my way on this—I asked Ash what he'd meant, that he would have been with me sooner.

"You remember that?" He smiled down at me with the warm affection I'd starved for. "I thought you were out of your head."

"She still is," Ursula muttered behind us.

"Bits and pieces. You came through the storm—did Andi get my message?"

He rolled his eyes toward Ursula and lifted a questioning eyebrow.

"You might as well speak freely in front of her," I told him. "She finds out everything anyway."

Ursula snorted at that but didn't disagree, just shadowed us. She'd put her sword away, but I knew she remained on full alert.

"Andi received your message and was preparing to journey here."

That made me pause, a giddy happiness swelling in me. "She was?"

"Yes. She was greatly touched when you asked her to come. Even more excited when we received word that Princess Ursula was also on her way."

"How did you know that?" Ursula demanded. "We traveled in secret."

Ash glanced over his shoulder at her with a feral smile. "The Tala see all."

"Back to the story," I interrupted their bickering.

"She and Rayfe were ready to depart and had invited me to come along, when—"

"King Rayfe, too?" Ursula mused out loud, and I glared at her.

"He'd hardly let his queen travel alone," Ash replied. "Though they argued about it. Both are quite stubborn."

"*When*—" I inserted. Again.

He laughed, soundlessly, under his breath. "When they received some unsettling news that demanded careful attention. We spent some time investigating, and ultimately, the king and queen decided the situation required them to stay in Annfwn."

"The *situation*," Ursula repeated.

"As I said." Ash had that neutral tone that meant he would say no more on the topic. "She asked me to tell you that she stayed because her being there would do more to protect you and your daughter than her traveling here would."

"What in Danu is *that* supposed to mean!" Ursula snarled out the question, right as we emerged onto the cliffs, dazzled by the sun off the water and buffeted by the salt wind.

I turned to Ash, studying his face. "She knew this would happen."

His face creased with pain, he nodded. "Not this but something similar. She—King Rayfe, too—hoped to prevent this."

"So you believe me that my daughter isn't dead because of that?"

"No." He shook his head, side to side, slowly, gaze on mine. "I believe it because I know you."

A rush of love filled my heart. Another shade of what I felt kissing my son's forehead. Full-bodied and connected to something real and vital and meaningful.

"This way, then."

30

Going single file on the narrow path, I reached for Ash and he took my hand, reminding me of our journey up Odfell's Pass. It felt so good to touch him again, his large, coarse hand enfolding mine. He hadn't questioned my need to see the body of the child entombed with Hugh. He might not have wanted what we had together, but he believed in me. And he'd left paradise to come for me.

In many ways, that meant more.

We made our way into the tombs, the alkaline stone silent and shadowed, dried rose petals in drifts in the corners. The sounds of surf and the wind whispered around the corners, playing ghost with each other, invisible fingers stirring the petal drifts with dry rustles. But that's all the haunting there was. Hugh lingered here no more than where he died on the pass.

His bricked-in arch stood out, with the fresh mortar evident, though it had been smoothed away.

"How did you do this by yourself?" I asked Ursula, who lurked unhappily by the exit to the cliffs, as if she might flee at any moment.

"I didn't." She sounded almost angry. "Dafne swore one of the brick masons to secrecy and the two of us said Glorianna's prayers over the babe."

Ash seemed to read my thoughts. "I can do it," he said, "though you'll need your mason to seal it again." Pulling a work knife from his weapons belt, which Ursula had grudgingly dug out of a locker, but only when I insisted, he chipped away at the fresh mortar with that uncanny strength and speed.

"This is wrong," Ursula said, her voice strained.

I glanced at her and away again. "I didn't think you were superstitious."

"I don't have to be superstitious to know to leave the dead well enough alone."

A tendril of wind toyed with the dried rose petals, spinning them in a spiral. "I have to see. You don't have to stay, if you'll respect what I decide after this."

She didn't say anything for a while. Finally, with a heavy sigh, Ursula unstrapped her sword, set it down within reach, and helped with her own digging tool. Working together, they pulled out the bricks, handing them to me. I made a neat pile, trying not to think too hard about it all. *Just make it to the next step.*

"That's enough," I said, when they had an opening big enough for me to climb in. Ash cast me a look, then nodded. Taking a torch from the wall, he lit it with a flint from his belt, handed it to Ursula, and climbed in. She passed it back, then laced her hands in a basket, to boost me over, as she'd helped me onto my first pony, when I was little.

With my sister lifting me, and Ash supporting me over, I climbed into my dead husband's tomb, as I had dreamed of doing, all those awful lonely nights.

Ash watched me intently, then cupped my cheek. "Okay?"

"Yes." I turned my head and kissed his palm. He stepped aside.

Hugh's body had shrunk under the funeral robes, the dry scent of embalming spices filling the air. Tucked in the fold of his arm lay a pitifully small bundle, wrapped in a pink blanket. One of the ones I'd managed to finish knitting.

I laid my hand on it, not sure what I expected to feel.

With tenderness, I gathered up the blanket and set it on the robe covering Hugh's chest. Then began to unpeel the wrappings.

"Ami—" Ursula started, and choked off. She'd climbed over the wall but stood as far back as possible. "Please don't do this."

I smiled at her, to give comfort, and tasted the salt of tears on my lips. They flowed so effortlessly now, like the rise and fall of the tides. Like the love and life that surged through my heart. Not shredded. Alive and whole. I let them. "It's okay. The pain isn't here. Their bodies are shells. They have no power over us."

She regarded me with bewilderment, so I returned my attention to the blanket, so lovingly and carefully wrapped around the creature they thought had been my dead child.

I reached the inmost layer. Ursula made a stifled sound and I hesitated. Ash laid his hand on my back, steadying me. "Okay," he said, reminding me.

Resolved, I tore open the cloth, my eyes closed against what I would see.

Both of them were silent. Then Ash let out a long breath.

I looked.

On the inner cloth, inside the carefully folded blanket, lay a bundle of twigs and leaves. *Look for the trick.*

Nothing more.

I breathed again.

"What is this?" Ursula's demand lacked all vigor. Like Graves, for all that she'd fought the Tala, she still believed in flesh and blood, life and death, not the shining and shadowy regions that tied them together.

"Magic," Ash answered for me, rubbing my back. "Tala magic."

"The Tala took my daughter," I breathed, testing the words. "This is what Andi knew."

"Some of it," Ash qualified. "And only a certain . . . dissatisfied contingent. Even in paradise, there are those who must play politics."

"You're saying the child we found dead was some kind of . . . fake?" Ursula wedged herself in on the other side of the bier and poked a finger at the pile of twigs and leaves, like a cat testing a mouse to see if it might run.

"Yes. Someone with Tala magic took the young princess and left this—changeling—in its place."

"Someone with Tala magic, inside Windroven." Her face hardened with suspicion.

"Like me, yes. But I don't have these skills."

"So you say. But there are no other Tala in Windroven."

He laughed—one with full sound for once. "If you believe that, Your Highness, you're a fool. The Tala are all among you."

She hated that thought. It stood stark on her face and burned the air. "Not much magic, if it lasted such a short time."

Ash lifted a shoulder, let it fall. "The culprit—he or she—would have known that the people of Avonlidgh bury their dead immediately. The spell didn't need to last longer than that."

"Just long enough for me to bury her," I added, sifting through the leaves with my fingers. "While he took her away, thinking we'd never look."

"Marin!" Ursula's scowl deepened as she found a target for her anger. "She stole the Princess."

But I was already shaking my head at her. I knew of one trickster. The one who'd recognized me when no one else had. As if he'd known where to find me. Who'd been inside Windroven, biding his time. "Not Marin. Wyle."

They gazed at me with identical expressions of bewilderment. I sighed with impatience. "Ash—you wouldn't know him, but Ursula, he's that minstrel, with the short, very dark hair and very light blue eyes, almost silvery with it."

She shook her head, frowning as she searched her mind, but

Ash—he gripped my shoulder, turning me toward him, and I could sense his growing tension. "Describe this minstrel," he demanded.

I did, telling them both how he'd happened upon our party at the inn, singing me that song. "It wasn't about me, was it—that song? It was about my daughter." Automatically, I put my hand over my empty belly. *Gone is the maiden of roses. Swallowed up into the sea.* "He took her."

Ash was shaking his head. "I do know that man. Terin. King Rayfe suspected him of leading this secret resistance group within Annfwn. He disappeared right as I arrived. Now we understand why."

"And exactly what are they resisting?" Ursula rubbed her thumb over the cabochon jewel in her sword hilt, voice neutral, but eyes glittering like a naked blade. They kept returning to the blanket, as if she checked the contents against the mental image she remembered. She and Graves truly were two of a kind that way.

"This doesn't seem the place to be having such a discussion," Ash evaded.

Ursula, for all that she hadn't liked it before, disagreed. "This is an ideal spot. No one will overhear us. Let's hash this out."

"I agree." I folded up the blanket. "Hugh is beyond caring, and I want to find out what I need to know to get my daughter back."

Resigned, Ash nodded. "I knew what I'd face by coming here on my own."

"You seem to be quite cozy with Andi and Rayfe, all of a sudden," Ursula noted. "Especially as I understand you only first crossed into Annfwn some months ago."

He nodded wryly. "It's true. The manner of my entry, in Ami's company, gave Queen Andromeda reason to be interested in me. She has also been pursuing a . . . project, of sorts, with King Rayfe's approval, to find ways to locate and repatriate the part-blood Tala currently locked out of Annfwn. Thus I've been useful to her."

"That sounds so like Andi," Ursula murmured. "Every damn baby bird in Mohraya ended up in her bedchambers."

"The Tala have an affinity for animals," Ash replied. "And it makes her a fine queen."

I didn't need to hear the admiration in his voice to understand how totally Andi had won his loyalty. As much as part of me ached like an old bruise over it, my heart held enough love that it didn't pain me so much. "So. This Terin is leading a group that wants to remove Andi from the Tala throne, because she's not fully Tala, is my guess," I said.

"It's more complicated that than, but that captures the essence of the situation, yes."

"Will he take my daughter to Annfwn?"

Ash hesitated. "I'm not sure. It's not clear what their agenda is."

"But you can track him?"

"I will, yes."

"Then I'll go with you."

"You will not!" Ash and Ursula spoke as one, their voices identically emphatic. It made me laugh, their absolute synchronicity. It felt as good to laugh as it had to cry, as if everything inside me was coming to life again. A late spring and a welcome one. How I loved them both.

Ursula glared Ash into silence, reminding him of her rank, then turned on me. "Ami, you are, if not shortly Queen of Avonlidgh, then at least Duchess of Windroven and always the daughter of the High King—you have responsibilities here. Think of your son, too!"

"I am thinking of my son. I'll bring him with me."

That astonished them both so much that neither could do more than blink at me. I laughed, again, the absurdity of it all hitting me hard. "Glorianna! Look at the pair of you. He's a baby, not a hothouse rose—he won't wither up and die if I take him out of Windroven. And, amazingly, this is the perfect solution to my dilemma—and yours, Ursula."

"What are you talking about, Ami?" Ursula sounded weary. The circles under her eyes had deepened, if possible.

"I don't want either Uorsin or Erich taking possession of my son. Nor you, Ursula. That's not a choice I'd have you face. My other option is to hold them off with another siege, and while the two armies might destroy each other for me, they'll take the crops and livestock with them. Windroven, Avonlidgh—Glorianna, all the Twelve—can't afford to lose this summer's yields."

Ash remained silent, while Ursula mentally parsed my points. "What's your plan, then?" she finally asked.

Taken aback that I didn't have to debate her further, I had to realign my thoughts. "How far away are Erich and Uorsin's troops?"

She lifted a shoulder. "Two days, three at the most."

"Tomorrow we pledge my son to the goddesses and name him. We'll spread the word for the celebration today. Morning ceremony for Glorianna, noon for Danu, nightfall for Moranu."

"All three? Are you sure you don't want to add in the frost gods they say the people of the Northern Wastes worship?"

I didn't rise to her bait. "All three. The Twelve Kingdoms need balance again. It's the only way for us to thrive."

"This seems to be a very strange conversation to be having in a tomb," she remarked.

My eyes fell to Hugh's shrouded corpse, a pang of sorrow coiling through me. It felt mellower, not the agony of those early days, nor the chronic, slow bleed of the months after. Like my mother, he, too, would always go with me.

"Not so strange," I reflected. "Hugh should not have died. Had things been in balance, it would never have happened. It was a tragic error."

Ursula looked profoundly stricken, as if an arrow had hit her between the shoulder blades and plunged through her heart. I could no longer scent her emotions—or Ash's—the way I had, but I didn't need to. The guilt and regret crawled over her face.

"Andi didn't kill him. She could never have bested a fighter like Hugh. I can think of one person who could," I said softly. Ash's hand settled on the small of my back and I leaned into the solid strength he offered.

Ursula's gaze dragged to the shroud, horror contorting her mouth. "I did it. I killed him." She spoke to him. Giving him the bald confession.

"Tell me what happened." I'd said those words to her over his body before, the day she arrived at Windroven the first time. She'd chosen her phrasing carefully then. She and Andi both, conspiring to mislead me.

Her thumb rubbed over the much-smoothed jewel in her sword, drawing comfort from her talisman. "It happened so fast. Tensions were high. Hugh went for Rayfe and Andi put herself between them. So fast. He wouldn't have been able to not strike her. I acted before I even knew. I cut him down. It was me."

I closed my eyes, imagining the scene. Hugh would have done exactly that. And, if Andi truly loved Rayfe, as it seemed she did, she would have done exactly that, too. I would have, for Hugh—and I would for Ash—I knew it in that heartbeat of understanding.

And Ursula—always she had protected us. I'd always seen Andi as my replacement mother, but if that was so, Ursula was the father Uorsin could never be. She would die before she let anyone hurt either of us. Without a moment's thought.

Of course it had been her.

"I see."

The silence of the tomb settled around us. Ash rubbed my back, slow and soothing. Ursula waited, shoulders straight, prepared for whatever punishment I chose to level on her.

"It never should have happened," I repeated. "But why lie to me about it?"

"Andi—and I—thought that, in the excess of your grief, you might raise Avonlidgh against Ordnung, if you knew I'd done it. She had visions of civil war."

"Much as seems to be happening these days," I pointed out.

"This is posturing only," she snapped, with some of her old spark. "The High King won't let that happen. Peace has always been his highest ideal."

I regarded her, so strong in her unwavering belief in our father. All of it made me angry. I wanted to protest that I wouldn't have done what they predicted, but, looking back at who I'd been in those first awful days, how I'd contemplated competing with Ursula for the High Throne . . . I might have.

"All right, then. I understand why you lied to me—you and Andi both. I forgive you both, and the River Danu has carried it to the sea. But I want a promise from you."

Her breath slowly sighed out and a weight visibly lifted from her, even as she shook her head, puzzled. "How can you forgive me?" She gestured at the shrouded corpse. "He lies there moldering because of me! Because I swung my sword and—"

"I know well what you did," I cut her off. "More, I understand why you did it."

"Why?" She sounded as plaintive as a child. "Even I don't understand."

"You did it out of love, idiot! If I understand nothing else, I know something about love. Glorianna Herself couldn't have stopped you, if you were acting to save Andi."

Ursula still seemed bewildered, uncharacteristically unsure of herself. "Who knew Andi would step between them that way?" she whispered, almost to herself, replaying the scene in her mind. It finally made sense to me, too, Andi—not with an evil grimace of sadistic joy, but with the nobility of love on her face—moving in front of Rayfe. Love not only for him, but for Annfwn and for the unity we all needed.

"You said she loves him, didn't you? You and she are the same that way. Like our mother. I think Salena did it all out of love, in her own way."

"And you." Ursula's eyes traveled between me and Ash. Opaque, without judgment. "That's why you must go after your daughter and why you won't leave your son. Of course that's what you must do."

Relief sagged through me. I hadn't realized how much I'd been afraid of fighting her over this. Of her trying to take my son to Uorsin.

"Then you'll help?"

"Yes." She nodded. "I have no idea what in Danu's name I'll tell our father, but I'll cross that bridge later. I'll help you escape."

"Thank you."

She smiled and her eyes were as damp as mine. "However, Miss Ami—if you're having the naming ceremony tomorrow, you'd better get busy thinking up a damn name for the boy."

31

Dafne handed over the baby with relief when we returned to my chambers. Seeming unsurprised to see Ash with us—but did anything ever surprise Dafne?—she greeted him and listened to our findings with grave interest. And then tears of relief. Suddenly everyone around me seemed to be weeping all the time, but I didn't mind.

"Well!" She wiped the corners of her eyes with her cuffs. "If we're having a naming ceremony at dawn, then I'd best rally the troops."

Ursula watched her go, then fixed Ash with a steely glare. "I suppose you want the rest of your weapons and supplies, if you're going on this rescue mission."

"That would be ideal, yes," Ash replied, "but I'm not helpless without them, either."

"You think you can do this—protect her and the babes? You don't want to take extra help?"

He shook his head. "More people would slow us down. Besides"—he slanted me a wry smile—"Ami and I make a good team."

Ursula snorted. "Ami, is it?"

"Ursula." I sank into the chair, cuddling the boy close. My breasts ached and he fussed, scooching into me. "Ash got me in and out of Annfwn. I trust him with our lives."

Ash went still, eyes veiled. I wished I could scent what he was feeling, but I'd have to go about it the mossback way and ask him. Once I got rid of Ursula. "Go make yourself useful. I'm going to contemplate names."

"What about him?" Ursula fingered her sword. "He can hardly stay here alone with you."

"Of course he can."

"It's not appropriate."

"It's my castle." I raised my brows at her and she frowned.

"I still outrank you."

"You can scold me later. Go away. Take a nap if you've nothing else to do—you look like hell."

Shaking her head, but with a faint smile on her narrow lips, she bowed elaborately and left.

Ash stood awkwardly, seeming unsure what to do with himself, a flurry of emotions chasing themselves across his face. He'd changed in the last months, not as hard, less anguish in those apple-green eyes. The babe began to fuss and Ash looked mildly alarmed.

"I need to feed him." I tugged at the neckline of the gown, which, as I'd suspected, didn't budge with Ursula's military-tight lacing.

"Do you want me to leave? Or turn my back?"

I laughed, so happy to have him here. Ash would help me get my daughter back. This was my destiny, to sew the things together. Together we could do this.

"It's not as if you haven't seen it all before. But I need you to loosen my laces." I stood and presented him with my back.

He tugged at them, fumbled a bit, and cursed softly. The baby started to wail at the delay. "I'll have to cut them, I think."

"I'm not surprised," I replied in a dry tone. "Ursula tied the knots."

"Figures." In a moment, he'd produced a blade and sliced the ribbons, the neckline gaping away from my swollen breasts.

I sat again, wincing as the boy latched onto my nipple and nursed greedily. Looking up, I found Ash's gaze riveted on me and imagined I smelled the smoky scent of banked lust.

"How is it possible," Ash said, almost to himself, "that you are more beautiful than ever? You say you have no magic of your own, but surely this is witchcraft that you can be nursing a child and I can only think of burying myself inside you."

My breath caught, my body warming at the thought. "Even with your excellent healing abilities, I might yet have to wait a few days for that."

His eyes jerked up to mine, and, unaccountably, he flushed. "I didn't mean it that way. I misspoke—and I apologize."

"Why?" I studied him. "Do you mean you don't want me? Perhaps you've come to your senses and managed to resist my witchy lures."

"Moranu, no." He buried his face in his hands, elbows propped on his knees. "I want you more than ever. Every day, every passing moment, I thought of you, Ami." He laughed that soundless laugh I'd missed so. "There I was—in paradise, realizing my life-long dream, my father's dream—and all I could think of was leaving. Because you turned out to be the only thing I really wanted. The joke is on me."

"Why is that a joke?"

"Because, Ami." He dropped his hands and stared at me, growing irritated. "I went from one unattainable desire to another. I'm like a drowning man, casting aside every branch that comes to hand, so I can drown again."

I switched the boy to my other breast, Ash watching us with such a deep longing that I nearly smiled at him. But I needed to be more careful than that. "You once accused me of having no power of my own. You said it was all borrowed from others."

He scrubbed his scalp. "Yes. That was unfair. I—"

"No, no—you were absolutely correct. You made me think.

You've always done that, from our first conversation. Made me reconsider myself and what I thought was true. Now I know new things about power."

Sitting back in the chair, he relaxed a little. "Such as?"

I could let myself smile. "I know that my power comes from inside me, from making decisions and sticking to them. From knowing myself and understanding my world and my place in it. From life and love. I want you with me, Ash."

"The Queen of Avonlidgh and Glorianna's avatar cannot bed an escaped Tala convict," he gritted out. "The thought is absurd, and—as much as I want you, enough that I might die of it—I can't be your secret consort. I know myself that much."

I laughed and he looked hurt. "Oh, stop! Even I understand you that much. And yes, I will be the Queen of Avonlidgh and I've already taken steps to make myself the head of Glorianna's church. That's right." I nodded at him. "I'm cleaning that house. There will be no more tales like yours, if I have anything to say about it."

The babe had fallen asleep, so I rose and carried him into the bedchamber. I tucked him into the little cradle, whispering Glorianna's benediction over him. Then turned to see Ash had followed me in. My dress fell open, baring my breasts, and he seemed stricken, staring at me from the doorway.

"Do you mean it?" he asked on a hoarse whisper. "You'll have me openly, before your people, as your consort?"

"Yes. Though we'll be journeying first, of course, looking for our lost one. That will give you time to decide if I annoy you too much and you can back out before we make it public."

He smiled then, the bisecting scar twisting it to the side. "Somehow, even when you annoy me, I just love you more."

"That sounds like true love to me, then."

"Does it?"

"Believe me, I know. I used to think that it only happened once, your single opportunity to make good. But now I think— no, I know—that love is abundant. That's Glorianna's gift to us.

That we love, over and over, many times and many people. You're one of them. I love you, Ash."

He crossed to me, tentative, and lifted his hands to cup my naked breasts. "Your tits are so much larger," he commented.

I burst out laughing and wound my arms around his neck. "Trust you to say the least romantic thing possible."

He grinned at me crookedly. "But you love me for it."

"Yes," I said. "Yes, I do."

Then he kissed me, and it was everything I remembered it being.

Dawn burst, bright and glorious, over the ripening farmlands of Windroven. I held the babe, Ursula and Dafne at my side, while the new head of Glorianna's chapel at Windroven said the invocations. Nearby the surf crashed against the shore, the salt scent crisp and full of life.

Behind me, Ash stood with the other men, Graves and Skunk and the others, flanking my ladies. The priest asked me for the boy's name and I drew Glorianna's circle on his forehead.

"Astar," I spoke loudly. "For he shall be the star that guides us to the bright future the goddesses wish for us. *And Stella*, I said in my head and heart, naming her there, *who shall be the twin star to his, the two in one, who shall make us all one.*

A jubilant cheer went up from the crowd, wild with triumphant glee. I'd repeat their names twice more today, for Danu and for Moranu.

And then, before Glorianna's sun rose again, Ash and I would sneak away from Windroven, bringing only Astar with us.

Hold on, Stella. We're coming for you.